THE CAGED VIKING

VIKING NAVY SEALS BOOK 8

SANDRA HILL

D0873448

SH
BOOKS

*"And now in Norway a branch
of the gods' race had grown."*

— Ynglinga Saga
Snorri Sturlason

wonderful book that successfully mixes romance, adventure, and humor." FreshFiction.com

"A well-told story, funny and heartwarming. Ms. Hill has created characters who will stay with you long after you close the book. This is a time travel that shouldn't be missed." The Paperback Forum

"Sandra Hill has truly captured the lifestyle and language of medieval times. The story allows the reader to immerse herself in the spirit of the day. Her prose eloquently develops the fragile relationship between two people who have given up all hope of love…This enchanting work is worth reading again and again." I'll Take Romance Magazine

"Trademark Sandra Hill is filled with lots of humor, some of it laugh-out-loud fun. She has that magical touch when it comes to creating heroes who are warriors but have a vulnerability that appeals to readers." RT Book Reviews

ISBN: 978-1-950349-89-0 Ebook
ISBN: 978-1-950349-42 5 Print

Publisher: Parker Hayden Media
Imprint: Sandra Hill Books

Art credits:
Cover Design: LB Hayden
Man: fxquadro/DepositPhotos
Cage: foto-pixel.web.de/DepositPhotos

This book is dedicated to all those still recovering from the Coronavirus pandemic...and those who were out in the public exposing themselves to danger for the greater good, and those who quarantined themselves at home, also for the greater good. I hope this book will provide a bit of humor to lighten your heavy burdens. And aren't smiles and laughter the best medicine, anyhow, pre-, post-, or during a crisis?

PROLOGUE

Saxon England, AD 1014

Daddy, dearest?...

*B*ergliot, the serving girl, stood a fair distance from the cage and stared at the beast. It was a man, actually. A Norseman. But, after six months and more living in a cage, the pitiful creature was more animal than man.

Not that Bergliot felt any pity. Nay, she did not. What kind of man allowed himself to be captured and put on display in his enemy's hall? Especially a Viking. A disgrace he was!

Bergliot had been raised in a Saxon keep, though half Norse-blooded herself, and had been told from an early age that Vikings were the world's fiercest warriors, never given to surrender. They were also reputed to be more handsome than the average male. Hah! There was naught handsome about this hairy, smelly, snarling spectacle.

He was tall, but gaunt with nigh starvation. Hair once blond hung in greasy clumps about his face and down his back. Unshaven for many a month, his face was barely

1

discernible under a heavy beard. Despite the grime and filth that covered him, old and new scars were prominent from forehead to legs. He wore but a scrap of fur tied about his male parts. The only life left in him stemmed from piercing silvery blue eyes.

Not that those eyes took note of her. No one did. And that was all well and good. An over-tall maid with no bosom or curves to speak of, with hair chopped off unevenly, even to her scalp in places, adorned in a drab homespun garment that hung on her skinny body down to her bare feet, blended in well with the lower staff that labored for this vast royal household.

Bergliot had only been in the Winchester Castle a few sennights now, having been brought here as an indentured servant, and she, for a certainty, was not supposed to be in the great hall. But she'd been drawn to this spot and continued to stare, trying to comprehend why the beast fascinated—and repulsed—her so.

She knew why, of course, and spat on the rushes at her feet.

For his sins, the beast was her father.

Not that she would recognize him if she hadn't been told of his identity, and not just because of his present condition. She hadn't seen much of the man in all her twelve years, and not at all the past three. Some father!

In one hand, Bergliot held a boar leg bone, gnawing idly on the little remaining meat, whilst using the other hand to scratch her backside. The coarse wool of her gown caused a bothersome itch. That, and the fleas that infested her bed furs and took bites out of her fair skin.

Suddenly, she felt a hard whack to the back of her head, causing the bone to fly and her to stumble, almost falling flat on her face into the rushes. The bone was caught midair by one of the royal hounds permitted to prowl the great hall. The dog scooted under a trestle table, too far under for her to reach, if she was inclined to retrieve the bone, which she wasn't.

"Stop picking at yer arse," the raspy-voiced Egil, her self-proclaimed protector, hissed, waving the wooden end of an axe at her. *What kind of protector sells his ward into slavery? For her protection? A likely story! A good one for the skalds, but not for me,* Bergliot griped silently, but did not say aloud. She was not such a dullard that she did not know when to curb her tongue, if forewarned.

Egil, though a graybeard of considerable years...having seen at least fifty winters...was short and wiry in frame, one of a dozen woodcutters who provided the kindling for the many palace hearth fires. He was stronger than he looked, as Bergliot well knew from the bruises on her arms from his dragging her hither and yon, all for her supposed well-being.

"Have I not told ye a hundred times that 'tis unseemly fer a lass to touch her privates?" Egil waved his axe handle in her face to make sure she was paying attention.

"Huh?" Bergliot said, rubbing the back of her head. She would no doubt have a knot the size of an egg by nightfall. "What's a person to do when they have an itch, then?"

"Do it when yer alone and no one can see."

"Like the self-pleasuring I caught you in yestereve in your bed furs?" Bergliot laughed and ducked, just missing a second knot from Egil's axe handle.

"And why have ye washed yer face and hair? Are ye trying to look pretty?"

"What? Are you barmy? I am no more pretty than...than you are!"

Egil's lips twitched with a grin at her outrage. The codger knew how much Bergliot disliked being called pretty, her bane from the time she was a toddler.

"Pretty or not, do ye want some Saxon whoreson tupping ye in a dark corridor?"

Bergliot gasped with outrage. "They would not dare!"

"They would dare, believe you me, and they will not care if ye are barley-faced, or pretty as a gilly flower. Nor will they care which hole they plug either."

Now he had gone too far. Blood rushed to Bergliot's face and her hands fisted. She was about to launch herself at the old man, but he had turned abruptly at the hissing sound that came from the cage. The beast had made the sound, as if to signal Egil.

With a motion for her to remain where she was, Egil sidled over to the cage, looking right and left to make sure he was unobserved. It was early morning, and there were few people about, but still the household had been warned to stay clear of the cage.

The beast shuffled forward in his cage and whispered to Egil, who pretended to be examining the strength of the wood bars, something a skilled woodcutter might do. Egil nodded several times, then returned to her, his demeanor one of sadness or worry, she wasn't sure which.

"What did he want?" Bergliot asked as they walked out of the hall, he toward the wood lot and she toward the outside scullery where there were another five or fifty cauldrons for her to scour.

Egil declined to answer, but the nervous tic at the side of his mouth said it all. Egil was worried about something the beast had told him.

"Does he know he's my father?" Bergliot asked of a sudden.

Egil shook his head. "He thinks ye dead."

Bergliot shrugged. "He would not care anyway."

"Foolish boy!" Egil said, slicing her with a glare. "Ye are the reason he's in that bloody cage."

4

CHAPTER 1

I know how the caged bird (beast) feels...

*H*auk the Handsome was not so handsome anymore.

Truth to tell, not having bathed or shaved or cut his hair for more than six months (twenty-four sennights and three days, to be precise), he, who had once stunned one and all, especially women, with his godlike good looks, stunk to high Valhalla. A disgrace! Everyone knew that Vikings bathed more often than the average man and took special care with personal appearance. Unlike the stinksome Saxons who had no excuse for their foul odors.

In his defense, Hauk scarce got enough water for drinking, let alone bathing, residing as he did in a cage in a corner of the great hall of the royal court at Winchester, put on exhibition like some exotic animal. In fact, his wooden pen had once been occupied by a huge white bear, a hunter's trophy from a far-off arctic land. Beasts, both of them, according to his ignorant captor, King Aethelred. `

Despite the thin war braids he tried to maintain in his wild hair, framing his face for some semblance of dignity, lice had become his new best friends, cracking the nits his only source of entertainment. That, and the occasional beast-like growl he emitted just to amuse himself when lackbrain Saxons poked him through the bars with sharp lances or burning sticks. Actually, they didn't prod him much anymore, or leastways not from up close, ever since he grabbed one irksome house-carl by the wrist and bit off the man's foul thumb.

Hauk was so thin his hips scarce held up the loin cloth he'd fashioned out of a fur tossed his way on that freezing winter night, following the St. Brice's Day Massacre. And, yea, he had been known to let it drop a little lower when some tongue-sucking, pole-up-the-arse ladies of the court passed by.

His other pastime involved making mental lists of all those foemen he would torture and kill when he was free, starting with the king, who'd ordered the death of all Viking males in Britain on that infamous saint's feast day, even Norse settlers who had lived peaceably in England for decades. Among the horrendous acts committed was the burning of the locked St. Frideswide Church in Oxford, where dozens of Norse men, women, and children had taken refuge. In addition, there had been the noted hersirs and their warrior underlings, who'd managed to evade the fiery end but then were handed a worse fate. Face-front decapitations.

And they said Vikings were brutal pagans! What did that say about Christians?

Hauk could not dwell on the mind pictures that plagued him day and night, berating himself for not arriving earlier, or he would grow as demented as he pretended to be. For a certainty, he now understood the rage that drove some Vikings into berserkness. Hauk shook his shaggy head, loosening a few more pests in the process. With determined effort, he banked the embers of that roiling wrath, hiding the emotions which beset him suddenly, waiting for the right opportunity to strike. Every good warrior knew that timing was everything, whether in battle or a contest of wills.

It was a waiting game.

Sweyn Forkbeard, king of all the Norselands, would come to his rescue, eventually. Hauk was certain of that fact, not because Hauk was of such importance, but because no Viking worth his salt would allow the atrocities leveled at his family to go unavenged. Among those who had burned to death in the church had been Sweyn's sister Gunhilde, her husband Pallig Tokesen, a Danish ealdorman of Devonshire, and their child.

Included among those who'd reportedly been beheaded was Hauk's son Bjorn, who had seen only twelve winters, but had been big for his age. Bjorn had been fostering in Pallig's keep ever since his mother died three years past of a wasting disease. To his shame, Hauk had considered the youthling safer there than a-Viking with him in the Rus lands or ensconced in his small northern Hordaland estate. *Now, that is a lie! Truth to tell, I did not want to be bothered with the bratling, whose Saxon mother tricked me into a marriage I never sought or wanted. I neglected the child to punish her. And now...* He sighed. ... *and now 'tis too late to make amends.*

Hauk had been in Frankland when he'd first heard rumors of Aethelred's perfidy...not the massacre, no one could have predicted that, but rumblings of the inept Saxon king's wild imaginings that there would soon be an uprising of Norse settlers in Britain against him. By the time Hauk arrived in Oxfordshire, he'd been a day too late. The church had been a charred ruin. Piles of headless bodies lay untended as feasts for the vultures that hovered overhead in a dark cloud, the heads scattered about the fields.

A cleric, who'd stood praying over the corpses, even as he kept swatting at the angry birds, told him of his son's passing, or what he knew of it. Nay, the God-man had not stayed to witness the actual decapitations, but he recalled seeing Bjorn among the males being led to the slaughter.

In his grief over his son's death, and the guilt he felt over his neglect that led to the boy being in peril, Hauk hadn't exercised his usual caution. As a result, he'd been captured by some of Aethelred's guardsmen who'd returned to the site of their treachery, no doubt to plunder the bodies for treasure. Human vultures. Even the clothing of the corpses would have been taken by nightfall, he'd known from past experience.

But that was past. Hauk had to look forward. He only hoped he could hold on, that the Saxon curs would allow him to live long enough until Sweyn's arrival with the northern army that he was gathering. They should be underway shortly, gods willing. That news he got from the newly arrived Egil, one of his hersirs who'd been off in the Baltics on one of Hauk's longships gathering amber for trade and only recently heard of his master's fate.

Egil, pretending to be a woodsman until he put in place a plan for Hauk's escape, had with him a ragtag maid for which he claimed questionable guardianship. Hauk was suspicious and wouldn't be surprised if they were fur mates, despite the girling's youth. But why Egil wouldn't just admit such was beyond Hauk. All the maid did was gawk at Hauk with a sneer on her fool face.

Until Egil's arrival, all of Hauk's hopes had lain with Queen Emma, Aethelred's not-so-adoring child bride. To give her credit, Emma was partly responsible for Hauk's survival thus far. At the very least, she'd arranged for a serving boy to put a pile of clean straw outside his cage every few days and remove the pile of soiled rushes that he pushed through the bars. A pail of drinking water and the occasional hunk of bread or slab of cheese were also given to him by the same servant, when he remembered.

Emma had been given in marriage by her father, Duke Richard of Norsemandy, last spring when she was only twelve years old to the Saxon king who'd been well into his thirties and had already fathered ten children, none older than the young Emma. It was meant to be a powerful alliance between the two countries with Emma acting as peacemaker. Hah! Some peace, considering that Richard and his family came from a long line of Vikings, including Rollo, or Rolfr the Ganger, first Duke of Norsemandy.

The king had long been referred to as "Aethelred the Unready" because of all the poor decisions he had made. Yes, he had been a boyling when he took the crown and no doubt was ill-advised by his guardians on the Witan council, but what excuse was there for the rest of his reign? Really, what could the monarch have been thinking to order the massacre of Vikings a mere eight months after wedding a Norse bride? Could he not see that it represented a slap in the face to Vikings everywhere, and to Emma, a personal affront? Thirteen years old she might only be now, and already breeding a Saxon whelp, but she knew her own mind. And that had benefitted Hauk, thus far.

"You must be patient. Norsemen from Hordaland to Iceland are volunteering readily for Sweyn's sea army," Emma had whispered the last time he spoke with her two sennights past whilst her husband and other nobles on the high dais were being entertained by a troop of jugglers. "'Tis said the numbers are so massive, five hundred longships are required."

Hauk had shrugged. Not for the first time, he'd told her, "They consider your husband's Viking death decree to be a slur on our very culture."

"I know," she'd said with an exaggerated moue of sympathy. "I told Aethelred that my father would be furious, but he just waved my concerns aside."

Hauk wasn't so sure that the girling queen cared about such issues as their shared heritage, or even her father's temper. He'd noticed in the months of his captivity that her appearance had changed dramatically, with more and more adornments in the form of robes of samite silk and jeweled brooches. In fact, she wore a ruby encrusted circlet about her head all the time as a reminder of her rank. Perchance her sympathies would sway toward whichever side was favored to win.

"You are not to worry," Emma had assured him. "I will handle everything." On those unpromising words, the queen had sashayed back to her husband and the other royal folk.

So now, he relied more on Egil for his escape. And there the fool stood now, blathering to the fool maid. Hauk made a hissing sound, and Egil approached the cage.

"Best you give me a knife, Egil. In the event of attack, Aethelred or one of his cohorts might decide to kill me and hide the evidence of their vileness."

"Nay. Not yet. 'Tis I whose throat will be slit if they suspect my complicity and then where would ye be?"

"Where I've been for the past six months and more."

"When news comes of Sweyn's landing on Saxon soil, I'll release you. You'll have all the weapons you need then."

Hauk glared at his comrade-in-arms, not pleased to have his orders questioned.

"In the meantime," Egil went on, sensing Hauk's displeasure, "I'll arrange horses to carry us away from Winchester, and you can make plans for where ye want to meet up with the armies. We could go north to London or to Jorvik, where your longship *Sea Wolf* is still docked, and where Sweyn will no doubt land his ships. Or south to Plymouth or

Southampton where Duke Richard's army will cross the Channel."

"Just how soon do you expect this to happen?" Hauk barely restrained himself from reaching through the bars and throttling the old man.

"Soon. Soon."

"That's what you said a sennight ago."

"Now, do not be getting yer bowels in an uproar, milord."

Hauk was no more a lord than Egil. A karl, or chieftain of his small holdings, yes. A low-level jarl in some circles, by reason of his ancestry. But by no means a high-placed noble. Nor did he want to be. And Egil knew it, too. He used the form of address to annoy him.

"As ye well know, milord, patience is a virtue recommended by the gods."

"Patience!" Hauk snarled. Then, noticing several house-carls glancing their way, he lowered his voice. "I need to kill someone, Egil, and best you be careful it is not you."

Hauk felt impotent in his inability to escape on his own. He hated having to rely on others, especially when those others were a self-loving, thirteen-year-old queen and a scrawny, overaged, lackwit Viking with a sudden penchant for wielding power over his master.

Thor's Balls! I need a different kind of champion to rescue me.

"With luck, ye will be home in Hordaland by late summer," Egil had assured him.

"Luck, fuck!" Hauk had muttered.

"Leave everything to me," Egil concluded airily as he walked away toward the girling who still stood gawping at him.

Hauk stuck out his tongue at her, an immature act which he found oddly satisfying.

The impudent wench stuck her tongue back out at him.

He had to laugh.

Alone again, Hauk mused over Egil's words. He cared not about a return to his home. In fact, he could not foresee any life beyond the personal revenge he needed to fulfill. After that, he would willingly join his son in Valhalla.

Ah, Bjorn! I did love you. I did! He blinked against the sudden burning in his eyes, and a single tear slid down his grimy face.

CHAPTER 2

Blue Dragon Vineyard, Northern California, 2019

Tears of a Viking...

The Viking came to her again that night.

And Dr. Kirsten Magnusson was not a happy camper...rather, sleeper.

"Go plague someone else," she muttered.

The Viking just stood there, a Norse pain in the ass.

How did she know he was a Viking?

His facial features, what she could see of them, were pure, sculpted Nordic. He wore the arm rings of an ancient Viking warrior. Thin braids framed the sides of his face. And he was one tall drink of water...or would that be mead?

"This is getting ridiculous," she said on a groan. "Leave me alone!"

She rolled over in her bed and buried her head under the soft down pillow. When she peeked out, he was still there.

She tried self-hypnosis to lull herself back to sleep. A friend of hers, a fellow professor at UCLA, was big on transcendental meditation and some weird spiritual crap called "soul soaring." *Imagine you are floating in the sky, like a cloud. Softly. Softly. Softly. Listen to the silence. Be the silence.*

Buuullshit!

It would be different, explainable even, if it was a sex dream...if the guy was even attractive, as Vikings were known to be. Like the History Channel's Travis Fimmel who played the Viking Ragnor Lothbrok, sporting an intricately braided, manly, topknot ponytail, with his head shaven on the sides. Mischievous pale blue eyes. Biceps bulging over tight arm rings. Long hairy legs (but not too hairy) exposed by a knee-length, leather tunic. Yum! Now that was eye (or dream) candy she could get excited about!

But, no, her guy wasn't even attractive. How could he be? He was tall but so thin that his ribs stuck out. Old scars and new wounds marred much of his exposed skin. Despite the large amount of hair on his face, she could see the gauntness of his sunken cheekbones. The long hair on his head, probably blond at one time, was so greasy its color was indistinguishable. Sometimes it was pulled back into a rough, single braid, but other times, like now, it hung loose with thin plaits on either side of his face. War braids, they were called. He wore nothing but a fur wrapped around his private parts and rings on his upper arms.

Leaning back against the bars of a wooden cage, arms folded over his chest, ankles crossed, he stared at her. He said nothing, but his eyes (silvery blue, not unlike good ol' Rag's), filled with pain or anger, she wasn't sure which...held hers in a silent challenge. No pleading from this proud Viking. No, he was demanding something from her. That wasn't quite true, either. It wasn't so much that he wanted her help, it was that he needed her help.

But then came the zinger, something new in the chain of

dreams. A tear...one single tear...seeped out of the pale ocean eyes.

Have I ever seen a Viking cry?

Never! And I grew up in a big family of macho men of Norse descent.

Maybe she should get up and drink a glass of warm milk.

Yuck! A stiff drink might be better.

Or play some soft music.

Like what? A freakin' lullaby?

Nothing worked.

She had been plagued by the dream for months now...a dream that was much more than an imaginary series of events that normally occurred during sleep. Being a professor of Nordic Studies at UCLA, a research scientist, Kirsten should know better than to give such importance to the fantasies she was seeing in her head. But they were too vivid, too real, to be anything but...*okay, call me crazy*...a call to action. As far-fetched as it might seem, Kirsten sensed a magnetic pull toward someone in need of her help. But who? What? Where? How?

Maybe I should contact that Long Island Medium, the one that has a TV show on one of the cable networks. Imagine the ratings on that one. Modern academic woman connects with Viking hunk. A telepathic love connection across the ages. But, no, this isn't love. It's something else. So, no mediums.

Maybe I could hire a ghost hunter? Where does one find a ghost hunter anyhow? On the Internet, I'll bet. You can find anything on the Internet.

Better yet, maybe I need an exorcism?

Or maybe I'm just losing my mind.

She surrendered and eased into the dream. Again.

. . .

She was standing in the middle of some medieval hall where a feast was taking place. From her years of study, she recognized by the hall's furnishings and the people's attire that it was probably Saxon England, around the turn of the last century...1000 AD, give or take, but before the arrival of William the Conqueror in 1066 when everything changed, from architecture to clothing.

It was a castle, but not like most people today pictured a castle. No stone exterior with turrets and towers. No fancy marble columns. No oriental carpets on the floors or old masters paintings in gilt picture frames on the walls. In fact, no pictures at all, although there were a few museum-quality tapestries and ancient shields hanging on the walls for decoration. Instead, it was more like a large—very large—wooden fortress set upon a hill. The motte-and-bailey style popular during that time period...motte, as in mound, not a water barrier moat.

None of the hundred or so revelers remarked as she strolled between the long trestle tables, even in her Snoopy-flipping-the-bird sleep shirt, a gift from one of her brothers last Christmas. It was a dream, after all. To these medieval folks, she was invisible. She could be naked for all they would notice.

Good thing she wore slippers, though. The rush-covered floor was gross, with discarded bones and grease, and who-knew-what-else with dogs and cats ambling among the crowd, at will.

Too bad she didn't have her cell phone with her. If such a modern device would work in a dream! She would love to capture the images of this primitive hall, especially with the foods now being paraded around the room and then placed on the high table for display before eating. Not just the customary whole boar with an apple in its mouth, being carried on an iron spit by two male servants. There was also a pheasant in full colorful presentation, which had presumably been gutted, plucked, and roasted, then reassembled with head and feathers. A pyramid of honey oat cakes held place of honor on one of the lower tables where little swipes were evident along the sides, samples snuck by passing children and adults alike.

All of this extravagant food was indicative of not just a royal household, but some special occasion. Easter, Kirsten guessed, when she noticed the rounds of bread with a cross imprinted on them. Hot cross buns, anyone? That and the mountains of hard-boiled eggs were clues that it was a holy feast. She recalled that the tradition had been for people to give up eggs for Lent back in the Dark Ages, but not wanting them to spoil during those forty days of fasting, they were boiled and preserved in brine or some other manner until Easter when there would be an overabundance of the suckers to be consumed.

But none of this was important to Kirsten. The main point of this dream, its star, was in another part of the hall. Carefully, she made her way toward the lower, darker end of the massive room where a large wooden cage was situated. There was a sputtering wall torch nearby which gave her just enough light to make out the hazy figure inside.

"Hello," she said. Well, that was dumb. But, really, what does one say to a man in a cage? In a dream, no less.

No reaction. He just stared at her. Maybe he couldn't see her either. But, no, he pushed away from the back wall of his cage and walked toward her, stopping about a yard away from the nearer bars.

He was tall, at least six feet three, Kirsten gauged by her own five ten. Filthy and reeking of BO. Long hair, which might be blond under all that grime, was roughly braided tonight in one long coil down his back. Pale grayish-blue eyes were startling, especially contrasted by oddly dark lashes. He wore nothing but a scrap of fur around his hips. The rest of his skin was marred with old and new scars and bruises. He was far too thin for his tall physique.

"My name is Kirsten Magnusson, and you are...?"

Still no reaction.

She repeated her introduction in Old Norse.

Was that a tiny flutter of his eyelashes?

"You're a Viking, right? Me, too. Well, I like to say Norse-Ameri-

17

can. Same thing. You might have known my father at one time. Magnus Ericsson." She, who was comfortable addressing a symposium of two hundred students or a conference of colleagues, was babbling with nervousness.

And he was looking at her like the babbling idiot she was.

"This is just a dream," she said then, giving an unasked-for excuse for babbling. "I'm not sure why you're plaguing me every night, like some ghost or spirit or something."

That was definitely a movement of his eyelashes. In fact, she could swear he rolled his eyes.

"I think you've been calling to me to come save you."

His eyes scanned her body, head to toe and back up again, obviously finding her lacking in the Knight-ess in Shining Armor category. He glanced right and left to see if she had someone with her, like maybe a small army, then shook his head.

"I know. I don't have any troops to back me up. Not even my brothers who, believe me, are always up for a good fight. But I'm smart. Suffice it to say, I can probably figure something out."

Her Viking spoke for the first time then, in a voice raspy from lack of use, or maybe he'd been choked at one time. "Did Sweyn send you?"

"Swane who?"

"Sweyn Forkbeard."

"Oh. No, I came on my own." But at least now she had a better idea of the time period. Sweyn Forkbeard hadn't invaded England until 1014.

"Lucky me!" he remarked on her solitary rescue mission. "Key?" he asked.

She looked around but didn't see any evidence of a key. In fact, she couldn't imagine anyone entering this cage if they valued their life. They probably just passed food or water through the bars. Yes, there was that little door over there at the bottom corner, like a doggie gate.

"Knife?"

"No, but I could probably get one. Better yet, I could grab one of those swords off the wall over there, if they're not too heavy. Don't they have any lady swords? Ha, ha, ha."

"Halfwit!" His word was harshly uttered and blunt, and oddly sexy with its hoarseness.

"What? You think I can't do it?"

"Go. Away."

"I wish I could."

"Trouble!" he said with a snort of disgust.

She wasn't sure if he meant that he was in trouble...

Obviously!

...that trouble was coming...

What could be worse trouble than living in a cage?

...or that she was trouble.

That's gratitude for you!

At least she had him talking.

"Why dost thou carry the emblem of a dog? I have ne'er heard of a Viking realm named for such. Bearstead, Wolfshire, Fox Lair, Ravensmore...but ne'er a scrawny mongrel."

"Huh?" She followed the direction of his gaze and laughed. "That's just Snoopy. A pet dog known for his wit and philosophy of life."

"Why does it have his finger raised? Not that dogs have fingers."

She laughed. "It's an age-old gesture. Can be traced by to ancient Roman times, I think. Even Socrates mentioned it."

His eyes went wide when he understood her meaning. Then he shook his head again and muttered, "The Norns of Fate must be having a grand jest at my expense."

"I saw you weeping tonight," she told him then, reaching a hand through the bars to pat his arm in sympathy. "Do you want to talk about it? I'm good at listening."

"You dare much, milady," he snarled, grabbing hold of her wrist and yanking hard. "Lest you taste the flavor my wrath, you will ne'er mention that subject again."

"Ouch!"

He released her hand and she drew it back quickly, rubbing the soreness with her other hand. "Jeesh! Talk about overreacting! There's nothing wrong with a man crying on occasion. It doesn't make him any less manly. In fact—"

He said a one-word Anglo-Saxon expletive that had survived the centuries, right in line with her Snoopy shirt.

ON AND ON the dream went. Sometimes he didn't talk to her at all, just stared at her intensely. Other times, he spoke, a little. The gist of it all was that, despite his words to the contrary, he needed her.

That was her opinion anyway, and when it came to her dreams, she had the last word.

CHAPTER 3

Vikings here, Vikings there, Vikings everywhere...

 t was barely past dawn when Kirsten gave up the ghost, so to speak.

With sleep being impossible, she got up, brushed her teeth, pulled her long blonde hair into a pony tail, and went downstairs, still in her Snoopy sleepshirt covered by a terry cloth robe. In the pantry, a coffeemaker, on an automatic timer, was bubbling away. Pouring herself a mug and putting in a spoonful of sugar, she walked barefooted out onto the back porch where she found her father. Magnus Ericsson had always been an early riser, since the days when he'd been what he called "a simple farmer" back in the "old country" of Norway.

"Good morning, sweetling," he said. "You're up early."

"Couldn't sleep," she replied.

"Excited about your birthday celebration tonight?"

"Please! What woman welcomes a thirty-fifth birthday?"

He grinned, knowing that age didn't matter much to her. Not yet, anyway. She was too busy with her professional life.

Glancing pointedly at the rare blue amber in a white gold filigree setting that she wore on a chain around her neck, he asked, "Do you like your birthday gift?"

"I love it! I've never seen amber this color before."

"'Tis rare. In the old days when I did a bit of amber harvesting in the Baltics, after my crops were planted and before harvest, we found a few pieces of that color. Mostly shades of rust, but there was the occasional blue or green or red. I gave Madrene a red stone one time, called Dragon's Blood. Methinks her husband, that miscreant Karl, took it with the divorce."

Madrene's first husband, Karl, had divorced her because she was barren. Not so barren now, though. Obviously it had been Karl who'd been sterile.

Not wanting to get her father started on the subject of Karl and his misdeeds, Kirstin asked, "Do you miss amber harvesting?"

"Nay!" He shook his head for added emphasis. "I am a farmer at heart, and raising grapes satisfies that yearning. 'Tis important for a man to be satisfied with his work."

And a woman, too. That's why I'm a professor, and not a wife and mother. Although...no, that's another subject to avoid with my father.

They sat on cushioned wicker chairs facing the rail of a wide wraparound porch that overlooked the neat rows of Blue Dragon Vineyard grapevines. For a while, they just sipped at their coffees and admired the view.

It was that special time of the year, a fleeting week or two in mid-Spring called "Bloom" when the developing flowers got fertilized, and the air was redolent with subtle but tantalizing aromas of the goodness to come. This was not a heady scent like that in an orange grove or a peach orchard. It was more elusive. Fresher, because of its understatement. Like the first slice of a Honeycrisp apple, or the skin of a pear still on the limb, or an ice-cold melon cracked open and oozing sweetness on a hot summer day. She must have read that description somewhere.

Inhaling deeply, she noticed her father doing the same, his eyes closed to enhance the sense of smell. She understood how he felt.

She lived in Los Angeles, and was home only for the weekend family gathering for Easter Sunday, which fell this year the day after her birthday, that all important one, a turning point for most women. She would rather not have a fussy party or anything, but it was no hardship coming home. In fact, she looked forward to her time at Blue Dragon, which managed to stay the same in a world changing too fast.

It wasn't just the property that was comforting, she noted as she glanced around, but the old Victorian style house, too. A mansion, really. Her family had moved here more than twenty years ago when their father had married Angela Abruzzi, who stemmed from a long line of California vintners.

And a good thing it was that the house had been so big, Kirsten reflected. Magnus had eleven children, including Kirsten, when he'd arrived in America; twelve, after he'd married Angela. To say that her father was a "very virile Viking" would be a vast understatement. *Or very busy, to say the least,* she quipped to herself with a smile. *Enough on that subject!*

Still, it was ironic that her father had probably had ten children by the time he was her age, and she not even one. Nor did she have a prospective mate on hand, or even a sperm donor, not that she was thinking of anything like that. Yes, she'd had that on again/off again relationship with Navy SEAL Jacob Alvarez Mendozo, JAM, but it had ended last year, amicably from both sides. Turned out that it was not the perfect match they'd thought it would be. Part of the reason for that breakup and others was her not wanting any children of her own, ever. Not that she didn't like babies—other people's babies—just not for her.

She knew why her mind was veering in that direction, though. "The blasted man came to me again last night," she blurted out, before she had a chance to bite her tongue. Then, in for a penny, in for a pound, she elaborated, "I can barely sleep anymore with these nocturnal visits."

"A man came to you last night? Here? At Blue Dragon? Was it one of my workers?" Her father started to rise with paternal indignation. She wouldn't be surprised if he went off to get his sword from the hall umbrella stand. Thirty-five years old, and Daddy was going to protect her virtue!

She laughed and put up a halting hand. "No, no! I didn't mean in the physical sense. This guy could hardly do me any harm. Nope. My Viking is in a cage, for heaven's sake!"

"A Viking? Did you say a Viking? In a cage? Impossible!"

Kirsten rolled her eyes at the vanity of a Viking. Truly, you could take the man out of the Norselands, but he would always be a Viking.

Her father, who was close to sixty, wore his gray-threaded, light brown hair in a long single braid. Hard manual labor in the vineyards kept his large body fit. He still wore etched arm rings on his upper arms. Despite the jeans and Blue Dragon T-shirt and athletic shoes, he was Viking to the bone, and always would be.

"Not only is My Viking...that's what I call him...in a cage, but he's about a thousand years old," she told him with a laugh, then added, "Like us."

Her father gasped, knowing exactly what she referred to. More than twenty years ago, her family had, unbelievably, traveled from 1000 AD Norway, best known as Hordaland back then, to modern day Hollywood, California. They'd melded into this society and rarely spoke of their experience.

24

A miracle, something ordained by God, or the gods, had been the consensus back then, and still was today. There was no scientific explanation. Besides, if they told anyone about it, they would be deemed crazy. The whole family might end up in some secret facility for scientific experiments. Considering the secrecy and shenanigans of some government agencies, that prospect wasn't as far-fetched as it might first seem.

"Another time traveler? And he came to you here...but, no, you said he was in a cage." Her father frowned with confusion.

"It's a dream. Sort of. And I think it takes place in a Saxon castle, probably a royal one, about the time of King Aethelred."

"That idiot! He was called 'Aethelred the Unready' back in the day. More like 'Aethelred the Dunderhead' if you ask me. Hey, that rhymed." Her father grinned at his own wit, then took a long sip of his coffee, before asking, "How could you tell?"

"Daddy! I'm an expert on that time period. I've written books on the subject. Don't you think I would recognize the architecture, the tapestries, the furnishings, even the weapons?"

"Sorry, sweetling. I meant no insult. It's just...a Viking in a cage?"

"I know, but that's what I'm seeing."

"I have to admit, it's the kind of thing Aethelred would have done," he conceded. "Remember what we learned about the St. Brice's Day Massacre after we left? An outrage, it was! You probably know more about that event than I do."

She nodded. "Wait here a sec. I want to show you something." She went into the house and came back with a pad and pencil. Quickly, she sketched a design of writhing birds, one beak nipping at the tail feathers of the other in a circle. "The man in my dreams has arm rings with this raven design on them."

"Those aren't ravens. They're hawks, and I know who your Viking Man must be. Hauk Thorsson...spelled H A U K. in Old Norse, not H A W K. He was from Haukshire in the northern sector of the Norselands, farther north even than our farmstead. He was known as Hauk the Handsome."

"It can't be the same guy because my Viking is far from handsome."

"Are you sure about that?"

"No," she admitted. "You know how the halls were then. Dark, smoky, and my Viking has a lot of facial hair. He probably hasn't trimmed his beard or mustache in a long time, let alone shaved." She shrugged.

"*Your* Viking. I do not like the sound of that."

They would have said more on the subject, but the sound of an engine could be heard from out front, probably a pickup truck by the loudness. Within minutes, her brother Torolf, a Navy SEAL, came sprinting around the house and up the back steps.

"You're early," her father remarked.

"I was up all night with Katla. She's teething; so, I came on ahead of Helga and the other kids." He sank down into another of the wicker chairs. Dressed in a U.S. Navy T-shirt and running shorts, he extended his long, bare legs out to rest his boondockers on the porch rail. "I figure I can help you with some of the first mowing around the vines." He turned to Kirsten then and grinned. "Still an old maid, huh? And you now hitting the Big Three-Five. Uh-oh! Pretty soon you'll be living with a herd of cats and getting all crotchety. Maybe even turn to other women, if you get my meaning." Amusement flickered in his expressive eyes. Torolf loved to tease. All her brothers did. "No? Well, my offer's still open, sis. I can fix you up with one of my buddies."

"Oh, you! As if we need another SEAL in the family!" Her younger brother Hamr, a former NFL football player, was a

SEAL, too. Not to mention her brother-in-law Ian, a SEAL commander. And then there was her recently ended affair with JAM. "Suffice it to say, we have enough arrogant, conceited, violent, chauvinistic, hairy apes in this family." She slapped him on the arm with her tablet.

"Suffice it to say, la de da!" Torolf often mimicked what he called her high brow vocabulary

"Do you consider me a hairy ape?" her father asked.

"You're the exception," she lied and gave Torolf a dirty look.

"And what is this 'other women' business, Torolf? Do you mean her stepmother Angela, or her half-sisters Madrene or Dagny, or Lida, or Marie, or the various sisters-by-marriage in this family?"

"Um...uh...," Torolf stammered.

Their father was a modern man in many ways, but back in the Dark Ages in others.

"He means that I might become a lesbian," Kirsten explained bluntly before her brother could come up with some half-baked story to cover his ass.

"Traitor!" Torolf hissed at Kirsten.

"Torolf!" his father said at the same time. Then to Kirsten, he inquired, "You wouldn't, would you?"

"No, Daddy, I'm not gay. Not that homosexuality is bad. In fact, in some ways I wish I leaned in that direction, but it's not my thing!"

Her father breathed a visible sigh of relief and said, "Get your brother a coffee, sweetling."

"Why can't Torolf get his own coffee?"

"We have man things to discuss. Like what to do about your Viking."

"Man things?" Kirsten gritted her teeth. "Did I happen to mention chauvinism?"

"Kirsten has a Viking?" Torolf sat up straighter. "Hoo-yah!"

~

Was Dr. Phil of Norse descent?...

BY LATE THAT AFTERNOON, when the rest of her family showed up, everyone...mostly her brothers...had an opinion on Kirsten's "Viking Man." Any one of them could have prospered with their own newspaper advice columns, or blogs on the Internet.

Most people thought that the term busybody referred to women. Hah! They didn't know Norsemen! Seriously, a day in the life of the Magnusson clan was like a bad reality TV show.

The only one missing was Jogeir who was working on some experimental farm in Iceland. Everyone assumed that someday Jogeir, who had dirt in his blood just like their father, would come home to take over Blue Dragon after his father retired, if he ever did. Kirstin missed Jogeir, who had been lame with a club foot as a child back in the Norselands, but had had a surgery to correct the issue once in this country, and even went on to be an Olympic runner at one point. She hadn't seen Jogeir, who had become somewhat of a hermit, in years.

At the moment, a group of her family sat around the patio, drinking vast quantities of mead (beer) as they waited for the roast boar (pork ribs) that was cooking on the barbecue. Her stepmother Angela was inside working on the sides with Marie, who was studying to be a chef at some fancy culinary arts school. They would probably be having something like Truffled Potato Salad or wine-infused asparagus with black garlic croutons. You never knew when Marie was around.

Lida, an aspiring Broadway actress, who sometimes stayed in Kirsten's LA apartment when on the West Coast, was in the kitchen, too, but she was probably just observing, not wanting to mar the admittedly spectacular French manicure that she'd splurged on at some hoity-toity Manhattan spa. In fact, after she'd arrived in LA yesterday in order to drive up to the vineyard with Kirsten, she'd insisted on painting Kirsten's toenails with a crimson gel enamel from a sample the spa had given her, named "Hot Blood." Kirsten had refused to let her do her fingernails which she kept a clear gloss, or occasionally a pale pink, in keeping with her professorship role. Hot-blooded Lady/Professor was not the image she was going for when teaching "Sexual Attitudes in Viking Society" to outspoken, no-filter young people.

Among the first to give his opinion on Kirsten's Viking was Ragnor, her oldest brother, a highly intelligent computer guru of some kind. He was married to Alison MacLean, a physician who worked with the SEALs on the naval base at Coronado. Their combined IQ was probably about five hundred. You'd think they would have intellectual suggestions.

Instead, Ragnor commented, "It's springtime, her sap is rising, and only a Viking man has the cure." And he was serious

"No, it's her maternal clock ticking," observed Alison. "Mama wants to build a nest." Meanwhile, Alison was rocking an infant, an only child, so far. Alison was hugely pregnant with twins which she expected this summer. Meanwhile, masses of other children ran around the yard like little hoodlums chasing their cousins. An Easter egg hunt would be held that afternoon.

In Kirsten's opinion, the sap was rising too much in too many of the male Magnusson trees, and a few female clocks needed to be smashed to smithereens.

"Yeah, but this guy's in a cage, not a nest," pointed out Torolf, the blabbermouth who'd told the family about her dreams.

Her older sister, Madrene, known for her sharp tongue

and no-nonsense opinions, said, "You're a moron, Ragnor, always thinking with your dick. Modern women do not need a man to fulfill themselves. On the other hand..." She glanced over to her husband, Commander Ian MacLean, who was helping their three pre-teen children set up a sound system for later dancing on the patio. (*Yes, Vikings dancing! It had to be seen to be believed!*) Madrene gave her balding, forty-something husband a full body survey in his T-shirt and shorts, and grinned. "On the other hand, Dickie makes a nice play toy for a woman with a little creativity." She winked at Kirsten and Alison, "Do you agree, ladies?"

Neither of them could speak for their laughter.

"Madrene!" their father exclaimed. "Betimes you go too far! Play toy, indeed!"

"*Pfff!* Says the man whose toy has been played with by more women than he has hairs on his...other toys, as in balls! Twelve children! *Tsk-tsk-tsk!*"

"You are not too old for me to put you over my knee and paddle your ample arse," their father said.

"Ian is the only one who paddles my behind, Daddy. Isn't that right, honey?"

Ian had just come up, overheard his wife's words, went beet red, and walked back the way he'd come, without comment.

"How does this look so far?" Her younger sister Dagny joined the group, showing her a sketchpad with a penciled drawing of the man Kirsten had described. Dagny was an artist who worked for the FBI in forensic facial reconstruction, even as she was an accomplished painter in her own right.

Her composite was good, but not quite right. "I think the cheekbones are more defined and the chin a little less square."

Her brother Storvald, a wood and metal sculptor who worked at Rosestead, their Uncle Rolf's reconstructed Viking village in Maine, was more interested in the arm rings her father had told them about and Kirsten's rough sketch from this morning. Using charcoal and her tablet, he'd gotten the etched jewelry down exactly and was excited about casting some of the pieces for sale on his Internet website.

"Bottom line," Torolf told the group, "I think this calls for a military intervention."

Kirsten groaned.

"I'm in," interjected Hamr, who'd no doubt been hit on the head one too many times in football or in SEAL operations.

"A military intervention? Like what?" scoffed Njal, who had been one of the most mischievous of her brothers as a child, but was now a high-ranking, way-too-serious officer in the traditional Navy, not the SEALs, a source of consternation among some in the family. "You want us all to grab broadswords and battle axes and rush back a thousand years to rescue the guy? Earth to clueless Magnussons? It's impossible."

"I wouldn't say impossible," her father said, looking toward Torolf who'd actually done it one time. And managed to return. With a bride, no less. It was a subject they rarely discussed.

"I wouldn't recommend it, but I know from personal experience that it can be done," Torolf elaborated. "The problem is, there's no control over the year you would land in, how to travel back, or even if you'd be able to return."

"Face it, this is a God issue," said her brother Kolbein, a priest. Yes, a Viking priest. He got a kick out of the plaque he had hanging on the wall of his church office, a play on that old Saxon refrain from when everyone feared the invading pagans in longships, "From the fury of the Northmen, oh, Lord, deliver us."

Several of the men groaned, but Kirsten asked, "How do you figure?"

"Well, much as we all avoid talking about our own time-travel all those years ago, I can only conclude it was the hand of God guiding us toward some celestially ordained destiny."

"A miracle," Ragnor concurred with a shrug. "Works for me. There is no scientific explanation."

"So, you're saying God wants me to go back a thousand years to rescue a stranger?" Kirsten asked.

She already knew the answer.

CHAPTER 4

The winds of war...

*H*auk's future was in increasingly more peril as hourly updates came in on the impending arrival of the invaders...Sweyn's longships at Jorvik and Duke Richard's vessels which had presumably already begun to cross The Channel. You could nigh smell blood in the air.

Meanwhile, the inhabitants of Winchester Castle were running around like chickens with their heads cut off as war plans were made and discarded, right and left. You'd think they would have set defenses in place long ago. For a certainty, they had to know that retaliation would be coming eventually. Instead, more than once Hauk heard the muttered prayer, "Oh, Lord, from the fury of the Northmen, please spare us." As if prayers were a battle strategy!

Hah! Prayers did naught to spare the Vikings who were massacred by them, even if they were to the Norse gods and not their One-God.

In any case, the ravens of death would be flying over

Winchester within days. Mayhap even hours. Then it would be over.

In the midst of it all, he noticed eyes directed toward him, then darting away quickly. "What to do with the caged Viking?" they seemed to be asking with worry.

About time they worried!

In fact, just now, Lord Botswith, earl of Larchford, approached with the king. The two of them paused to stare at him and then proceeded to discuss him as if he were not even there.

"Not high enough in rank to be used as a hostage in negotiations, I suppose," the earl remarked.

What makes him think Vikings would negotiate at this point? The halfbrain!

"Pff. Not even a high jarl," King Aethelred replied. "Just a karl, according to my wife."

"Karl?"

"A jarl is comparable to our English earl, whilst a karl is just a wealthy landowner, or chieftain."

Just? I would like to give him "just"! And I am so a jarl. A lowly one, but a jarl just the same. It was ironical that he would now claim his jarlness, if only in his head, when he denied it otherwise, like whenever Egil called him "Lord."

"Should we just kill him and hide the body?" Lord Botswith asked.

Nay, nay, nay! No killing me!

He must have made a sound because both men jolted to attention and gave him a closer scrutiny, from their safe distance on the other side of the cage bars.

"Dost think he understands English?"

"Nay! All Viking are dumb, hardly more than animals," the king said.

Hauk would have leapt through the bars and strangled the

34

fool monarch if he could. Dumb was Aethelred's middle name, not his.

"Not yet," the king answered the earl's question about killing him, but continued to ponder the thought as he pressed a forefinger to his lips pensively. "Word may have reached Sweyn and Duke Richard of a Viking noble being kept here in a cage for torture and humiliation. You know good and well that someone in my castle would reveal the truth at the mere pulling of a fingernail or the heat of a hot iron near an eyeball."

"With God's support, the pagans may never reach Winchester," Lord Bothwith opined.

Don't count on it.

The king, in his usual pattern of procrastination, said, "We will decide the Viking's fate at the Witan meeting on the morrow. Let the body of Saxon thanes share in that decision, as well as final battle plans. Personally, methinks 'tis best to risk the ire of the invaders by killing this one Viking, mayhap even hanging his head from the ramparts as a warning to the heathen attackers. Yes, I like the sound of that. But let the deed be enforced from a Witan order, not mine alone."

And so they pondered Hauk's fate.

And here I stand like a fox in a field of archers, just waiting for one overeager housecarl to take a shot. With only two lackwits to save my sorry hide! The lackwit Viking queen, who is about to pop out a royal whelp, and the lackwit woodcutter/hersir who dawdles like a youthling contemplating his first swive.

When Egil came to him later that afternoon, Hauk repeated what he'd overheard. "It has to be tonight."

Egil nodded, for once, and said, "'Tis the same I'm hearing round and 'bout. Rumor is, one mucky lord has suggested they release you into the woods outside the castle and set up a chase with dozens of armed men on horseback and hounds to track you down."

"Like a bloody fox." Hauk spat into the rushes.

"That way they kin allus say ye died tryin' to escape."

Hauk shook his head at the idiocy of the Saxons who wasted time on such games when their very lives were in peril.

"Be ready after the castle settles down fer the night."

"Do you have the two horses ready for us to get away?"

"Three."

"What?"

"I have three horses for you, me, and...Bergliot."

"What? We can't be slowed down by some silly maid."

"She comes," Egil insisted.

"Stop thinking with your cock, you old fool."

"She comes, and that is that."

Hauk rolled his eyes. Later he would deal with Egil's fanciful notion.

They discussed details for their escape then, until one of the passing housecarls looked their way with suspicion. With their plans set in place, Hauk was hopeful for the first time in months.

But then, early that evening, an unwelcome visitor changed everything.

～

It wasn't Johnny Cash, but there were rings of fire...

IT WAS three months before Kirstin saw her family as a whole again, and this time it was at her Uncle Rolf's Rosestead village in Maine.

To mark the twentieth anniversary of the opening of the Viking re-enactment community, a week-long Norse Festival was being held. All of the extended family, which numbered more than fifty, stemming from the three Ericsson brothers who'd come from the Norselands to America...Geirolf, Jorund, and Magnus...were pitching in to help the resident staff of twenty-five handle the twenty thousand visitors who were expected from around the world.

Thankfully, term break at UCLA afforded Kirstin a full week away from her duties. After that, she'd be doing research for the next two months for a paper she was writing on "Viking Women in a War Society," having taken a hiatus on her teaching schedule until the fall.

Maybe she'd even find material here among her Viking clan to add to her scholarly documentation. Madrene, for one, would have a thing or two to say about the popular misconception that Norse women stayed home docilely, "barefoot and pregnant," while their men went off a-Viking. Madrene often likened herself to Lagertha, that warrior-ess or shield maiden who'd brought Ragnor to his knees in more ways than one, on the battlefield as well as the bed furs, in that TV series.

In fact, Madrene was dressed to the part today in tights covered by a fitted corset made of leather and intricate, light-weight chainmail coming down to her thighs. Slouch boots and etched bronze bracers on her forearms completed the picture, along with a round wooden shield decorated with a chasing dragon design and an authentic short sword, which she carried in a sheath attached to a wide leather belt. Her blonde hair had been done up Lagertha style, too, with a dozen elaborately woven tight braids on the sides and on top of her head, leading to a high ponytail, which swished as she walked...in a swagger, of course.

The eyes of her husband, Commander MacLean, who'd reluctantly dressed as a Viking warrior himself today, about bulged out every time she walked by. And he glared at any men who dared ogle her in her form-fitting attire. He could be heard muttering something that sounded like "Holy Thor!" but was probably "Hoo-yah!"

Kirstin was in period Viking dress, as well, though her gown, or gunna as it was called then, was more in keeping with some noble event in a Norse Jarl's great hall, rather than a battlefield. An ankle-length, royal blue silk, it was heavily embroidered along the scooped neckline, wrists, and hem with a border outlined in metallic silver thread of a Valknut design using a repetitive pattern of three interlocking triangles, sometimes known as Odin's Rune, against a lighter sapphire blue background. On her feet were flat ballet slippers; she'd chosen comfort over historical accuracy there. Her loose hair was pulled off her face into a single French braid that hung down her back to mid-shoulders, for comfort in the summer heat and humidity. Her only jewelry was the blue amber pendant around her neck, the birthday gift from her father, and a wrist watch which she could tuck into a side pocket of her gown before her talk, pockets being an anachronistic but handy addition she'd insisted on with her dressmaker.

In the old days, hard as it was for most people to believe, especially her students, pockets didn't exist; they hadn't been invented yet. Instead, men and women alike carried small leather or cloth bags tied to their belts, sort of medieval versions of fanny packs.

"Kirstin! Hey, wait up!"

Kirstin turned to see her sister Dagny rushing toward her from the parking lot.

"You made it," Kirstin said with a sigh of relief.

"Am I too late?"

"No. Uncle Rolf changed the schedule. My workshop on Viking fashions doesn't start for another hour."

"Good." Dagny looked her over and then asked, "How come you get to look all fancy and pretty, and I get the dowdy housewife outfit?"

"I'd hardly call that dowdy. Not with those amethyst

brooches and all that gold."

Dagny was dressed in the more traditional Norse woman's everyday attire. A full-length gunna, in this case a deep violet color, was covered with a long, open-sided white apron, the straps of which were attached over each shoulder with brooches of deep purple stones in gold settings. A heavy gold chain, holding various household-type keys and precious objects, like a thimble and needle case, hung in a wide loop over her chest from each of the brooches. Her honey-bright hair was braided into a coronet atop her head.

"Did you come like that on the plane?" Kirstin laughed as she linked her arm with her sister's and began to walk through the village fairground toward the great hall where her fashion seminar would be held.

"No. I changed in the airport ladies' room. Not that I didn't get lots of strange looks after that at the car rental desk. But then, crazies abound in airports these days."

"Tell me about it! It's like doing a gauntlet at some weird convention sometimes, especially in LA. Forget DragonCon or Comic Con. Did you know there is a con called BlobFest for fans of that old Steve McQueen movie *The Blob* and BlizzCon for men who are over thirty and live in their parents' basement. And get this, I heard last week about the World Toilet Summit and Expo for people who celebrate...well, pee-yew!"

Dagny laughed. "I saw some kids today carrying a sign that read, 'Welcome Home from Prison, Grandma'. Then, there was the old lady who looked like a homeless person carrying a five-hundred-dollar Gucci handbag. Not to mention a group of Stormtroopers. *Pff!* A medieval Viking maiden was almost normal."

"A maiden are you now?"

Dagny elbowed her for teasing. "I assume everyone else in the family is geared up, ala Frederick's of the Fjord."

"Of course." She had talked a bunch of her family members into participating in her Viking fashion show. They would be dressed as authentically as possible. "What made you so late?"

"Missed my first flight from Dulles. Some last minute forensic art needed on a terrorist case that just came in."

"You'll have to tell me about it later," Kirstin said as they entered the crowds that were walking and stopping before the dozens of booths that had been set up. Some of the jobs Dagny worked on at the FBI as a forensic artist were very interesting, fodder for many a family gab fest, certainly an exciting contrast to the solitary art work she did in her DC home studio.

"Oh, my God! This is amazing," Dagny remarked suddenly. "I haven't been here for five years, and it's grown so much."

"I know. Remember the first time we came...maybe fifteen years ago? There were only a few tents, with the highlight being Uncle Rolf's ship-building exhibition. Now, there are fifty-some booths, and they have to turn people away. The neat thing is that lots of them are working booths. People get to see the products being made, not just on display for sale. Like soap, and cheese, and swords, and candles, including those amazing time-keeping ones. We had those back on the farm in the Norselands, remember? No need for clocks then! But that's not all here at Rosestead. Now, they also feature weaving, mead brewing, jewelry, woodcarving, leatherwork... oh, everything!"

Dagny grinned at Kirsten's enthusiasm.

Kirstin wasn't offended. "I do go on, I know, but this isn't just my history, and yours. It's my field of expertise. Seriously, I'm already making plans in my head for a proposal to bring some of my UCLA students here next year, a kind of work-study program."

"Makes sense," Dagny agreed.

"Yep. And did I forget to mention...the History Channel

and the Food Network have both sent crews here this year to film all the happenings. Talk about Uncle Rolf hitting the bigtime!"

"Will they film your workshop, too?"

"Maybe." Kirstin smiled.

"Do you think Travis Fimmel or Alexander Ludwig might show up?"

"In your dreams."

They smiled at each other. Both of them had exchanged many a conversation about which was the hottest actor, the one playing Ragnor Lothbrok, or his son, Bjorn.

"Speaking of dreams...how are you and your Viking Man getting along?" Dagny asked.

"Haven't had any dreams since I told you all about it back at Blue Dragon."

"Good. Guess that means that the guy escaped his cage all on his own. Didn't need your help at all."

For some reason, Kirstin was a bit saddened by that. Not that she would want the dreams to continue, or the guy to suffer. But she felt as if she'd let him down or something. Which was silly, of course.

"Anyhow, the TV crews will probably want to catch your kulning act this evening," Kirstin told Dagny.

Dagny groaned. "Not only do I get caught in this House-wives of the Norselands outfit, but throw in a few smelly animals. That's all I need for my image. Calling the cows home with my singing. If some of the Fibbies back at the agency hear about this, I'll be subjected to cow and bull jokes like you wouldn't believe."

Kulning was an ancient Norse ritual employing a unique, high-pitched, almost haunting vocal technique for cattle herding. Rather like yodeling but much prettier, it echoed through the valleys and fjords. As if enchanted, the cows walked to the caller.

"But you do it so well. Even back in the Norselands, on father's farmstead, you kulned better than me or Madrene."

"You're just saying that because neither of you wanted the job."

Kirstin laughed. "There is that, too."

"I'm starved. Any chance of grabbing a bite first?"

"There'll be a big feast tonight. Aunt Meredith has had a wild boar roasting in a pit since last night. But that's for dinner. Oh, look. I see some gammelost over there. And manchet bread."

"Stinky cheese and bland, unleavened bread? I'll wait."

Hours later, Kirstin was packing up the fabrics and display boards from her workshop in the great hall, a massive long house in the Norse style that could hold up to two hundred people, easily. Her seminar, held at one end of the hall, had gone exceptionally well. In fact, what should have been a one-hour talk before fifty attendees had run into almost two hours with the lively question-and-answer period afterward.

Her family members, true to form, had added humor to the event. Her father, for example, wearing a belted, thigh-length, leather tunic over tight leather braies, and his gray-threaded, light brown hair adorned with war braids sparkling with colored crystals, told the crowd that he was once known as "The Very Virile Viking."

Then Madrene and Ian had come out together. With a twinkle in her blue eyes, Madrene proceeded to embarrass her husband, but had the audience howling with laughter, when she said that Ian had plans for her in that outfit later that night. Ian surprised his wife, though, when he told the crowd it was the other way around, that his wife was looking forward to being seduced by a fierce Viking warrior. Ian had winked mischievously after he spoke, in case anyone missed his meaning.

And then, Kirstin's brother Torolf had added to the

hilarity by announcing that he was the new breed of Norseman, a Viking Navy SEAL. Like Scots Vikings of old, he didn't mind telling them what he wore under his short tunic. Nothing. His wife Hilda shook her head at his antics.

Afterward, most of her family and audience members had rushed off to the fields beyond the fairgrounds so they could witness Dagny's kulning demonstration. Kirstin would have liked to go, too, but since her workshop had run over its time slot, she needed to get her stuff out of the way. Rosestead staff were scurrying about to set up the trestle tables and benches for the evening's dinner and entertainment. And members of the public, those dressed in Viking attire and those all touristy in shorts and jeans and summer dresses, were coming in early to get the best seats.

Once she was done, she stood for a moment and was momentarily taken aback when she stared about the massive room. Its construction was so authentic, exactly like some royal hall, even a Saxon one, would have looked like at the turn of the century, the tenth century, that was. Made of half logs, not stone, with a turf roof. There were no central raised hearths like there would have been in a Norse household, used for cooking as well as heat. There were hearths at either end of the hall, and a number of raised daises, or high tables, for the "nobles" or special guests, instead of the usual single one. Meals were prepared in a separate kitchen building.

"Hey, sis! I thought you were going to stop by my booth."

Kirstin turned to see her brother Storvald approaching. In many ways, he resembled their father when he was younger, especially in the belted Viking tunic over slim braies and with his light brown hair pulled off his face low on his nape in a long ponytail. The rimless glasses, which he wore for close work because of a longtime vision problem, didn't detract at all from his attractiveness. He was only a year younger than Kirstin and had never been married.

"Sorry. I didn't have time." She made a little moue of apology. "How's business?"

"Wonderful! That's why I wanted to talk to you. The idea you gave me last spring turned out great. I must have sold a couple thousand dollars' worth of arm rings and brooches and belt buckles with that design, just today."

"Really? You mean the chasing hawks?"

"Uh-huh. I have a special gift for you, a belated birthday present, to thank you."

She arched her brows in surprise and took the box from him which was imprinted with the Rosestead logo. In it were two arm rings in sterling silver with the intertwined hawk motif etched around all the sides. "Oh, Storvald! The design is beautiful. Exactly the way I pictured it in my dreams, although his arm rings were all tarnished and drab."

"So, still dreaming about your Viking, huh?"

"Actually, no." But then, she put on the bracelets, which seemly oddly warm, pushing them up until they fit snugly on her upper arms. She jerked when she felt sparks, almost like electricity where the metal touched her skin. And the room seemed to spin. But maybe it was her imagination.

"Kirstie! Are you okay?"

"Yeah. I got dizzy for a moment. Haven't eaten since this morning, and it's really getting hot in here." Summer temperatures in Maine weren't all that high, not like Southern California, but with all the people crowding inside, the air was getting thick, and someone's perfume was rather cloying. Hopefully, the air conditioning would kick on soon.

"Come on outside. I'll buy you a hot dog...a boar hot dog."

She laughed and said, "No thanks. I can wait till dinner. You go ahead. And Storvald..." She gave him a quick hug. "... thank you so much for the gift. The bracelets are exquisite."

"Arm rings," he corrected her.

She smiled and said, "I'll treasure them always."

"Are you sure you're okay?"

"I'm sure," she told him, and he went back outside to his booth which he'd left in the hands of one of their cousins.

But she wasn't all right. Something strange was happening to her, and whatever it was seemed to emanate from the arm rings.

She tried to take them off, but they wouldn't budge. She could understand her feet swelling from all the walking she'd done today around the village, but upper arms? That was a new one. They just wouldn't move, and they were growing warmer and sending some kind of electrical impulses through her body. She felt lightheaded once again and leaned back against the log wall, closing her eyes.

When she opened her eyes, it was a good thing she had the wall against her back for support because she might have fallen over with shock. The hall was the same, but different. Larger. More elaborate, even with the rushes on the floor, unlike Rosestead's oak planks. And there were antique weapons and tapestries on the walls. Only one high table, not the four that were at Rosestead. All of the people who milled about talking and laughing and drinking wore period clothing. Even the serving guys and girls, who were clearing away remnants of the evening meal, wore homespun garments, while there were exquisite silks and brocades and brushed leather on the upper classes, of which there were many.

Kirstin blinked several times to clear her head.

Now I'm dreaming in the daytime. Standing up. She tried to laugh, but it came out as a choke, especially when she pinched her arm to wake up and touched the hot metal of an arm ring.

Her eyes widened with sudden understanding. In her mind, she was picturing that popular Netflix series, *The Last Kingdom*, and how its creators had depicted a royal residence. What she was seeing before her looked very much the same. Not exactly. But similar.

She frowned as she studied the furnishings, the people, the clothing, the language.

Oh, no! Oh, no, no, no! Kirstin knew in that instant where she was. The great hall of Winchester Castle in the year 1015, give or take. Just before the Viking invasion.

How can I be so sure, down almost to the precise year?

Well, duh! Isn't this what I've been studying for the past ten or so years? Isn't this what I actually lived a long time ago?

Could I have landed on some television production set?

No, that isn't it. There isn't a camera in sight. Or behind-the-scenes workers in regular contemporary clothing.

Somehow, some way, I have time-traveled, in reverse, she concluded.

She had joked with her father and other family members several months ago about traveling back in time to save the Viking of her dreams. But she hadn't really been serious. After all, she wasn't a soldier or special ops person equipped in any way to rescue a captive. Besides, her dreams had stopped.

End of story.

Or so she'd thought.

Looking around her, once she was convinced she wasn't dreaming, or hallucinating, or anything like that, she berated herself for not being prepared. Even Claire, in that famous *Outlander* series, had planned for her adventure by packing a bag of photographs, modern medicines, ancient coins, and other necessities. All Kirstin had was what she wore.

But I have my brain, Kirstin told herself. *Time to use it to figure out why I'm here, and how to get back home.* She breathed in and out, determined not to panic. At heart, she knew why she was here...or rather who was responsible for her time-travel.

*The question is...*she began to study the crowd in more detail, to no avail...*where is My Viking?*

CHAPTER 5

The best-laid plans of mice and Viking men...

onight was the night, and not a moment too soon. If all went according to plan, Hauk would be out of his cage and riding off with Egil to join the Viking hirdsmen for the attack on Winchester Castle and its Saxon surroundings. He already had a knife, hidden in his loincloth, and horses and other weapons should be a'ready in a nearby woodland.

There was a worry, though. The Saxon nobles and their fighting men who remained in Aethelred's great hall following the evening meal were imbibing more ale than usual in their attempt to put on brave fronts. The more they drank, the louder their boasts of past victories and of ones to come in the days ahead. Also, the more they drank, glances kept darting his way, with angry remarks, as if he were a symbol for all heathen Vikings who dared to invade their country. If one of them got any more *drukkin*, the mead-brave lackwit might just attempt something foolish, like dragging Hauk out for the amusement of his comrades-in-ale.

Hauk breathed in deeply, then exhaled slowly, repeating the process several times in an attempt to slow his racing heartbeat. Energy abounded in his body, like it always did before a battle.

Just then, Egil sidled up and whispered, "Who is she?"

"Who? What?" Hauk was more than annoyed with the man. He'd warned Egil not to approach his cage anymore today, lest he raise suspicions about their relationship at this late date.

"The woman who is asking for you?"

"Huh?"

Egil pointed to the far end of the hall where a woman in a blue gown was talking to some nobles who appeared to be amused by what she was saying. He didn't recognize her, but then, it was hard to tell what she looked like from this distance and from the dark, smoky atmosphere of the cavernous hall.

Hauk waved a hand dismissively and asked, "Everything is arranged?"

Egil nodded. "Bergliot is taking the horses to the forest, as we speak."

That bedmate of Egil's! Hauk bit his lip to prevent telling Egil once again how halfbrained it was to drag a female with them. "Clothing for me?"

"Yea, and weapons. All is set. Just waiting for these Saxon whoresons to make for their beds."

Hauk would like to kill a few of these Saxon nobles before he left the castle, especially those involved in the St. Brice's Day Massacre, especially King Aethelred, but good sense curbed his appetite for revenge. For now. They would pay, though. That, Hauk vowed.

There was a sudden stir in the center of the hall as the woman in blue approached the high table, where King Aethelred still sat with his wife and several of his thanes. Was she demented? A person didn't address the royal family unless invited, and it appeared as if she'd just marched up, big as you please, and demanded an audience.

Oh, good gods! Hauk recognized the woman now. It was the female who'd appeared before his cage some sennights ago, the one who'd worn the symbol of a dog on her shert. He'd assumed it had just been a dream. That she was a fantasy of his tortured brain.

Queen Emma leaned forward over the high table, not an easy feat with her big belly, as she listened to the lady in blue speaking to her, gesticulating with her hands as she spoke. Others at the high table appeared interested, too, in whatever the lady was saying. Even those below the salt, sodden with drink, were listening, no doubt bored and open to new entertainment.

"She appears to be a Norsewoman," Egil observed.

'Twas true. She had pale blonde hair like many of his culture and the sculpted cheekbones that marked people of the North.

"A Viking woman in a Saxon hall?" Hauk remarked. "I smell trouble."

But that was the least of Hauk's troubles. Just then, the woman, the queen, and all those eavesdroppers turned to look in his direction.

And the woman smiled.

At him!

Trouble, for a certainty.

～

Phi Beta Warrioress...

Time to get *this show on the road.*

Kirstin inhaled deeply, then exhaled. With chin up and

shoulders back, she stepped forward. She was never one to avoid problems. Even seemingly insurmountable ones, like, oh, let's say, time travel and all the complications it would surely involve. The best way, she'd learned, was to meet a dilemma head-on.

And use my head, for goodness sake! In a war of brainpower versus brawn power, of which she had almost none, intelligence would win out every time.

She hoped.

For that reason, she approached the person closest to her, a housecarl by the looks of him, dressed in a belted tunic over slim pants and seated several tables below the salt. She tapped him on the shoulder to get his attention.

A housecarl was a permanent member of a noble's household guard. In medieval times, salt was a valued commodity which was placed in the center of one of the tables closest to the dais. The upper classes were seated above the salt, the common folks, below. Thus, she concluded, this was a guardsman of lower status. She knew these things because of personal experience, as well as her medieval studies, which hopefully would be handy in this time period.

See, my history, as well as my academic background, is already proving an asset in this situation. Who needs weapons and big macho men, like my brothers proclaim? If I was sent here to rescue a Viking idiot dumb enough to be captured by the Saxons, that's what I'll do, dammit! I am woman, hear me roar. Or something like that.

Bolstered with that confidence, she felt better about her prospects and asked the startled housecarl, "Can you direct me to the Viking being held in a cage?"

The man stood and gawked at her for a moment before saying, "Huh?" Obviously three sheets to the wind, he belched and almost knocked her over with his boozy breath.

His pal, another housecarl, stood as well and leered at her.

"Did ye not hear, Osric? She wants the Viking beast. Looks like she has a bit of the Norse blood in her, too."

"Ye could be right, Elfrid. Mayhap we should take her to our bed furs and show her the Saxon way. Ha, ha, ha!"

The two elbowed each other.

"No, thank you," Kirstin said and moved away quickly before they got aggressive.

She made her way directly toward the high table and heard murmurs following after her.

"A Norse woman. What's she doing here?"

"Where did she come from?"

"Appears to be seeking the Viking in the cage."

"Uh-oh!"

"Mayhap she is a spy for the heathen invaders."

"Best we inform the king of this."

"Put her to the rack, he will."

"Or worse. Some say Viking women are more vicious than their men."

"All women are. Ouch! Why did ye pinch me arm, Dorrie?"

"I'll pinch more than your arm if ye don't shut your yapper."

Kirstin ignored the comments until she stood below the dais and called up to the young woman in the center, a teenager, really, but wearing the garb and crown of royalty. If this was the time period she'd calculated when her father had first mentioned Hauk Thorsson to her, she knew exactly who this must be. "Queen Emma!"

When the queen failed to respond and instead kept chatting with an older woman on her left, Kirstin yelled, "Queen Emma, could I have a word with you?"

Now, Kirstin had the attention of not just the queen, but everyone around the queen, including the man on her right who must be her husband, King Aethelred.

The queen tilted her head in question and stared at Kirstin. "Dost speak to me?"

"I do. My name is Kirstin Magnusson, and I'm looking for the Viking being held here in a cage." Kirstin figured she couldn't be any more direct than that.

There were gasps around her, and she noticed the king make a motion with a flick of the fingertips of one hand toward some guardsmen on her left... to take her into captivity, for daring to address royalty without permission, no doubt, or maybe because she was clearly of Norse descent, or, oh, yeah, because she was asking about their prisoner. Immediately, two burly men took hold of her by the upper arms and tried to drag her away.

"Wait!" the queen said as she stood and attempted to see Kirstin better by leaning forward over the table, which wasn't far, considering her condition. Her purple gown, trimmed in gold thread, had a sort of empire waist which could not hide her huge baby bump. "Magnusson? Do I know you?"

Kirstin tried to shrug out of the grip of the two guardsmen, who turned out to be her two pals, Osric and Elfrid, to no avail. So, in a rush of words she tried to explain, "No, we've never met, but you must know my aunt, Lady Katla, who is married to Jarl Harald Gudsson of Norsemandy, or my cousins Thorfinn and Steven, Lady Katla's sons. My father is Magnus Ericsson. I know, it's usually the boys who take their father's names and the girls who take their mother's, but in my family we all use dad's first name as our surname. Much simpler, especially in our case where we all had different mothers." Kirstin bit her bottom lip to stop her nervous chatter.

Emma's eyes went wide as she picked out one part of Kirstin's blathering. "Lady Katla is my mother's godmother."

Well, yippee! Kirstin breathed a sigh of relief. When it came to Vikings, the usual six degrees of separation was knocked back to about three. She should have realized that from the start.

"Who is she? Where did she come from?" the befuddled king asked, looking first at his wife, then at the guardsmen.

"She asked for directions to the Viking beast," one of her guardsmen told the king.

The king's bushy eyebrows shot up with suspicion and he rose to his feet next to his wife. "For what purpose?" he demanded of Kirstin.

Kirstin knew she had to think quickly. She couldn't say she was a traveler from the future; too much explanation would be required on her part and too much disbelief would follow on theirs. And she couldn't say that she'd come to rescue the prisoner; she'd probably end up behind bars, too, or worse. So, she blurted out the first thing that came to mind, "He's my fiancée."

"Your what?" the king questioned.

"Betrothed. Hauk and I were betrothed by our fathers, as children. I haven't seen or heard from Hauk in years, and, frankly, I'm a little tired of waiting for him to drag his sorry ass to the altar. Oops! Sorry for the bad language. Anyhow, I figured I should check and see if he's dead or alive. If he's dead, time for me to move on." She shrugged. "If he's alive, well, that poses another problem, seeing as how he's living in a cage. Hard to set up housekeeping in that small a space. Ha, ha, ha."

Well, that bit of flippancy went over like a lead balloon, Kirstin realized as about a dozen people, including the king and queen, gaped at her. Not one of them smiled. No sense of humor, at all.

"How romantic!" Queen Emma said then.

"What?" Kirstin exclaimed and that sentiment was echoed by the king who looked at his wife as if she'd just hopped on the crazy train.

"We should have a wedding," Emma proposed.

"Are you gone barmy, wife?" Aethelred asked.

"No. Think about it, husband. If they wed, this woman will get the marriage she was promised. And my father and Sweyn can hardly complain about Hauk's confinement if they find him happily wed during his sojourn here."

Sojourn? Is that what they're calling imprisonment now? Like, "Hey, Mister President, how long will those terrorists be sojourning in Guantanemo?"

There were cheers from everyone within hearing distance. Finally, the drunken mass was to be given new entertainment. "A wedding! A wedding! A wedding!" they all chanted, banging their wooden goblets on the tables.

"Someone get the bishop," the king declared with an evil smile. "If he's not available, any priest will do. My wife gives good advice. Perhaps the heathen invaders will think twice about attacking if they find out we've treated one of their own so well."

No wonder Aethelred is described by historians as dumber than dirt, so to speak. And Emma is just as bad. As if one marriage could make up for months of incarceration for one high-placed Viking or for the massacre of so many Norse people living in England! "No, no, no!" Kirstin shouted over all the chatter. She doubted whether the king would be dissuaded by her pointing out that his transgressions would far outweigh this one act. So, she tried a more logical approach. "We can't have a wedding *now*. The banns have to be called in church for several weeks and other preparations need to be made for the ceremony. Plus, I have no wedding gown."

"I'm the king. I waive the need for banns," the king declared, raising his right hand as if making a royal proclamation.

"And your gown is perfect for a wedding," Emma decided,

smiling at Kirstin as if she should be happy at this turn of events.

"Um, do you mind if I go give my groom the good news?" she asked, playing for time.

"Is that wise?" the king asked. "Best you take a guardsman with you. If you get too close, he might bite off a body part, like he did a finger on that foolish lad who kept prodding him with a stick."

"I promise I won't prod him with a stick," she said, but thought, *Eeew!* "Besides, I would have to get close to him sometime if we're going to be husband and wife, right?" She batted her eyelashes suggestively. "No, it's best if I approach him alone at first." *And try to figure a way to get out of this mess.*

"Go at your own peril," the king said, then yelled at her two guards, who still held onto her upper arms. "Go find that bloody priest."

The morons just blinked at their monarch in a "Who? Me?" fashion.

"Now!" Aethelred screamed, spittle flying.

The two men released her, each going off in a different direction.

Emma was already ordering servants to clear a space in front of the dais for the wedding ceremony. "Britta, find some flowers. And you men, pull a table over here to set up an altar. Eadyth, go to the chapel and get an altar cloth. Whilst there, grab a chalice and communion wine. Rings must be exchanged; I can probably find those. Oh, so much to do!"

"Forget the communion wine. Bring more ale," yelled the king, whose crown was sitting lopsided on his head, whether from inebriation or all that yelling. Then, he plopped back down into his chair and glared at Kirstin.

She took that glare as her cue to exit the royal presence.

Making her way in the general direction of the cage, Kirstin plotted what she should do, concluding that getting Hauk out of the cage was a first priority, no matter how that was pulled off. Even if it was for a fake wedding. Once free of his jail, she and Hauk could figure out, together, how to escape the castle.

And then Kirstin could go home. Mission accomplished. *Easy peasy.*

On the other hand, maybe she didn't need to consult Hauk about a solution. She would take the man back to the future with her. Deposit him at Blue Dragon where her father and the other Viking-Americans could help him assimilate. That was the solution, of course. She just needed to get him somewhere alone to start the process with her arm rings, which were the means of her time travel. She assumed. Or hoped.

She was close enough to the cage now to see Hauk-the-Not-So-Handsome leaning against the bars at the back of the cage, arms folded over his chest, frowning at her.

Maybe not so easy peasy.

"Spare me, gods, 'tis the dog lady again," he grumbled.

"I beg your pardon. Did you call me a dog? You, who look like a hairy Big Foot creature, are saying I look like a dog? Maybe I won't rescue you, after all."

He rolled his eyes. "I meant the dog symbol you wore on your shert last time you bothered me."

"Bothered? Bothered? I'd like to tell you about bother," she sputtered. Then, taking deep breaths to calm herself, she explained, "That was Snoopy, who isn't a real dog. Just a comic...oh, never mind. We don't have much time, and I have to explain what's happening."

He ignored what she'd said and homed in on an earlier remark. "As for rescue, please spare me your halfbrained scheme. I have my own halfbrained scheme with my own halfbrained rescuer, thank you very much." He looked pointedly at the short man approaching who carried a sling full of kindling over his shoulder, which was odd in itself, it being so warm this evening and no fires having been lit in any of the hearths.

"M'lord, ye will not believe what I just heard," the kindling holder said, coming right up to the cage. Apparently this guy wasn't concerned about losing a body part. "The king and queen are planning a wedding. For this very evening. The bishop has been called, and a space is being cleared in front of the high table."

"Egil! Why should I care if someone is being married? Unless..." He narrowed his eyes and stepped toward the front of the cage.

Kirstin could swear she saw fleas bouncing off him as he got closer.

"Unless," Hauk continued, "it would somehow interfere with our plans for escape."

"Well...um...uh." The little man hmmmed and hawed, shifting from one foot to the other.

"Exactly who is being wed?" Hauk asked.

"You." Egil ducked his head as if fearing Hauk would reach through the bars and clout him a good one.

"Me? Nice to know. And who is the happy bride-to-be?"

Egil looked at Kirstin.

And Hauk laughed. He actually laughed. "Is this your half-brained scheme, dog lady? Will we consummate the marriage in my cage? Mayhap we can even have babies right here in this cozy little space."

"Don't be silly."

"Silly? I swear, ne'er in my misbegotten life have I been called silly. Do you have a death wish?" He peered closer. "Why are you wearing my arm rings?"

Even in this dim light, he could clearly see the chasing hawk design etched on each of them. An exact match for the rings on Hauk's own upper arms, though his were, of course, wider and bigger.

Kirstin crossed her arms over her chest and touched each of the silver rings on her upper arms. At once, she flinched at the mild shock, then shook her hands to clear the fingers of some invisible…something. "They're not yours," she declared. "They're mine. My brother Storvald gave them to me for a birthday gift."

He looked skeptical, then waved a hand dismissively. "Go. Away. You are going to ruin our plans for tonight."

"Actually, m'lord, mayhap this is not such a…," Egil started to say.

"Stop calling me a lord," Hauk grumbled.

"You're not a lord?" Kirstin asked.

"Aaarrgh!" Hauk said and pulled at his own hair, causing more fleas to dance around his head or were they lice? Maybe both. "No, I am not a lord. Egil just says that to annoy me."

"Ye are sort of a lord," Egil protested.

"Would you both stop this nonsense? It matters not a whit if I am a lord or a leper."

"You wouldn't say that if you were actually a leper," Kirstin pointed out. "Leprosy eats away at the body till all your flesh is rotted away and—"

"Aaarrgh! I know what leprosy is." Hauk was pulling at his own filthy hair again.

"As I was saying," Egil went on. "Mayhap this is not such a bad idea. It would get you out of the cage far easier than me breaking out some of the bars without anyone noticing."

"We've already half-sawed those bars," Hauk pointed out.

"Still, we need to get out of the hall, through the corridors, pass through the scullery to the back bailey, and on to the woodland, without anyone noticing. If ye wed the wench, yer presence outside the cage would be expected, to some extent."

Hauk pondered the possibilities. "Why would the king agree to this farce?"

Egil looked at Hauk as if he should know.

And he did. "Another source of entertainment for the idiots. Make a spectacle of the Viking. *Pfff!*"

"Plus," Kirstin added, "he's convinced that Sweyn and Duke Richard will be so impressed with his generosity in allowing a wedding that they'll overlook the indignity of the cage and your ill-treatment, maybe even be misled into thinking that the massacre wasn't really a massacre."

He stared at her for a long moment before repeating his earlier assessment, "Idiots!"

She wasn't sure if he was referring to the king or her as the idiot. No matter! "Use their idiocy to your own advantage," Kirstin advised.

Hauk gazed at her with speculation. "Seriously? And what do you gain from this arrangement?"

She shrugged. "Angel points." She looked upward. "I figure God sent me here to save you. Once you're saved, I can go home again."

"And your home is where?"

"You won't believe this, but it's America."

"That country beyond Iceland? The far-off land discovered by Leif Eriksson?"

"Yes!" She was glad he understood without lots of explanations.

"Isn't that a bit far for a rescue mission? I assume you have a longship nearby with at least thirty, preferably fifty, seamen aboard. And weapons aplenty because, sure as sin, Aethelred and his army will follow after me. I commend your foresight in preparing so for my rescue."

"No need to be sarcastic. A wise man accepts help graciously, no matter its source. Even in a dream."

"Graciousness is overrated, in my opinion." He mumbled something then, under his breath, something about damn dreams, damn gods, and damn women who gave themselves angel airs. She could tell that he, like most Viking males, didn't like the idea of being saved by a woman, or the idea that she was sent by God, or any of the gods, for that matter.

But then, he said, "'Twould seem you are gaining yourself a husband, m'lady warrioress. May the gods help you."

"Amen," she said, and she meant that as a prayer. "And, by the way, I'm no lady, either."

He just grinned. "Lucky me!"

CHAPTER 6

Now, that's what I call a honeymoon...

*a*nd so it was that Hauk prepared to be wed for the second time in his sorry life. He could only hope it did not end as badly as the first, for truthfully they were both forced marriages.

The woman...Kirstin...was not to his tastes, personally, being tall and blonde, like many Norsewomen. Not that there was anything wrong with pale versions of the female sex, but a man got tired of the same diet in the bed furs day after day. On the other hand, how could he complain? He was light-haired himself. Still, he much preferred dark-haired females with a smaller, more curvaceous frame. And Kirstin was no longer a young woman, either, being closer to his own age of thirty and five, he would warrant.

But female attributes were the least of his concerns. And who was he to be particular in his present position?

He had to give Kirstin credit, though. She had a skillful tongue when it came to dealing with the bothersome Saxons who thought to manage this charade of a nuptial affair. If only said tongue would rest on occasion! Instead, it was blather, blather, blather. And she had no qualms about addressing the king or queen in familiar terms, even the occasional, oddly-worded "You who!" when the royal pair failed to respond quickly enough to her comments.

The first obstacle arose when the king had demanded that, before opening the cage, Hauk be fully restrained with ropes holding his hands behind his back and ropes tied to both ankles so that he could scarce walk. Not to mention a leather collar and a chain held by a brute the size of a small mountain.

"What? You can't be serious," Kirstin had exclaimed. "How will he bathe before the ceremony?"

"What need is there for a bath?" the king had inquired.

"Cleanliness?" she'd replied sweetly.

"Aethelred!" his wife had berated the king. "You cannot expect a highborn lady to consummate her marriage with a man who reeks."

"Wouldn't be the first time," the king had muttered. Then he'd turned to several of the housecarls who were standing about drinking and enjoying the spectacle. "Take him outside and clean him up. A couple buckets of water and some soap should do the job. And get rid of that fur thing. It looks like a squirrel tupping his cock."

"Aethelred!" Emma had chided her husband again.

"What?"

"Must you be so crude?"

"More wine," the king had ordered.

"It's fox, not squirrel," Hauk had contributed. Not that anyone seemed to care.

The bath itself would have been laughable if Hauk were in the mood for laughter. The guards had not so much poured buckets of water over him but threw them, not wanting to get too close. Even with his arm and ankle restraints, Hauk had been fairly confident he could break free from these dolts and make a run for the trees, especially since the chain just dangled from his neck whilst the giant went off to the garderobe to settle a case of roiling bowels.

Hauk had considered the option of a rush to freedom, but only for a moment. He couldn't abandon Egil in the castle, and, truth to tell, the dog lady, either. If Aethelred suspected her help with his escape, the lady might very well end up in the cage herself. Furthermore, with his luck of late, Hauk would probably be stuck with Egil's girling, who was presumably tending the horses for their escape.

When he'd been led back to the great hall, Kirstin looked at him with disgust and remarked, "You look worse than you did before. Instead of being just dirty and greasy, now your hair is hanging in wet clumps, and I doubt you'll ever get the tangles out of your beard. Eew, don't get so close. Your lice might hop over onto me."

"Does your tongue ever stop flapping?"

"Nice talk for a bridegroom!"

"And by the by, you never did answer my question afore. According to your plan, how far do we have to go to ensure our escape?"

"Um."

Obviously, she had no plan. "Where exactly is your longship anchored?"

"I didn't come by boat."

He'd frowned with confusion. Knowing where America was located, roughly...beyond Iceland...he'd pictured the route from England to Iceland and beyond. Nothing but waterways came to mind. The English Channel, the North Sea, the Atlantic ocean. There was no direct path overland. "Dost care to explain?"

"Air?" she'd said, more as a question than a statement.

"You're asking me how you got here?"

"By sky then. Jeesh!"

He'd rolled his eyes. 'Twas as he suspected. The wench was barmy.

In an obvious attempt to change the subject, she'd called up to the king, who'd been talking to the newly arrived bishop, presumably yanked from his bed by the looks of the sleep shert peeking out from his wrinkled vestments and the mitre sitting lopsided on his bald head. "Could you not find any suitable clothing for my betrothed?"

When the king hadn't immediately answered, she'd yelled a little louder. "You-who, Aethelred!"

The king's eyes had gone wide when he realized that she addressed him thus.

Did that stop the wench? Oh, nay! She'd just blathered on, "Lord Hauk is a man of noble status in the Norselands. He cannot be wed in a threadbare, dirty tunic. And barefooted, to boot."

"What boot?" Hauk had asked.

Everyone nearby glanced down at his filthy feet and long toenails. A few of the women gagged and stepped back, as if the toenails might reach out and grab them. In his experience, females had an odd aversion to untended feet. Hah! They should meet Olev the Hermit whose toenails were so crusty and bone-like that he had to use a hand saw to cut them, which is why he had nine and a half toes. As for smelly feet, personally he was more sensitive to the scent of hairy arses or unwashed ballocks, or that gods-awful gammelost, the stinky cheese some chieftains fed their warriors betimes before battle so they would go berserk.

Back to his jabbering betrothed, who had obviously failed to realize that Aethelred's housecarls had to release his hands and feet in order to get a shert and braies on him, risking bodily harm or his escape. Instead, they'd thrown an open-sided, knee-length garment over his head and tied it at the waist with a thin rope.

"They are not about to release me," he'd started to explain, "so you can adorn me to your standards." He smiled to ease his criticism of her well-intended remarks.

"Shhh!" she'd said.

Truly, the wench went too far, shushing him. He'd been about to tell her so, but the king, by then recovered from his initial startlement, responded, "What difference does his clothing make? He will be naked within the hour. Unless..." He'd glanced to some of his drunken cohorts for support. "... unless Viking men have a way of consummating a marriage with their cocks covered. Which wouldn't surprise me. It's cold enough in the Norselands to freeze a bear's ballocks, let alone a man's staff, which on a Norseman probably resembles a skinny icicle. Ha, ha, ha!"

Much laughter had followed. Even the bishop, who'd been handed a cup of ale, had appeared amused.

"Actually, where I come from, condoms do cover the male penis during sex," Kirstin had said, "and no one would argue that protected sex is not intercourse. Tell that to thousands of college guys who buy condoms by the dozens. Ha, ha."

Hauk had no idea what a condom was or exactly what she had implied, but even he had been shocked that a woman would discuss sex, or male parts, in mixed company. "Have you no shame, woman?"

"Oh, please! Get over yourself!"

He'd recalled of a sudden how Ivan the Ignorant always said that the best wench he'd ever met had no tongue. Could be there was wisdom in Ivan's ignorance. He'd been confirmed in that conviction when she began you-who-ing again, this time to the queen, wanting to know if a bridal bower was being prepared. Little did she know that the cage and a pile of fresh straw was probably to be her wedding bed.

But now the ceremony was about to begin. Somehow, someone had gathered some flowers together and woven them into a crown of sorts that sat on Kirstin's head, which gave her a bridal look. And, in truth, made her look younger. Almost maidenly.

"By the by," he whispered, "are you a virgin?"

"No. Are you?"

Again, he was taken aback by her bluntness. "What a question!" he declared indignantly. "Untried at thirty and five years? What kind of man do you think I am?"

"I don't know. That remains to be seen."

Did she imply...? Holy Thor! She did! "I could show you right now what kind of man—"

She elbowed him into silence as the God-man began to expound on the heavenly responsibilities of marriage. He elbowed her back, just to show he would not be managed, but his elbow hit one of her arm rings and he nigh fell over at the stinging sensation, which felt like a thousand bees biting him at once, accompanied by a brief sizzling noise, like water on a white-hot blacksmith's iron. It wasn't that it hurt so badly, but that he was shocked by the sensation.

He glowered at her, but she just stared ahead, unaffected. He was beginning to wonder if she was some otherworldly creature, sent by the gods, mayhap the jester god Loki, or the Christian One-God, as she'd said. *And I am to be wed to her... this magical wench? Where was I when the luck tokens were being passed out by the Norns of Fate? What will happen when I put my cock inside her? Will she sting and scald me there, like she did my elbow, till I am a bare nub of my former glory?* He edged away from her a bit.

"What God has joined together, let no man put asunder," the bishop pronounced. "You may kiss your new wife, Viking."

The crowd roared and pounded the trestle tables with their fists and wooden mugs. The king was starting to look bored, which was not a good sign. Only Odin knew what a bored king would want next.

Hauk turned to Kirstin and said, "This is a new custom to me. The wedding kiss. In my land, the groom chases the bride across the courtyard, then swats her on the arse with the flat side of his broadsword, to show who will be master of his home."

"I know. It's called the *brud-hlaup*, or bride-running."

Why was he not surprised that she would know that? In fact, she started to expound on related matters, "When my father married for the fourth, or was it the fifth time, he—" Blather, blather, blather.

Hauk yanked her into his arms by looping his bound wrists over her head and behind her lower back, pinning her arms to her sides. She gasped, but before she could utter another word, he laid his lips on hers.

And it was sweet.

Way sweeter than he'd expected.

Way sweeter than he'd ever experienced.

Kisses were a waste of time, in his opinion. A boring prelude to better things. Leastways, that's what he'd thought in the past, from way back when he'd first tried his charms as a fourteen-year-old youthling on Inga, King Olaf's chambermaid.

Now...well, now, he knew that a kiss could be a bliss in itself. A simple brush of lips, at first, like a greeting. *Hallo, Inga! Nice seeing you again! Wouldst care to tup?* But then lips moving of their own volition, shaping until a perfect fit was made. *That's the way, Inga. Move to the left a little. Nay, you're hitting my nose. Yea. Like that.* And there was delving, too, as the tongue sought its natural channel, creating a wet path of what some might call slobber, but was more like what the skalds poetically called "sex dew." *Inga, Inga, Inga! Naughty, naughty, naughty!*

But this was not Inga. It was Kirstin. And, best of all, the woman had stopped talking. Another benefit of kissing he'd failed to appreciate until now. But wait, was that a low moan of pleasure emanating from deep in her throat? Thank you, Odin...it was, it was! He felt that moan like an echo all the way across his tongue, down his throat, downward, downward, downward, till it lodged where least expected and let out a wild, silent, vibrating yodel, a long drawn-out kulning.

Truly, this new view of kissing was something Hauk needed to examine in more detail. But not now, and not here, where hundreds of randy men, and dozens of equally randy women, chanted their approval of the spectacle he was creating.

He drew back slightly to stare at his new bride.

She was equally stunned, or aroused, if her glazed blue eyes and parted lips were any indication.

"More! More!" the raucous, laughing crowd demanded.

Hauk wasn't sure if they wanted more kissing, or more bodily contact, like mayhap an actual consummation taking place right here in front of one and all. Either way, he had no intention of giving the bloody Saxons any more entertainment. He began to raise his hands, but the bare skin of his inner forearms brushed against her arm rings. A hot tingling sensation was his first warning. But it came too late. Instinctively, he widened his arms to avoid contact, but in the process his own arm ring seemed to weld themselves to hers, just above the elbow. Try as hard as he could, the attachment held.

Then everything happened at once. His entire body went hot and tingling. His tongue felt numb, and he could not speak. In his confusion, he felt light-headed and dizzy. He could swear that he began to rise above the crowd, Kirstin still in his embrace. And they were swirling about, like a fast country dance. Or like a tornadic waterspout he'd seen years ago on the Baltic Sea, spiraling like a funnel out of the black clouds during a thunderstorm, except in this case the air was moving them up, not down.

Higher and higher, he and Kirstin went. Faster and faster. Up through the ceiling and roof of the great hall, into the night sky, which seemed bright as day. Even the stars were dancing. Or so it seemed. And the moon was a huge golden ball dripping honey. Strange. Very strange.

That is a lot of honey! he mused, ducking his head to avoid any of the drips.

Perhaps this was his barmy new wife's introduction to the honeymoon. In some Norse clans, family and friends of the bride and groom gifted them with enough honey mead to last a month. Since Vikings drank a lot of mead, and since it was believed that a month was the measure of time it would take for the moon to revolve around the earth, well, that period of newly wedded bliss came to be called the honeymoon. It was no coincidence that a month was enough time to conceive a child afore the man was free to go off a-Viking again.

And isn't it ironical that I would have these thoughts whilst twirling up in the sky. Truly, this is the strangest day of my life.

But then they began to drop. Fast. His senses went blank as they landed, he flat on his back on a hard surface with Kirstin atop him. Not the way he'd imagined their wedding night to play out. Well, mayhap her manning the rudder, so to speak, but not quite in this way.

Plus, he was fairly certain it was Kirstin who was screaming, "You idiot! Look what you've done!"

Definitely the strangest honeymoon in the history of Vikings, Hauk decided, and wagered that there were more than a few gods up there laughing their arses off.

~

There are road trips, and then there are road trips...

EGIL STOOD with Bergliot at the edge of the forest, staring, gape-mouthed, at the whirling dervish that appeared in the sky above them and came crashing down to the ground at their feet. They had been waiting, hoping, that Hauk would be able to find a way to escape the Winchester castle.

Looks like he did!

Bergliot...rather, Bjorn, still in female clothing... exclaimed, "Frigg's foot! Wish I could do that."

The lackwit!

The lady in blue had landed atop Lord Hauk, but already she was raising his bound hands over her back as she shimmied downward to escape his restraint. At one point, her mouth, still spewing forth curses, was aligned above a part of Hauk's body, which, under other circumstances, he might appreciate. But not now, of course.

Once free, she stood between his splayed legs and straightened the floral circlet on her head. Gazing around, she gave a groan of dismay and kept muttering something about idiots and this being the wrong place and time.

Meanwhile, the master still lay, eyes closed, spread-eagled on the ground.

"Is he dead?" Bjorn asked.

"No. Just unconscious, I think," the woman answered, nudging Hauk on the hip with the toe of her shoe, at first lightly, then harder. When she got no reaction, she looked over at Egil and Bjorn. "We're going to have an army of drunk Saxons after us any minute now. Do you think the three of us can get him up onto a horse?"

With all the weight the master had lost these months in captivity, Egil was fairly certain they could manage. Bjorn was stronger than she...he...looked. So, it was with much grunting —and more cursing from the woman, who knew some famous Anglo-Saxon words for fornication—they managed to get Hauk's body up and over the bare back of a swaybacked mare, arse upward, with his head and arms hanging over one side and his legs down the other. In the process, his open-sided tunic had come undone, and, with the slight breeze that rose suddenly, they all got a good whiff of his still dirty body.

"Eew!" Bergliot said.

"You don't smell like a flower yourself," the woman remarked.

"Huh?"

The woman quickly introduced herself as Kirstin Magnusson, daughter of Magnus Ericsson.

"Egil Karlsson here. One of Lord Hauk's hersirs when he is about fighting wars and such," he said, then added, "And this is Bergliot, my ward."

Kirstin nodded, then with a narrow-eyed scrutiny of Bjorn, observed, "Nice disguise, Bergie! Though you ought to cut back on the crotch scratching."

"Bugger off!" Bjorn replied.

"What a sweet *girl!*" Kirstin observed.

What? In all the weeks they'd been at Winchester Castle, no one had questioned Bjorn's gender, and, yet, this woman in one glance knew the truth.

"You make a great pair. The weird witch and the cowardly caged Viking!" Bjorn interjected, still annoyed over the lady's criticism of his crotch scratching...something Egil had been remarking on for weeks, for Thor's sake! The boy was stubborn as a fenced bull during the rut season.

Bad enough Hauk would be hearing such comments from others, but it was unacceptable from his son. Egil reached over and smacked Bjorn's head for calling Hauk a coward. That insult of his master he could not abide.

Then, turning to the lady, Egil wanted to ask her how she could tell the she was a he, as regards Bjorn, other than the cock scratching, but decided to save that question for later. Already, they were hearing a rustle of activity from within the castle.

"I'm not a very experienced rider," she told him. "In fact, I haven't been on a horse since I was twelve years old."

"You'll have to ride behind the master, then," Egil told her. "That beast is the tamest of the three horses and shouldn't bolt when being pursued." *I hope*, he added under his breath.

Although she appeared about to protest, she arranged her gown up under her bottom and between her knees, tucking the hem forward and into her belt, before letting him boost her up. And the three of them were on their way. Not as fast as he would like, with Kirstin and Lord Hauk moving at a slower pace, always lagging at least five horse lengths behind. There was a fear that a Saxon troop might close in on them using younger steeds.

"Where are we going?" Kirstin asked when her mare managed to catch up with him and Bjorn. They had been traveling for hours on a dirt road, unoccupied at this time of night. It had been well after midnight when they'd left Winchester. The sun should be rising soon, which would make their travel easier. But also easier for the Saxons to shorten the distance.

"To Jorvik."

"Hmm. That's modern-day York."

"What?"

"Never mind. Why Jorvik? Isn't there any place closer that would be safe?"

"That's where Sweyn's ship army should be arriving, if they are not already on their way here. We could go to South-hampton, of course, where Duke Richard's ships should have already unloaded an army of fighting men, but, no, Lord Hauk would much prefer to march with Sweyn, I'm thinking."

"Actually, Duke Richard isn't coming, but he has sent men

to help his daughter Emma and the king to escape to exile in Normandy."

"What? Who told you that?"

"Oops...I mean, it wouldn't be surprising, would it, if the royal couple found refuge in her homeland?"

Egil narrowed his eyes with suspicion. "Did Queen Emma tell you of such a plan? If so, 'tis important that my Lord Hauk know of this so he can stop the bloody bastard from escaping his wrath."

They both looked at Lord Hauk who was still dead to the world, atop her horse.

"You're right. We should just proceed toward Sweyn's army," she said then, as if her agreement meant aught.

But then, she seemed to think of something else. "Don't tell me you're going to join in the battle right away. Hauk needs time to rest and recover from his ordeal."

"Of course we will be raising our swords. Lord Hauk can rest once the battle is won. Believe you me, he will insist on participating."

"Why? Why does he have to be in the fight?"

"He is a Viking."

She shrugged, as if she understood.

"Besides, my master has more reason than most to want to spill Saxon blood. And not just because of their placing him in a cage." He glanced pointedly toward Bjorn.

Lady Kirstin shrugged again.

"So, you are Magnus Ericsson's daughter? I fought with him at the Battle of Stone Hill years ago. Will the old warrior be joining in this fight?"

"I'm sure he'd love to, but he's too far away. In America. No, I'm on my own."

"Why exactly are you here? In Britain, I mean."

"To save Hauk."

"Me, too," he said. "Were you really his betrothed at one time?"

"*Pfff!* Hardly. No, I was sent to save him."

"By whom?"

"God, I think."

"Ah, the Christian One-God." Egil had heard many a Papist lay all kinds of claims on their deity, who was supposedly three gods in one being. But why would their god not send a weaponed warrior, or an army, to save Lord Hauk, rather than this one puny woman?

He sighed. Who could guess the way of the gods?

"The question is, whether I'm supposed to leave him here, or take him back to the fut...to America with me," she pondered aloud, not appearing to want or expect an opinion from Egil.

Still, he asked, "Should a bride not leave that decision to her man?"

"Not in my world!" He must have looked at her with disbelief because she added, "In my country, women are equal to men, in all ways."

He could swear he heard Hauk mutter, "Gods forbid!"

Kirstin must have heard the same thing because she swatted the master on his arse with the palm of her hand and said, "Behave."

Egil was beginning to wonder which world she came from, like mayhap a barmy place in the Other World, not that Ah-mare-ick-ha discovered by his old comrade, Leif Ericsson.

All speculation in that regard ended, though, because approaching them from up ahead, coming in the opposite direction, was an army led by none other than Sweyn Forkbeard, easily identifiable in the misty dawn by his flaming red hair and his long, cleft beard. Before Egil had a chance to register this good fortune, he watched Sweyn raise a sword ahigh and kick his horse into a gallop, then yell, "Kill the Saxons!"

What Saxons? Egil wondered, pivoting his head to look behind, until he realized that Sweyn thought they were the enemy. And that demented Kirstin Magnusson was waving her arm and yelling, "You who! Hold your fire!"

"What fire?" Egil asked, just before an arrow pierced his shoulder, his horse reared up, and he fell to the ground with a thud. 'Twas just a flesh wound, he realized immediately, yanked the arrow out, and stood to glare at the miscreant who'd shot him.

Meanwhile, he heard Kirstin screeching at Sweyn, "Friendly fire, is it, you idiot? These are your fellow Vikings, and they have important information for you. Are you blind? Or just the usual thick-headed macho man?"

"Watch your words, wench, lest I slice off your tongue which outruns good sense. Like the usual lamebrain woman who knows naught of warfare and man business but thinks she must wag her tongue nonetheless!" He turned to one of his comrades-in-arms and asked, "What is a match-ho?" which gained him a shrug.

"Wench? Did you call me a wench? I'll have you know I have a doctorate degree in higher education. I have more smarts in my little finger than you have in your whole hairy body."

"Was that an insult?" Sweyn asked the same aide. And gained another shrug.

But then, Hauk, who had still been lying atop the mare in front of Kirstin, slid off the horse and stood, leaning against the animal for balance, momentarily, before stepping forward. "Greetings, Sweyn. 'Tis past time you got here. I was beginning to think I would have to fight the bloody Saxons on my own."

"Hauk? Is that you, Hauk? Not so handsome anymore, eh?

75

I heard you were living in a cage. I can see it must be true. I can smell you from here. Ha, ha, ha! The skalds will be busy for years telling tales of The Caged Viking. Ha, ha, ha! I heard you tried to eat through the bars." Sweyn dismounted and began to walk toward them.

"And I heard your third wife divorced you for a younger, more cock-worthy Viking," Hauk countered.

"'Twas just a rumor. I still have only two wives," then added under his breath, "which is two too many."

"Just so you know, you do not smell like flowers, either, Sweyn. More like horse and sennights of brewed man-sweat."

The two men laughed and embraced in a manly hug.

"Will you join us in the fight?" Hauk asked.

"You could not stop me if you tried."

"My sword, Neck Biter, has a hunger for Saxon blood."

"Sorry, but I get first claim on the king's fool head. I plan to mount it on the prow of my longship for the sharks and sea birds to nibble on as I journey home."

"Methought you would like to put him in a cage."

"There is merit in that idea, too. Naked, wearing his bloody crown."

"Mayhap I would spare him to you for that purpose, but only if you give me a limb or two for keepsakes."

"Will an eyeball do?"

"Men!" Kirstin muttered from where she still sat atop the sorry-looking mare.

But they all heard her and turned to stare.

"And who is this wench?" Sweyn asked.

Hauk rolled his eyes and revealed, "My wife. A gift from Aethelred."

"Wedlock? For you who always disdained the chains of matrimony? And I thought the cage had been your greatest torture!"

Egil could understand Sweyn's misthinking about Hauk's

marital history. Not many people knew that the master had married a Saxon lady all those years ago, never having lived with her or taken her to his home. And then she'd died. It was as if she'd never existed. Except for…

"'Twas my second greatest torture. My greatest torture was riding the skies in a magical whirlwind."

"Was that you?" Sweyn inquired, throwing his head back to laugh uproariously. "Methought 'twas an omen from the gods prophesying my upcoming luck in battle."

"Nay. 'Twas me. And my *wenchy* wife." Or did he say "witchy"? Egil wasn't sure.

Hauk looked at Kirstin to see if she was amused at his words.

She was not, the frown on her face a clear clue to her displeasure.

So Hauk glared at her, no doubt remembering that he should be displeased over the manner of his escape from the Saxon castle and her spouting off her opinions to Sweyn.

She glared right back at him.

"You did that strange trick without my permission," he lashed out indignantly. "What will you do next, turn me into a toad?"

She muttered something about him already being a toad.

"Because I object to being hurled about like a jester's puppet?"

"You escaped, didn't you?"

"I would have escaped anyway, in my own way, and my own more seemly manner," he insisted.

"Yeah, yeah, yeah. A little gratitude would be nice, baby."

"*Baby?*"

"If the name fits!"

They faced off at each other, of an equal height with her still on the horse, him pressed against the animal's side, and

77

continued to glare, one more stubborn than the other, not wanting to be the first to look away.

Egil suspected that his master had met his match, in more ways than one. He could scarce wait to see what they would do next.

But first, Egil had other matters to be concerned over. He must tell Hauk about Bergliot. Soon. Afore he discovered elsewhere that the maid was actually Bjorn. His son.

Help me, gods! he thought, suspecting that Hauk would be a mite displeased at his withholding that information. He sighed. *Where is a mead barrel when a man has a mighty thirst...or the need for ale-bravery?*

CHAPTER 7

He'd thought a cage was his biggest problem until...

"Let me see if I understand," Hauk said, his lips twitching with a combination of barely suppressed amusement and mounting impatience. "You traveled here from the future, *a thousand bloody years in the future*, your sole purpose to save *me?*"

"Exactly. The year two thousand and nineteen. Whew! I'm glad you finally understand."

He rolled his eyes. This was the first chance he'd had to be alone with Kirstin and demand an explanation for the amazing feat that had the two of them twirling up in the air and out of the castle in some kind of magic whirlwind. And this was the answer she gave him? Time travel! *Pff!* More likely, she was a witch. Which was equally unacceptable.

He had to be careful. Yea, he owed her for her help. But he could not chance another sky ride. Leastways, not until the battle was over, and he'd sent King Dumb-as-Dirt to an early grave, hopefully in a dozen pieces.

They were in a small tent which had been assigned to

Hauk and his entourage of Kirstin, Egil, and the lackwit maid Bergliot in the midst of the huge temporary settlement erected by Sweyn a considerable distance from Winchester. Hundreds of warriors had gathered already...a scene of organized pre-battle chaos, to be sure. But promising for the battle to come, which would be the following morning, if all went according to plan. They were waiting for Duke Richard of Norsemandy and his troops to join up with them.

Hauk was sitting on a chest, using a whetstone to sharpen his short sword. She was sitting on a pile of furs, opposite him, rebraiding her hair. Seen in the light of day, with the sun's rays peeking through an opening in the tent, the pale blonde strands shimmered like spun silver. With her sapphire-blue eyes enhanced by the sky-blue of the suddenly (well, 'twas the first he'd noticed) form-fitting bodice of her gown and the deep blue stone hanging about her neck, she was more than comely.

And she was his.

He had mixed feelings about that.

So, she was not as uncomely as he'd first thought.

But she was strange, to say the least.

On the other hand, having a wife could be a convenience betimes.

But mostly they were a pain in the arse.

He cleared his throat and inquired with casualness that was forced, "And this...uh...what did you call it?...time travel...it happened just because you wished it?"

"Dreamed it," she corrected.

"Wish, dream, summon, conjure, cast a witchy spell." He drew the whetstone over the blade as he spoke. Rasp, rasp, rasp.

"Don't get snarky on me. I'm pretty sure my time travel had something to do with these arm rings my brother Storvald made for me. That and the Viking reproduction hall in

80

Maine where I was standing. Uncle Rolf's hall somehow resembles the one in Winchester Castle. Suffice it to say, that's why it's important that I keep the bracelets on me, and that I don't wander too far from Aethelred's royal estate."

Rasp, rasp, rasp. He continued to work with the sword, seemingly only half listening, to cover his distress. What had he gotten himself into? Out of a cage into...another kind of prison. Wedlock with a witch! So, she wanted to stay close to Winchester. Could it be this was all a plot, and she was a spy for Aethelred? "Why would you need to stay close to Winchester?"

"Well, duh! Otherwise, I might not be able to return home. Or, rather, *we* might not be able to return to my home in California. Since that's where my bridge in time or wormhole, or whatever you want to call it, took place."

"Worm hole? You crawled here through a worm hole?" he sputtered, then stood, dropping the sword and whetstone to the ground. "We?" he inquired with sudden alarm, taking a step back.

"Aren't you curious to see what it's like in the future?" She stared up at him through amazingly beautiful blue eyes, waiting for his answer, a picture of innocence. Which could be a deception, of course.

"Not in the least." What a pointless exercise! He would have to accept her outrageous notions before he entertained speculation on what the future would be like. *When boars fly!*

"Believe me, there are fascinating advances," she driveled on. The woman did talk a lot. And it was clear she considered herself of greater intellect, whereas everyone knew that women had smaller brains. "Life is much easier. For example, you wouldn't need a couple dozen rowers for your longship. All you'd have to do is turn on the motor and steer the craft. Vroom-vroom."

He looked at her as if she was demented. She was. Not that

he knew what a moat-whore was. "Even if I believe this time-travel nonsense, which I do not, are you capable of moving from one time period to another, at will? I mean, can you guarantee I would be able to return here, if I did not like the future?"

She blushed.

As well she should!

"I don't know for sure," she admitted. "This is actually the first time I've done it, on my own, and I certainly didn't ask for it to happen. It was an accident."

He threw his hands in the air. The woman was beyond unbelievable. "Listen to me well, wench." And, yes, he had deliberately used the word wench to show her he was the one in charge here. "I am all for an adventure, but I am not sure I would want to risk my future in that extreme a fashion."

She shrugged. "You can decide later."

Easy for her to say when she'd just admitted that she'd ended up a thousand years in the past by *accident*. The gods only knew where he might end up, by *accident*. Mayhap that Biblical Garden of Eden that Christians believed in. Or in the other direction, mayhap the Norse estate of his very own great-grandson, assuming he ever had living children. *Try explaining kinship to a great-grandson who is older than you.*

Hah! A smart Viking did not depend on mischance for his future. "I doubt I will feel differently later. I have neglected my estates back in the Norselands far too long. 'Tis past time I returned to Haukshire and took care of my responsibilities. Gods only know what conditions I will find."

Although the tent gave them some privacy, they could hear clearly the loud noises outside of wooden tent stakes being pounded into the ground with mallets, the neighing of huge war horses, the bellow of oxen pulling equipment wagons, the clanging of cooking cauldrons over open fires, the whistles of swords and arrows being engaged in battle exercises, shouts, and laughter.

Hauk felt almost human after having bathed in a nearby stream, shaved, then bathed again. With his long hair hanging in a single plait down his back, except for two slim war braids framing his face, wearing a clean tunic, braies and boots borrowed from Sweyn, he might not be as handsome as he'd once been proclaimed, and he'd lost a good two stone in body weight, but that mattered not when it came to the upcoming battle.

Mayhap later, when the sex urge rose like sap in a maple tree as it did for many soldiers following a good fight, he would be concerned with his appearance and his appeal to willing wenches. He was a Viking, after all, and vanity was a gods-given right to that favored race of men. Truth to tell, bedmates came easy for Norsemen, handsome or not.

Which brought him to his wife. "I would be barmy to believe your story of time travel."

"I know how ludicrous it sounds. How do you think I felt almost twenty-one years ago, when I was only fourteen years old, living in the Norselands, and suddenly found myself along with my family on the other side of the world, America, a thousand years in the future?"

Hauk thought it best to humor the woman, who was clearly deluded, if not a mite insane. At the same time, he did a mental calculation. *Almost twenty-one years ago she'd been fourteen. Which means, she is thirty-five now, or almost thirty-five. Long in the tooth, as I suspected.* He was thirty-five, too, but age was different for men than it was for women. He was in his prime, or would be once he recovered from his ordeal.

"Are you saying that in your land…uh, time…when you left yesterday, it was…?"

"The twenty-first century. Yes, as I told you before."

"Unbelievable!" he muttered. "But your family's time travel

or whatever it was is neither here nor there. It does not explain what just happened to us. Did you and your family travel to the future in a whirlwind like we just did? Which would be something to see! Your father is known to be the size of a horse. Ha, ha, ha!"

She shook her head, and did not smile at his jibe about her father's weight. "No. There was a shipwreck off the coast of Iceland and we landed on a Hollywood movie set."

"Uh-huh." He had no idea what she meant.

"After that, we lived on a California vineyard, where my father remarried, had another child, and still lives."

"Your father, who already had ten or more children, as I recall, is still breeding in the future? Your father, a noted farmer, now grows grapes?" Her tale grew more and more unbelievable. He laughed.

"Yes," she replied. Still no smile at his humor. "He's adapted."

"Vikings do not adapt. They conquer. They do not surrender and adapt." He spat the last word as if he had a bad taste in his mouth. For a moment, he realized that was just how his Viking comrades would regard his being a caged Viking...surrender. They would make mock of him and say he should have fought harder and died in battle afore giving in to his captors.

She shrugged. "My father is an enlightened Viking."

Did she imply that he was not enlightened, whatever that meant? At least she was not calling him a coward, as some might, or a weak specimen of a man. "And you...have you a husband waiting for you in the future?"

She shook her head.

"Dead?"

She shook her head some more. "No, I never married."

"And you live with your father and his new family on this vineyard?"

"No! Of course not. Not anymore. I'm a college professor. I live alone in the city."

He blinked at her with confusion.

"A professor is a teacher of high education. And a college is a place where students...boys and girls both...go to study for various professions after twelve years of high school."

"Good gods! Are people so dumb in your time that they need twelve years of study?"

"Sixteen or more years, actually, if you include college."

He rolled his eyes. "What could they possibly study over all that time? Never mind. What do you teach?"

"Ancient Nordic Studies. In other words, this time period."

Is she saying I am ancient? He sighed. Talking with her was like swimming through mud. Hopeless. "If reverse travel through time is possible..." He couldn't believe he was actually saying that. "...why did your father and your entire family, for that matter, not return to the Norselands long ago?"

"Because life in the future is so much better...well, easier."

"No wars?" *I have no idea why I mentioned wars first off. Vikings ever do love a good battle; therefore, a world without wars would not be "better" for a Norseman. What would a Norseman do with his time, if there were no wars? Ride his longship for trading only? Or visit foreign lands just to chatter with new people? Or farm? How boring! Holy Thor! I am blathering in my head now, as bad as my wife with her running tongue.*

"Well, yes, there are still wars," she said.

"Whew! Thank the gods for that."

"In fact, three of my brothers are in the military."

"More wealth then? Is that what makes your country...uh, time...better?"

"My father was wealthy enough here."

"Adventure? Vikings are ever up for a good adventure on their longships."

"Hah! My dad is pretty much land-bound. In fact, I can't recall the last time he was on a boat."

"And yet you consider it a better place...uh, time...to live."

"It's hard to explain. There are so many modern conveniences, like horseless carriages and, suffice it to say, inventions that would boggle the mind. Like...oh, never mind. I can tell you everything later. For now, all you need to know is that I was sent here to save you."

And I was a dunderhead just sitting there waiting to be saved by a female? Hah! I beg to differ. Still, he wanted to be polite until he understood his path in this mire of confusion. "By whom, pray tell?"

"God, I think."

He laughed. "The Christian One-God has a care for a pagan Viking? Why? What is so special about me?"

"I can't explain why. I just saw you in my dreams and here I am."

The dream story again! "I hope I performed well." His mouth twitched with amusement.

She waved a hand dismissively. "There *are* some things you should know about the *near* future. What's going to happen right here in your time period. Like, I know that Sweyn is waiting for Duke Richard's forces to join up with him before attacking the Saxon castle. But news flash! The duke is playing both sides of the field. He's probably already sent men in to rescue his daughter, her husband Aethelred, and others in the royal household, scooting them off to Normandy for safe exile."

"What? Are you certain?" He paused and stared at her to see if she was serious. She was. "I should go tell Sweyn immediately. But, Frigg's Foot! Sweyn will want to know how I gained this information, and how will I explain that my witchy wife from the future told me so?"

She arched her brows at him, for doubting her words, no

doubt, or perchance because he'd referred to her as witchy. "You could tell him and let the facts prove their truth.

"You are so sure of the facts?"

She nodded. "I am. And here's another fact. A few years from now, the Normans will invade Britain and conquer the entire realm. For a period of time, starting with William the Conqueror in 1066, Vikings will actually rule the English world."

His eyes about bugged out at her amazing prediction...and that is all it could be, of course...a prediction. "And do we Vikings still rule these parts in your time?"

"Oh, no! The Vikings die off as a separate culture soon after that."

"Die off?" he sputtered.

"Well, not die off precisely. More like they meld into other cultures. Marriage, settlement, and so on. In fact, modern-day Iceland is the closest we have to Vikings."

He laughed "You should be a skald. Your sagas are as absurd as any I have ever heard the poets and storytellers relate during the long winter nights afore the hearth fires."

"Believe it or not, it's the truth. You'll find out. At least some of these things will be proven true soon enough."

He tried to decide what to do. Tell Sweyn about Richard's possible defection and risk ridicule. Or tell him nothing, and have them all waste precious time awaiting the duke's arrival. "Come," he said, taking her by the elbow, "Let us go brave the lion, and inform Sweyn of your news. But, please, enough of this nonsense about time travel! Instead, just say that you know by way of Queen Emma, or other family members."

She appeared unsure of his plan, but allowed him to lead her out of the tent, making their way through the various camp sites.

"So, you are not a witch. That is a relief," he said as they walked along. "I have no liking for mating with a witch.

Afeared I would be that the least misstep and my witchy wife could turn my favorite body part into a black cat." He was teasing, but she did not smile.

"There's going to be no 'mating,' let's understand that right away."

"Oh, really?" He'd only been teasing with the "mating" remark. Holy Thor! He'd had no time in the past twelve hours to even think of sex.

But now...

He eyed his new wife up and down in deliberate scrutiny. As he continued to stare at her, he felt a clutching sensation in his chest, which moved lower. Probably hunger. Of one kind or another.

Until now, he'd had mixed feelings about her. Yea, she was passably pretty. And, yea, he would have no trouble swiving her when the occasion arose. But then, considering the length of his prison celibacy, most any woman would do.

Or not.

Was she insinuating that she did not want him? Hauk knew his worth and she dared to rebuff him? The nerve of the wench! "Are you saying that I am not comely...that you do not find me attractive?"

"Hardly!" she said with a note of disgust. "You're so hot you would make any girl's bones melt."

He assumed that "hot" was a compliment, and a slow smile grew on his lips.

"Not that you don't know that already."

Of course he did, or leastways he used to. "And your bones...are they melting?"

"That's not the point," she said huffily. "What's with this sudden interest in me...*that way?*"

"Which way?"

"You know...sexually."

Truly, this woman was more blunt and outspoken than he

was accustomed to, especially a woman of the upper class. Not that he was objecting. He rather liked the honesty of her words. "'Tis well that you ask that question about my interest! Look around. Dost notice men staring at you with lust?"

She waved a hand airily. "That's just because I look different from the camp followers."

He shook his head. "Egil tells me that you were accosted at least a dozen times as you walked, unescorted, around the camping grounds today, despite my orders to the contrary, by the by, that you stay in the tent. He followed you and witnessed several arse pinches, two embraces that lifted you off your feet, a half dozen offers of coin for tupping, and many rude insults."

"Egil has a big mouth."

"You are just now realizing that?"

She sighed with impatience. "Get to the point. I can't stay in hiding forever. What's going to change their attitude?"

"Consummation."

"Whaat? Do you mean sex?"

"That is what I said, is it not?"

"Actually it wasn't. You tossed that out there as if consummating a marriage was an everyday occurrence. You could just as easily have said, 'We need to bake some bread.'"

"Did you hit your head when we did that whirly dance through the sky and fell to the ground?"

"You know, your attitude is really annoying me. Certainly not a way to woo a woman to your bed."

Well, she certainly put him in his place. He blinked with surprise.

"So, consummation would change the way men view me?"

"Probably. Word has spread that you and I were just wed, with no chance for the ritual bedding. Until that happens, some consider you fair game. 'Tis a well-known fact that the sap rises in warriors as they prepare for battle. Any willing, or unwilling, female will do. And there you are like a bloody haunch of roast reindeer on a silver platter."

"Thanks a lot for the compliment. So, we should just do it? Now? Should we duck into some empty tent? Or go behind a tree? Assuming your sap is up and running, like all the other randy men. And, by the way, do women have sap, too?" She fluttered her eyelashes at him in an exaggerated fashion.

"Sarcasm ill-suits you, wife."

"Likewise, husband. That's another thing. I'm not really your wife. That farce of a wedding...? *Pfff!*"

"Oh, that your assumption were true!"

"What do you mean?"

"Are you forgetting that the rites were performed by a priest? I saw him sign a document, which I assume gets a church seal."

Any further discussion on that subject was interrupted by Egil rushing up to them, huffing to catch his breath. "My Lord, *please* stop and listen. There is something of importance I must discuss with ye."

Egil had been trying to speak with him about some "important matter" all day. When Egil had admitted that it was not a matter of life or death, Hauk had put him off. "Later."

"Nay, m'lord. It must be now," Egil contended.

Hauk groaned. "Egil, please. I must needs meet with Sweyn first about something my wife just told me. Then, Sweyn wants my help with battle strategy, and a map of the inner design of the castle to weed out any stragglers once they break in. You could help with that, Egil, since you moved freely about the lower regions of the castle. After that, he expects me to regale him with a history of all that I suffered under Aethelred's imprisonment. And, you can be sure, he'll want an explanation of that Holy Fuck dance I just did up in the air." He glanced at Kirstin on mention of this last thing. "Sweyn will want to know if you can you do that at will, wife, and if so, he will think that such a skill could come in handy during battle."

"What will you say to that?" she asked.

"I will say, Sweyn, my friend, if you think I will willingly subject myself to that terror again, I have a bridge to sell you over the North Sea. If he wants to win this battle, he will need weaponed men, the more the better. Not tricks."

"Speaking of seasoned fighters," Egil broke in, "some of yer shiphird, who have been hanging about Jorvik these many months manning your longship, *Sea Wolf*, have arrived and are looking to join the ranks. They need direction on where to gather. There aren't many of them left, actually, about two dozen or so, but..."

Hauk pointed a hand in the opposite direction. "Find an empty space in my formation for all of them, and I will come by shortly to talk to each of them. Make sure they are fed and have places to lay their furs for rest."

He could use both of those himself...food and sleep. A short nap somewhere private to prepare for battle. Anywhere would do. Even the hard ground, against a tree if there were any left in this clearing with all the cook fires now blazing, or spooned against some mongrel dog in an open field. Or a wife, he thought, and immediately wiped that idea from his lame brain, but it made him smile.

Egil mistook his smile for agreement to talk with him, now. "It all started about a year ago when I happened—"

Hauk cut him off with a halting hand. "Is this about that bedmate of yours again?" he growled. "I swear, I have seen and heard enough of—."

"Yea, 'tis about Bergliot, but not what you think," Egil inserted quickly.

If you only knew what I think! "Where is the maid?"

"Guarding your tent, after you left. You have no idea how scarce such accommodation is, even ones so meager."

In addition, there was a pouch of gold coins in the chest inside the tent, of which Egil was unaware. "You left a girl to guard my few possessions from a horde of thieves mixed in with this lot?"

"Well, see, that is the thing. Bergliot is not a girl."

"Well, for a certainty, she is not a woman full grown. How old is she? Thirteen? Fourteen?"

"Twelve. And she is a he...a lad." Egil ducked his head at that latter announcement.

Hauk cocked his head to the side. Already, various folks were gathered, wanting his attention. One of Sweyn's hersirs motioned for him to follow, a guardsman from Haukshire who must be newly arrived was waving a greeting, and a buxom wench was inviting his custom with obscene gestures toward her nether region.

"Bergliot is a male, is that what you are telling me?" Hauk asked with not a little consternation.

"Yea, that is exactly what I am saying." Egil appeared relieved that Hauk understood his meaning.

Now that he thought on it, he could see the signs had been there all along. How could he have missed them? "Good gods! You are a sodomite now?"

"Nay! Of course not. 'Twas just a ruse."

Hauk put a hand to his face and counted to five, silently, *ein, tver, þrir, fjórir, fimm,* before looking at Egil. "Why would you need a ruse?"

"To protect the boy."

Hauk picked up Egil with hands under his armpits. Staring at the little man face to face, he demanded. "Spit it out so I can get on with the business of this mad day."

"Bergliot is actually Bjorn. Your son."

Hauk's brain went numb for a moment and he shook his head to clear it. "Bjorn?"

"Yea. I found him wandering in a daze outside Oxfordshire the day of the head loppings." When Hauk continued to gape at the little man, Egil continued, "I saved him. Hid him under a wagonload of headless bodies, I did. Never saw a person vomit so much in all me life. Me, not the boy, who was brave as Thor. You would have been so proud."

Oh. My. Gods! Hauk thought for several long seconds before dropping Egil to the ground and putting a boot on his chest, preventing him from jumping to his feet. "Is this a jest?"

"No jest," Egil said. "I could not tell ye when ye were still in the cage. Afeared I was that ye would attempt to break loose and get yerself killed afore we could escape."

Hauk grunted his disgust and lifted his leg, letting Egil scramble to his feet. Turning, Hauk began to stomp back toward his small tent at the far end of the field.

Egil continued to talk to him as he ran to catch up. "This is good news, m'lord. A happy reunion. But best ye be prepared, Bjorn has a gripe against ye for years of neglect."

Hauk stopped suddenly and Egil ran into him. Kirstin had followed after them and was listening with interest, nodding her agreement. "Don't blame Egil for what was obvious."

He turned slowly to stare at her. "So, you were aware of this deception, too?"

"Well, any fool could see that she was a boy, but, no, I didn't know he was your son. How wonderful!"

Righting himself, Egil raised his chin and said, "I did what I thought was best to protect you and yer son."

"Hmpfh!" was the most Hauk was willing to concede. With a sigh, Hauk said to Egil, "Go, tell Sweyn that I will be there shortly...with my wife. First, I must see for myself that the maid is my...my...son."

Even as he spoke with reasonable calm over the lump in

his throat, Hauk's mind swirled with this unexpected turn of events.

Bjorn is alive!

My son.

A second chance to make things right?

Bjorn is alive!

Praise the gods!

And, yes, a bit of praise for Egil, too.

Happy at his apparent pardon, Egil scampered off in his crab-like gait, gained after years of riding one longship after another over rolling waves. Thus, Hauk was alone, somewhat, except for his wife who trailed behind him, when he approached the tent and saw his son, clearly a boyling now, dressed in a belted tunic over slim braies and ankle boots. His blond hair was pulled off his face and tied at the nape with a leather thong. There was a strong resemblance that should have been apparent to Hauk before.

"Bjorn!" he called out.

The boy turned abruptly at his greeting, his expression wary. He was skinny as a pike, just as Hauk had been at that age.

"I had no idea...Egil just told me," Hauk choked out. "By thunder! This is the best news I've had in years."

Bjorn's chin went up and he backed away from Hauk's extended arms.

"Son?" Hauk said. "You have naught to be afeared of. I am your father."

"Hah! You are no father to me." He spat on the ground for emphasis. "Where have you been these ten years and more? Where were you when my mother was dying? Where were you when the bloody Saxons murdered my foster father, Pallig Tokeson, and his family? And then you let yourself be caged like a tame dog. No matter." He waved a hand dismissively, as if Hauk and his misdeeds were of no importance to him and continued to back away.

Hauk grabbed Bjorn's upper arm and yanked him to a halt.

"Bugger off!" The boy tried to squirm out of his hold, to no avail.

His insolence and lack of respect would merit a whomping if they came from anyone else. Should he try to explain his absence? Should he force the squirming Bjorn to stand still, and to hell and Muspell with any explanations? Should he tell him of his regrets and how much he loved him? Should he try to explain how he'd been taken by the Saxons? With a grunt of disgust at his wavering thoughts, he pulled the boy into a tight bear hug, murmuring, "My son! Alive! And you helped Egil rescue me? Praise the gods!"

Bjorn bit his shoulder and muttered, "Kiss my arse!"

Hauk chuckled. He had to admire the boy's spunk.

But then, said spunky boy kneed him in the ballocks, *hard*. Reflexively, Hauk loosened his embrace, and Bjorn took advantage of the lapse, running off, laughing.

Hauk was bent over at the waist, cupping his private parts, gasping for breath, when Kirstin came up to him. She dared to grin at his position. "Still think you could handle consummation?"

Not any time soon, he thought, but what he said was, "Betimes, a man must endure a little pain to gain his reward."

Then he winked at her, just in case she didn't get his meaning.

She must have because she gave him a look of disgust, which was not the usual reaction he got from women when he winked at them.

He gave her a shove into the tent and followed after her. "Heed me well, you headstrong, willful woman. Before we go to meet with Sweyn, you must needs listen to me. If you speak to Sweyn the way you do to me, he will discount anything that comes from your mouth as that of a barmy person who is wasting his precious time. Or he may deem you a spy for the Saxons, which would be just as bad for you. Believe you me, Sweyn is not known for his patience or kindness. On a whim he could slit your tongue, or strip you naked and let his archers use you for target practice."

"Blah, blah, blah! I don't care a fig about Sweyn or what he thinks of me," the impudent wench said, plopping down on the travel chest. "I came to rescue you, and now that you're free, there's no reason for me to be here anymore. Suffice it to say, mission accomplished!"

He paced the small space inside the tent and glanced intermittently at her, trying to figure her out. Why was she not shivering with fear, as any normal female would, or many a male, as well?

"If you hadn't touched my arm rings and thought of escape to the outside of the castle," she continued, speaking slowly as if he were a slow-witted youthling, "we could have been far, far away from here. Maybe back in America, which is what I would have pictured in my mind."

He gave her a glance of horror. Did she honestly believe that was a situation he would desire?

"But do you care? No. You are where you want to be and that is all that matters. So, go off and do your war things." She made a shooing motion with her hands. "I'll go home on my own, somehow."

"Barmy as a bat drukkinn on mead," he muttered.

"Really. Go off and fight your silly war and probably end up dead, defeating the whole purpose of my rescue mission."

"You are not going anywhere until I discover why you are here, *wife*."

"As if you have any say in the matter! As long as I have my arm rings, I can go wherever I want," she asserted.

But that was her mistake, giving him information to use

against her. "Is that so?" Hauk said, and before she could run away, he wrapped his hands in scraps of linen and pulled her arm rings off, tucking the bundles inside his tunic. "For safe-keeping," he assured her with a self-satisfied grin.

She attempted to hit him then, but he ducked and she ended up tossing the shield which she probably intended for his head but instead landed at his feet. He laughed, he couldn't help himself.

"Where is that cockson Hauk Thorsson?" a male voice boomed outside the tent, interrupting whatever his wife intended next.

It was Sweyn and he was not in good humor, as evidenced by the sounds of Egil trying to explain their delay. "There was a family crisis, which required my master to handle some other priorities."

"Other priorities? How dare he fail to obey my summons to council? How dare he force me to come to him?"

"I'm sure he will apologize profusely when he gets a chance—"

"Apologize? Apologize? I'll give the loutling an apology with the side of my sword across his arse. And where is that blonde sorceress? The witch best not have flown away afore I have a chance to examine her myself. Legend says witches have three tits? What think you, Egil?"

"Um," Egil said. "They are both inside the tent."

"Praise the gods! I am in the mood to lop off a head, or two."

CHAPTER 8

This was "Living History" at its best...or worst...

irstin was sitting next to Hauk in the midst of
Sweyn Forkbeard's war council. Under a large,
open-sided tent, a huge makeshift table (the bed of a weapons
cart) rested on several hastily constructed trestles. Thanks to
two sets of planks from the sides of the cart, braced on a
number of war chests, a dozen or so Viking hersirs lined both
sides of the table. She was the only woman present, except for
three maids serving munchies...hunks of flat manchet bread,
slices of hard cheese, some ribs or legs of rare (okay, bloody)
animals...boar, rabbit, whatever, or pouring many pitchers of
mead or ale into wooden goblets or the men's own horns
which they carried on loops at their belts.

Wow! In her wildest dreams (and, yes, this was a dream,
sort of, maybe), she...a professor of Nordic Studies... couldn't
have imagined such a living vision of the past. She wished she
had her iPad with her so that she could take notes...better yet,
a video camera... for when she got back home.

If I ever get back home, she reminded herself.

She immediately wiped that thought from her mind, not wanting to contemplate such a horrific possibility. Besides, there were more important, more immediate problems. She was still trying to come to terms with that magical out-of-body experience that had occurred last night during the wedding. The spin through space and walls that had landed them, not back at Blue Dragon, which is what she'd hoped would happen after rescuing Hauk, but outside the castle, and now in the middle of the huge tent city of Sweyn Forkbeard's army, roughly five hundred warriors, who were preparing for the upcoming battle.

There were a numbers of issues Kirstin had to deal with, ASAP.

First of all, what had happened to her, and Hauk, last night was unlike her first time-travel experience, from Rosestead to Winchester. Just poof! One place to the other! Easy peasy! But this time, there had been no poof involved. Instead, it had been a whirling, wide-awake thrust over a short distance, from inside to outside a building. Not really time travel. More like teletransport, or something.

Aarrgh! Where is Spock or a scientist to explain this phenomenon? If there is any explanation. She was still leaning toward the celestial involvement theory.

Secondly, this latest event had happened without her being in charge of the rudder, so to speak. A dangerous thing, that.

Can I trust a man...a Viking man...an ancient Viking man...to determine my fate?

Hell, no!

Nothing personal, Hauk. It's a female independence thing. I wouldn't let my brothers arrange a blind date for me, let alone arrange my future. As for my father, he'd probably have me wedded and bedded and heavy with child, if he had his way.

Third, she was now without the arm rings that presumably were the key to her reverse time travel.

What will I do if Hauk gets himself killed and I can't get to his body before the scavengers arrive to loot the corpses? Morbid, yes, but I've got to get those arm rings back before tomorrow.

All these were problems to be pondered or solved later. For now, she had to appreciate the irony of the moment, a professor of Ancient Norse listening to people speak Old Norse, the real deal. Actually, she probably would have understood most of it anyway because Old Norse (which in no way resembled modern Norwegian) had a sprinkling of English words in it. In fact, many English words stemmed from Old Norse. The closest there was to Old Norse in modern times was Icelandic.

Anyway, sitting here among these Dark Age Vikings, well, it was like being in a History Channel video on medieval warfare. Or a reality TV show. And she was the star. Or one of them.

The other star was sitting next to her, calm as you please, unlike how he'd been on the way here, upset over his encounter with his son and then several almost-fights with Viking acquaintances who'd made jokes about "a caged Viking," calling out such things as, "How does a caged Viking have sex?" The answer made had been, "Like a dog. He licks his own balls." And yet another fool Viking had remarked, "Hmmm. To develop that skill I might live in a cage, too. Ha, ha, ha!"

Although there had been no all-out brawls, several Vikings were now sporting bloody noses or black eyes. And Hauk's knuckles were scraped and swollen.

Men!

She and Hauk were listening to Sweyn prattle on about the events leading up to this day, mostly patting himself on the back for all his heroic efforts in pillaging many English monasteries and villages these past ten years. Presumably this was leading up to his current battle plans.

Ho hum!

If he'd let her speak, she could get them out of this mess. Lickety-split. Maybe. But no, she had to be careful not to say or do something that could alter the path of history. At least, she didn't think she should do that, or could do that. After all, if that were possible, someone could go back and eliminate Adolph Hitler before the Holocaust, or go back to the fourteenth century and warn everyone that it was fleas that would cause the Black Death or Plague, which wiped out up to two hundred million people. The Stock Market Crash and the Depression...

Hauk took hold of her hand, linking their fingers, and squeezed hard. Under his breath, without looking her way, he whispered, "Pay attention. Sweyn was talking to you."

A zing of pleasure swept over her, from her palm, up her arm, and throughout her whole body, leaving her warm and tingling. She glanced down at their still-entwined hands which he held over his thigh, which was pressed against her thigh. Then she looked up at him. He ignored her, listening intently to Sweyn, but she noticed a slight tic in his tightened jaw. He was as aware of her as she was of him.

Hauk must have found some place to bathe because he looked like a different person than the creature she'd found in the cage. With his newly washed blond hair pulled off his clean-shaven face, except for two thin war braids on either side, and borrowed clothing befitting a Viking of upper status, he was certainly attractive. Not godly handsome like he'd been reputed to be, but once he regained his lost weight and his prison pallor faded, he would no doubt pose quite a figure.

Suddenly she had an image of herself lying on soft-as-silk furs, with him leaning over her, minus said garments, whispering wicked words, just before his lips pressed...

Oh, my God! Seriously! In the midst of this mayhem, I'm thinking about sex. I must be losing my mind.

Hauk did look at her then, and he knew what she'd been thinking if that twinkle in his eyes was any indication.

Was he having similar thoughts?

Oh, boy! She did not need these complications. With deliberate care, she turned her attention to Sweyn, who sat at the head of the table on a high-back chair he must have brought with him. He was indeed expounding on something related to her. He said that he'd been told third-hand, via an aide who'd spoken to Egil who'd been told by Hauk who'd relayed what Kirstin had said about Duke Richard of Normandy reneging on his agreement to stand with Sweyn in this upcoming battle. "The interesting thing is, my comrades-in-arms, a scout just arrived with news from Gastonbury where our allies were presumably landing. Finan, speak."

A middle-aged man took a last swig from his horn and stood, swiping with the back of his hand across his heavily mustached mouth. "No sign of the duke. He ain't comin'." He then started to sit back down.

"Whoa, whoa, whoa!" Sweyn said. "You must have discovered more than that."

Finan straightened and said, "Well, yea, a bit more. Whilst there were no signs of the Normans, there was talk of some sighting of a boat hidden in a cove nearby. Not a longship. One of those Frankish designs with a room built below deck to hold passengers. When I checked the area, there was no sign of a boat, though." He took another draw on his horn and frowned, realizing that he'd emptied it already. "Also, I spoke to some villagers nearby and they claimed to have seen some foreign-looking men with that strange hair style them in the Franklands favor. You know, the one where they comb their hair forward and cut a line across their forehead and they also lob off the hair shoulder-length in a straight line, too. Makes 'em look like lackwits, if ye ask me. You know what I mean," he said, demonstrating by drawing a line across his forehead.

Others at the table nodded, understanding what he'd meant. He meant a pageboy hairstyle with bangs, a medieval version of the later mushroom haircut popularized by the Beatles.

"I'd shave me head afore I'd cut my hair so," said one burly Viking who had a wild bush of graying brown hair.

"Makes 'em look foppish," another man, whose blond beard was braided intricately with colored beads, said. Like a braided beard wasn't a tad foppish!

"Next they'll be wearing ruffles on their tunics and bells on their boots. Ha, ha, ha!" This from a man with no teeth, who'd been sucking on what looked like a dragon bone, it was so big.

"Enough!" Sweyn bellowed. "It appears that what the woman, Hauk's wife, has said is proven true. What say you?" Sweyn and every other person at the table turned to look at her.

Hauk squeezed, then released her hand, helping her to stand. Not that she needed any help, but she appreciated him standing beside her. Finan breathed a sigh of relief that he was no longer being grilled and sat down, waving at a maid for more ale.

"What did she tell you, Hauk?" Sweyn asked, while he gazed at Kirstin's chest area, no doubt looking for signs of a third breast. If she'd had time, or had thought ahead, she would have put some padding there, just to confuse the fool.

But Hauk was speaking.

She listened carefully.

"All she told me was that Duke Richard would not be coming or sending troops to stand with you in this assault. Oh, and mayhap I forgot to mention...she said that the king and queen would be offered exile in Norsemandy should the assault prove successful."

Everyone seemed to realize at once that the boat Finan had mentioned must have been sent for the royal couple.

"Arne, go at once to investigate and take a hird of soldiers with you. Find the bloody boat and make sure the vessel is destroyed. If ye find any Frankish men about, take them captive and bring them here for questioning."

A tall, black-haired Viking with a vicious scar running from his left eye, down his cheek and onto his neck stood and left immediately. Outside the tent, he could be heard calling out orders.

"Now then...m'lady Kirstin, isn't it?...start from the beginning and tell us everything." The steely glint in Sweyn's eyes told her that Hauk had been right. This was a man who would as easily kill you as listen patiently.

"There isn't much to tell," she said. "All I know is that Aethelred, Emma, and the king's children will escape to Normandy...uh, Norsemandy...while you overtake the castle."

"And this is an accomplished fact, in your informed opinion?"

"Well, I meant that this is what is planned," she amended.

"You speak familiarly of Aethelred and Emma, as if you are personally acquainted with them." He narrowed his eyes with suspicion, no doubt still thinking she might be a spy, or on the side of the Saxons.

"Well, Emma *is* related to me..." Hauk groaned softly beside her, and she realized she was giving too much information. But she couldn't stop now. "My aunt, Lady Katla, is Emma's godmother."

Sweyn's eyes widened with surprise.

In for a penny, in for a pound, she decided then. "My father is Magnus Ericsson. I grew up...my early years anyway...in the Norselands."

Hauk stiffened beside her, fearing she would tell the time-travel story. She knew better than that.

"Is your father here with you?"

"No, he is—"

Sweyn waved a hand dismissively. "'Tis of no importance now. Tell us how you knew of these plans for escape."

"Emma told me. In fact, she invited me to go with them," Kirstin lied, "but I couldn't abandon my betrothed." She batted her eyelashes at Hauk, as if she was love-struck.

Hauk pinched her butt. Luckily no one stood behind them who could see.

She put a hand over her mouth and whispered to Hauk, "Should I tell him that he will be crowned king of all England before Christmas, but that he will die about a month later?"

Shocked, Hauk said, "No!" Failing to lower his voice, as she had, everyone heard his response and looked at him with curiosity.

"What did your wife just say to you?" Sweyn demanded.

Hauk glared at her, then told Sweyn, "It's rather intimate."

"So?"

Now everyone was *really* interested.

Hauk sighed in an exaggerated fashion before telling him, "She said, with all the male virility around this table, her woman dew is pooling like hot honey. She wondered if we could take a short break and go swive somewhere."

Kirstin gasped and elbowed him. Then, realizing they were being watched closely, she pretended embarrassment and said, "You didn't have to tell everyone, you lout!"

"Sorry, sweetling," he replied, not at all sorry.

Puzzled, Sweyn stared at the two of them. "I thought your marriage had not yet been consummated. You two seem very familiar with each other."

"Oh, the marriage might not have been consummated, but that does not mean that we haven't been engaged in some...activity." Hauk rolled his eyes suggestively and added, "You'd be surprised what can be done between the bars of a cage."

At first, there was a stunned silence as each of them tried

to figure out what Hauk meant, but then everyone burst out laughing. Even Kirstin.

After that, they discussed at length specific plans for the morning's assault. Kirstin had to give these Vikings credit. They didn't rush into battle like wild berserkers, although there were no doubt plenty of those. Instead, they took the time to plan battle strategy, optimum times and locations, weapon readiness, even specific fighting techniques, like the famous *skjaldborg* or shield wall, or the *svinfylking* or wedge formation. They would move toward Winchester during the night, with the assault to begin at dawn.

Once everyone was clear on their roles and where they should be at the call to move out some ten or so hours from now...roughly three a.m., by Kirstin's estimate, it being five p.m. now...the council broke up. Sweyn gave her a look that said he wasn't done with her yet, but he let her go for now. Hauk held her hand again as he led her out, probably fearing she would bolt. She would, if she knew where to go. Or if she had her arm rings.

Hauk just plodded on, wending their way through the troops and camp fires, presumably heading toward his tent. He remained silent and frowny faced.

"Moody much?"

He ignored her question.

"Have I done something to annoy you?"

He gave her a look that pretty much said, "Are you kidding?" What he said was, "You, m'lady, have become the biggest thorn in my arse."

"What? Me? After all I've done for you. Now you're pissed off at me for some little annoyance or other? Big whoop!"

He arched his brows at her, but after that remained deliberately silent, forcing her to skip to keep up with him. He didn't let go of her hand, though.

She tried the silent treatment in reverse, but he couldn't

care less, probably welcomed her mute tongue. So, she gave in. "Well, that went well," she said. "The council, I mean."

"You talk too much."

Ah! So that's what had him out of sorts. "I hardly said anything," she replied huffily. "I didn't give any specifics of tomorrow's battle. I didn't mention Sweyn's upcoming untimely death. I didn't warn him to stay away from horses, especially ones that might cause him mortal injuries. I didn't tell him about his sons. I didn't—"

"Like I said, you talk too much."

"I want my arm rings back."

"I want to be back at my estate in the Norselands enjoying a warm hearth, a good mead, and my mistress."

"You have a mistress?"

"I used to."

"What? You don't think she'd stick around and wait for you?"

"Are you still talking?"

"And you aren't talking at all, most of the time," she pointed out. "Tall, dark, and brooding went out with the Regency novel, Heathcliff."

"What cliff?" he asked. Then, "Never mind."

"So, what has your loincloth in a twist, husband? You have every reason in the world to be happy. You're free of your cage. You've discovered a son you'd thought was dead. In no time at all, you and your mistress will be boinking like bunnies. But instead you go all grumpy-faced."

His lips twitched as he fought a grin.

She was making headway.

As they continued to walk...well, he walked, she trotted...she noticed Bjorn off to the right a short distance, practicing swordplay with some young Vikings. Without appearing to notice, Hauk veered to the right, taking her with him, grabbed his son by the scruff of his neck and dragged him along with them, his sword dragging on the ground.

And God bless Hauk, but he remained silent while Bjorn hollered and called him a long line of colorful insults and threatened all kinds of retaliation. They drew the attention and laughter of everyone they passed.

"Do you really think this is the way to handle your son?" she asked.

He stopped, turned slowly inch by inch, Bjorn dangling with his boots a foot in the air, and said to her, "Stop. Talking."

Okaaay. It's his funeral.

When they got to the tent, Hauk directed Egil and Kirstin to do something about a fire and food. "Meanwhile, my son and I are going to have a talk. Isn't that right, Bjorn?"

Bjorn, who was still dangling, nodded.

Hauk released him, heading in the opposite direction, and Bjorn had the good sense to follow after him. Kirstin looked at Egil then and shrugged. "What should we do?"

"Fire first," Egil said.

Which wasn't as easy as it should have been in the middle of a forest. Since so many trees had been felled to make the clearing and were now smoldering away on numerous camp fires, they had to go into the woods to find deadfall which the two of them dragged toward their tent. Once they had enough to start a fire, Egil worked at getting it started while Kirstin made two more trips for extra wood. By now Kirstin's wonderful reproduction gown designed for Rosestead was looking dirty and bedraggled, and her underarms were beginning to reek, despite her twenty-four hour deodorant, which was hardly noticeable in a field of five hundred or so mostly unwashed male bodies. Later, she'd see about bathing in the stream which apparently ran about a quarter mile away, if she could find a private spot.

Once Egil got the fire going, the two of them went out

through the various campsites until they found one where an elderly woman was stirring a broth. She looked relatively clean, which was a big plus for Kirstin. Egil pulled out a small sack of coins and was able to convince the woman to part with several circles of flat, manchet bread and a small cauldron of what was some of kind of rabbit stew...chunks of meat in a broth thickened with oats, dotted with wild onions and carrots, and even a dash of precious salt. The woman even gave them four wooden bowls, for coins, of course. They wouldn't need utensils since the bread could be used as scoops and the liquid could be slurped.

By the time they got back, Hauk and Bjorn were sitting on the ground before the fire, which Hauk was poking with a long stick. Although they weren't sitting close together, they weren't snarling at each other. They appeared to have come to some kind of understanding.

Egil managed to construct a sort of tripod which would hold the cauldron over the fire. Once the stew came back to a boil, Kirstin served everyone including herself. It wasn't too bad, and the men came back for second and third helpings until the pot was empty.

They talked then, or rather Hauk gave out one order after another.

"Bjorn, you are to stay here tomorrow and protect your stepmother."

Kirstin and Bjorn looked at each other with surprise. She hadn't thought of herself in that way, and neither had he, obviously.

But then Bjorn erupted, "Nay! You will not keep me from the fight."

"You are a youthling," his father pointed out.

"I'm old enough. How old were you when you were first blooded?"

The sudden color in Hauk's cheek said it all. "This is not

up for debate. There is no shame in guard duty. And, besides, I need someone responsible to take my wife to safety if the battle goes against us. I will leave you with coin enough to get yourselves to Jorvik and from there take ship to Haukshire."

"How do you know I want to go to your estate?" Kirstin asked. "If you're gone, I'm going home to America. Speaking of which, you need to give me back my arm rings. In case you don't return."

He gave her a long look. "I'll give the arm rings to Bjorn for safekeeping. He will return the arm rings if I am in Valhalla."

Bjorn was still grumbling over being left behind but he nodded at his father's order.

Hauk looked to Egil and suggested, "Get our battle gear set out tonight...chain mail, helmets, shields, weapons. Try to get a few hours sleep."

"As you say, master," Egil said.

Hauk stood then and told Bjorn, "Come with me while I meet with my men...those who stayed with my longship in Jorvik these many months whilst I've been imprisoned."

Bjorn, for once, didn't balk but rose to his feet to follow his father. There was a similarity between the two of them, although Bjorn, at twelve, was of course a foot shorter and slender in an adolescent way with little muscle definition, unlike his father who was slim from near starvation but still retaining muscle. Despite his already voiced animosity toward his father, the way the boy stared up at him bespoke admiration, too. Their relationship was getting off to a good start in healing, Kirstin could see. Now, if only their bond had a chance to grow, as in the battle leaving Hauk unharmed. *Please God*, she found herself praying.

"Egil, do we have soap anywhere?" she asked.

"Nay," he replied but then added, "Wait." He went inside the tent and came back with a hunk of a hard gray substance that she assumed was soap, probably made from ashes and suet and lye.

Yuck! But she couldn't be choosy and said, "Thank you. Why don't I go clean up these dishes and you can take care of Hauk's battle stuff?"

Egil appeared hesitant at first.

"I'll be careful to stay away from the men," she assured him. "Most of them are off in their various camps preparing for tomorrow anyhow." Although some of those preps involved drinking, she noted to herself.

Since all of the rabbit stew had been eaten, the small cauldron was empty. She put the ladle inside the pot, along with the four bowls, topped with the cake of soap and a scrap of linen she'd used to lift the hot handle. And off she went to the stream which was mostly deserted, except for a few women... camp followers...who'd had the same idea. After she'd cleaned the dinner paraphernalia as best she could, she moved a little farther away around a bend in the stream for privacy, and worked quickly with the rag and soap to wash her face and neck and arms, even undoing her gown to her waist to take care of underarms and breasts. There wasn't much lather, and no lovely floral scent like her favorite Dove beauty bar, but the hard soap did its job. She hesitated for a moment, then lifted her gown, and gave a quick wash between her legs.

Feeling refreshed, she went back to the campsite. By then it was dusk and everywhere folks seemed to be settling down. There were still the sounds of conversation, occasional laughter, and such, but mostly it was subdued, as she imagined most places, whether they be a Viking camp site or a modern military outpost, would be on the night before a battle. She knew for a fact that at the SEAL base, last wills and financial arrangements would be made, along with praying for those so inclined, which was almost all of them when possible death was on the horizon...that famous foxhole religion.

She found Egil inside the tent where he'd placed all of his and Hauk's fighting gear down the middle of the space. The long pile was almost three feet high, comprising the swords, knives, lances, battle-axes, shields, chain mail, and helmets, not to mention harnesses, saddles, and saddle bags for two of the horses they would be taking. A fat, burning candle sat on a level area atop a flat shield, providing a dim light in the tent. On either side of the dividing line, Egil had laid out all the bed furs.

Egil was lying on one side. He'd left enough room beside him for another body...Hauk...when he returned. As she stood on her side, Egil raised his head, bracing himself on his elbows, and told her, "I'm jist restin' me head a bit. 'Twas a long day, and I 'spect 'twill be much longer on the morrow."

"Hauk and Bjorn haven't returned yet?"

"Nay. The master will be introducin' his son to his old comrades, ensuring their loyalty to his son, whether Hauk returns or not."

"Do you think they've reconciled...I mean, that Bjorn will have accepted his father?"

"No doubt. If not now, then soon. A son will forgive a father for much, and vicey versa."

That was true. "Have you been with Hauk for a long time?"

"Since he was a boyling. I served his father before that, and talk about forgiveness! There was a man who deserved no forgiveness! Meaner than a snake, he was, even with his own family. Methinks the master Hauk stayed away from his boy Bjorn for so long 'cause he was afeared he had no fathering skills, like his own heartless father."

"Where was his mother?"

"Died in his birthin', she did."

"And he was raised by...?"

Egil shrugged. "The other wives and mistresses. Mostly he

was ignored, 'cept when his father was at home, hollarin' or beatin' on him or anyone who got too close."

Kirstin's father, bless his virile body, had had a number of mistresses and several wives over the years, though not all at once, thank God! Thus, his twelve children. But he'd treated all of the kids as if they were precious, even the ones who were probably not his, but had been foisted off on him by women who didn't want the responsibility of a baby. Unfortunately, or fortunately, Madrene and Kirstin, as the two oldest daughters, had been forced to care for all their younger siblings while their father went about the business of farming and amber trading. That was probably why Kirstin had never had a particular interest in having children of her own. In any case, her father might have been careless at times, but never cruel. They'd been a family.

Poor Hauk! She could picture him as a child, hiding in dark corners from the wrath of a hateful father. But always looking to forgive at the least sign of kindness on his father's part.

"Hauk's father had no other children, some say because he had a sickness that caused his ballocks to swell when he was a young man a-Viking in some foreign land, some say because he was in disfavor with the gods. For some demented reason, the miscreant blamed Hauk for his sterility."

"Is he still alive?"

Egil shook his head. "Nay. Died a straw death five years past. Well-deserved, if ye ask me. The beast did not deserve Valhalla. The things I could tell you about what he did to his own son! Oh, I forgot to mention. There was another babe born to one of his mistresses almost a year after his death. She tried to hide the birth date, and claimed the boyling was sired by the old lord, but the months do not match up." He shrugged. "The child, Gorm, who would be about four now, is still there, but the mother took off with a passing trader two years past."

"And who cares for the boy...never mind." Kirstin shook her head with disgust, knowing full well that even in a compassionate household such as her father's had been, babes could be squalling and toddlers waddling about at will and their care fell to whomever was closest. Usually her. Forget "It takes a village." To Vikings, "It takes a longhouse," was the norm, long before that other expression came into popularity.

It wasn't that Viking men didn't love their children. In truth, they were great family men, even if the family extended to include other wives, concubines, legitimate and illegitimate children. It was just that care of the little ones fell to the women of the household until they reached age ten or so when they were considered young men, of a suitable age to be taught about weapons and sailing. Or, in the case of girls, skills to prepare them for marriage and managing a household.

As to the boy, Gorm, born posthumously, Kirstin knew all about that, too. At least a few of the babies passed onto her father as his were probably fathered by someone else, but he'd accepted them nonetheless. That's the kind of man he was.

"So, now Hauk is the jarl?"

"That he is, though he has not been there for many a year."

Kirstin frowned. "But Hauk mentioned that he has a mistress waiting there."

"Oh, her! Zoya is a passing fancy, though she counts herself queen of the Norselands in his absence," Egil said with obvious distaste. "Hauk made one last visit to harvest amber in the Baltics, planning to trade the goods in the markets at Hedeby for coin to make much needed repairs to his estates. He sent many of his men ahead to begin the renovations, along with Zoya whom he'd met in the Rus lands, whilst he sent me to Britain to get his son and bring him home. Alas, when he finally got to the Saxon lands, having heard of the St. Brice's Day massacre, he did not find me or Bjorn, and, in fact, was told that the boy was dead. That's when the Saxon soldiers captured him."

"Aaah!" Kirstin said, understanding more of the man than she had before. "You've been a good friend to Hauk, Egil."

Egil beamed, obviously pleased at her compliment.

But then she yawned widely, apologizing, "Sorry."

"Ye've had a long day, m'lady. Ye should rest."

"I will." In fact, Kirstin couldn't believe that only twenty-four hours had passed since she was back in her own time at Rosestead. So much had happened! So much was about to happen!

Turning away, she toed off her slippers and took off her gown, draping it over the far end of the weaponry wall. With the damp rag she'd used as a washcloth, she wiped over the silk fabric and attempted to smooth out the wrinkles. She dropped down to the furs on her side, wearing only her underwear, but that was okay. Hauk would be sleeping next to Egil, and she could don her gown quickly once she heard them getting ready to leave during the night.

She could no longer see Egil but she told him, "Good luck tomorrow."

Her answer was a loud snore.

A short time later, she was snoring, too...a soft feminine snore.

CHAPTER 9

Who is the victor if both parties surrender?...

auk and Bjorn returned to the tent later than Hauk had planned. Bjorn was a little bit *drukkinn* from the small amount of ale they'd imbibed, but Hauk was proud of his son. As Hauk had introduced Bjorn to his comrades-in-arms, he ensured that their loyalty would be for the son as well as the father, which was especially important on the eve of battle. Bjorn helped by being respectful and listening without interruption as many of the more garrulous lot expounded on past victories, often exaggerating, which was of course a fighting man's right, whatever the country... or time, for that matter, he would warrant.

Hauk was about to tell Bjorn how he felt, but before he could say anything to his son, the boy sank to his knees, fell flat on his face onto the furs next to a sleeping Egil, and immediately added his snores to the old man's raucous melody. Hauk smiled and stretched widely. It had been a long and eventful day for all of them. And who knew what the morrow would bring? He couldn't wait. Like all Vikings, he loved a good fight, and he had more reasons than most to anticipate this one with relish.

He noted that Egil, may the gods bless his eager heart, had made a neat pile of all the weaponry and battle gear they would need for the upcoming battle, providing a dividing line across the middle of the small tent. On the other side, his wife slept huddled under a bed fur up to her neck, though the night was not particularly cool. She probably considered it a barrier to any lusty Viking who might drop by. Like him.

He chuckled, and shook his head at her foolishness. As if a mere fur would impede him if he were in a lusty mood, which he was not at the moment.

She, too, snored, but the sound that came from her parted lips was soft and almost like a moan. *A moan of ecstasy or a moan of pain at whatever she was dreaming? Loveplay or torture of some sort, maybe even the horrid cage?* He preferred the former, he decided with another chuckle, realizing that mayhap he was in the mood, after all.

Should I or should I not? he pondered. *Have I not been telling the wench that consummation is a necessity for her survival here?*

But I was just teasing.

Or was I?

Hah!

I deserve this.

Ha, ha!

I should get some rest.

How long would it take? I could do it, quick like, and still get some rest. Besides, mayhap my body humours would be more relaxed. All the kinks of inactivity from these long months of captivity would be untangled.

Ha, ha, ha! I should mention that theory when engaged in a drink fest at the next Thing. I can imagine the laughter I would rouse. The skalds might even create a saga called "Viking Kinks," or some such thing.

No matter. Kirstin would no doubt argue with my reasoning, anyhow. She argues about everything.

Enough arguing with myself! Should I or should I not?

His gaze traveled around the tent. A fat candle that Egil had planted on a shield provided a dim light. Kirstin's gown was draped over one end of the pile. Her slippers were arranged neatly, side by side, on the ground below the gown. Which meant that she was naked under the furs, he concluded.

That is my answer! Praise the gods! Must be she is too shy to initiate sex herself. Must be she is hot for the bedding but too stubborn to ask for it. Must be this is her way of inviting me to couple with her.

Quick as spit, he was undressed and about to join his wife. Lifting the edge of the robe, he stopped short. Kirstin, lying on her back, was not naked...not precisely. Instead, she wore a scrap of white lace on top, cupping her breasts with straps over the shoulders. Down below was another scrap of white lace which covered her mons but did not even reach her navel or the tops of her thighs, riding high on her hips. What was the purpose of either of those undergarments? Though, come to think on it, they *were* rather enticing, more alluring than the naked body itself. Well, *almost* more alluring.

Tossing the top fur aside, Hauk eased himself down and rolled Kirstin over on her side so that he was front to her back. "Sweetling?" he whispered against her ear.

She let out another little snore/moan.

Is she awake?

He listened to her breathing. *No, she is still sleeping.*

He nestled closer, placed his left arm above her head, and ran his right hand lightly over her right arm from shoulder to wrist, up her leg from knee to upper thigh. "So soft! Your skin is so soft."

She didn't wake, but the fine hairs rose on her skin. Her

body was reacting, even if she wasn't. Which was fine with Hauk. If she was awake, she would be talking, and that meant she would be telling him what he was doing wrong and how much better everything, even sex, was in the future.

So, he continued his soft, gentle exploration. His hands might be rough and calloused, but his movements were light as a butterfly's wings.

It was at times like this that Hauk was thankful that Vikings were born masters at loveplay, and that was not an exaggeration. Everyone said so. Whether in battle or the bed furs, Viking men knew all about timing, when to be aggressive and when to use stealth.

Like now. He took the time to be fascinated and, yes, aroused by the contrast in textures of their skins, leather to velvet. Where his forearm rested on her abdomen alongside her forearm, he couldn't help but notice his dark bristly hairs whilst hers were like strands of gold silk, almost invisible.

And the contours of their bodies! Blunt, bulky edges against smooth curves. Hard muscles against cushiony softness.

Masculine against feminine.

With a sigh, she dropped her hand to her side, thus giving him the opportunity to place a palm against her waist and moved it upward till he cupped one breast outside its lace covering. The breast was not large, but big enough to fill his hand. He lifted it and used a thumb to flick the center, which caused the nipple to rise against the lace and press against his palm. He did the same to the other breast.

She gasped and went stiff.

Now she was awake!

In one swift move, she rolled onto her back, rose to a sitting position, and gaped at him wide-eyed. "What are you doing here?" she shrieked.

He pushed her back down, pressing her shoulders to the

furs. Leaning over her, he whispered in her ear, "Shhh! You'll wake Egil and Bjorn."

"I'll wake the whole damn camp if you don't get off of me," she warned, putting both hands on his chest in an attempt to shove him off. To no avail, of course. "I could even—"

He cut off what was bound to be a tirade by putting his lips over her open mouth, then quickly adjusting his placement, molding her mouth in changing patterns till they met perfectly. Then he kissed her with an expertise honed by years of experience, but also complemented by the sweetness of her taste and pliancy...and surrender, which surprised him this early in the game. In fact, she took his head in both her hands and initiated a duel of tongues that was nothing short of amazing.

His heart hammered against his rib cage, and blood pounded through his veins. If he were standing, he would no doubt be light-headed.

He drew away reluctantly to look at her, his head tilted to the side. "You agree to the coupling?" Meanwhile, he outlined the edges of her mouth with a fingertip, spreading the moisture. His and hers both.

"Don't act so surprised, Mister I-Am-Viking, therefore I-Am-Irresistible."

She had insulted him, but it was a half-hearted insult. Not worth a reaction. He noticed that she licked her lips, not once, but twice. A good sign, for both of them, he realized, because her eagerness appealed to him mightily. "You do not answer my question," he rasped out. "Why are you suddenly so biddable?"

"Seriously, Hauk! I don't know about biddable, but you've been plaguing my dreams for months. At this point, suffice it to say, I deserve to experience the real thing...to see if you're as good as your dream self."

120

His eyes widened, and a slow smile emerged. "I was that good?"

She swatted his shoulder. "Oh, please! Stop wasting time. Do your thing."

"I have a thing?"

"Fer the gods' sake, do *something*!" Egil called out. "Ye're keepin' me and Bjorn awake with all yer chatter."

"I don't mind. I am learning...*things*," Bjorn said.

"See! I told you to shhh, did I not?" Hauk whispered into her ear.

"Shhh yourself," she whispered against his ear, then followed by blowing into his ear, once, twice, before inserting the wet tip of her tongue inside the whorls and jiggling it.

He about hurtled to a premature peaking like an untried youthling at the intense pleasure that shot from his ear to his cock. For a certainty, his eyes must be rolling back in his head. He muttered that famous Anglo-Saxon swear word, then repeated it in five other languages.

She smiled up at him, a little wicked smile of female satisfaction. She was not as shy as he'd thought, obviously.

"Witch!" he said softly and kneed her legs apart, arranging his heavier self carefully over her, very much aware that he was nude and his "enthusiasm" showed like a flag waving on the wind, whilst she was at least partially covered, and her "enthusiasm" not so apparent. Enthusiasm was the Viking word for arousal. "How do you remove this thing?" he muttered, tugging the edge of her upper garment between her breasts. He was surprised when the fabric sprang back.

She raised her body slightly and did some maneuver with her hands behind her back causing the garment to go loose. She then lifted it off her body and tossed it over her head, exposing two of the prettiest breasts he'd ever seen. Well, mayhap his perception was colored by his long time since seeing such splendors. Still, they were very nice. Not too big.

Not too small. With promising, already engorged nipples, which caused him to give himself a silent clap on the back. Her "enthusiasm" was showing, too!

He decided to start there. First, cupping her breasts from underneath and squeezing them. Then tracing the areola with a forefinger.

She was holding her breath.

But not for long.

He strummed the nipples with his fingertips like a stringed instrument.

With a little yelp, she shot upward, trying to sit. But he wouldn't allow that. Pressing her downward, he murmured, "Shh. Stay. Let me."

Panting deliberately, in and out, she closed her eyes. He took that as her acceptance, for now, of his leadership in this sex play. He also, being a Viking, made note, in that part of his brain which men set aside for such details, that breasts were particular erotic spots on Kirstin's body. That was not true for all women. He knew a few who balked at being touched there.

Which prompted him to continue playing with her breasts, finally leaning down to take one whole breast in his widened mouth, then drawing it out with a suctioning pull till he had the nipple between his lips. Then he fluttered the tip with his tongue until Kirstin was arching up off the furs and keening her arousal.

He put a hand over her mouth and whispered against her ear, repeating his earlier command, "Shhh. You will wake Egil and Bjorn."

Both of them were snoring, but they wouldn't be for long at this rate.

Then he moved to the other breast and did the same thing, but he held one hand against her belly and moved it lower, edging under the stretchy fabric of her garment, thus distracting her. It was a well-known ploy, in warfare or bedfare, attack at several sources at once to divide the enemy's attention. Not that Kirstin was his enemy. But the principle was the same.

He could tell he was successful when one hand fluttered over her breasts, the other over her mons, unsure which of his hands were causing more distress. She removed his hand from her breast and he just slid it under her hips to caress her buttocks. When she tried to move his hand from her female area, he returned it to her breasts.

She succumbed to all the sensations then and laid back with a moan, raising her arms above her head. "Oh...oh...oh."

After testing the wetness between her legs, he tore off the scrap of cloth and arranged himself more comfortably. He put a hand to her face, forcing her to look at him, and said in a husky whisper. "Do you come to me willingly, wife?"

She stared up at him through eyes that were hazy with arousal. She nodded.

Taking himself in hand, he entered her slowly. He had to be careful. It had been so long since he'd been with a woman, and her channel was so tight, and he feared this might end in an embarrassing one-thrust wonder. But she made it hard for him to slow down as her inner muscles clasped and unclasped around him, stretching to accommodate his length and breadth, which were mighty after such a prolonged abstinence. But finally he was imbedded in her to the hilt. Even then her female channel shifted to make room for his size.

For a long moment, he just lay over her, forehead to forehead, elbows braced on the furs above her shoulders. When he was able to speak without blubbering, he gazed down at her and said, "You feel so good. Slick as honey, warm as cream fresh from the cow."

"I like that combination. Honey and cream. But I don't know about the cow." She laughed, then rolled her hips in a most enticing manner, almost as if she was caressing him from the inside.

A hissing sound escaped from behind his gritted teeth before he was able to ask, "What...was...that?"

She looked embarrassed as she revealed, "Churning the butter."

He let out a hoot of laughter. He had not expected her to be so...earthy.

She was the one to say "Shhh" then as they both paused and listened, relaxing only when they heard the two discordant snores from the other side.

"We do fit rather well together," she told him.

He had to smile at that. "As if any man and any woman wouldn't fit!"

She shrugged.

"What? In your time, some men and women do not fit together?"

"Some fit better than others," she contended. "I'm just sayin'."

Once he pondered that idea, he decided that they did fit well...very well. Mayhap this *was* different, better than other matings. A fanciful idea, that! But then, he thought, *My wife*, and a warmth seemed to fill him, pumping out from his heart to all his extremities.

"You have a beautiful smile," she said.

He smiled wider. "I wish we had more time."

"Sometimes short and sweet is enough."

Sweet was not his goal, and short was no man's ideal time in the tupping.

"Have you rested enough? Can we start now?" she inquired with exaggerated sweetness.

He growled and said, "I was not resting. I was giving you time to adjust to my...um, magnitude." Before she could make a comment about that, he withdrew his staff almost to her entrance. Then he began the long in-and-out strokes that had probably been invented by Adam and Eve in that Biblical Garden of Eden.

Kirstin did not just lay back but participated in the coupling, linking her hands behind his nape, which gave him access to her moist, eager lips, raising her knees to hug his hips, which gave him more room to plunge deeper.

Way too soon, the long, slow strokes turned short and fast. He couldn't help himself. And her almost continuous moans did not help him reduce his pace. In truth, her excitement excited him.

With the utmost effort, he paused and concentrated on what he was doing, after which he managed to flex himself inside of her.

She countered by rippling around him, but, in her defense, he did not think she did it deliberately. Her body was as out-of-control as his own.

Beads of sweat stood out on his forehead, and his arms quivered with the tension of remaining rigid and still. But somehow he managed to stay unmoving inside of her.

"What are you doing to me, you brute?" she asked.

"What are you doing to me, sweetling?"

"Sweetling? I like that."

"I like *you*," he said.

"And that surprises you?"

"It does. You are bothersome and talkative and half-demented and…"

"…and?"

"…and I want you so badly I cannot think straight."

"Well, you are so attractive you make my bones melt."

He grinned, inordinately pleased at her compliment. So, he reciprocated by explaining his attraction to her, "You are prettier than I originally thought, and sexier than any woman I have ever been with, despite your skinny frame and less than buxom breasts."

She laughed. "Those are the lamest compliments I have ever heard."

"I was being honest."

She rolled her eyes. "That reminds me of my grandmother, my mother's mother from Hordaland. She hurled out the most outrageous insults, usually to her daughter-in-law, Girda, and felt it was okay as long as she added, 'I'm only being honest.'"

"Your arse is as big as a boat, Girda. What? I'm only being honest."

"Your cauldron is so dirty I could cut the grease with a knife. What? I'm only being honest."

"Your gunna is cut so low I can see your nether hair when you bend over. What? I am only being honest."

"Why do you have spots on your face at your age? Mayhap you do not wash enough. What? I am only being honest.'"

"I can't believe we are having this conversation in the midst of bedsport," Hauk interrupted. "If my cock could talk, it would be asking, 'Have you lost your senses, man? I'm here, planted where I want to be, hard as a sword in a tight woman sheath, bigger than any man, any Viking, for the love of Thor, has a right to be, and you engage in chatter about face spots and kitchen grease.'"

"Your cock is very articulate," Kirstin commented.

He wasn't sure what that word meant, probably something akin to "impressive." So, he just nodded his acknowledgement of her praise. "Are you ready now? Because once I start this time, I will not be able to stop."

She glanced downward at him, arched her brows, and commented, "A Blue Steeler. Wow!" Followed by, "Lucky me!"

Once again, he had no idea what her words meant, and he did not care. He slammed into her, causing her head to snap back onto the furs and her back to arch. Then he rock-rock-rocked in and out rapidly and could not stop or slow down the motions even if he wanted to, so inflamed were his senses.

His eyes caught hers and held. She appeared stunned, a glint of wonder in her expression, and her fingers dug even deeper into the muscles of his shoulders. Panting softly, she revealed, "You make me tremble."

And he made a revelation as well. "I have never felt like this before."

Amazingly, even as he spoke, he continued to thrust and withdraw in an increasingly more rapid fashion. And she convulsed around him, in one peaking after another.

Remarkable!

Is it a dream?

Or a fantasy?

Or a gift from the gods...or her One-God?

The sweet agony rose to a fever pitch till he teetered on the edge. Then, his head reared back as he catapulted, roaring out his triumph...or was it her triumph? He spilled himself inside her hot depths as she melted around him, which was another remarkable revelation to him...that a woman could spill her essence, just like a man.

Once he was no longer breathing like a warhorse in the midst of battle, and they were both clearly sated, he eased his limp staff out of her. Then he rolled to his back and turned her so that she was on her side, her face resting on his chest, and he lifted her one leg over his. He kissed the top of her fur-mussed hair and whispered, "Wife." That was all he could get out through the thick lump in his throat. But it was enough.

Because she whispered back, "Husband."

CHAPTER 10

Siren or moron? Is there a difference?...

Their next bout of lovemaking was initiated by Kirstin, to her later embarrassment, no doubt. Was she losing her mind, or God forbid, her heart? To an arrogant, ungrateful, bloodthirsty, eleventh century Viking, of all things! Just because he had a knack for turning her on! How dumb was that?

Kirstin didn't think she'd ever been the one to make the first move in bed before. At this time, though...an hour or more after they'd both surrendered their satisfied bodies to the peace of post-coital slumber, Kirstin roused herself enough to realize that she was practically wrapped around a sleeping Hauk, clinging to him like a limpet that would never let go. And both of them naked!

Even worse, she found herself horny, *again*, after the best lovemaking of her life.

Which prompted that little imp in her head, the one that plagued all women at one time or another, to whisper, "Why not?"

Hauk was splatted on his back, his legs spread, his arms flung overhead in complete abandon, and she reclined half on her side, half over him with her face planted in the curve of his neck and shoulder (*I hope I'm not drooling!*), one breast resting on his chest (*Oh, no! Why is my nipple so big and rosy? As if I don't know! Hope the other looks the same or I'll have a mismatched pair. Ha, ha, ha! Aaarrgh!*), one arm wrapped around his waist with her fingers digging into the flesh (*He'll probably have bruises from my nails!*), one knee nudging his flaccid penis (*How cute!*). There was no way he could get up and escape without alerting her first, (as some jerkoff men were wont to do once the deed was done—not to her, but she'd heard of such creeps).

Bracing herself on one elbow, she was able to raise her head enough to get a better look. Hauk Thorsson was a prime specimen of masculinity, despite his apparent weight loss and the numerous scars that didn't so much mar his body as give it character. He had to be six feet three, at least, and built like a quarterback with broad shoulders and slim hips and long muscle-sculpted legs. His narrow feet were rather sexy, too.

She glanced at his face, which was Nordic perfection. Even in sleep, he appeared tense, probably a symptom of soldiers and warriors throughout time on the eve of a battle. But then, he had other reasons to be stressed, as well. He'd just escaped from months of captivity, had been shocked by their teletransport, or whatever it was, and learned his dead son was actually alive. His future was uncertain, to say the least.

I should let him sleep, get whatever rest he can. That thought was immediately followed by a memory of her father saying that the one word Norsemen hated most was "should," as in people telling them what they should or should not do because, of course, that prompted them to do just the opposite.

I might not be a Viking man, but don't tell me I should leave him be. A little exploration won't hurt, she told herself.

She checked to make sure that Hauk still slept deeply, then ran a fingertip over the long white scar that ran from his collarbone, across his chest, then stopped at his opposite hip. She wanted to kiss the scar, and she would if there wasn't a risk of Hauk waking and observing her emotional reaction to one of his wounds. He wouldn't appreciate her response, she guessed, and would probably consider it pity. Typical man!

She released a sigh of relief when there was no change in his breathing. She was about to lie back down when she noticed that while he remained dead to the world, another part of his body was not. Even as she watched, his penis swelled and straightened. Her head swiveled quickly to the right and she saw him staring at her, wide awake, and grinning.

"Siren," he said. "Do you deliberately tempt me?"

"Are you tempted?"

He arched his brows and inclined his head downward.

Yep, it…he was growing more tempted by the moment.

"I should let you rest."

"Should? Do you know what Vikings think of that word?"

She laughed. "Actually, I do."

"So, my siren wife," he drawled, folding his arms behind his head, "what do you have in mind?"

"In mind?"

"Since you so rudely roused me from sleep?"

"Rudely?"

"Well, mayhap *joyfully* roused would be a better description."

"Joyful huh?"

"That remains to be seen."

She sat up, knelt, then swung a leg over his hips so that she sat astride his belly, his erection growing against her buttocks.

Where this new lack of inhibition was coming from, she had no idea. Perhaps her inner Viking was emerging. "You were saying?"

"I'm getting more and more joyful by the moment," he said in a sex-husky voice and lifted her by the hips, up high, and then onto his now fully erect penis. Slowly, very slooooowly, he eased her downward inch by inch until her pubic bone rested against his pubic bone, his golden curls mixing with her silver blonde ones.

After that, Kirstin showed Hauk a few things a woman could do while on top in what she told him was a reverse missionary position. Which he thought was hilarious...that missionaries in her time had favorite activities in the bedsport.

While Hauk claimed to enjoy all her efforts, he soon rolled her over, claiming he had a better idea.

So far, she was rather fond of his ideas...when it came to sex.

"We're going a-Viking, sweetling," he told her as he arranged her on her back with her arms and legs where he wanted them.

"But we have no longship," she said, getting into the game.

"Hah!" he replied, glancing downward. "I see something long, and believe you me, this ship is looking for a harbor. But first, this Viking needs to do a bit of exploring afore he heads home."

"Goody!"

They both went all Marco Polo then, leisurely exploring each other's bodies, commenting here and then on what they saw and what they liked, laughing sometimes, gasping at others, ending with a slow, very sexy intercourse that was even more powerful than their earlier more frenetic pace. And that was dangerous because it felt almost like...horrors!...falling in love.

131

Afterward, they just stared at each other with a mixture of mutual wonder and perhaps a little fear. No words were necessary.

She was awake at three a.m. when Hauk and Egil arose. She knew the time because she still had her wrist watch. But they seemed to awaken to some inner alarm clocks, or maybe it was the sound of movement outside around the camp.

She quickly dressed, although her gown was still damp from her wiping, and minus her panties which would never stay up due to Hauk's rough treatment of the elastic. She watched with distress as the men dressed for war. With what was probably hysterical irrelevance, Kirstin thought once again of that popular *Outlander* series and noted that if she'd known she was going to time-travel, she would have planned accordingly, like Claire had. Sewing supplies, soap, gold coins, a first aid kit, antibiotics for heaven's sake! So many things that would come in handy.

Bjorn was awake, as well, arguing with his father about accompanying the soldiers in the assault, even if only with a rear guard. Hauk was adamant; his son would stay behind and protect her. Kirstin would have protested that she didn't need protection, but she didn't want the boy fighting, either.

Before he left, Hauk stood before her, looking like the quintessential Viking warrior wearing a chain mail shirt with scabbarded broadsword and short sword, carrying a leather helmet and a shield with his family's coat of arms, the chasing hawks design, like that on his arm rings. He put a hand on her shoulder and tipped her chin up with the other hand. "Will you stay until I return?"

"I can hardly leave without my arm rings," she griped.

He leaned down and kissed the side of her mouth, softly. "Perhaps there are other ways. Promise me that you won't try."

"Why?" She tilted her head so he would kiss the other side of her mouth.

"Because you and I have unfinished business." He kissed her full on the mouth then.

Bjorn made a gagging sound, and Egil chuckled, but Kirstin didn't care what anyone thought. "Like what?" she murmured, giving his bottom lip a little nip.

Hauk nipped her back and smiled. "You know. Do not deny this...thing...that simmers betwixt us."

She couldn't deny it.

Even if there was no attraction, she couldn't leave the past until she was sure she'd accomplished her goal, whatever it was. But that wasn't the entire truth. If she were given the chance, would she want to leave without Hauk...that simmering thing unresolved?

And there was something else. Hauk wasn't important enough of a figure to show up in any history. If she left now, she would never know if he survived this battle. Yes, the Vikings would be the victors, but the fate of individuals... Hauk, Bjorn, Egil? Could she live with not knowing?

He kissed her then, a final connection, and the kiss was sweet with promise, not good-bye. "Don't leave," he repeated.

She didn't answer.

He looked disappointed, but then he was gone.

Several hours later, she awakened from a nap. She'd decided to lie down when the camp was empty of almost everyone, knowing the battle wouldn't take place until after dawn. She hadn't expected to fall asleep.

The first thing she noticed was her two arm rings sitting on the bed furs at her feet. She jumped up and grabbed them. Had Hauk decided to leave them, giving her the choice to go or stay?

But, no, when he'd left, the bracelets were still in Bjorn's custody.

SANDRA HILL

Which meant…

"Oh, my God!" she exclaimed as she looked at the other side of the tent and saw empty bed furs. Rushing outside, she noticed immediately that the horse was gone.

Which meant...oh, my God! Bjorn was gone! He must have followed after his father and the troops. The boy was not an experienced fighter. Oh, this was a disaster in the making.

She looked down at the arm rings that she still held in her hands. Then she looked off into the distance, toward Winchester.

Maybe this is a sign.

Maybe I should just try to get back home, and call this whole experience a strange detour in my destiny. Over and done with! A success since Hauk was out of the cage.

Maybe this is all just a dream, anyway.

But it doesn't feel like a dream.

And he asked me to wait.

What to do, what to do?

She groaned.

First things first, she put on her flats and went out to the woods to relieve herself. Then she used some water that had been left in a bucket back at the tent to wash her face and hands. She finger-combed her hair, which was a mass of tangles, off her face into a low ponytail that she tied with a strip of leather that she'd found hanging from the tent flap. She slid the arm rings on, not wanting to risk having them inaccessible again, just in case.

As she nibbled at a hunk of manchet bread that had been left over from last night, she decided to explore what was left of the campsite. There were several dozen people working at campfires…women, older men, and some boys… mostly thralls, or slaves. Preparations were already being made to cook cauldrons of broths and stews to be served that evening, assuming the returning troops would have time to stop and eat and not be on the run from the Saxon army.

Most interesting to Kirstin was the huge tent which would serve as the "hospitium" to treat the inevitable wounded. Like the war council she'd sat in on, she wished she could imprint the scene around her with all its "historic" details. The folks setting up here were friendly enough, answering Kirstin's questions, but everything was pretty much self-explainable. One table which held sharp knives and saws would be used for amputations. Another held salves, long strips of linen for bandages, splints for broken limbs and moss to stanch bleeding. More ominous was the hot fire being built up, next to which sat a number of flat-bladed tools for cauterizing wounds.

One man said he was the *laeknir*, or the healer, in charge; there were two others serving under him. Another man was the bonesetter. What they described in answer to her questions was a pretty well-organized operation for the time period when medical education was nonexistent. Despite the orderly arrangement, she couldn't help but notice that the devices, the tabletops, and their hands were dirty. She shuddered to think what the mortality rate would be under these conditions.

Next to this large tent was a smaller one in which an aged crone of a woman, a sorceress, was setting up runic charms to ward off fever and putrid oozings. She also made offerings, for coin on behalf of a patient, to the statue of Eir, the god of healing. The crude wooden figurines of the god, who looked like a skinny Buddha with long Viking hair and a lazy eye, were strung on leather thongs to be worn around the neck as an amulet.

If any of her group came back with wounds, Kirstin was going to suggest they steer clear of the "hospitium," keep everything clean, and hope for the best. Once again, Kirstin thought of Claire's preparation for time-travel, and realized that antibiotics, or at the least a first-aid kit, would have been helpful. But then, unlike Claire in her second journey to the past, Kirstin hadn't known ahead of time that she would be shot back in time.

Back at Hauk's tent, Kirstin spent some time straightening the bed furs, where she found her mangled panties that Hauk had torn off. A lost cause until she found a needle and thread, she decided, then had to smile as she recalled something a college roommate of hers had said one time. Sonia, who was a free spirit if there ever was one, rarely wore underwear, claiming that the vagina had to breathe sometime, too. Well, Kirstin would be doing a lot of lower breathing today.

After everything was spiffy inside the tent, she went outside and starting a pot of water in the cauldron over a small fire she finally managed to get started with the help of Viggo, a boy of about eight who'd been standing around laughing at her twenty or so attempts to accomplish the simple task on her own. The scrawny bird was purchased from Viggo's mother, Estrid, with a coin Kirstin had purloined from a small leather bag of various coins she'd found in Hauk's chest. She had no idea if she'd overpaid or not. For all she knew, she might have paid what was comparable to a hundred dollars. Estrid had also tossed in a handful of wild roots and herbs...limp celery, carrots, onions, and what smelled like thyme. Most precious of all was a golf-ball-size block of salt.

Since she had no means of making noodles, not that she really knew how to make them from scratch, she decided to try some spaetzle, little dough balls, like her stepmother—Angela's mother—used to make. "I don't suppose you have any flour or an egg you could spare?" she asked Estrid.

"In fact, I do," Estrid replied, her eyebrows arched in question.

When Kirstin explained, Estrid said, "Make enough for my pot, too."

It was probably foolish of Kirstin to be preparing a meal, but she needed to be doing something, or she'd go mad wondering what was happening a mere five miles away. Besides, wasn't chicken soup supposed to have some medicinal qualities? Why else would they give it to people when they were down with the flu or some kind of fever?

The flour she used for the spaetzle was oat and gritty, but the end result was rather good, if she did say so herself. Once she had the coals hot enough to maintain the broth at a simmer, Kirstin walked over to Estrid's fire and said, "Mind if I join you?"

Estrid nodded toward a log that had been pulled close to her fire and handed Kirstin a wooden mug of mead. The honeyed ale would probably taste good if it were cold, but without refrigeration, it resembled a lukewarm, thin syrup with a kick. Kirstin liked beer, on occasion, and she knew good mead; her father brewed several batches a year at the vineyard, in addition to all the fine wines.

"Wow! That's some cauldron you have there. You cooking for the entire camp?" Kirstin asked, motioning with her mug toward Estrid's iron pot that must hold at least twenty-five gallons. Was she a thrall cooking for some clan?

Estrid, who was probably in her midforties, wore the typical Norse woman's clothing...a long homespun gunna covered by a once-white, calf-length, open-sided apron attached at the shoulders with bronze brooches in a circular design. Her gray-threaded blonde hair was braided and wound into a coronet atop her head. She was of medium height, slightly plump. Not the usual camp follower. "Nay. Jist fer my family."

Kirstin was a little embarrassed, to have made an assumption about her, in fact, about any of the women here. "Are they all here? Your family, I mean."

Estrid shook her head as she stirred her pot. "Nay. Back home in Vestfold, my eldest son Jerrik takes care of our farmstead. My daughters Bodil and Girt are off to their own homes with their own families. Come to think on it, Girt is about to pop out another babe any day now, her fourth. Mayhap it's already born. And Bodil is a fussy one, can't stand the sight of blood. She'd be of no use near a battlefield. Nay, I am here with my husband and five of our sons, including Viggo over there, our late-in-life surprise." She smiled toward Viggo, who was emerging from the woods, carrying an armload of kindling almost bigger than he was.

Kirstin thought for a moment, then exclaimed, "Eight children! And four of them are soldiers fighting alongside your husband? Holy cow!" Kirstin didn't ask, but odds were that there were several others who had died in the womb or shortly after birth, given the life expectancy of fetuses and infants in this time period.

Estrid arched her brows, again, this time as if eight children were nothing out of the ordinary.

She tried to elaborate on her reaction by saying, "This is like a medieval version of *Saving Private Ryan*."

"Who?"

"Never mind," Kirstin said, not wanting to explain that all but one of the Ryan sons died in that Tom Hanks World War II movie.

"So, you're with The Caged Viking, eh?" Estrid asked with a grin.

"Yes. For now. Though I wouldn't mention it around him. It's rather a sore point."

"Do ye have children?" Estrid asked hesitantly. She had to know that Kirstin had just married Hauk, but that would be all she knew about her history.

"No children," Kirstin told her, "and never been married...before."

"Really? How old are ye?"

"Thirty-five."

"What's wrong with the men where you come from? Yer passable comely and still have yer teeth and a few good breeding years yet."

Kirstin choked on her mead, then wiped her mouth on the back of her hand. *Now that is what my brothers would call an ass-backward, fucked-up compliment.* She noticed that Estrid assumed that Kirstin would want to be married, the goal of all females, and that no man had wanted her. Estrid would not be able to fathom a society where many women chose the single life. "And you...how old are you, Estrid?"

"Thirty-five."

Oh, my goodness! She's the same age as me! Kirstin hadn't expected that, and tried her best not to show her shock. Estrid looked to be in her midforties or more. *Well, what did I expect? Eight plus children and a hard life on a farm in the north!*

"How old were you when you got married?"

"Fourteen."

That was pretty much what Kirstin had expected from her study of the time period, and not just for the Vikings. "Um... do you mind if I ask? Does your husband have more than one wife?"

Kirstin knew that many Vikings practiced the *more danico*, or multiple wives. It wasn't as rude a question as it might seem.

"Hah! If Hulgar dared take another wife, I'd cut off his staff and feed it ta the pigs. Told him that when we were first wed, and he hasn't strayed yet...that I know of."

"So, do you always travel with your husband and sons when they go to war?"

"In recent years, yea, I do. 'Twasn't as easy when I had

bratlings at home tugging on my teats from one side and on my apron from another."

"You know what to expect then. Do you have any idea when we'll know how the battle is going?"

"Should be some men straggling back about midday, methinks. Leastways, there will be wounded by then."

Kirstin glanced at her wrist watch and saw that it was almost noon. "So, if you're anticipating wounded men, you must not be optimistic about the results of the battle."

Estrid shook her head. "Nay, that's not what I meant. There are wounded on both sides in any battle. Always. The question will be which side has the bigger pile of bones, so ta speak."

Nice image! "You seem so calm. Aren't you afraid for your family?"

"'Course I am. That's why I'm here and not home dryin' lutefisk or knittin' socks. Holy Thor! The amount of socks my boys go through each winter! Comes from not changin' the smelly things often enough, is what I keep tellin' them. How are they gonna attract good wives if they smell like the back side of a boar, is another thing I keep tellin' the fools. Luckily, we keep sheep on our stead! Lots of wool!"

Kirstin smiled at the obvious fondness in Estrid's voice as she spoke of her family. And her "boys" were no doubt adult men if they were off fighting a war. They continued to converse about everyday things, and Kirstin kept checking her watch. It was one-thirty, well past the time Estrid had predicted that they would have news.

Just then, as if she'd conjured them up, the rumble of horse-drawn wagons could be heard on the road, coming from the direction of Winchester. Everyone in the camp rushed to get news. The three wagons passed through a gauntlet of people, peering forward to see if they recognized anyone among the wounded, some of them so severely they were unconscious. Luckily, neither Estrid or Kirstin saw any of their "family."

They soon learned that the battle had been won already, many of the Saxons having flown the coop beforehand and others surrendering once they realized there was no hope of winning. The men in the wagons were the first of the injured coming back to the hospitium. Others too injured for transport were being set up in the great hall and in rooms at the castle where Saxon healers were being forced to undertake their care. The Viking dead would be prepared for funeral rites on site; the Saxon dead would be burned in huge pyres.

All this she learned from Estrid who gave her a nervous running commentary. It was only then that Kirstin realized that while there was relief that none of their men were among the wounded, now there was the possibility that one or all of them were dead.

Another nerve-wracking hour went by with Kirstin imagining all kinds of dire circumstances. But then, she saw a number of horsemen approaching. One of them was Egil. But not Hauk or Bjorn.

Oh, God! Oh, God! Please, God! Her heart hammered against her chest walls, and she felt light-headed as she approached the little man who was dismounting from his horse. The expression on his face was not promising.

"What...who...?" she choked out.

"'Tis Bjorn. He's hurt bad. A gut wound."

Tears immediately filled her eyes. It was heartbreaking to think how Hauk must feel, having just found his son was alive, and now to lose him. "Where is he?"

"In a room inside the castle."

"What can I do?"

Egil nodded at her ready offer to help. "Hauk sent me to get whatever medical supplies I can, and you, if ye have any talent in caring for the wounded."

"I don't have any nursing experience, but I can help. Don't bother with any of those potions or salves in the hospitium, but grab as many of the strips of clean linen for bandages. When we get there, I'll need hot water and maybe something to stitch the wound."

"I must needs rent a wagon for the master, in case Bjorn recovers enough that we are able to take him to Jorvik for better care at the minster hospitium there and, please gods, eventually the longship, *Sea Wolf*, to Haukshire. There should be coin enough in the pouch he left behind."

While Egil went to the campsite hospitium to get those supplies, she entered the tent to get Hauk's travel chest containing spare clothing and she picked up the bed furs, assuming they would not be coming back here. To Egil's chagrin, she insisted on taking her cauldron of chicken soup which she arranged carefully in the back of the wagon.

"Ye're barmy ta be takin' such with us. There's plenty of food in the castle."

"But not chicken soup."

"Chicken slop?" He rolled his eyes.

"Soup is what I said, not slop. And, just so you know, chicken soup could very well be better medicine than any other stuff you have around here."

"Holy Thor!" he muttered under his breath. "The demented lady 'spects ta cure the master's son with chicken *slop*."

Shortly after, they were on their way to Winchester, with her seated beside Egil, bare-assed except for her gown under her butt, she noted. She hoped she didn't get any splinters. But she couldn't think about that now.

Her attention was drawn, with horror, to their surroundings as they traveled the five miles back to the castle, so different than when they'd passed this way the previous day. Here and there, more and more the closer they got to

Winchester, lay dead men, both Vikings and Saxons, but mostly Saxons. She even saw a few headless bodies and turned away quickly as bile rose in her throat.

Overhead, black vultures were already circling.

Was it a sign?

Is this how her time in the past would end?

CHAPTER 11

Sometimes prayer is the best medicine, even for a Viking...

*B*jorn awakened from unconsciousness, finally.
 For that, Hauk was happy.

But Bjorn awakened from unconsciousness behaving like a spoiled bratling.

For that, Hauk was not happy.

"I need to get up," Bjorn insisted, trying to rise from the pallet in the servant's quarter of Winchester Castle where he'd been taken from the bailey after he'd fallen, a Saxon sword pinning his body to the bloody ground...not all of the wound dew being Bjorn's, thank the gods. The room, as sparse as it was, must belong to a higher-level servant because most underlings slept in the great hall on broad, low benches built into the long walls or enclosed bed nooks, or sleep bowers, if they were fortunate. Even nobles rarely had their own private bedchambers. "All the loot will be picked over if I don't get out there."

"Loot? What is loot?"

"Spoils of war. Rewards for service. Treasures, like gold,

silver, jewels, even slaves. Lady Kirstin told me...back at campsite...that loot is another name for battle treasures." All this he gasped out, then added with a whine, "I...want...my... loot." With that effort, he fell back on his bed.

Kirstin! He should have known. She who was an expert on everything, and blathered about them at the least prompting, or lack of prompting. He couldn't imagine the context of that subject coming up, but his wife didn't seem to have a reason for many of her actions. "Forget the damn loot. And forget about slaves. I do not deal in slaves, ever. Look at you. Just sitting up and talking has caused the blood to start surging again." A pile of red-soaked rags rested on the rush-covered floor in the corner, a testament to how much blade flow his son had already lost. "Your life is more important than some gold goblet or silver-embossed sword hilt."

"You...go...get us some...loot...while I...rest." Bjorn coughed and, with a groan, succumbed to unconscious again.

As if I would leave you, son, for even a moment in this condition!

Two more times, Bjorn awakened for a short period, jabbered on about the loot, lost more blood, than sank back into oblivion. One thing Hauk grew to suspect in the course of these events was that it wasn't the wound that was causing these lapses in consciousness, it was the bump the size of a plum on the back of his head. Apparently he'd hit a rock when he fell in the battle.

The way he's talking about loot, though...Holy Thor, he must have a rock for a brain, Hauk thought. Vikings liked the spoils of war, of course they did, but a good Viking fought for the love of fighting itself. If a man fought for profit alone, he might as well sign on to some rogue band as a mercenary. No future in that! Or go off and join up with the Varangians and live in foreign lands.

Egil and Kirstin arrived then, and Hauk found himself surprisingly thankful to see his wife. He wasn't sure why. It wasn't as if she was a healer, but perchance she had some modern ideas that could help him with Bjorn. Besides, he was tired of arguing alone with his son. Let someone else take on that tiresome task. Then, too, there had been that amazing bedplay betwixt them back in the tent.

"Thank the gods you're here," he said to both of them. "What took you so long?"

"Egil had to hit every pot hole in the road."

"She complained every bit of the trip."

"Did you know horses can fart? Well, Egil found the one in all of England that does, and I think he did it deliberately."

Egil rolled his eyes.

"What's in that pot?" Hauk asked, motioning toward the cauldron that Egil held in front of himself with both hands.

"Chicken slop," Egil answered with disgust.

"Chicken *soup*," Kirstin corrected, elbowing Egil, causing him to almost drop the pot. "It has medicinal value," she added as she placed a pile of clean rags she was carrying on the bottom of the bed and went up to look over Bjorn's inert form. "How is he?"

"He has awakened a number of times, but he's lost a large amount of blood," he replied, looking toward the bloody rag pile. "He has a wound in his belly but it appears that the blade missed vital organs. In my opinion. But what do I know? Methinks that the hit to his head is what might be his bigger problem. Also, my unlearned opinion."

"A head wound? That *can* be serious," Kirstin said as if she knew what she was talking about.

That encouraged Hauk. A bit.

"Well, let's see what we have to deal with first. Egil, put down that cauldron and go to the kitchen. Get a pot of hot water. As hot as possible." She gave orders like a Viking chieftain.

But Egil did as he was told.

Kirstin immediately got to work, first checking the bump on Bjorn's head. "The head swelling *is* a concern, but it didn't break the skin. That's good news, but still it needs to be watched. At the very least, he probably has a concussion."

"That's what's causing the lapses in consciousness?"

"Probably. Let's see the sword wound." She gasped when he pulled the bandages, bloody again, off his belly. "Did it go through the other side?"

He shook his head. "Nay. And I do not think it hit any organs. Otherwise, he would be sitting in Valhalla by now."

"Okay. We're going to clean the wound thoroughly. Yes, again. Then stitch it up. I assume you can find a needle and thread somewhere in this castle. After that, we'll wrap it up with clean strips of linen. Any chance there's any alcohol around...like whiskey? It would be a good substitute for an antiseptic. And get some honey, if you can."

Hauk frowned, not understanding half her words. The one, he did, Whiskey. She referred to that potent Scottish brew called *uisge beatha*, breath of life. One dram of that could knock even a tall Viking to his knees. "I'll see what I can find. Then...?"

"...hope for the best."

"*Pfff!* Is that all you can offer?"

"Sorry. I'm not a doctor, and there are no antibiotics or magical medicines available at this time. Suffice it to say, it wouldn't hurt for us to pray. Even some physicians claim that prayers perform miracles with some of their patients."

"And which god would I pay to?"

"There is only one God."

"So you say."

She thought for a moment then added, "Of course, I could always try to take Bjorn back to the future with me. Treatment for his injuries would be a breeze there."

Hauk drew himself up with affront. "Bjorn is going nowhere without me."

She shrugged. "Then the three of us could try to go back."

He gazed at her with horror. "Let us hope that won't become necessary."

Once Egil returned, lugging a pail of steaming water, Hauk ordered him to go off and find some "loot" for Bjorn. He explained about Bjorn's ramblings over war plunder every time he became lucid.

Kirstin made *tsk*ing sounds at the mention of loot and plunder, but she immediately began to cleanse Bjorn's stomach, especially the wound itself which she said might have debris from the sword...dirt, other people's blood, and something called back-tier-yah. Bjorn flinched at the ministrations but did not wake up.

Hauk went off to search for a needle and thread, which he found in a nearby room, and a small pottery container of whiskey in the castellan's private chest of treasures, but there was also an especially welcome prize...a small vial of poppy juice, which he recognized by its milky white appearance and strong scent. If he'd been unsure of his deduction, the vial had two poppy flowers painted on it, with their distinctive black dots denoting seeds. He brought the whole chest with him in hopes of satisfying at least some of Bjorn's yearning for loot. He also stopped by the kitchen storeroom and grabbed a honeycomb wrapped in waxed parchment, an item overlooked thus far by the "looters" more interested in valuables. When he returned, Kirstin was laying out strips of white linen on the bed, preparatory to closing the wound.

To his surprise, she did not give the whiskey to Bjorn to drink, but instead she spread the liquid all over his skin from neck to groin. At the end, she did try to get some in Bjorn's mouth, but most of it dribbled out. Only then did she insert only a single drop of the poppy juice onto his tongue with a

148

warning to Hauk, "It's important that we only give him a tiny amount at a time, and that we don't continue it for a long time. What you call poppy juice is pretty much pure opium, and it's highly addictive."

Like Hauk didn't already know that! He was aware of several Vikings who'd traveled to eastern lands and came back good for nigh nothing except lying about on their bed furs in a daze. Same thing...addiction...happened to those fool enough to love their ale more than life itself. "I hope Bjorn lives long enough for addiction to become an issue," he muttered.

"You're right," she conceded, patting him on the arm. "Still, we should be careful."

"Have you ever done this before?" he asked once she'd threaded the thick needle...a tapestry needle, according to Kirstin, and inhaled deeply for strength.

"No, have you?"

He shook his head, then noticed how pale she was looking. "I'll do it," he said. "You can catch me if I faint."

She smiled at his weak attempt at humor.

He leaned forward and took her face between his two hands. "Just so you know, I appreciate all you are doing." He kissed her then, lightly, but with all the emotion he was holding in. He could tell that she was equally affected. First chance he got, he was going to tup her until her eyes rolled back in her head. A good way to sever this odd attraction betwixt them, he decided. It was distracting, to say the least. Besides, he had not had nearly enough of her the one night they'd made love.

"Maybe this is why I was sent back in time...to save Bjorn, not to save you," she mused.

Hauk still wasn't buying her barmy theories, but he conceded, "Mayhap you were sent to save us both." *And to tup me.*

He began the stitching then. Viking men knew how to sew, or at least the rudiments, often having to mend sails on their longships. Hauk's sutures were rough but sufficient to hold the flaps of flesh together. The scar would be impressive enough for Bjorn to brag on, assuming he survived this ordeal, please gods.

Bjorn awakened with a scream of pain at the first piercing of skin with the needle. Then he fell back, unconscious again. At least he wasn't babbling about loot. Hauk worked quickly to complete the task, fearing he might have to vomit at any minute. He was suffering almost as much as his son.

Kirstin cleaned the whole area again with a cloth dipped in the pail of water and wrung out, followed by a whiskey wash over the wound section. After that, the two of them worked to bind the wound with strips of linen wrapped all around his body, over and under.

When they were done, Hauk dropped down into the rushes and leaned back against the wall, his legs outstretched. Bone-weary from lack of sleep, the battle, and the stress over Bjorn, Hauk inhaled and exhaled with relief. "I need to rest for a few minutes," he told Kirstin. "Can you watch over Bjorn if I should doze off?"

"Of course," she said, looking at him with concern. "Maybe you should go off and find a bed somewhere."

"Nay. This is sufficient."

"Well, relax for now. Bjorn seems to be sleeping normally. If he doesn't get an infection, there's a good chance he'll survive. In my opinion."

"Thank you," he said, then yawned widely.

While she had the needle and thread, she decided to repair her ripped undergarment...what she called pant-hes. Hauk watched with interest while she sewed. A rough job with the thick black thread against the white silky fabric. "At least, my privates will be private again," she told him.

Hauk sighed as he nestled lower against the wall, and, wondered how soon he could explore those privates again. Just before he fell asleep, he murmured, "I'm glad you're here, Kirstin. I'm glad you're my wife." He wasn't sure if he'd spoken aloud or just thought those words. *In any case, I'll thank you later, in my own way. Ha, ha.* Everything went gray and then black as he fell fast asleep.

A thought swam through his dream-state, *Only the Norns of Fate know what will happen now. It's in the hands of the gods.*

Ironically, another voice in his head laughed and said, *The One-God guides thy destiny now, Viking. Pray!*

Good idea! Hauk decided to pray to all the gods, and at the same time, there was a plan forming in the back of Hauk's mind. He was very good at making plans. *Gods bless this particular plan!*

Uh-hum! the voice in his head piped in.

I mean, God bless this particular plan.

That is better.

~

To be or not to be...in love, that is...

I'M glad you're my wife. Kirstin repeated Hauk's words in her head.

She wasn't sure how she felt about his declaration. Well, that wasn't quite true. She was flattered. Maybe a little worried, too, because Hauk might decide to keep her here, or try to. She wouldn't put it past him. She touched her arm rings, just to reassure herself she was safe, for now.

The question is: Am I glad that he's my husband?

She glanced over to where he half-reclined against the wall, sleeping deeply, his head tilted slightly forward. It had to be an uncomfortable position, but the man was exhausted beyond caring.

Life in the eleventh century was hard at the best of times, and they'd been particularly bad for Hauk. Loss of his son, imprisonment, escape by a means that was frightening even to Kirstin, finding his son was alive, and then the battle. She couldn't help but notice the rips in his tunic and braies seeping blood from presumably small wounds, the black and blue marks on his face and arms that would soon turn purple. New scars would surely join those already marring his body... a body still displaying the ravages of near-starvation.

The poor man!

Dear God, she prayed, *please don't let him lose his son on top of everything else. He appears to be a good man. Help him, Lord.* Kirstin was not an overly religious person, but she was convinced that God had something to do with this time travel of hers. Who else to go to for help, then?

Well, there was one thing she could do to help. Now that Bjorn seemed to be out of the woods, for the time being, she could feed him...all of them, in fact...her chicken soup. But no one would want to eat cold broth with fat congealing on the top. So, she picked up the cauldron by its handle with both hands and made her way carefully across the room. She needed to look for the nearest fire. Since it was summer and fairly warm, even inside this dank castle, hearths wouldn't be lit for heat. She decided the kitchen or scullery would be her best bet.

Before she left, she repeated her earlier question to herself. Studying Hauk in this most vulnerable position she would probably ever find him in, she asked, *Am I glad that he's my husband?*

The answer, to her dismay, was yes. Absolutely yes.

But that didn't mean she was in love with the man.

Did it?

It occurred to her as she walked down the hallway that she was in Winchester Castle, near the great hall where her time-travel experience began. She was wearing the arm rings. This would be the perfect opportunity for her to attempt to go home.

Her heart lurched and she felt a humming in her ears. An almost magnetic pull drew her to the archway leading into the great hall. Over there, a mere thirty feet away, was the spot where she'd first emerged from her time travel.

I could step across the room right now, and within moments be back home, or at Rosestead, or somewhere in the future, wherever I pictured in my mind.

It's too soon, the other side of her brain demurred. *I have to prepare for this departure.*

Why? Hauk is no longer in his cage. He is free to go home.

But am I free?

Depends on what you mean by free.

It would be cruel for me to just leave without saying good-bye to him, or to Bjorn, who is incidentally not wholly recovered.

Excuses!

I'm just not sure what to do.

Just do it, for God's sake! It's the only logical thing to do.

Instead, she spun on her heels and walked in the other direction.

To her surprise, Hauk was standing a short distance away, just watching her. She could swear there were tears in his eyes. But then he glanced downward and grinned. "Were you planning to take your chicken slop with you?"

~

IN THE HEAT *of the night...*

Hauk was sitting on the side of Bjorn's pallet with a wet rag in his hand when Kirstin returned, lugging her cauldron in both hands, some of the liquid sloshing over the sides and wetting her gown. With a long sigh, she set it on the floor and, noticing what he was doing, exclaimed, "Oh, no! Does he have a fever?"

"Nay. I've just been laying cool cloths on his forehead in hopes of forestalling a fever," he told her. "I know, foolish of me."

"Hey, whatever works. You should have some of this soup while it's still hot. Maybe we can get some into Bjorn, too. It really does have medicinal value. And it is chicken *soup*, not *slop*, no matter what Egil calls it."

He winked at her to let her know he'd been aware of Egil's teasing and took the bowl she handed to him, watching while she ladled its contents. He was still reeling from having discovered her near the great hall a short time ago, contemplating a reversal of her time-travel. If he hadn't found her there, would she be gone by now? For some reason, that possibility was too harsh to contemplate. Instead, he chose to lighten her obviously somber mood. "What are those white things floating on top? Please don't tell me they are slugs?"

"No!" She smacked him on the shoulder with her ladle. "They're spaetzle, or dough balls. Would you eat them if they were slugs?"

"*Pff!* I've eaten worse. Gammelost, for example. Since I haven't put anything in my stomach since last night, I'm not about to be fussy, even spit-cells." He shrugged and pretended to be holding his nose with trepidation. But then, as he took his first slurp, his eyes widened. "Mmmm. This is good, even if they are made with spit."

She thought about correcting him, that they were spaetzle, not spit-cells, but decided not to bother. "Why are you surprised? It's not rocket science to make soup. All it takes is—"

He put his fingertips to her lips. "Not everything has to be a lecture, Kirstin. Just say thank you."

She blushed prettily and said, "Thank you."

Egil returned, dragging a burlap-style, coarse-woven bag that clanked metallically on the stone floor in the corridor. "This is the best I could do out in the field," he said. "Sweyn has ordered any treasures found within the castle to be brought to him and he will decide who gets what. Apparently, some miscreant was caught stealing off with the king's gold crown. He now has only one hand."

Kirstin gasped at that news, and he and Egil looked at her with question. "What do you expect?" Hauk asked. "Thievery must be punished. Even in your time, I daresay."

"Not like that!" she protested. "That's...that's barbaric."

He pondered, then shrugged. "Barbarians...that is what the Saxons call us."

"You say that as if it's a compliment."

"Is it not?" He blinked at her with exaggerated innocence.

"Loot!" Bjorn said, sitting up suddenly and glancing over at Egil's sack and the castellan's treasure chest.

Hauk gave Kirstin a meaningful glare at having taught his son that word, but then used the opportunity to get some of the broth into his son's mouth. Bjorn resisted but Hauk told him that Egil would show them all the "loot" if he ate.

Thus, Hauk sat on the edge of the pallet, holding Bjorn's shoulders so that he was half-sitting, and Kirstin took over, using a wooden spoon to feed the broth into his mouth. Half of it ended up running down the dusting of fine hairs on his chin, not yet whiskers, onto his neck and tunic, even into his ears.

Egil made much ado out of everything he pulled out and spread about the floor within view of Bjorn's bed. It was a motley assortment of goods...everything from a heavy cloak embroidered on the edges with gold thread, a fancy short sword and several heavily embossed knives, a leather helmet, a half dozen shoulder brooches, two rings, a handful or two of assorted coins, and that was just from Egil's battlefield foraging. From the castellan's chest, he displayed some valuable spices, more coins, a heavy gold chain, two matching brooches with precious stones, a bottle of wine, and a rare book, which Kirstin told him was a gospel or writings by a saint.

As much as he wanted to see everything, Bjorn was weak and soon succumbed to sleep again. Hauk helped Egil put everything away while Kirstin used a damp cloth to clean up Bjorn's face and neck to make him more comfortable. "He looks just like you," she observed.

"He does?" Hauk stared at his son, but could not see the resemblance, except mayhap for the hair color and shape of his nose.

She nodded. "He'll be a chick magnet, just like you."

He wasn't sure what that meant, but he was fairly certain she meant that he was comely in appearance, and so he winked at her.

She made that *tsk*ing sound she was wont to make around him and said, "Don't waste your charms on me, Viking."

"Why? Dost deem yourself untemptable?"

"Hah! You know very well that I can be tempted."

He smiled then, inordinately pleased. Why, he wasn't sure. He'd never had trouble attracting females, and it was too late for him to claim modesty. But his wife's admission that he tempted her...ah, it made his heart swell with pride.

Egil had been following their exchange with interest, his head swiveling from one to the other as he spoke. "Dost want me to leave for a while so you can tup?"

"What?" Kirstin squealed.

Hauk just grinned.

"Can you all stop talking? You're making my head ache,"

Bjorn said, then, remarkably, fell right back to sleep, snoring softly.

They all laughed then.

"'Tis good to hear you laugh, wife," Hauk said. "You know, you are always talking about the future in somber tones. Does nothing funny happen there?"

"Oh, lots of things would be funny to you. Let me think... okay, physical exercise is very important in modern times. Lots of people, men and women, jog every day. Jogging means running, not running from something or toward something, just running. In fact, dedicated athletes often jog for several miles at a time."

"Why?" Egil asked.

"To get in better shape, or for some because they get a high from it, a rush of pleasure."

"Barmy," Egil concluded.

"What else?" Hauk asked.

"Did I mention that children go to school for at least twelve years? Some, sixteen or twenty years if they choose some particular career path."

"Whaaat?" Bjorn quaked out. Apparently he'd awakened. "I had a priest teacher for three years and he nigh made my head burst with megrims."

Kirstin smiled kindly at Bjorn, then went on, "Vikings have skalds to entertain you in your great halls. We have lots of kinds of entertainment, but one of them comes from comedians, whose sole job is to make people laugh. They tell jokes."

"Like a jester?" Egil inquired.

"Not quite. A jester plays a fool in colorful clothing with a donkey-ears cap. They sing bawdy or mocking songs. Perform magic. Play instruments. Juggle. Whereas, the modern comedian just tells jokes, for the most part. Some of them are extremely wealthy."

"From making jests?" Egil scoffed.

Kirstin nodded.

"Such as?" Hauk was peeling a rather wilted apple he'd brought up with the noon meal and was cutting it into slices, some of which he offered to Bjorn.

"I thought you'd never ask," Kirstin said, smirking at him. "What do you call a pony with a cough?" She paused and answered, "A little horse."

Hauk just raised his eyebrows.

"Okay, how about this one? Why did the skeleton go to the feast alone? Don't know? Because he had no body to go with him."

She giggled, enjoying her own jokes.

"Oooh, this one is a favorite of my nephews and nieces. What did one egg say to the other? Well, eggs-cuse me!"

When no one laughed, she tried to explain, "Eggs/ex...get it?"

"We got it, but it's just not funny."

"How about...why doesn't anyone want to shear a crazy... um, demented sheep? Because it's a baaaaaa-d idea."

"What's bad is your idea of humor," Egil said, but he was grinning.

"How about some knock-knock jokes, then?"

"How about I knock you over your fool head?"

"You wouldn't!"

"You are correct. I wouldn't. But that does not mean I am not tempted."

"So, you don't appreciate my attempt at basic jokes and you don't want knock-knocks...bet you wouldn't go for slap-stick, either. No, I don't mean slapping two sticks together. Jeesh! I give up! Okay, forget about modern jokes then. You asked what things are amusing in the future. Well, some of our music would seem funny to you. In fact, the most popular is called rock and roll music. But especially funny is country music, which my brother Torolf and his buddies love." She hummed, then sang the words to a song called "Achy Breaky Heart" and another about badonkadonks, which was apparently a modern name for women's arses.

Even Bjorn rose slightly from his bed to laugh at that one, although, unlike him and Egil, Bjorn hadn't yet heard her tales of time travel. He just thought she was speaking of some far-off country she came from.

Then there's one called "Who Let the Dogs Out?"

When she made dog barking sounds, he and Egil and Bjorn just stared at her.

"Okay, speaking of dogs...here's something that you might find comical. People keep dogs as pets in their homes in the future, but they take them outside on leashes for walks to do their business. Then they pick up their poop in plastic sacks and carry it home for disposal."

"You are making this all up," Hauk said. "No man...no Viking man...would ever do that."

"Wanna bet?" she countered. But then, she seemed to come to some conclusion. "Listen, it's six o'clock already," she said, glancing at the gold band on her wrist which she claimed told all the hours and minutes and seconds of the day. "Why don't you two go to the hall and celebrate the victory with your friends, enjoy a few yucks with the boys. I can stay with Bjorn. Suffice it to say, if there's a problem, I can come for you."

"Yucks? Is that the same as fucks?" Egil asked, and then, at Kirstin's gasp of affront, he whispered to Hauk, loud enough for all to hear, "She is barmy."

"I like her, probably because I like dogs," Bjorn said, making a barking noise, but then clutching at his gut for the pain that small movement caused.

"At least someone appreciates me," she said with an exaggerated woeful expression on her face.

Hauk smiled. "Are you sure you don't want to come to the hall, to share a cup of mead? Egil can keep watch over Bjorn."

"Not on your life! Me in a hall full of drinking men? I don't think so!"

She was probably right. Besides, Hauk wasn't sure he wanted her so close to the spot where her "time travel" or whatever the hell it was, had begun. There were too many questions to be answered before she disappeared. At least, he told himself that's why he didn't want to risk losing her.

"You could always tell the crowd one of your jokes," Hauk teased. "Otherwise, we will be forced to listen to the skald compose praise-poems to Sweyn's heroics."

"Thanks, but no thanks."

Hauk left with Egil a short time later. They spent several hours in the hall, imbibing the Saxon royal ale, and sharing good cheer with the ten men of his shiphird who had taken part in the battle and still remained. More than once he'd glared at comrades-in-arms who tried to make jests about his time living in a cage. Hauk liked to laugh like any Viking, who enjoyed humor, even when at their expense, but enough was enough on the cage jests.

After a while and much imbibing of ale, the men in the hall, including him and Hauk, accepted their share of the spoils, which were not overly generous in their case since they were not part of Sweyn's regular army and had only joined the fight late in the day. Hauk got two gold plates, several ells of rich samite cloth, a sable-lined cape, and a handful of loose gems. To Sweyn's amusement, Hauk also grabbed several gowns for Kirstin and a pair of lady's half boots. Egil got a small pouch of gold coins. Each of the twenty Haukshire shiphird got a silver arm ring each. The meagerness of their reward wasn't worth an argument, Hauk decided. Besides, they'd taken the castellan's chest without Sweyn's knowledge. And both Egil and Hauk's seamen, along with many other Vikings, had done some scavenging on the battlefield afore Sweyn put a halt to that activity.

Normally, Hauk would have enjoyed this fellowship with his comrades-in-arms, but tonight, everything seemed too loud, the food too greasy, and the boasting too embellished. And way too much farting and belching, even for his less than refined tastes. He directed all but two of his men to return to Jorvik on the morrow and prepare the ship for eventual voyage back to the Norselands.

Sweyn stopped him when he was about to leave the hall. "You are going so early to your bed furs? What is amiss? Are you displeased?" Sweyn's breath was heavy with drink and his tone combative. Like many Vikings when drukkinn, he was looking for a good fight.

Well, Hauk wasn't in the mood to give it to him. "The company is fine. The disbursement of treasure satisfies me. I am just overtired. And I need to check on my son who is wounded."

"Ah, I forgot," Sweyn said. "I will give him my personal thanks first chance I get."

Hauk added, "Keep in mind, I have been living in a cage for nigh on six months. Spending more time in this hall provides bad memories."

"Ah, I forgot that too," Sweyn said with a big grin. "I know, let us go burn the thing down."

"You might very well catch the whole castle afire."

"Well, then, perchance one of our Saxon prisoners would like to reside within the cage. What think you, Hauk?"

"If King Aethaelred or one of his nobles were about, I would agree, but a housecarl of lower rank...? Nay. Not worth the bother."

On those words he began to walk away and noticed that Sweyn's attention was already diverted to a Saxon serving maid who'd caught his eye. Best Sweyn be careful, or another part of his body would catch something. Hauk had noticed from his cage that this particular wench bedded many men, several in one night.

When he got back to his bedchamber, he found Kirstin, fully dressed except for her shoes, curled up on the castellan's fine wool cloak which she'd spread out on the rushes. A quick check of Bjorn found him soundly asleep, drool dribbling from the side of his open mouth, due to the poppy juice, no doubt, which they were weaning him from, but not yet totally.

Hauk toed off his half boots, undid his belt, and pulled his tunic up and over his head, leaving him bare-chested but with his braies still on. He considered taking those off, too, then decided to leave them on. With a wide yawn, he sank down to the cloak and pulled his wife into his side, with her head resting on his shoulder and his arm around her back. With his free hand, he pulled the edges of the cloak over them both.

He sighed then, feeling at utter peace for the first time since he couldn't recall when. Perhaps since before he'd heard of Bjorn's presumed death. Mayhap it was a sign of his getting older. Under normal circumstances, he would be enjoying himself with heavy drinking and boisterous bedplay after a battle. He kissed the top of his wife's head…and sighed again.

He could not lose her.

Holy Thor! When had he turned into such a weakling? He *would not* lose her. All he needed was a plan.

An idea came unbidden to him then, and he grinned.

Dare I do such?

Dare I nót?

She will be so peeved with me.

When is she not peeved with me?

Having made a fateful decision, he allowed himself to succumb to sleep.

The voice in his head chuckled and pronounced, *Man plans. God laughs.*

Huh? he said, but got no answer; so, once again he relaxed his body into sleep. The next moment he was aware of Egil was shaking him and shouting, "Master, wake up! Oooh, this is bad! Hurry! Wake up!"

He shot to a sitting position, knocking Kirstin to the side. Apparently she'd been wrapped around him in their joint slumber.

"What? What is it?" Hauk jumped to his feet, grabbing for a weapon, looking behind Egil to see if he'd been followed by some villains looking for trouble.

Egil had a wall torch in his hand, which he must have used to light his way back to the bedchamber. He was waving it about as he explained hysterically, "I jist got back and I suspected there was something wrong when the boy was rolling about on his bed. So, I decided to check on him afore I lay meself down. That's when I—"

Hauk put up a halting hand. He had no idea what Egil was blathering about, except that his distress seemed to be related to Bjorn, not some troublemakers. He immediately moved over to the pallet, and he didn't need the light from Egil's torch to see what the problem was.

His son was burning up with fever.

CHAPTER 12

Beware lusty men with plans...

*F*or the next two days, all their efforts...hers, Hauk's, and Egil's...were concentrated on Bjorn and reducing his fever. Finally, they succeeded, but Bjorn was so weak he could only sit up for moments at a time, and he slept on and off through the day and night, even though they'd reduced the amount they gave him of the so-called poppy juice. Very potent! Now would be the time when her hearty chicken soup would come in handy to strengthen the boy. Unfortunately, Kirstin hadn't been able to find the ingredients in her explorations of the castle, and, frankly, she couldn't imagine cooking in the chaos that reigned in the castle kitchen, where Saxon servants had been turned into Viking thralls. She would have been more comfortable cooking over an open fire out by the moat.

Hauk and Egil went to the great hall each evening, claiming a need to mix with their comrades-in-arms and not give offense to Sweyn. They invited Kirstin to accompany them, but she felt too uncomfortable in the heavily masculine, rowdy atmosphere and chose to eat in the bedchamber. Usually a slice of manchet bread, a hunk of hard cheese or some *skyrr*, which was similar to yogurt, and a mug of ale. Hauk rarely stayed away more than two hours and never came back drunk, although she was sure many of the Vikings were three sheets to the wind before they hit their beds, or fell asleep with their faces on the greasy trestle tables..

Occasionally, during the day, Kirstin crept about the castle, wanting to memorize details for future reference. Winchester was not a crude timber castle like many were at that time, more closely resembling forts, but it was not all stone either. A combination of both. Any splendor it might have had was sorely missing now after the Viking plunder. Precious illuminated manuscripts on parchment being compiled in the castle librarium by monk historians, who had the good sense to make themselves scarce among the men they'd deemed despicable pagans, lay torn or burnt on the floors, which of course was a crying shame. If she could have saved some of them, she would have. Alas...!

The walls of the great hall and solars were mostly bare, any weapons or adornments having been removed by Aethelred when fleeing or Sweyn's men as battle rewards. There was a stale smell like a beer dive after hours in the hall, and the rushes were ripe with scraps of food and animal waste; the whole place needed a good cleaning. Many of the Winchester servants had been thralls, or slaves under the Saxons, but were all deemed slaves under Viking rule. None of them felt the need to be extra vigilant in their work. The only place where there was much activity was in the kitchens and laundry where a Norse soldier stood guard with his trusty long-handled, twin-bladed battle axe in hand, scowling or cursing out orders.

Sweyn and his troops would be leaving soon to conquer other parts of England, and, as Kirstin knew from her history lessons, to be eventually declared king of all Britain. Not that he knew that. Or that he was going to die soon after.

But Kirstin couldn't be concerned about that man whom she was convinced was a megalomaniac, half narcissist and half serial killer. His changeable moods were downright scary; he could jump from happy-happy to sword-wielding nutcase with no notice, and beware anyone who stood in his path.

No, Kirstin was more concerned with her own problems. No avoiding the fact that she was going to have to return to the future. *Soon.* She'd noticed Hauk looking at her on occasion, when he didn't think she was aware, and she could tell that he was waiting for her to announce her departure. The only question was: *When?*

"I have a surprise for you," Hauk said when she came back from the garderobe that afternoon. And wasn't that an experience, by the way! If the hall was rank, the medieval indoor privy was a nightmare of filthy odors. A modern bathroom would be the thing she missed most if she were stuck in the past, something she had no intention of doing.

"More loot?" Bjorn interjected from his cot, although it had been clear that Hauk was addressing her.

"Nay," Hauk said, scowling his son's way. "Enough with the loot!"

Bjorn just grinned.

"Come with me," Hauk said, his lips twitching at some secret. "Grab some clean clothing. One of those gowns from the treasure pile will do."

She gazed at him suspiciously.

"You will like my surprise, I promise."

She was still suspicious, but she let him take her hand, and lead her out of the room. They went only a short distance to another bedchamber, which was empty except for a large brass tub with steaming water more than halfway to its brim. On the floor were a number of toweling linens, a large-toothed ivory comb, and most precious of all…a small bowl of soft soap, which, *be still my sybaritic heart*, was clearly not made of the usual lye.

"Oooooh!" she sighed and turned to him with thanks. "How did you manage this?" she asked, quickly adding, "No, don't tell me. You are Viking. Anything is possible."

"Was that an insult?"

She squeezed his arm and said, "No. I'm thankful. Now, go so that I can bathe in private."

"What? You do not need my help in scrubbing your unreachable parts?"

"No, thank you."

"Perchance I could join you if we squeeze together just so?"

"Not a chance!" She laughed.

He left her alone and she trusted that he would leave her alone for a while, but she made quick work of removing her dirty clothes and getting into the warm water, just in case, sudsing herself up with the soap, washing her hair, rinsing herself with a small bucket several times before she leaned back and sighed. This was better than the most indulgent bubble bath in her modern soaking tub, even though this brass container had her sitting with her knees raised and the water was less than a foot and a half deep. She would have liked to relax longer, but the water was already turning cold.

She dressed in a green wool dress so finely woven it was almost like silk and not as warm as you would expect from wool. It had a round neckline and long sleeves, rather full to the ankles, but she was able to tighten it at the waist with a braided gold cord belt, which she tied off with a bow. When Hauk came back…without knocking, she noticed…she was attempting to run the comb through her snarled, damp hair. Without conditioner, it was almost impossible.

Immediately seeing her dilemma, Hauk said, "Let me." He

forced her to sit on a stool while he faced her back, resting his buttocks on the lip of the tub, and began to work on the tangles, one at a time. Meanwhile, he chatted amiably. "I've decided to go back to Haukshire."

A chill ran over Kirstin. So, the time had finally come. Hauk intended to leave Winchester Castle. And where did that leave her? Was he abandoning her, or planning to wait until she time-traveled back home? But she would address that later. For now, she asked, "With Bjorn?"

"Of course. I think he is well enough to travel to Jorvik in the back of the wagon."

"Jorvik. That's York. For goodness sakes, Hauk, that's about two hundred miles. It would probably take you a week to get there."

"I don't think so. If Egil and I take turns driving, we can make use of all the daylight hours. Four days at most, mayhap five, but not a full sennight."

"I think you're being overly optimistic, but even so, a week or four days, Bjorn is in no condition to travel," she said and winced when he pulled on a particularly difficult tangle. "Ouch!"

"Sorry."

"I assume that Jorvik is where your longship is docked, or wharfed, or anchored...or whatever you call it."

He smiled at her fumbling over boat terms. "It is."

"Isn't there somewhere closer where you could move the longship?"

"Now that you mention it...yea, I think that is a good suggestion, considering Bjorn's condition. I will send the two men of my shiphird still remaining here to ride to Jorvik immediately where the rest of my men are already preparing for a voyage. *Sea Wolf* is a fairly small longship, and no doubt I will need to hire on another six or more sea men. They will be directed to bring the longship to London.

On horseback, the men should need only two days to get to Jorvik, and in the meantime, it will take Egil and I only a day and half to get Bjorn to the wharf." He kissed the back of her neck and murmured against her ears, "Thank you, dearling."

Before she could swat him away, or ponder just how good his lips felt against her skin, he stepped back. "I think I got all the tangles." He ran the comb smoothly down through the long strands several more times just to be sure.

She shivered at the almost erotic delight of the comb's teeth stroking her scalp. She'd heard about scalp massages being sensuous experiences offered in luxury spas, but had never experienced before. *Wow!*

He turned the stool so he was facing her. His eyes took in her gown, and her scrubbed face, and hair which hung in a straight damp swath from behind her ears down to her shoulders.

"You are beautiful," he observed.

Clean and presentable, she thought. Even in the best of circumstances, back in her own time, with make-up and all the modern enhancements, she would have described herself as attractive, never beautiful. But instead of arguing, she said, "Thank you."

"We need to talk," he said, running his fingertips along her jaw and over her lips. Then he took both her hands in his.

"About my going home?"

He nodded.

"If you're committed to beginning a trip to London tomorrow, I should probably attempt to go back sometime today, or tonight."

"Are you committed to that course?"

She hesitated, but then nodded. What other choice did she have, really?

"Even though we are wed?"

"I'm not sure that would be considered a legal marriage in my time."

He raised his eyebrows at that argument. "And if you are with child? You would take my son or daughter to a place where I could never meet them?"

"I am not pregnant," she stated.

"Are you certain of that?"

She could feel heat flood her cheeks. "Almost certain. Besides, if I stayed here, I might get pregnant, and then I might not ever be able to return."

He frowned. "'Might' is a far cry from certain."

"Come on, Hauk. Be honest. You don't really want a wife."

"Oh, I do not know about that. I admit that I once felt that way, but I have grown accustomed to your stubborn ways and high conceit. And talkative? Truly, dost have an opinion on everything, sweetling?"

She made a *tsk*ing sound of disgust. "That doesn't sound very attractive."

"You are attractive, believe you me. It took all my impressive self-control and raging enthusiasm," he glanced pointedly at the bulge in his slim pants, "not to barge in whilst you were bathing and take you wet and all, mayhap against the wall, or on my lap sitting on your stool, or kneeling on the stone floor, face to face, or, wait, wait for this, better yet, both of us kneeling on the floor with me at your back, and—"

"Oh, you!" she said with a laugh, then pulled her hands out of his grasp and cupped his cheeks, giving him a quick kiss. "You are a charmer, all right."

"But not charming enough to convince you to stay?"

"Oh, I'm tempted. Maybe if you were staying here, or near Winchester Castle where my time-travel portal is...I don't know...maybe I would stay for a while to see where things could go."

He stood suddenly, causing her hands to drop at her sides.

He looked down at her and shrugged. "So be it," he said. "I can't stay. I've already neglected Haukshire far too long. By the time I get back there, assess how bad the situation is, go off to one of the market towns, Hedeby or Birka, to replenish stock before the winter snows come in, well, there is just not enough time. My lands are in the north...not so far as the endless daylight region...but brutal cold, just the same. And so mountainous that farming is nigh impossible; I have no plow lands to speak of. We must rely on hunting and trapping for sustenance and skins to trade, supplemented by goods purchased for provender...oats, vegetables, and such."

"And all this takes time," she concluded, smarting over his seeming indifference. "That time crunch thing again."

"Yea," he agreed. "But, most important, I think Bjorn will recover better in a secure, more quiet setting. In addition, I have a neighbor who is a threat. Last time Egil was there, Jarl Ingolf of Stormstead was seen prowling about my estates in a proprietary manner."

He sounded so calm and rational. Did he really care so little that they might never see each other again? Meanwhile, her heart was breaking. Yes, the separation needed to happen, but that didn't mean it would be easy. Not for her anyway.

"A stalemate then, between you and me," she said and quickly explained, "A standstill, or impossible situation."

"Just so we are clear...are you saying, regarding the bond between you and me, that time is the issue for you? Not enough time to know each other?"

"Basically. I mean, there are other issues, of course, which may or may not be resolved eventually, but, yes, all of it would take time. Which we don't have."

He nodded, as if her words confirmed something he'd already thought. "So, tonight it is then?"

"Yes," she said. "Bjorn is getting better. The battle is over. My job is done."

"Is it now?" He was examining his fingernails, as if to see if they needed paring. "I suppose you are right."

She was surprised that he seemed so accepting of her departure. While her heart felt like it was breaking, Hauk seemed resigned to her leaving, maybe a little relieved. They hadn't made love since the one night in the tent, and no opportunity to repeat that experience while here at Winchester with four of them crammed in one room, one of them almost dying. That meant they wouldn't have any opportunity before tonight, either.

Unless...

"So, this is good-bye," she said casually, then slanted him what she hoped was a sultry invitation. "You know what you said about what you could do with me on your lap?"

A smile slowly emerged on his lips.

~

Crazy in love, or just plain crazy...

"You've gone barmy," Egil concluded as he watched Hauk pour several drops of poppy juice in one of three cups of wine.

"Hey, only three cups! Don't I get some, too?" Bjorn asked as he half sat, half reclined on the cot, his condition having improved dramatically throughout the day, as the young were wont to do.

"You've had more than enough strong drink, my son," Hauk declared, "and, besides, there's almost no wine left." With that, he poured the last few drops into a fourth cup, anyway, just for appearance sake...and to please the boy. This was intended to be a farewell toast to Kirstin, once she returned from a last trip to the garderobe before she made her exit back to her time and place in the future. *Gods! I still cannot believe I have accepted her stories.*

"I cannot believe you have accepted her stories," Egil said, as if reading his mind.

Hauk shrugged. "What else can I believe?"

"That she is barmy as a bat?" Egil offered.

"Well, that's two of us then, according to your theory," Hauk said. "Didn't you just call me barmy for fixing her wine?"

"Fixin', eh? She'll be the one fixin', once she discovers what ye've done. Fixin' yer arse."

"By then, it will be too late. We'll be at sea and far from Winchester and her supposed time portal, or whatever she calls it."

"I still do not understand why ye can't jist take the arm rings from her, like ye did afore."

"Because then she would know what I am about and start haranguing me hither and yon to give them back. My way, it will be too late afore she can protest."

Bjorn laughed. "I did not realize having a father would be so much fun."

Hauk was fairly certain his son was making mock of him, but he had no time to pursue the subject because Kirstin had returned. She was wearing one of the gowns he'd gotten from Sweyn's plunder pile, a garment of a silky-like fabric in a pretty sky-blue color that matched her eyes and the rare blue amber pendant that hung about her neck on a gold chain. She had taken time to plait her hair into one long braid. The arm rings were on her upper arms.

"What is this?" she asked, noticing the four cups sitting on top of his travel chest.

"Wine, a farewell toast to you afore we go to the hall," Hauk said, leaning down to give her a quick kiss on the cheek. She did not duck as she usually did when he got too close.

How could she after what they'd shared in the bathing chamber this afternoon? *I thought I knew everything about the sex arts. I had no idea women could do that...that thing.*

She eyed him suspiciously, but took the cup he handed her. He took another for himself and handed one each to Egil and Bjorn. She took a tiny sip and made a grimace of distaste. "It's not very good wine, is it?"

He shrugged. "It will do."

Bjorn made a choking sound which Kirstin took to be equal distaste for the wine.

"'Tis been a pleasure meeting you, m'lady," Egil said, tipping his cup in salute to her.

They all took sips of their wine.

"I'll never forget watching you and my father spin through space," Bjorn told her. "And here I was hoping for a step-mother who could teach me such fancy tricks. Oh, well!"

More sips of wine.

Hauk cleared his throat and took one of her hands in his. "I wish you would stay, at least for a while, but I have to thank you for all you've done for us...releasing me from the cage, getting us out of the castle, curing Bjorn of his injuries."

"Hah!" she said. "You wish I would stay *for a while...*until you got bored. You can't fool me."

"But mayhap you would be the one to get bored," he pointed out, although he did not really believe that. Leastways, it had never happened to him with other women.

"Well then, I would just have to make sure you worked extra hard to keep me unbored." She grinned at him to demonstrate her meaning, as if he hadn't understood that she meant sexplay. "Lucky you, that you won't have to work so hard."

She had tears in her eyes as she teased him, and he knew the parting was affecting her, too. Not enough to change her mind, but hopefully enough to temper her wrath later.

He released her hand, and they all drank the rest of their wine. Bjorn would stay in the room while he, Egil, and Kirstin went to the hall. Leastways, that was the plan they'd laid out to Kirstin earlier.

"Come, wife," he said, his voice gravelly with emotion, and held out a hand.

Instead of taking his hand, she wobbled on her feet, swayed, then fell forward into his arms. Just before she fell into a drugged sleep, she looked up at him. "You didn't!" she accused him.

"I did," he admitted, "and may the gods help me."

He heard that annoying "ahem" noise in his head again, and he self-corrected, "May *God* help me."

"Thou art on thy own, Viking."

CHAPTER 13

Not the trip she'd expected...

*K*irstin was nauseated, and her eyes seemed to be glued shut. It felt like an axe was imbedded in her skull. Like the worst hangover. Not that she'd ever experienced many of those, not being much of a drinker, but red wine tended to affect her in that way, or at least with a bad headache, or some vomiting.

No wonder! Now that she thought on it, she had drunk that cup of the grape in a farewell toast, hadn't she? She should have expected this.

Back and forth, back and forth, the contents of her stomach sloshed. She licked her lips, expecting the fuzzy-tongued yucky taste of stale booze, but instead she tasted...salt?

She kept her eyes closed, at first, trying to make sense of what had happened.

I was about to go to the hall to make my trip back to the future.
Am I in the future?
If so, it's final. I've left Hauk...my husband...behind. Her heart

squeezed at that prospect. *It's over. All chances of a happily ever after with him, gone!*

Not that he ever promised that.

Or that I expected it.

But still...

Or was it all a dream?

If so, I need to see a therapist. These dreams are getting out of hand.

Is there such a thing as a dream therapist? Bet there is. Gotta go Google that.

She tried to get up, but realized she wasn't lying down. She was standing up, but...she tried to wipe the sleep gunk from her eyes...and discovered that she couldn't move her arms from her sides. Alarmed, she squeezed her eyes several times, creating moisture, and was able to open her eyelids a bit.

That's when she let out a scream. A loud scream. A loud unending scream.

Hauk came over to stand before her where she was tied to the mast pole of a ship.

A moving ship.

On the open frickin' sea.

That explained the salty crust on her lips and eyes.

Panic overcame her as she realized where she was, soon supplanted by anger. She sputtered with disbelief, "You...you..."

He hunkered down a bit so that he was eye level with her. "Shhh, dearling! You'll scare the sea birds."

He jokes? At a time like this? She screamed louder.

"Now, Kirstin, hold your screeching. Let me explain."

"Explain? Explain? You kidnapped me. How do you explain that?"

He batted his eyelashes and had the nerve to look offended. "I only did what you wanted."

"What? Here's a news flash, dumbbell. I never asked you to kidnap me."

"You missay me, m'lady." He did more of that I-am-unfairly-accused-innocent eyelash batting. "What I meant was, you said you needed time, I have given you time." He smiled and raised his hands in a voilà! manner.

She screamed again, then barfed all over her gown.

"At least it's you that got the barrage this time. Twice now, you have decorated my boots. I did not think you had anything left in your stomach." At the look of outrage on her face, he added, "Not that I am complaining."

She noticed then that Egil, who was manning the rudder, and Bjorn, who was reclining on a pile of furs nearby, along with the twenty or so rowers, were staring and listening to the exchange between her and Hauk, mostly with amusement. They thought her kidnapping was hilarious, no doubt, and not at all out of character for a Viking. Her rebellion entertained them, as well.

"Why am I tied up?" she asked.

"We had rough seas yestereve, and this being one of my smallest longships, thus light on the waves, not an attribute to be desired in a storm, well, I did not want to risk your falling overboard. Is that not considerate of me?"

"Release. Me. Now!" she demanded through gritted teeth.

"Are you going to hit me?" he asked with a teasing grin.

"As many times and as hard as I can."

He pondered her reply, then nodded. "But first I must wash you off."

Before she had a chance to tell him that she would do her own washing, he picked up a big wooden bucket and dumped several gallons of water all over the front of her gown.

"You...you...you...," she sputtered. Glancing downward, she saw that her gown, which was already bedraggled thanks to God only knew what the past two days while she'd been

178

drugged, was now sodden. And the wet fabric molded her body in ways that clearly aroused him. *Good! Let him have a hard-on from here to Valhalla before he'll get it anywhere near me again.*

As he worked at the knots in her ropes, trying to hide the tent in his britches by standing behind her, she asked, "How many days is it since we left Winchester?"

"Two days. Another day and a half and we should see the Norselands. The gods have blessed us with good winds today." Now that he mentioned it, she could see that the sailors were sitting on their sea chests which acted as benches positioned before each of the boat's oarlocks, ten on each side, at ease. No rowing at the moment, with the red and white square sails unfurling in the wind.

"Two...two days?" she sputtered. "You've been drugging me for two days?"

"Only a little at a time," he said. "I heeded your warning about using too much."

"That was in regard to a seriously ill person, you idiot."

"Oh." He thought for a moment. "Do you think you are addicted already?"

She made a growling sound and rolled her eyes. Instead of hitting him once she was free, she put her hands on her hips and glared. "Turn this boat around and take me back to England. Now!"

"Nay."

That was all. Just a refusal.

But then, he added, "Later, if you still want to return to your time, I will take you back."

"How much later?"

"After the winter season."

"Aaarrgh!" she said, doing a mental count in her head. This was only late July or August. That would mean eight months or so till spring. "And in the meantime...?"

"Perchance you will grow to love m...my castle."

She could tell he was about to say love him, not his castle. Not that it made any difference. "Do you have a castle?"

"Nay, but you know what they say...every man's home is his castle." He grinned, pleased with himself.

"A poet now!" she scoffed. Then, "Would you really want me to fall in love with y...your castle?" she asked. He had to know what she meant. And, really, would he want the impediment of a clinging, love obsessed wife?

"I do not know," he answered honestly. "'Tis like you said, we need time to see where this attraction leads us."

Again, he was trying to lay the blame on her for this fiasco. "How do you know that I won't be able to teletransport from another place...like your castle?"

Her question made him uncomfortable, as evidenced by the tic in his jaw, which she'd noticed had a tendency to emerge whenever he was frustrated or exasperated with her and was fighting an outburst of anger. "Tell-a-tramp-sport? That is a new word for your time-travel business?"

"Yes, it must have come to me when I was in my drugged state. It's a made-up word my brothers used occasionally for our experience based on `teleport' in the Star Wars movies. Oh, never mind, it's too hard to explain. Suffice it to say, it describes perfectly what happened to me."

"Suffice it to say," he muttered under his breath.

It was an expression she used a lot, a bad habit, but she was giving him no leeway after what he'd done. The lout! She began to stomp away toward the other end of the boat, holding onto the rail of the swaying boat with one hand for balance, when he asked, "Where are you going?"

She paused and turned to address him. "I don't know. Anywhere away from you. The sight of you turns my stomach."

"Now, sweetling, you don't mean that." He started to follow her.

"Wanna bet?" She put one hand over her belly and pretended to gag. "Do you really want to come closer?"

He stopped in his tracks.

She spun on her heels and started to walk away again, still holding onto the rail, though the waves weren't rough, more like rolling. Thus, her rolling stomach. Kirstin had never been prone to sea sickness or motion sickness, but this had to be a combination of the red wine and poppy juice, on top of the rocking sensation.

But if she'd thought she had the last word, she was mistaken.

"By the by, you might want to grab a cloak or something," he called out to her back.

The sun was out and the air was comfortable with a warm breeze. In fact, the square red and white sails were partially unfurled and the rowers were standing about, or sitting on their sea chests honing weapons or carving pieces of wood. The breeze and the current were doing their work, for now. In any case, she had no idea why she would need the warmth of a cloak.

"Your pretty nipples are showing," he answered her unspoken question. With a smirk.

She glanced down to the front of her soaked gown and, yep, her nipples were standing out prominently. Looking right and left, she also confirmed that the men were enjoying the view.

"But then, mayhap you want to give my seamen such a treat. Mayhap modern women do such. I do not like sharing my wife's charms, but I am an enlightened Viking. 'Tis your decision."

She recalled then how she'd mentioned that her father, in adapting to his new land, was an enlightened Viking. "Aaarrgh!" She turned her back on him and pulled the bodice away from her skin, fluttering it a bit to air-dry the damp fabric. Making her way to the back of the boat where Egil was manning the rudder which controlled a huge steering oar, she pointed to the waterskin that hung from his belt. "Can I have a drink of that?"

"Of course, m'lady." He unhooked the skin from its leather loop and handed it to her.

She walked over to the rail and took a drink, gargled, then spit over the side. She did that several times before actually taking a long swallow of the tepid water. Then she poured some into the palm of one of her hands, tossing it over her face. Using the hem of her gown, she rubbed her eyes and face. She repeated that procedure several times before returning the water skin to Egil. "I used most of it. I'm sorry," she apologized and sank down onto a pile of coiled ropes.

"'Tis no problem. I will refill it shortly."

For a while, she said nothing, just watched Egil's expert maneuvering and took in the scenery. The sea was a gorgeous clear green and the sky a brilliant blue. Kirstin knew from her youth in the Norselands and from her research as a historian that the Viking longships were nautical marvels, especially for their time. Works of art, really, with finely carved figureheads and trim work, not to mention the painted shields which hung on specially designed racks over the rails pointing toward the seas. The shallow vessels could travel in both ocean depths and inland fjords, by rowing or sailing, or a combination of both. And they were light enough that they could be carried over land for short distances when necessary.

And, oh, but the fjords were works of art, too! God's works of art. The coasts of Norway were pitted with hundreds of deep streams, branching off the seas, surrounded by majestic mountains and cliffs, all created by glaciers which covered the earth millions of years ago.

This vessel of Hauk's was a fairly small one with only twenty rowers, ten on each side. Some of the boats could man more than thirty rowers, with another thirty or so seamen on board to provide alternate shifts of the brutally tiresome work. The oars could be as long as the boat itself.

Wherever possible, the longships followed the land lines, often beaching at night to sleep on sandy shores. Since she could see no land at the moment, she assumed they were making the cross over the North Sea that separated Britain from the Scandinavian countries.

"Were you a part of this plot to kidnap me, too?" she finally asked Egil.

"Me? Hah! I tol' the master he was barmy fer doin' such."

"Oh?"

"Best he left ye to go back to where ye came from, I tol' him. No offense meant, m'lady, but the master has enough problems on his hands without a wife to deal with."

"Not that I disagree with you, but aren't wives supposed to be helpmates, of benefit to their husbands? Marital bliss and all that?"

"Ye'd think so, but not in my experience. More bother than bliss."

"Have you never married yourself?"

"I have. Three times."

"Three?" she exclaimed. "You have three wives? The *more danico* then." She shook her head with disgust at the Viking practice of multiple wives.

"Not all at the same time," he said. "One died, one divorced me fer being gone a-Viking too much...abandonment, she called it, and the third is in Frankland. I have no idea if Estelle is dead or alive and no interest in finding out; I was forced into that one by an angry papa. I have women aplenty, when I want, but no more wives, thank ye very much."

Kirstin had to smile. Picturing Egil as a ladies' man was difficult, if not impossible.

"And children...do you have children?"

"Not that I am aware, though Estelle was big with child when I escaped her clutches."

"And you don't want to find out?"

He thought for a moment and said, "Nay."

"How long ago was that?"

He shrugged. "Ten years or more."

That meant he might have a son or daughter a little younger than Bjorn.

Seeing her disapproval, he elaborated, "I have no home to speak of. By choice. I like the roaming life. I like the tupping, good and well, but afterward I have not much use fer women. Oh, I know, 'tis not an attractive trait. But, truth to tell, women are too waspish by nature and demanding. 'Do this, do that, I want, I need, where were you, who were you with?' What man willingly submits himself to that?"

Kirstin laughed.

Midway down the ship, Hauk's head went up at the sound of her laughter. He smiled, probably thinking that her anger was melting. She scowled his way just to let him know he was still on her shit list.

"Smitten!" Egil murmured with a decided tone of disgust.

"What?"

"The master. Head over arse smitten with ye, he is."

"You think so?"

"Why else would ye be here on his longship, on the way to his broken down, long-neglected estate where a mistress with a witchy attitude awaits yer arrival? A saner man woulda left ye behind to get his affairs in order afore bringing ye home, but, nay, Hauk is too...smitten."

She gazed at Egil with horror.

Then she turned to stare at Hauk, also with horror.

~

Not the homecoming he expected...

FINALLY, they had almost reached their destination, Haukshire.

Traveling down Friggsfjord, Hauk noted the stand of ancient blue spruce trees that marked the beginning of his estate. The waterway lapped at the rocks that festooned either bank, leading upward to more rocks. What greenery there was thrived only in the branches of the trees, the soil being too rocky and infertile except for the most hardy plants. But then, the vast number of evergreens here in the north were a boon in that they provided winter cover for plentiful game, like deer, hare, bears, wolves, and other fur-bearing animals.

One of the first things Hauk would have to do is send out hunters to bring in a goodly amount of meat for the snow-bound months to come. Mayhap they would travel even farther north for bear and *hreindyri*, or what the English called reindeer, if there was time. *And the furs would be good for barter in the markets of many countries.*

Soon, around the next bend, his home would be visible up on the rise.

It had been five years since he been back to his birthplace. His father had been alive then, and the fight they'd engaged in had turned physical. The subject of the argument was long forgotten, but, no, Hauk recalled that his father had been considering the purchase of several slaves to farm a parcel of land on the western portion of his property. A futile venture as many landowners had learned in this region over the decades. It was slaves, not farming, they'd argued over that day. Hauk had vowed never to return. According to Egil, his father had never gotten around to the slaves, thank the gods for that at least. Mayhap he'd brought up the subject just to provoke him, which had been like him.

Now that he was approaching Haukshire, he felt an odd lightness. Not the usual heart-clenching dread he experienced on coming home. And he realized that it was because his father would not be there. No tiptoeing around to avoid his volatile temper outbursts. No hiding when a beating was threatened. No criticism of every single thing he did.

With this realization that he was free to view Haukshire in a different light, he found himself seeing for the first time the stark beauty of his land. It was not pretty as some southern estates were, with lush lawns and vibrant colored flowers. Still, there was a beauty in the stately evergreens and sharp-edged cliffs, the sparkling water of the fjords, the icy blue skies. It was a harsh land which bred strong men.

He looked to Kirstin at his side to see how she reacted to their surroundings. She had not spoken to him in two days.

"'Tis the silent treatment," Egil had informed him last night when he complained about her continuing anger over his effort to give her more time by bringing her to the Norse-lands. "When men or women are upset with each other in her country, they use the silent treatment until the other person surrenders or makes things right."

Was he supposed to say he was sorry for bringing her to his home, even if he was not sorry at all? As for making things right, that would mean returning her to Winchester, which Hauk could not...*would not*...do. Not yet, leastways. Instead, he'd continued his conversation with Egil. "What kind of weapon is silence?" he'd asked. "A Viking woman would hit her man over the head with his battle shield. Or screech to High Valhalla about all his deficiencies. Or slap his arse with the flat side of a broadsword."

"Well, she is a modern Viking woman," Egil had pointed out, as if Hauk didn't know that. If Egil had used the word "enlightened," Hauk might very well knock him over the head with a nearby oar.

Actually, he was beginning to see how painful silence could be. He wanted Kirstin to forgive his clumsy efforts. He wanted her to like his home, even though he'd had no fondness for it himself, which would change now...he hoped. He wanted her to give him a second chance at...something.

"This is Haukshire land we travel through now," he told her now.

She raised her chin and said nothing. But she was looking intently, her head turning right and left, then upwards to the land.

"Over there is where I shot my first deer with a bow and arrow I made myself. I was only ten at the time. Of course, my father proclaimed it a sorry excuse for a kill, scarce big enough to warrant butchering."

She looked at him as if she had something to say on the subject, but still said nothing.

"I learned to swim in this very fjord, when I was three."

"Yer father tossed ye in the waters, as I recall," Egil said from Kirstin's other side. "It was either sink or swim, and the bastard didn't care either way, damn his sorry soul."

Kirstin pressed her lips together tightly to prevent her voice escaping.

"I see plenty of fish down there, master," Egil said, leaning forward to speak over Kirstin. "Once we are settled in, we must set lines and nets to catch what we can afore the fjord freezes over."

Hauk nodded, adding fishing to the jobs to be done right off, although it was possible to fish through the ice betimes. It was not a pleasurable experience, though, in the ballocks-frosty air.

And then they arrived at the Haukshire wharf. He noticed two of his other longships still upended on the far bank to the left. Apparently, work hadn't been done to caulk and water-proof the vessels after their last voyages. Someone would have to answer for that.

Once *Sea Wolf* was tied off and the anchor dropped, the crew began to disembark, carrying their sea chests on their shoulders. Friends and family were there to welcome them home with hugs, claps on the shoulders, laughter, and good cheer.

By the time Hauk and Egil were ready to leave the ship, with Egil leading Kirstin, and Hauk helping Bjorn to walk with an arm around his waist, he was surprised to see there was still a sizeable crowd standing by. He hadn't expected this kind of loyalty from the people of Haukshire, especially after serving under the harsh hand of his father. There was Half-dan, the longtime steward, and Frida, the cook, along with some of the household staff he recognized. The longbeards had to have been here in his grandsire's day.

But then, at the forefront, he noticed Zoya, his mistress, or former mistress. She was dressed in finery more fitting a royal event, certainly a sharp contrast to the others here.

"Uh-oh!" Egil said, and made quick work of changing places with Hauk so that Bjorn was being helped by Egil, and Hauk stood next to Kirstin. When Hauk tried to wrap an arm over her shoulder to show her importance to him, she shrugged him off and told him, "Don't even think it!"

At least she was talking now.

And he was thinking, all right. Thinking it was time to put this woman in her place. He placed his arm around her shoulder again and this time he held on tight. "Behave thyself, wife. I must needs introduce you to my people."

"Does 'your people' include that glowering, black-haired witch with the half-exposed boobs?"

He was fairly certain he knew what boobs were, and, yea, Zoya's gunna was cut very low in front. She glared at Kirstin but then she smiled coyly at him, licking her lips in a manner meant to be seductive but only appeared to him as if she had dry lips. He had the good sense not to smile back.

He walked up to where Egil stood talking with Halfdan. Putting his free arm around Bjorn's shoulder, whilst maintaining a hold on Kirstin with the other, he announced to the crowd. "Greetings, everyone. It is good to be back at Haukshire. There is much for all of us to do before winter, but tonight we celebrate."

There was a loud cheer from the crowd.

"But, first, let me introduce you to my son Bjorn who fought bravely in Sweyn's battle against the Saxons and sustained some injuries from which he is still recovering."

There was more cheering, this time for the valiant son.

"Also, meet Kirstin, daughter of the great Magnus Ericsson...my wife." He leaned down and kissed the top of Kirstin's head, holding tight to her the whole time, as she struggled to be free.

There was a pause as his people digested the news, then loud cheers of congratulations. A few even cast gloating smirks at Zoya, implying that she would no longer be able to rule them. Zoya herself gave him a scowl, then spun on her heel and stomped back up the hill toward the largest of all the longhouses.

Bjorn was making his way toward an outbuilding with Egil and some of the men carrying supplies from the ship. Those of his seamen who had wives and children went off with them to separate longhouses that scattered about in the distance, creating almost a sort of village setting.

"Well, that went well," Kirstin said when he removed his arm from her shoulder.

"Sarcasm ill-suits you, m'lady."

She arched her brows with indifference.

"There is much work to be done, wife. Let us get on with

it," he said then, and smacked her across her bottom with the flat of his hand, pushing her forward.

Her jaw dropped with shock, as she put a hand to her arse.

As Hauk walked toward the back courtyard, he smiled to himself, not bothering to see if Kirstin followed him. In truth, she had nowhere else to go.

Betimes a man got the last word in without speaking a word.

CHAPTER 14

Where're Molly Maids when you need them...

*K*irstin had expected things to be bad, after all the years of Hauk's or his father's absence, but not this bad. She looked about the great hall of Haukshire and thought, *Phew! It stinks!*

Not only had the floor rushes not been replaced in ages... at least a year by her guess, when they were normally changed every season...but the trestle tables were covered with a layer of greasy grime. Some of the benches were broken. The hearth ashes were a foot high. Several flea-ridden dogs lay sprawled near the door leading to the scullery. And, even as she watched, a cat strolled onto the dais and peed on a tapestry that had fallen from the wall onto the floor.

Hauk had gone off to one of the barns with Halfdan, the steward, with the remark to Kirstin, "I'll see how bad the situation is outside with the animals and hay and outbuildings. Can you check the inside for me? Make a list of what needs to be done and what we must buy from the market in Hedeby."

"Me?" she'd asked. "I'm in charge?"

"Well, you are my wife."

"And Zoya?"

"She will be gone soon."

"Really?"

"Really." He had been about to depart, but he paused and said, "Look, I realize that I might not have thought through this plan of mine, but—"

"You think?"

"More sarcasm. *Tsk-tsk-tsk!*" he'd said, tapping her on the chin with playful admonition. "What I started to say was…yea, I brought you to my home against your will to give us time, but the home I've brought you to is not in good order, not by any means. For that, I apologize."

"You apologize for the condition of your home but not for bringing me here?"

"Well, yea, that is correct."

"You're a piece of work, Hauk Thorsson."

"Thank you," he'd said and gone off.

She glanced around the hall once again. In many ways, when she'd first seen Haukshire from the longship, she'd been reminded of Kattegat, that fictional village in the Viking TV series. A number of rustic longhouses and outbuildings surrounded the much bigger longhouse belonging to the king, or in this case the jarl. Even here in the great hall, she could see similarities to the Kattegat royal residence, the layout, the dim light, and the intricate carving on the wood. But that's where the resemblance ended. This place was a mess. She hadn't even checked the other rooms yet or the food cellar. They would probably be just as bad, or worse.

And Hauk expects me to fix this? I'm an academic, not a Molly Maid. Not that there's anything wrong with a cleaning person, but I work with my brain, not my hands.

With a sigh, Kirstin chided herself, *So, use your brain, girl.* Raising her chin with determination, she headed toward the kitchen. Many estates of this time period had kitchens separate from the rest of the timber-framed buildings, a safety measure in case of fire. This house did not, although the cooking area did appear to have stone walls.

She found the cook there, stirring something in a huge cauldron hanging over a fire in a hearth so big it could easily hold a side of beef. She'd been introduced to Frida earlier.

"Hello, Frida," she said. "I need your advice."

"Oh? For a certainty, m'lady, if I can be of help." Frida was a middle-aged lady, maybe fifty or so, tall, and slim as an arrow, with gray-threaded blonde hair which was in two braids pinned into a coronet atop her head. The long, white open-sided apron, which hung over a plain brown robe or gunna, was clean, as was the kitchen, for the most part. Frida poured some mead into two wooden cups and motioned for her to sit on the bench on the opposite side of the table from her. "How can I help you?"

Kirstin took a sip of the mead, which was surprisingly good, cool and hearty with a distinctive honey tone. "Well, first off, I notice how clean and tidy your kitchen looks. I congratulate you. That can't be easy, having to haul water and everything."

Frida nodded her thanks at the compliment.

"But the rest of the building...the great hall...is awful. Just filthy."

"Doan be blamin' me. The kitchen is my responsibility, and that is all."

"I wasn't being critical, just pointing out the difference. Who is in charge?"

Frida shrugged. "Who knows anymore? I do not. In the early days, back when Hauk's mother was alive, I was a mere girling but saw how she managed the house with efficiency. After her passing, the household reins passed to the other wives and mistresses, who took increasingly less interest. Until now only one person is left."

"Zoya?" Kirsten guessed.

"Exactly. Oh, she keeps her bedchamber...the master's bedchamber...clean enough, and occasionally she comes down to the hall, especially if a guest arrives...passing traders and such...and orders everyone about to clear a space for her to dine. She has a heavy hand, that one does, when her temper is riled. Me husband Efrim has a scar across his face from the whip she wielded when he could not find her flowers to arrange on the high table when she was entertaining one of her visitors. Flowers in November! *Pfff!*"

It took Kirstin a moment to digest all that Frida had revealed in her long discourse. So, Zoya was planted in Hauk's bedchamber. Well, let him deal with that. And Zoya was in charge of the household. Hah! She doubted the diva would object to Kirstin taking over that duty. With that in mind, Kirstin asked, "How many servants do I have to work with here, inside?"

Frida thought a moment before telling her, "Twelve, including two old men, and three boys."

Kirstin thought of something. "What about the steward... Halfdan? What does he do?"

"Not much," Frida said, and folded her arms over her chest in an "Enough said!" manner.

Oookay. "Is there any woman who could act as housekeeper?"

"Housekeeper?"

"Um, the person in charge of supervising the overall daily duties inside a house or keep, like cleaning, laundry, cooking, weaving, scullery maids, food servers, whatever. Not here in your kitchen. I'm sure you can get all the help you need."

"Signe," Frida said without hesitation. "Signe is big enough and loud enough to order anyone about. Should have been a shield maiden." Without missing a beat, Frida called out to one of the boys lugging in a huge pail of water that had to weigh almost as much as he did, "Gorm, go get Signe and tell her to come here."

Gorm dropped the bucket with a thud, a large amount of the water splashing over the side, and stared blankly at Frida. He was covered with dirt from his bare feet to his calf-length tunic, which was tied at the waist with a rope. His stringy, once blond hair hung in dark swaths down to his shoulders. "Where be I findin' Signe?" he asked, as he swiped an arm across his nose which was seeping blood. In fact, he appeared to have a blackened eye, though it was hard to tell under that grime, and there were bruises on his arms and legs.

"In the milk shed," Frida answered the boy, "and wash yer face and yer arms like I told you do this mornin'."

He looked at his arms and made a rude noise of dissent, then turned and stomped off, muttering something about, "Clean this, clean that."

"Gorm? Is that the child who was born after Hauk's father died?"

Frida nodded. "And bears a strong resemblance to that second son of Jarl Cnut who visited here at just the right time."

"Why does he have all those bruises?"

Frida waved a hand dismissively. "Some of the older boys pick on him because he is so small."

Kirstin gasped. "And you don't intervene to protect him?"

Frida looked at her with surprise. "Intervene? Nay. He needs to learn to protect himself, like all Vikings in this hard place. And the bratling does very well most times." Frida said the word "bratling" with affection, thus leading Kirstin to believe he got at least a modicum of care.

Just then a big-boned, tall woman with a long, brown

braid hanging over one shoulder came in and said, "You seek me, Frida?"

"I did. Come sit down, Signe." Frida poured another mug of ale and offered it to the new arrival who sat on the bench next to the cook. "This is Lady Kirstin, Master Hauk's wife."

Signe acknowledged the introduction with a nod, but a frown of confusion at the reason for her being called.

"I'll let Lady Kirstin explain," Frida said.

Kirstin did not like being called "Lady" but she let that go for now. "Signe, this jarl house is a filthy mess, and what it needs is a housekeeper or someone to supervise all the jobs that need to be done. Do you think you could handle that?"

Signe looked to Frida. "What about the dairy...the milking, the cheese and butter making?"

"Esme is young, but she helps you betimes," Frida commented. "Methinks she could take over those duties, don't you?"

Signe nodded, then straightened with pride, realizing she was being offered a sort of promotion. "Yea, I can do it."

"Why don't you two go into the great hall to discuss this? I have a side of venison to prepare for the evening meal and the gods only know what else for all these unexpected arrivals. I will have to see what we have in the storerooms."

Vikings usually served two meals every day...one early in the morning, before the work began, and one in the evening, after the day's labor

"Oh, that's another thing," Kirstin said, standing. "Hauk asked for a list of all the goods you have on hand so that he'll know how much game and fish they'll need to get, and what will be needed from one last trip to the market at Hedeby.

"Good, good! Halfdan kin handle that. He needs to do somethin' to warrant his steward title."

"And explain why so much is missing," Signe added in an undertone.

Kirstin sensed a little hostility there.

Signe took a long draw on her ale and stood to follow Kirstin. Once inside the hall, Kirstin said, "I think the first thing that needs done here is raking up all these dirty rushes. If there are no clean rushes at this time of year to put down, let's leave the floor bare." She pushed some of the rushes aside to reveal a stone floor. It wouldn't be comfortable in the winter but better than the filth, in her opinion.

"Ubbi," Signe called to a young male who was passing with a pile of dirty mugs and plates, headed toward the scullery. "I want you and Toste to get some rakes and come back here to rake up all the rushes. Then push them out the doors," she pointed to the closed double doors on the other side of the hall, "and burn them."

"Yea, I will, Signe."

Kirstin noticed how quickly the boy acceded to Signe's command. That was good. "And take these dogs and cats out to the barn until they are house trained," Kirstin added.

Signe and Ubbi both looked at her as if she was crazy, but she didn't care. She wasn't going to clean up after animals once the place was rid of their pee and poop.

"Next, I would like all the tables scrubbed down," Kirstin said to Signe, "though I'm not sure even hot water will penetrate this built-up grease."

"Ah," Signe said and took a knife from a scabbard on her belt. Using the flat side of the blade, she dug it deep into the table, then scraped, taking it right down to the bare wood.

"That will work," Kirstin said with a smile.

"I'll have some of the youthlings work on this. They will consider it a game."

Oh, great. Kids playing with knives, Kirstin thought, but decided to show deference to Signe's ideas.

Hauk's home was built in the longhouse style of the Vikings, although much bigger than most, being that of the

197

jarl. At one end of the hall was a raised dais on which the "nobles" dined. At the other end, there were several private sleeping chambers, one of which was currently being inhabited by Zoya, she assumed. Three raised hearths ran down the center of the hall, which would be used for heat during the winter months, and occasionally some cooking. It would take a monumental amount of wood to last all that time, but that was Hauk's and the steward's concern, not hers. Fortunately, there were a number of holes in the high roof above those hearths which would help relieve some of the smoke. A number of bladder windows (stretched and scraped pig stomachs, rather than glass) let in a translucent light even on dark days.

After that, they checked out two of the three bedchambers, not the one occupied by Zoya. Everyone else slept on the broad benches, as much as a yard wide, that lined the great hall, or they slept in the few bed closets that were so small they held only a bed. Some of the married couples and families had small longhouses within the "community." Plans were made to gather all the dirty linens and replace them with clean. Signe assigned a maid, Dora, who was already the laundress, to be in charge of the bedchambers, as well, which was apparently a step up in the hierarchy of the estate, if Dora's toothless smile was any indication.

"We should take all the bed furs out, as well, to be brushed of fleas and lice," Signe mused. "Kaelen, the healer, is complaining about an excess of skin bites, especially on the little ones."

Fleas and lice? Kirstin shivered with revulsion…and a real or imagined itch all over her body. She had to keep reminding herself that this was a different time than the one she'd become accustomed to.

"Soon it will be too cold to work outside," Signe continued. "Winter comes early in the Norselands, but the weather is perfectly warm for air drying today."

Really? Kirstin thought it was chilly, probably about fifty degrees. But then, she guessed that would be balmy for people who lived with below-zero temps, snowbound, for many months. She had been spoiled, living in California.

Luckily, one of the bedchambers, the smallest, was cleaned by the time Bjorn staggered in. Apparently, he'd been following his father about while he assessed the situation at Haukshire, and his continuing need for recovery from his injuries caught up with him. After they helped him into the bed, Kirstin made sure that he wasn't suffering fever again, and then decided sleep would be the best remedy since they had no medicine she knew of. That was another thing she would have to check... Signe had mentioned a healer. Would the healer have some medical supplies that could help Bjorn, even primitive ones?

Soon after that, Hauk stomped in to the hall where she was talking to Signe while she oversaw the raking of rushes and scraping of the tables. A boy was pushing a wooden wheelbarrow of ashes out to a bin beyond the back courtyard where they would eventually be used to make soap. It was the little boy, Gorm. Hauk did a double-take on seeing Gorm, the little guy pushing a heavy wheelbarrow, his bruises, his still running half-bloody nose. Was he seeing himself at that age?

Hauk was accompanied by the steward, Halfdan, who was clearly upset about something, as evidenced by his red face under his bushy gray beard. Even his bald head was red. "I understand you have appointed a housekeeper to replace my steward," Hauk snapped at her.

Halfdan gave her a look that translated to, Now the you-know-what is going to hit the fan.

She gave Hauk no chance to say more. "I did no such thing," she declared, putting her hands on her hips, "or if I did,

I merely relieved Halfdan of some of the duties he so clearly had no time to handle." *Talk about lame subtlety! A diplomat I will never be.*

Hauk's eyes swept the large room, taking in the contrast between the clean and the uncleaned-as-yet tables, as well as the piles of filthy rushes which reeked especially bad now that they had been stirred up. In fact, he leaned on one of the tables and jerked back when his hand came away covered with a layer of the greasy goop. He wiped that hand on his pant leg and turned with arched eyebrows to his steward.

"I...um...well...mayhap there was too much to do with overseeing the inside and outside the buildings," Halfdan stammered.

"Hmpfh! The outside isn't much better. Why have those boats not been recaulked yet? And why are there so few laying hens in the coop? And the roof on the hay shed is leaking." When Halfdan just stared downward and did not answer, Hauk said, "Let us check the storeroom with Frida." By the frown on Hauk's face, Kirstin guessed that Hauk was not optimistic about what he would find there.

Just then, several men walked into the hall, swords dangling from their belts, wearing leather armor. They made their way to one of the clean tables on which pitchers of ale, manchet bread, slices of hard cheese and cold meat of some kind had been laid out for those who had missed the noontime meal. After taking a few bites and a long draw on a horn of the ale, the tallest of the men glanced over and noticed them standing at the other end of the hall. "Hauk!" he exclaimed and made his way with long strides toward them. "When did you get back?"

"Earlier today," Hauk replied with a smile. "Where have you been, Thorkel?"

"Off fighting Jarl Ingolf's men of Stormstead. Again! They have developed a habit of sneaking onto Haukshire land and stealing whatever is foraging in the woods...cattle, hogs, sheep."

"Egil told me about Ingolf's misdeeds some time ago. I thought he would have given up by now."

"Nay. He was depending on you not coming back anytime soon before he took over here."

"'Tis good I have returned then," Hauk said.

"Yea, 'tis good you are back," Thorkel agreed and gave him a man hug. "And who is this lovely lady?"

"This is my wife, Kirstin," Hauk told him in an exaggerated menacing tone.

Thorkel's eyebrows rose in surprise. Then he turned to Kirstin and said, "Welcome, m'lady." To Hauk, he murmured, "You always were lucky with women. You have a prize here."

"I assume you know my steward, and this is Signe, I believe."

Thorkel ignored Halfdan but grinned at Signe, who developed a sudden blush. "Oh, I *know* Signe."

"Hah! You'd like to *know* me, you loathsome lout." And she stomped away toward the kitchens.

"She likes me," Thorkel told the rest of them, widening his blue eyes with exaggerated innocence. He was a good-looking man and tall enough to tower over Signe, not that appearance was important, or the most important thing. And obviously Signe was not pleased with his attention.

"Oh?" Kirstin remarked.

"She just does not know it yet."

Typical overconfident Viking male! she thought. And she should know, having lived in a home with about a dozen of them over the years.

Hauk prepared to leave, but before he left, he surveyed the hall once again, then looked at her and nodded.

If that was his idea of an apology after his initial criticism of her taking over Halfdan's job, Kirstin had a thing or two to say to him. Later. She must have made a growling sound, though, because he turned around, came back, and kissed her, hard and quick. Just as abruptly, he pulled back, gave her a wink, and left.

Now that was an apology she liked, to her chagrin.

To even more chagrin, she noticed that Hauk had changed direction. He had been going to the storage room with Half-dan, but now he was heading toward his bedchamber, the one occupied by Zoya, who opened the door at his first knock and threw herself up and into his embrace, her arms wrapped around his shoulders. And the jerk didn't put her down. Instead, he stepped inside and closed the door behind them.

Sigurd looked amused. And Halfdan looked like he'd just escaped the guillotine.

CHAPTER 15

Resisting the irresistible...

K irstin was exhausted beyond anything she'd experienced in years, even worse than the time two years ago when she and several of her colleagues made the Camino de Santiago pilgrimage in Spain. They hadn't completed the entire trail, but hiking twelve miles a day for five days had left them practically dead on their feet, and they'd all been physically fit. Tonight, there wasn't a part of her body that didn't hurt, what with helping to scrub, haul, and empty buckets of water, launder linens and clothing, and dust cobwebs with a long-handled broom.

On the other hand, Kirstin felt more satisfaction than she could recall, even from her teaching, which she happened to love. There was something to be said for seeing the actual immediate results of hard work. Hauk's home didn't sparkle by any means, and it would never be a precious diamond, but it was on its way...a rough cut semi-precious stone, so to speak. Like the amber that Vikings so prized, muddy colors hiding something in its center.

Signe had told her that there were bathing huts for the men and women, with firepits to keep the water warm. They were located beyond the back courtyard, between the main longhouse and the "village," comprised of a half dozen or so smaller longhouses for families. Since the evening meal would be served soon, that was Kirstin's goal: to bathe and put on clean clothing.

She had to wonder if Zoya would be joining them for dinner, and where she would be seated, in relation to Kirstin. She also had to wonder what happened with Hauk and Zoya when he'd closed his bedchamber door behind them earlier today. She hadn't seen either of them since then.

She shouldn't care about such petty things as who sat next to whom, but she did. Jealousy struck even if their marriage wasn't real, or whatever you called a couple a thousand years apart. Jeesh! Instead of fixating on her jealousy, Kirstin focused on the discomfort Hauk would be facing over the seating arrangements; with that in mind, she smiled inwardly as she made her way to the small bedchamber on the other side of Bjorn's where their trunks had been taken. When she got there, she was pleased to see that it was clean and smelled of fresh-aired linens and, thank God, brushed bed furs. She took a clean gown out of the trunk, one of the gowns Hauk had gotten for her from the plunder pile, and laid it on the bed. She still wore the same patched underwear, which she would wash when she bathed, and she determined to find some fabric and make herself extra sets, though she was no seamstress.

She sat down on the side of the bed and removed her slippers and the long hose which she'd tied above her knees. She yawned and decided to lie down, just for a moment. Then she decided to cover herself, just for a moment, with the fur, which was so cozy, just like the Sherpa fleece coverlet her sister Madrene had given her last Christmas. That was the last she recalled until she heard someone calling her name.

"Kirstin, wake up."

She burrowed deeper under the warm blanket and sniffed. Hmm. Wasn't Sherpa fleece supposed to be fake lamb's wool? She'd never known hers to have the scent of animal. Oh, well! She shrugged and rolled over on her side.

"Dinner is ready," a male voice said.

"Go away, Daddy," she said on a moan. "I'm not hungry."

A booted foot shoved her in the behind and laughed. "C'mon, sweetling. Either you get up, or I join you."

What? Kirstin's eyes shot open. First of all, although her father occasionally called her sweetling, he would never threaten to slip into bed with her. Rolling over to her back, she stared up at Hauk who was standing at the edge of the mattress, smiling down at her.

"Don't you dare," she said.

He dared, and lifted the bed fur, sliding under beside her, boots and all.

"Those boots better not be dirtying these clean sheets, or you are in big trouble, mister."

"Sorry!" he said, and chuckled, not at all repentant.

She turned away from him and repeated, "Go away."

"Mmm," he murmured, spooning his big body behind her, nuzzling her hair aside so he could kiss her neck, "Mayhap I am not hungry right now either. Not for food, leastways."

She stiffened and tried to pry away the arms wrapped around her middle, to no avail. "You've got to be kidding. You were locked away in a bedroom with a woman with whom you have a history, probably boinking each other's brains out, and you expect me to be all horny and hot for you."

"Huh?" he said. "If boink mean what I think it does, you are wrong. I did naught with Zoya except peel her arms off me and tell her she would be leaving for Hedeby with Egil when he goes for supplies."

Kirstin was relieved. She hadn't really believed Hauk would hook up with Zoya, after the efforts he'd made to bring Kirstin here, but she knew that some, no, many Viking men practiced the *more danico*. So, there had been a niggling little doubt.

"Did I mention I am staying here and sending Egil in my stead? There is too much needs done here for me to leave so soon. In any case, Zoya will be gone shortly."

Kirstin felt another rush of relief. Yes, over Zoya being gone. But more because she'd been afraid to be alone, back here in this time period. Hauk was her anchor. A scary prospect, that! But she could see that Hauk was trying to make her feel better; so, she smiled, tentatively.

In response, he leaned over to lick her ear and tug on the lobe with his teeth, causing shots of intense pleasure to shoot through her body and her to shiver with a reluctant delight. He chuckled again, this time at the obvious reaction he'd gotten. "Any chance you want to bonk with me?"

"It's boink, not bonk, you idiot," she said and moved his hand which had somehow found its way to her one breast where it had been rubbing in a circular fashion.

Oddly, now that she knew Zoya wouldn't be an issue for her at Haukshire, Kirstin was concerned for the woman...a bit. She turned over to look at him. "What will Zoya do in Hedeby? You brought her here from her country, the Russian lands, didn't you? You can't just drop her in the market town. Even if you gave her some money, a woman alone in these times...no, that wouldn't be right."

"You are defending Zoya? Do you hate me so much you would want her to stay?"

She didn't hate him at all. Unfortunately. "That's not the

issue. I'm a woman. I don't want to see any woman mistreated."

"Hah! Zoya is the one who has apparently been mistreating...anyone within her reach here at Haukshire. She will not suffer...under me, leastways. Truth to tell, she has a brother who lives in Hedeby. He operates one of the trading booths, selling samovars and exotic teas. She could go to her brother. Or I could make arrangements for her to return to her homeland. Or I could possibly find her a mate. She has a choice."

She giggled.

"What is so funny?"

"The idea of you being a matchmaker."

He shrugged. "I misdoubt she would accept any hersirs I might offer anyhow. None of them have enough coin or lands."

"So, Zoya has meekly agreed to your plans?"

"Not so meekly," he admitted with a shrug, "but she has to realize that she has no choice."

Men! Clueless, whether eleventh century Vikings or twenty-first century Vikings. "So where is Zoya now?"

"You should ask! She has planted her pretty arse in the middle of the high table, waiting to be served."

Just as I suspected would happen. "She has a pretty ass and you want to send her away?"

"M'lady, all my bed partners have pretty arses. Even you." He waggled his eyebrows at her.

The man was charming and hard to resist. Kirstin had to steel herself against him. "So, you want me to come to dinner and sit next to my...what? Enemy? Rival?"

"Rival would be good. That would mean that you want me. But, nay, I don't expect you to sit next to Zoya. She might try to scratch your eyes out, or so she has threatened. I will sit between the two of you."

"Over my dead body."

"Well, I could ask for food to be brought to this bedchamber so that we can dine after..." More waggling of his eyebrows as he attempted to pull her into a tighter embrace.

She shrugged away and scolded, "Behave!" Then, she observed, "You're in an awfully jolly mood. You must have had a good day."

"*Pfff!* I have had an awful day, not awfully jolly in any way. Halfdan is gone, by the by. When he realized that I was beginning to uncover his misdeeds, he stole a horse and rode away, probably to Jarl Ingolf's estate."

"Will you chase after him?"

He shook his head. "Not yet. Too many things more important at the moment."

"Like what?" she asked and sat up, propping another smaller bed fur behind her for a pillow behind her for support.

He leaned on one elbow, trailing a fingertip along her arm from her elbow to her wrist, smiling at the fine hairs that stood up in its wake.

She repeated, "Like what?"

His face went serious then, and he sat up as well, propping himself against another fur pillow. "I feel so guilty."

"For kidnapping me?"

"Nay, never that, my wife." He put an arm around her shoulders and forced her to accept the embrace. "I should not have stayed away so long. It was selfish of me. 'Tis a burden on my heart that I thought only of myself, and forgot there are people here who depend on me. Many of them have been living in squalor, their homes barely habitable. The storerooms are almost depleted. Gods know, but there might have been starvation this winter if I had not returned. With the longships not being sea ready, the people couldn't have escaped if they wanted to."

"Couldn't they go to a neighboring estate for help?"

"The only one approachable by land is Ingolf's Stormstead, and he would have used that as an opportunity to take over Haukshire."

"Then it's good you returned when you did."

"It is." He squeezed her shoulder. "And I appreciate all you did today."

"I didn't think you noticed."

"I noticed," he said and leaned over to give her a quick kiss, drawing back before she could smack him away. "Does that mean you want to bonk now?"

She suspected he deliberately mispronounced the word. "No," she said, emphatically. "Besides, I stink. I was about to go to the bathhouse before I made the mistake of lying down on the bed for a moment."

He pretended to sniff her hair, then pronounced, "Phew! You do stink. Methinks we both need to visit the bath hut."

She drew away to survey him. He wore a clean, dark blue tunic over black braies. His hair was clubbed off his face into a long braid. And he'd shaved. "Looks to me like you've already bathed."

He took her hand and stood, pulling her with him. "I may have missed a few spots on my body. You can help me find those secret places, and I'll find yours."

A man can never be too clean...

ONE DAY HOME at Haukshire had impacted Hauk in ways he hadn't expected. He felt like he'd come to a turning point in his life and he wasn't sure what the future held for him.

He'd already been carrying a persistent burning in his gut of guilt over Bjorn. When he'd seen the state of neglect at Haukshire for the first time this morn, the fire flamed higher.

But the sight of some of his cotters wearing ragged tunics and gunnas, living in hovels, some of the children looking undernourished, well, he feared for the state of his innards with all this heat.

Shame was a close cousin to guilt, and that was untenable. He was a Viking. Vikings did not go all weepy over their mistakes. In fact, they rarely admitted their mistakes. Even so, Hauk had come to the conclusion that he must drop anchor and stay put at Haukshire until he made things right, mayhap even permanently. A landed Viking he would become. No more sailing the seas for battle, or trading, or adventure...not until he got things under control here at Haukshire. Unfortunately, when he thought of his future, an image of his new wife came into his fool head, especially after seeing all the good she'd accomplished in his home after only one day.

"This is heavenly," said wife murmured, jarring him from the reverie. Hauk had almost dozed off on the bench in the bathing hut, which was basically a small longhouse, where he sat watching his wife. And no wonder, it had been a long day and the humid heat here was relaxing him a bit too much. Even though he'd teased Kirstin about bathing together, he was frankly too tired to take off his clothes, bathe, and put them on again, even if there was some sex play in between. He would never admit that to his male comrades, of course. A Viking too tired for sex? Never! Actually, he was looking forward to making love to his wife again in the comfort of a bed with the time and energy to enjoy it to the fullest.

Kirstin was submerged up to her neck in the small stone pool, leaning her neck against the surrounding ledge.

"Heavenly, is it?" he said. "Mayhap I should join you after all, and we can be naughty angels in heaven."

Instead of reacting to his teasing words, she commented, "This bathing place really is a unique marvel for this time period. I know from having lived in the Norselands until I was fourteen and from my research, that some estates in the Scandinavian countries made use of natural hot springs on their properties, but I've never heard of any making use of a well."

Oh, good gods! She is going to give me another of her lectures. Even so, he told her, "My grandsire designed this many years ago to please his new bride. I think he saw something similar in Frankland."

Only about three arm-lengths wide, the bathing pool held three or four adults in a tight fit, or a half dozen children. A plug on the one side drained all of the dirty water out, or regulated how much hot water could be added without over-flowing. There was another smaller pool in the bathing house, built over a fire pit. Water came into that pool from a deep well outside, where it could be warmed up, then added to the larger pool via a covered clay trench.

"I agree," he said, "Very ingenious. It's lauded by everyone who ever uses it. I wouldn't be surprised if this is one of the reasons Ingolf envies my property."

Soaping up her arms and neck, she sniffed and made an expression of distaste. "Your soap is so harsh. It's the lye in it, which is fine when washing clothes and pots and pans, I suppose, but really not very good for the skin. I wonder if I could experiment with adding oil, or even lard, and then some scents. Floral would be one possibility, but maybe pine from all those evergreen trees out there would appeal more to men. Fruit, too, would good, but out of season now. Ooh, ooh, maybe some of those wilted apples down in the storeroom would work. And honey, definitely honey."

His wife did talk a lot, he noticed, not for the first, or fiftieth time. Even so, he had to smile, "You would have us virile Viking men smelling like apples?"

"Better that then BO," she replied vehemently. "That's body odor. Pee- you!"

"Actually, I do know a man…Brandr Igorsson, who married a strange woman who made scented soaps. Mayhap I can introduce you next spring."

"Why do you say she is strange?"

"She can rappel up and down the outside of a castle, and she taught the ladies at Bear's Lair how to dance in a line to some song about achy breaky hearts. Come to think on it, you sang a song for us by that name, didn't you?"

"What? Oh, my God! Maybe she's a time traveler, too."

"Nay, I don't think so. Ne'er have I heard mention of her moving up in the air through a twirling funnel."

"That's not the only way…oh, never mind. Back to soap…I have to admit, Vikings *do* have an appreciation for cleanliness, far more than men of other countries." She grinned and added, "No wonder women from other countries welcome them to their bed furs."

He put a hand over his heart, as if wounded. "I can think of some other reasons why women welcome us to their bed furs." Then he ogled her body with fake lasciviousness.

"I know. From personal experience," she said, disconcerting him with her directness. Then further disconcerting him when she added, "We've only made love two times, but I have to admit you have a few moves."

"A few?" he exclaimed with a laugh. "'Twould seem I have work to do."

Standing, he began to remove his clothing. Suddenly, he was not as tired as he'd thought.

～

Oops, she did it again!...

DESPITE ALL HER best intentions not to have sex with Hauk again after his kidnapping her, Kirstin had succumbed to the man. Again!

Face it: he was temptation on the hoof where she was concerned. And, oh, what he'd just done to her in the bathing hut! It had been beyond amazing. Turned out he had more than the few moves she'd implied. A shiver of pleasure passed over her at the memory. In fact, her toes still curled when she thought about it, which she feared was going to be too often.

"Are you cold?" Hauk asked, putting an arm around her shoulders and drawing her into his side as they walked back to the main longhouse of the estate.

"No," she said.

"You shivered."

"Yeah, well, maybe I shivered at the prospect of having to spend months in this lousy place before I can go home."

He stopped to look at her, releasing her from his hold. "Lousy? Is this true? You hate Haukshire that much?" What he didn't ask was whether she hated him that much, but the question was there in the wounded expression on his clean-shaven face.

And her fool heart hurt at having hurt him. She wasn't sure what she felt for this man, but, whatever the reason, she did not want to hurt him.

With an honesty that came naturally to her, she admitted, "No."

She could tell that he wanted her to explain: no, she didn't hate Haukshire, or no, she didn't hate him, or no to both. When she didn't elaborate, his jaw went rigid, and he took her hand in his, continuing their walk to the back door of the main longhouse. Under his breath, he muttered, "Guess I'll have to work harder to make her like me."

And she thought, *Holy moley! Can I take any more of his*

efforts to seduce me? I'll be a puddle of melting hormones. She shivered again.

Hauk's jaw relaxed, and he grinned.

They entered the brighter light of the kitchen, which was illumined by the hearth fire and several wall torches. Frida was sitting at the table, a cup of mead or ale in front of her. The evening meal had apparently already been made and served, if all the empty pots and serving utensils were any indication, the cleanup not yet begun. Kirstin had been hoping to grab a bite here and not have to sit down in the hall where Zoya was probably holding court.

Frida looked up at them, then looked again, before bursting out in a chortle. Kirstin didn't know what Frida was reacting to until she glanced at Hauk. Then she did a double take, too. The skin of his clean-shaven face down to the rounded neck of his tunic had a definite ruddy glow to it.

Glancing downward, all she could see on herself was her upper chest, exposed by the neckline of her gown, and, yep, the skin showed little spots which together gave her a pinkish tone.

A sex flush!

Yep, she and Hauk were displaying the quintessential sex flush. How telling! Everyone who saw them would know what they'd been up to.

No way was she going to let everyone see her...them...like this! Vikings loved nothing more than to laugh at each other, and themselves. She knew exactly how her brothers would react if she and Hauk walked into a room like this. The knowing...the teasing...of the men in the great hall would be no different than her brothers...loud and crude. So, she dug in her heels as Hauk continued to lead her by the hand through the kitchen toward the hall.

"What now?" he asked. "Are you still upset that I showed

you more of my....uh, moves?" Then he grinned with self-satisfaction.

"Oh, you!" She smacked him on the arm for the grin. "I was never upset by...um, never mind. I think I'll just grab something to eat in the kitchen and go to bed early." She yawned to accent her tiredness.

"Nay."

"What do you mean 'nay'?"

"Nay means nay. We will dine in the hall with my people. It is expected."

"By whom?"

"Everyone. It's my first evening home. It is your first introduction to my people as my wife and mistress of Haukshire. It would be impolite if you, or I, declined to eat with them.'

"It seems to me that they've already eaten, or begun eating," she pointed out.

He waved a hand in the air dismissively. "Give me one good reason why you would not sit down with them? To eat or just to share fellowship?"

"I'm embarrassed," she said, weakly

He stopped to stare at her. "About what?"

"You know. Everyone will know what we were doing."

"And that is a bad thing?" He tried but was unable to hold back a smile.

She hated when he smiled like that. Actually she hated/loved his smiles. "Yes, that is a bad thing. Embarrassing."

He sighed, obviously unable to understand, or maybe he just didn't agree. With exaggerated patience, he asked, "How will they know, dearling?"

She hated/loved when he used such endearments with her. With a *tsk*ing sound of disgust, she waved a hand in front of her neck and chest. "The sex flush. It happens when a person has engaged in intercourse and climaxed. Blood rushes to the surface, and...oh, what difference does it make how it happens. Just know, it's a telltale sign."

He was frowning with confusion. "So, it doesn't just happen when two people engage in sexplay? Just *good* sexplay? The kind that leads to a peaking?"

"Well, yes."

He grinned some more.

She slapped his arm for the grin. "Stop smirking."

He pressed his lips together to stop his grin. Then he studied her face and chest area. "I thought you were blushing," he said and began to grin again.

She smacked him on the arm, again. "Don't gloat. You're flushing, too."

"I am?" he glanced downward but was unable to see himself. "I have a sex flush?"

"Yep. So, let's just eat something in the kitchen."

Instead of being embarrassed like she was, he began to smile, slow and sexy. "You are a font of information, my wife. This time I enjoyed your lecture. Immensely. A sex flush! Imagine that!" He beamed at her, grabbed her hand, and yanked her forward to enter the hall where loud cheers greeted their entrance.

There were about fifty people sitting in loose groups on benches on both sides of the four long lines of trestle tables, half as many people as would be there normally, many having left during the lean years with no jarl in residence. Hauk had told her earlier that most of them would return in the spring, once word got out that Haukshire was again a thriving estate. Kirstin had to admire his confidence.

There were few women in the hall, aside from the serving maids, which didn't surprise Kirstin, but she *was* surprised to see that many of the diners were servants. In many estates, even in the Norselands, a class system existed, and only the jarl and his family, his hersirs, and fighting men with their wives would be seated in the great hall. Once again, she had to admire Hauk, this time for his democratic attitude toward his people.

Just then, a bundle of brown fabric flew by them. It was the little boy, Gorm, whose homespun tunic was blowing back as he ran past them, his skinny legs pumping like mad. Immediately following were two boys, considerably larger, one of them with a goose egg prominent on his forehead, and the other sporting a bloody lip.

"Whoa, whoa, whoa!" Hauk said, grabbing the older boys by the back of their tunics, lifting them a foot off the floor. "What are you bratlings doing? Each of you has at least two stone on that little mite."

"Little mite? Little mite? That dirty bugger. I'm gonna kill Gorm and feed his guts to the pigs."

"I'm gonna stomp on him like a maggot. A little mite maggot. Squish!"

Hauk set the boys in front of him and kept them in place with a heavy hand on each of their shoulders. "What did Gorm do to you that prompted this chase?"

"He hit me with a rock in a sling," the boy with the goose egg told him with disgust.

"He put me boots in the manure pile," the other boy said, swiping with the back of his hand at his bloody mouth.

Kirstin saw Hauk's lips twitch with a barely suppressed smile.

"And what did *you* do to him *first*?"

The boys ducked their heads sheepishly, not even trying to deny Hauk's good guess at culpability.

"'Tweren't nothin'," they claimed at the same time.

"We jist put a little bit of water in his bed furs."

"What kind of water?" Hauk asked, narrowing his eyes with suspicion.

The little idiots looked downward toward their groins.

She looked at Hauk. "Did they pee on his bed furs?"

Once again, Hauk's lips twitched. "It appears so."

"Yeech!"

Hauk hunkered down to the boys' level, still keeping a hand on each of their shoulders. "Listen, you two bratlings. I want you to stop beating on Gorm. 'Tis cowardly of you, being so much bigger than he is. I'll be talking to him, and he'll stop provoking you, or have a blistered arse. But I want your promise to stop bedeviling him, as well."

The two boys shuffled their feet and then nodded.

"Maybe you can all be friends," Kirstin interjected.

The boys looked horrified, as if she'd suggested they eat worms, or something equally objectionable.

"Well, if not that, then I think a perfect punishment for all of you is to finish scraping the grease off these tables tomorrow." Kirstin pointed to the last two greasy tables to her right.

"Good idea!" Hauk said. "Dost agree?"

The boys nodded, reluctantly, then bloody lip asked, "What about Gorm? What's his punishment?"

Kirstin thought for a moment and said, "He's going to help me make soap."

Once the boys scampered off, Hauk turned to her. "Do you know how to make soap?"

"No, but I'm going to learn."

Hauk took her hand once again. She'd thought he would head toward the dais at the other end of the hall, but instead he led her down a short corridor toward the garderobe. There was a door just before that, behind which was a small room… a closet, really…that held piles of bedding and odd fabrics.

Hiding under one of the piles was the little gremlin who'd caused all the trouble. Before he could run away, Hauk grabbed him by an upper arm and lifted him out to stand on his bare feet.

The boy's grimy face had tear tracks on it, and like before,

Kirstin noticed a number of bruises on his body. At first, he cowered with an arm over his face, as if to fend off a blow.

What had he been subjected to here to make him fear an adult, as well as those bully youthlings?

Quick as a wink, Hauk leaned down and pulled the boy up off his feet to dangle, with his arms pinioned to his sides.

Despite the fear evident in the boy's wide eyes, he squirmed in Hauk's hold and called him every foul name he could think of. "Dirty bugger! Big sod! Slimey snake! Pig arse! Wormy cock!"

Hauk just laughed, holding tight to the squirming boy. "Gorm. Gorm. Settle down. I'm not going to hurt you."

Once Gorm finally calmed downed, Hawk told him, "Those boys are not going to bother you anymore. They have promised. But what I need from you is a similar promise."

Gorm's face immediately took on a stubborn expression. "They started it."

Hauk shook his head. "Doesn't matter who started it. It ends now." He gave the boy a few quick shakes, but before he let him go, called out to a male house servant walking by, "Gunnar, take this boyling to the bath hut and scrub him until he shines. Then toss his garments into a fire and put clean clothes on him. He smells like a cesspit."

"Wha-what?" Gorm exclaimed as he slowly began to realize what Hauk was ordering. "Nay, nay, nay!"

Gunnar, who was an older man but of considerable size… well over six feet tall and built like a body builder…stepped closer and picked up Gorm by the waist, tossing him over his shoulder. Gorm's screams of outrage could be heard as Gunnar strolled down the corridor toward the kitchen and out to the back courtyard. A loud smack could be heard, presumably on Gorm's rump.

Now that the screeching could no longer be heard, Hauk took her hand again, and stepped outside the room, closing the door behind them. Hauk's treatment of the two bullies and of Gorm caused Kirstin to give Hauk still more credit.

"How did you know to look there for Gorm?" she asked.

"'Tis the same place I used to hide from my father when I was about his age."

Hauk made that revelation casually, as if of no import, but Kirstin sensed the pain in his voice.

"Be careful, Hauk, I'm starting to like you," Kirstin said before she could bite her fool tongue.

Hauk stopped and look at her. "*Now* you are blushing, on top of the sex flush."

She felt her face heat even more.

"Does that mean you want to stay here...that you love me?"

"I said like, not love."

"Ah," he drawled out, "'twould seem I have more work to do." Then he added, "I can't wait."

CHAPTER 16

Doctor Seuss never had this in mind...

As Hauk approached the dais, leading Kirstin by the hand, he saw that Zoya did indeed sit in the center of the high table, as he'd feared, and was giving orders and smiling down on her "subjects." He thought he'd made it clear when he talked to Zoya earlier that she would be leaving Haukshire soon, and had hinted that mayhap she should stay out of sight until then. He should have known better; apparently she hadn't gotten the hint.

To his disgust, the others at the table, Egil, Thorkel, and Bjorn, were grinning at him, like *skyrr*-eating piglets, just waiting to see what he would do next.

He wished he knew.

Suddenly, he had an idea and stopped in his tracks. He ordered two nearby housecarls to pull one of the empty trestle tables and a bench up front in the space before the dais. He then directed Signe, who was about to pass by on the way to her seat at the far end of the hall, to go into the treasure room and gather a few objects.

Signe smiled as she became aware of what Hauk was up to.

Soon there was a new table arranged cross-wise to all the lines of trestle tables, and on it had been placed a tablecloth (a luxury even many noble estates did not have), several gold goblets, and even some sterling forks and knives. A new "high table."

He did not need to look up to know that Zoya would be outraged at being outsmarted.

"Well done!" Kirstin congratulated him, as they sat down facing all his laughing and cheering people, helped along by the large amount of ale they'd already consumed.

"Does that mean you like me even more?" he asked, putting a hand over his heart.

"Maybe a little," she conceded.

That was good enough for him. Battles were often won by small well-fought skirmishes over time.

"This reminds me of Sneeches," she said while several housecarls were carrying platters of food and pitchers of ale to their table.

"Sneeches?"

"They're bird-like creatures in a famous children's story of modern times. In this book, the star-bellied Sneeches are lording it over the inferior plain-bellied Sneeches. So, some inventive fellow creates a way to put stars on bellies, and soon everyone is equal, which infuriates the original starred birds, and they look for a way to remove their stars so that then the superior Sneeches will be those without stars."

He frowned with confusion. "What has that to do with us?"

"Well, Zoya was lording it over us by seating herself at the high table, but then you created a new 'high table'. I guarantee that Zoya will be envious and want to sit here now. Oh, I know it's a stretch, not a really good comparison." She waved a hand dismissively.

"Nay, you are correct. Value is in the eye or head of the beholder, and can change at the flick of a wrist. I know a man who collected feathers, all kinds, hundreds of them and he valued them more than other treasures, which caused his comrades to mock him at every chance. Then, one day he decided to sell the collection to some Saxon earl, who paid him fifty mancuses of gold. Guess what his comrades started collecting after that?"

"Feathers," she guessed. "Actually, the book is considered a lesson in equality, how everyone is the same."

"That, too, I understand. In fact, I think my setting a table here on the same level with my people sets a good example of how I view them."

"Exactly," she said.

He was fairly certain she was liking him even more now.

Thorkel soon joined them and reached for a goblet of ale, downing it in one long swallow.

"What is amiss now?" Hauk asked.

"Zoya...she keeps putting her hand on my thigh, far up. Very far up."

Hauk grinned. "And that bothers you...why? Seems to me you have always been *up* for new quarry."

"I am trying to woo Signe."

"Woo?"

"Seduce."

"With serious intent?"

Thorkel hesitated, but then nodded. "'Tis past time I wed and start a family."

This was something new for his friend who had quite a reputation for his numerous female conquests. Rumor was that he'd once served three women in his bed furs, at the same time. "And Signe is not jumping with delight?"

"*Pfff!* Not even a little."

"Why? You are passable in appearance." In truth, he was

godly handsome. "And you should have wealth enough by now to establish your own homestead."

Thorkel nodded his agreement with Hauk's assessment, but then he explained, "She says I am like a randy bull who will mount any cow that lifts its tail."

Hauk let loose with a hoot of laughter, but Thorkel appeared so doleful that Hauk put a hand over his mouth to hide his mirth.

Kirstin leaned forward to look at Thorkel and advised, "Have you tried celibacy for a while?"

Both Hauk and Thorkel drew back with horror. Hauk knew from recent experience how difficult it was to go without sex for a long period of time, but in his case the celibacy had been forced. He couldn't imagine doing it willingly.

"You would not be practicing the *more danico* if Signe agreed to marry you, would you?" Kirstin persisted.

Thorkel's face heated with color. "I hadn't considered that question."

"Well, you should. If Signe objects to your past horndog behavior, she would certainly insist on fidelity in marriage. That's just my opinion, of course."

Both Hauk and Thorkel mouthed "horndog?" at each other, then grinned when they understood.

"My wife has very strong opinions," Hauk told Thorkel.

Kirsten elbowed him.

"What? That was a compliment."

"A half-assed one."

"You do have a way with words, wife," he said, hugging her to his side and kissing the top of her head.

Zoya soon stormed out of the hall, her chin in the air. To her chagrin, no doubt, no one protested her leaving early. But now that Zoya was gone, the rest of the evening proceeded without problems.

"Too bad you don't have a skald," Kirstin said. "It would be nice entertainment."

"Hah! The first thing any poet would do is tell some saga about a Viking in a cage. I can think of a dozen other things, mayhap two dozen, that would give me more pleasure." In fact, just sitting here in his hall, minus any entertainment, was one of the best evenings Hauk had enjoyed in a long time, not the least of which was attributed to the presence of his wife beside him and the promise of what was to come when they left the hall.

"I think you're too sensitive over the cage thing," she said.

He shrugged, not wanting to discuss that horrible cage and how annoyed he got every time someone brought it up in jest. Looking for a change of subject, he glanced around the hall at all the happy faces and told her, "You've stolen my people's hearts."

"Me? Are you sure? How do you know?"

"Look how many toasts they've raised to you."

"Hah! They're Vikings. They would raise a toast to a troll if it meant more booze. That means ale or mead or wine or whiskey."

He tilted his head in agreement. "You may be right."

Actually, there had been an uncommon number of toasts, and everyone, even Kirstin and himself, was halfway to drukkinn. "Methinks it's time for us to end this feast. I must be up early to travel with the hunters."

"Y'know, Hauk," Thorkel slurred out, "by marryin' in the Saxon lands, you deprived us of the brud-hlaup." He belched before adding. "A good bride-runnin', thass what we..." His words trailed off as he seemed to forget what he was saying, or maybe he was distracted by Signe walking by and deliberately ignoring him and yet swaying her hips suggestively.

Hauk looked at Kirstin and raised his eyebrows with exaggerated interest. "A bride-running?"

"Don't you dare," she said. But then, she jumped up and began to run along an outer aisle on the left side of the hall.

He laughed and ran after her in another aisle, leaping onto a bench and launching himself over to the other side of the table. Everyone in the crowd was laughing and cheering him on, a few of them making ribald suggestions. He arrived at the guest bedchamber just before Kirstin. He opened the door and stood aside, waving a hand to bow her in.

She gazed at him suspiciously.

The ritual called for the husband to smack his new wife's arse with the flat side of a sword to indicate he was the master of their household. Since he had no sword on him, he used the flat of his hand to swat her bottom. "Now we are truly wedded, wife."

"Hah! Just because you touch my ass doesn't make you a husband."

They were both in the bedchamber by now, and he slammed the door behind him. Leaning back, he crossed his arms over his chest and asked, "What would make me truly your husband, in your mind?"

She told him in terms so explicit that his jaw dropped.

He didn't even know what one of those words meant. Still, he boasted, "Any time, sweetling." He was a Viking, after all. He would figure it out.

~

Beware the very virile Viking...

KIRSTIN WAS CONFUSED. And being confused when a superb specimen of Norse virility was stripping in front of her and urging her to do the same...well, her brain just wasn't working properly. In fact, women often said that men's brains were located about three feet below their heads; the same could be said of her at the moment. And she was a person who'd always placed such emphasis on her brain.

Jeesh!

Maybe she could blame the amount of ale she'd imbibed with her dinner. She *was* a little tipsy. And she *did* feel dizzy, like she had an internal pendulum. Yes, I will/No, I won't. I should/I shouldn't. What would be the harm/The harm would be monumental. It would be fun/Fun is overrated. Come to Mama/No, no, no, I am not a Mama.

Jeesh!

There were two candles burning in the room, along with a small wall torch...extravagances that people rarely used in this time period. Hauk had gone to a lot of trouble for some very obvious purpose. *Me.*

Jeesh!

"Hauk...," she started to say.

"Nay, nay, nay. Do not say we need to talk. No more talking! I am not listening." He put his hands over his ears.

How did he know I was going to say that?

Jeesh!

He must have read her thoughts, because he just smiled, even as he was stepping out of his braies, at the same time doing some more beckoning of his fingertips for her to take her turn in stripping, now that he'd dropped his hands from his ears. He stood in front of her, wearing only his small-clothes, sort of a loincloth type of garment. He'd already removed his belt, tunic, and boots.

Jeesh, jeesh, jeesh!

She backed up a step and hit the side of the bed, almost toppling over. It's not that she didn't intend to make love with him, despite all her vacillating. That was a foregone conclusion hours ago, probably back when he'd dealt so sensitively with the little boy, Gorm, then cemented when he managed to handle the Zoya situation without Kirstin being humiliated.

Besides, she'd already made love with him back in the bathing hut, even though it had been a mistake. In truth, every time she succumbed to his temptations, it was a mistake, knowing that she would eventually be returning to the future. Probably. And she was risking pregnancy. Possibly.

Her reluctance at this moment was due to something else entirely. Her overactive hormones. She didn't want to appear overeager and jump his bones without any foreplay. Now *that* would be humiliating.

Pushing himself away from the door and taking one step, and one step only, he asked in a voice that sounded sex-husky, "Do you know what I want to do tonight?"

She glanced pointedly at the tent in his loincloth and arched her brows.

He laughed. "Nay, not *that*. Well, yea, *that*, but later. I want to take my time tonight. Deep, wet, tongue kisses, the kind you taught me to appreciate, you know, the ones that go on and on and on until you are mewling your need. Then caresses of your body that alternate between soft and skimming, with hard and squeezing. All this I will do until you are begging me to enter you, but I will make you wait while I pleasure-torture you some more. Finally I will enter you, and I promise, my stubborn wife, I will remain hard through many, many thrusts, long and short, gentle and strong, slow and fast till you are screaming with your peakings, coming one on top of another."

Oh. My. Goodess. Kirstin was wet just listening to the man.

She must have a stunned expression on her face because he asked, "Why do you resist me at every turn? You already know that we can flush each other."

She laughed. "That sounds like a toilet."

"What?"

"Nothing." This was silly. She was thirty-five years old, not some shy virgin teenager.

But then he unwound the loincloth thingee and she got an up close and personal look at his very impressive erection. She might have blinked several times to make sure she was seeing clearly.

"Stop looking at me, or this bedsport will be over before we begin."

He was right. As she stared...or rather gaped...he grew even more. "You have the same effect on me," she blurted out.

"I do?" He tilted his head to the side as he studied her, looking for some physical sign of her arousal, which of course he wouldn't see until she disrobed. Her nipples, for example, felt turgid and achy, against the silk fabric of her gown.

What the hell! she thought and undid the laces down the sides of her gown, then tugged the garments off her arms to pool at her hips. She didn't look down at herself, knowing what she would see, but she did look at Hauk, and was rewarded with the flare of his nostrils and the licking of his suddenly dry lips.

He was disconcerted for only a moment, though. He stepped right up to her and ran the back of his finger up and down over her nipples.

She stiffened her body and arched her head back, but she couldn't stop the little moan of pleasure that escaped her lips.

He started to chuckle.

But she couldn't have that. "That just makes us even," she said, glancing pointedly at his penis which was pointing upward at her.

"Ah, I did not know this was a contest," he said with obvious satisfaction. Before she could guess his next move, he yanked her gown the rest of the way down and lifted her out of the puddle of fabric on the floor before tossing her onto the mattress, then coming up and over her.

The sound of straw being crushed filled the room, that and the sound of their heavy breathing.

Hauk was propped on extended arms, his body arranged between her thighs, which he spread wider with his legs. Raising his head to look down at her, he moved his hips from side to side to better arrange his erection against the most sensitive part of her, then said, "Greetings, wife."

What could she say to that? "I like the way you say hello."

"I can tell."

"How can you tell?" The minute she asked, she wished she could take the words back.

Sure enough, he smiled and winked at her. "Your woman dew is nigh soaking the mattress."

"Oooh!" she said, mortified, and tried to shove him off.

To no avail. He pressed his hips harder against hers.

But then she relaxed and confessed, "That's why I was hesitant to make love with you. I was already so turned on by you that I was afraid I would be embarrassed."

"You and your embarrassments!" He nipped her bare shoulder with his teeth in punishment, then licked the spot to soothe it. "So, your enthusiasm rose in response to the size of my...um, endowments?"

She laughed and leaned up to nip his shoulder, too, but not bothering with the licking. "No. Actually, I was most turned on by your words, promising what you planned to do to me."

"Really?" he said, frowning with concentration as he no doubt filed that information for future reference. She could just about hear his mind working. Best seduction technique: words, not cock. All guys, whether twenty-first or eleventh century era, had those kind of mental playbooks.

"Not that your...um, endowments...aren't amazing."

He nodded, as if that was a given. He was still digesting her remarks about his words wooing her more than the size of his amazingness.

"Isn't it time for you to get on with your promises?" she asked then.

"Isn't it time for you to rest your tongue," he countered, "unless it is in my mouth. Then it can definitely move."

"Seems to me that you're the one with a whole lot of talk and a lot less action."

"A challenge?" He grinned and made a growling sound against her neck.

She laughed, especially because his breath tickled her ear. "Should I be afraid?"

"Very afraid."

Every Viking wanted to get the last word in, and Kirstin was a Viking, no matter her gender. So, not to be outdone, she said, "I can't wait."

Hauk smiled then, slow and lazy and supremely sexy before he raised his hips and surprised her by thrusting himself into her, to the hilt. No foreplay. No warning. Just "Go in and go big." Especially big.

Kirstin realized that she'd stepped into his trap.

Beware the virile Viking.

CHAPTER 17

Not his most shining moment, or was it?...

Oops! Hauk thought on finding himself imbedded in Kirstin's moist depths.

Without one bit of foresport on my part!

Like an untried youthling!

"Oops" was the word Kirstin used when she accidentally did something, wasn't it?

But Hauk wasn't about to admit to that kind of mistake, not out loud. He smiled and pretended it had been a deliberate action. Thankfully, Kirstin's female channel had been ready for him, melting around him like molten honey.

He almost said something embarrassing, like, "Loki made me do it," but then he noticed the expression on his wife's face. Wide-eyed with wonder.

Well, praise the gods and pass the mead! Apparently he'd done something right, without even intending to. That would be a good "oops," he supposed.

It took every bit of his self-control to remain still, the instinct to begin the age-old thrusting rhythm almost overwhelming. He bit his bottom lip to the point of nearly breaking the skin and tried to think of other things, like turnips, which he considered a gagsome vegetable, or riding a longship during a fierce sea storm, or waking after a night of drinking in the bed furs of an ugly, wart-nosed, gray-haired woman. Not that he had ever experienced the latter, but many of his friends had. The skalds told sagas about such lame-brained men.

But then, Kirstin moaned with pleasure, breaking into his reverie.

And Hauk tasted blood.

"I wasn't expecting that," she said breathlessly.

I wasn't either. "'Tis one of my talents."

"You have a lot of those, do you?"

Oh, gods! She is going to talk now! "Do you doubt it?"

"Not for a Viking minute. Wanna see one of mine?"

Is she serious? What kind of question is that to ask a Viking man, especially one who is knee-deep, rather cock-deep, in enthusiasm? "Mayhap." Perchance a one-word answer would halt her chatter.

Which it did, except that now she did something with her inner muscles, causing them to flex, several times, which caused him to move a little bit deeper inside. Who knew that was even possible? His eyes were probably rolling back in his head. "What was that?" he choked out.

"That was my va-jay-jay saying 'Howdy' to your happy tail."

He had no idea what those words meant, specifically, but he suspected they were bawdy names for body parts, and that "Howdy" was a word of welcome. The blush that emerged on her face confirmed his suspicion.

"Why do you keep trying to shock me?" he asked.

At first, she stiffened at his question...he was still lying over her, still buried inside her nether parts...but then she told him, "It's probably the result of growing up with nine brothers. They had no mercy for feminine sensibilities. So my best defense became a frontal assault. Shock them before they could shock me."

"But I am not your brother." He smiled, then turned serious. "I want to make love with you."

She reached a hand up to cup his cheek. "I want to make love with you, too."

Thank you, gods...or God. He turned his face to kiss her palm. "Then let us make love to each other, heartling."

Whatever the cause, Hauk knew in that instant that Kirstin was a gift he'd been given for some predestined reason. Was it a forever gift, or one that would be taken away without notice? He had no idea. Facing that uncertainty frightened him more than a berserker's axe or a rash on certain body parts. He must do everything in his power to convince her to stay, or leastways he must cherish each moment that he had with her.

With that in mind, he eased himself out of her, almost but not quite the whole way.

She sighed her appreciation, or mayhap she was trying to bridle her own passions.

He stroked in and out of her. Unhurriedly. But only a few times because his body demanded faster and deeper. "I need to slow down," he rasped out.

"Faster," she demanded, and clasped his buttocks with her two hands and pressed tightly. He would probably have finger marks.

He tried to laugh but it came out as a chortle. "I'll hurt you if I lose control, sweetling."

"I'll hurt you if you don't go harder, ding-a-ling."

She didn't know what she was asking. He was half again as big as she was. He tried a different tack. "I'll be done too soon."

"Did I tell you that in modern times, they have invented a little blue pill that helps men to get and stay hard?"

"That is not my problem at the moment," he told her.

"I noticed."

He looked cross-eyed at her. "Truly, we are going to talk? When I am locked in you like a sword in a blacksmith's vise?"

"Nice image!"

"Aaarrgh! Truly, do you deliberately chatter in an effort to incite me to end too soon?"

"That's the best thing about sex. We can do it again. And again and again and again."

There were a few too many "agains" in there for Hauk's comfort. But the most important thing was that she had her way, which was of course his way, too.

Succumbing to the growing urgency that swept over him, he was mindless with the savage need for completion. With chest heaving and blood roaring in his ears, he pounded into her woman heat. Once, twice, thrice, and his neck arched back as he roared out his ecstasy. Thankfully, Kirstin's sheath clasped him spasmodically as she reached her own peak.

He collapsed onto her body with his face resting in the arch of her neck. Despite the coolness of the bedchamber, both of their bodies were covered with perspiration. He might have actually fallen asleep for a second or two, as some men were wont to do when satisfied in the bedplay.

But then he felt her body shaking under him. Was she crying? Oh, gods! Had he hurt her?

He raised his body on straightened arms and looked down at her. She was not weeping. She was laughing.

Now that was an ardor crusher for a man, if ever there was one. In truth, he could not recall any woman ever laughing at him after bedplay.

He arched his brows at her. "My lovemaking is cause for mirth? You laugh at me?"

"I'm not laughing at you. I'm laughing at myself."

He frowned with confusion. "Huh?"

"I've been so hot for you all night, and I promised myself I wouldn't jump your bones, but that's exactly what I did, so to speak. I'm a disgrace to the single women's rule book that says men prefer their partners to let them lead the way, to seduce them."

What? It's not me she's laughing at? Whew! "That bloody rule book is wrong. Men love sex no matter how it comes."

She put a hand to his face and smiled. "In any case, that was amazing."

"It was? Even short as it was?"

"Long, short, hard, gentle, standing up, lying down, on top, on bottom, whatever...there's an attraction to all of those, isn't there?"

He nodded, and moved his chest back and forth over her breasts, the bristly hairs causing her nipples to engorge. He could swear he almost felt the points pressing against his skin.

"I don't know how you're going to outdo, or even match, what you've already done...here, in the bathing hut, back at the castle, in the tent." She fluttered her eyelashes at him coquettishly.

Is she challenging me? Has she not learned that lesson yet? He was still inside her female channel, though limp and needing a rest. Still, he thought of something. "Have you ever heard of the famous Viking S-Spot?"

Her inner muscles flexed, hard. Just once.

But that was enough. His cock stood to attention and probably said that word that Kirstin had used, "Howdy!" Apparently Hauk did not need a rest, after all.

Role reversal: a modern concept, a timeless practice...

ACTUALLY, Kirstin had heard of the famous Viking S-Spot before. Her brothers were always talking about it with each other, always in a lusty, boastful manner, always in hushed tones so that she and her sisters wouldn't overhear. As if that wasn't the inducement for them to make sure they overheard!

Not that Kirstin had ever experienced it herself, if it really existed. She'd never done the deed with a real Viking...until Hauk. A college professor, a Navy SEAL, a wine merchant, and a journalist, but never a true blue Norseman. And, hooboy, it was true what they said about Vikings, by the way.

But she decided to give Hauk a break. "Lie back," she urged, pushing upward.

He eased himself out of her with a grimace of supposed pain and rolled to his back, taking her with him to rest on her side with her head on his shoulder and an arm over his chest. "Like this?" he asked.

"Exactly," she said, kissing his chin. "Let's just relax a minute. This isn't a race. We have all night."

"Ah, so I wore you out already?" He chuckled with sheer male overconfidence and squeezed her tighter so that her breasts were pressed against his side.

Let him think that.

"You didn't answer my question." The fingers of his free hand trailed over her shoulder and down her back to the small of her waist and the top of her crack. He hesitated *there*...thank God! She didn't know a woman alive who wanted to be touched *there*. But then, he repeated the trail upward, back to her shoulder. He left a ripple of goosebumps in the wake of his wicked fingers.

"Yes, I've heard of the Viking S-Spot, from my bragging brothers, but I'm convinced it's just a bunch of Viking baloney. The kind of skill men claim to have but are never called on."

"Are you saying you have never experienced it yourself?"

"Hey, there aren't that many Vikings in modern-day California."

He grinned and started to rise, putting his hands on both her shoulders, presumably to arrange her on the bed.

"Not yet," she said.

He paused, only half reclining by now, and arched his brows at her.

"I have something else in mind for the moment. Something that will require no work on your part. Give you time to recover from your last orgasm."

"Who said I needed time...ah, whatever you want, dearling. What would you suggest?"

"A bit of role reversal."

"Hmmm," he said, obviously having no clue what she meant. Even so, he volunteered, "I am always *up* for games in the bedsport." He smiled and glanced downward to his rising enthusiasm. "Orgy-asm, though? I like the sound of that."

"You'll like what I'm planning even better."

"Oh?"

"I want you to sit on the edge of the bed."

He frowned with confusion, but did as she asked. His bare feet were firmly planted on the floor, knees spread in a manly fashion.

She scooted over and off the mattress, standing in front of him. For a moment, she let his eyes travel over her, while his enthusiasm got more enthusiastic.

Then she knelt.

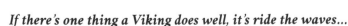

If there's one thing a Viking does well, it's ride the waves...

HAUK WAS SHOCKED.

And he was pleased.

Nay, "pleased" was too small a word to describe how he felt. In fact, he was chest-thumping, mouth-roaring, head-lifting jubilant. All those emotions being held inside, that this woman...his wife...would do that for him, made his heart feel too big, kind of achy. It would be foolish to attribute such an act to love, or some such fanciful notion. Still...

It's not that he'd never had his cock in a woman's mouth before. He had. Well, truth to tell, it had only been a few times in his thirty-five years, and one of those had been when he was a youthling and it had involved a great deal of begging and a small bribe...a slightly soiled blue riband...to a dairy maid who reeked of cow, as he recalled.

With Kirstin it had been an entirely different experience. Afterward, he dropped back onto the mattress with a whooshing exhale and watched, stunned, as she pulled a gunna over her head and said, cheerily, "Hold that thought, honey. I'll be right back."

She could talk after that? Whilst he could scarce put two words together? Was this not such a momentous event to her, as it had been to him? Apparently not. "Where are you going?"

"Gotta go pee." With those words and a saucy wave, she left, giving her hips an extra swing. Or so it seemed to him. She could have relieved herself in the bucket behind the screen in the corner, but then women were squeamish about such things, preferring the garderobe or the outside privy.

Upon her return a short time later, she washed her hands with water that she poured from a pitcher into the bowl on the wall shelf. Drying her hands on her gunna, she then turned to look at him.

He was leaning back on an extra bed fur he'd placed at the headboard, his arms folded behind his head. His body was covered with another fur up to his waist. "Thank you," he said.

She arched her brows but didn't ask what he meant.

Instead, she smiled and said, "My pleasure. You can reciprocate later."

*Reciprocate? Does she mean...? How do I do that? Mayhap she
refers to the Viking S-Spot, which involves the tongue, but, nay that
is different. Oh, well, I'll figure it out. Or Kirstin, bless her blathering heart, will tell me what to do.* He lifted the side of the bed
fur and invited her in. To her credit, or his, she removed the
gunna before ducking under the fur with a shiver. Unfortunately, she didn't stand long enough for him to enjoy the view,
but then, the air was cold. Even that short exposure chilled
her skin. But not for long. He pulled her tight against his side,
again, and she, brazen wench that she was...praise the
gods!...lifted her knee up and over his thighs, thus placing her
even tighten against him. They created a wonderful heat
together.

She yawned and cuddled her face into his neck. To his
further amazement, and disappointment, she fell asleep
almost immediately.

He remained awake for a long time, though. Thinking,
thinking, thinking. Even as he worried, a sense of serenity fell
over him, like a blanket, or the bed fur he had drawn up over
both of them, to the neck. Partly, it was gratification, the
physical kind gained after good sex. But more than that, he
felt contentment filling him. Well, not totally. Yea, he was
content being back at Haukshire, to his ever-increasing
surprise, and he was hopeful that with his hunting trip on the
morrow and Egil's trip to Hedeby for supplies, and the
removal of Zoya from his premises, he and his people would
make it through the autumn and winter. After that, springtime and the inevitable return of many of his cotters and
warriors, would bring prosperity, not just survival. There was
a purpose to his life that had not been there before.

The only thing blocking his complete contentment was
lying beside him, snoring softly against his chest hairs.

Kirstin. His wife. Even saying, or thinking, the word "wife" caused a lump to form in his throat and his eyes to water. She was coming to mean way too much to him. And he knew without a doubt that she still planned to leave at the first opportunity.

I need to convince her to stay.

And how will thou do that? that infernal voice in his head asked. Was it Odin or the Christian One-God or just himself questioning himself?

I've already tried forcing her. She is here because I drugged her, not by her own choice.

And how has that worked out, Viking, if she is still planning to leave?

Definitely the One-God, he decided. *Um, do you have inside information on her plans?*

None that I would disclose to you.

Oh, well! Time, that is my friend just now. I have time to seduce...uh, sway her emotions toward me.

Seems to me, thou art the one being seduced...uh, swayed.

Do Christians know their God is so sarcastic?

Dost think it wise to alienate the One being who can help you?

You would help me...a heathen?

Oh, I forgot thou art a pagan.

I could convert, he added quickly.

He thought he heard a smile in the voice when it replied, *Of course thou could.* The One-God had to know that many Vikings allowed themselves to be baptized to gain lands or treaties, while at the same time maintaining their old ways.

Hauk hated these wavering emotions that were assailing him. He'd always been confident of his abilities, both as a warrior and a lover, but he was oddly insecure now, when it came to Kirstin. Mayhap it was because the outcome mattered so much to him.

She woke then, and they talked of inconsequential things,

SANDRA HILL

skirting around what was surely on both their minds. The future. *Their* future.

"I must leave at first light."

"How long will you be gone?"

"Three or four days...a sennight at the most."

"Depending on...?"

He shrugged. "How much game we can get close to home?"

"How far have you had to go in the past?"

"Well, I haven't hunted here for many years, but in the old days, when game was most plentiful, two days of walking. Beyond that the cold and terrain become too difficult."

"Is there danger?"

"There's danger in everything."

"How about Bjorn? Will you take him with you?"

He shook his head. "He is improved, but I fear that so much walking could reverse all his progress. I've asked him to supervise the fishing."

"And he was okay with that?"

"*Pfff!* Not at all! But I told him that men were needed here to provide protection. Also, I promised him that he could go a-Viking with me next spring if he is able to obey orders."

She nodded and remained silent, though she probably had thoughts on what a by then thirteen-year-old boy should be doing with his time. But that was neither here nor there. He wanted to ask her if she would be here when he returned, but instead he said, "How will you keep busy whilst I'm gone?"

"Hah! There's plenty to do. We'll probably make soap tomorrow if the weather is all right."

"Flavored soap?" he inquired with a grin.

She pinched his belly for his teasing. Which, of course, caused a body part somewhat lower to rise with attention. "*Tsk!* Scented, not flavored," she said. "And, actually, yes, I might try some scents. I'm thinking you might be a perfect candidate for something like, oh, I don't know. Maybe turnip."

242

"Turnip? Turnip?" he exclaimed, then realized that she must have discovered his aversion to that particular vegetable. "Do not dare!"

She giggled and told him, "Just kidding."

"How about mead? That would be a smell men might not mind."

"There you go! But they might be walking around half-blitzed all the time, or have a constant craving for alcohol," she said with a laugh. "Seriously, though. I might try honey, or mint if I can find any wild plants that haven't yet died off, or evergreen. It will be fun experimenting."

He wasn't sure about that. "Your idea of fun and mine are vastly different." He paused, then added, "Though there are some things we both appear to enjoy."

He proceeded then to show her one of them.

"What do you call that?" she gasped out.

"Rocking the boat."

She tried to laugh, but it came out as a snort. "Am I the boat, or are you?"

"I am the longship. You are the fjord," he told her, then showed her some other ways to rock a boat on unruly seas.

She was unable to speak for several long moments after that, except to mutter something that sounded like, "Ahoy, matie!"

He figured "matie" must be another of her endearment terms, like sweetie or darling. As for "Ahoy"...well, that had to be the same as her "Howdy" or "You-Who"! Now that he was learning Ah-mare-ee-can, he was becoming a very modern Viking, if he did say so himself.

CHAPTER 18

Falling, or fallen? That is the question...

"Stay."

Kirstin wasn't asleep when she heard that single, huskily spoken word, or thought she heard it. She was just basking in the afterglow of the most incredible sex she'd ever experienced. If nothing else, she'd never had three bouts of sex with a man in one night.

Cracking an eyelid open slightly, she saw that it was still nighttime. There was a dim light, even though the torch was out and the candles had burned almost the whole way down. But then, her eyes shot wide as she noticed that Hauk sat on a chair he had pulled closer, with the heels of his extended legs braced on the side of the bed, sipping at a mug of what was probably ale. A wool blanket was wrapped around his shoulders and pooled on his thighs against the cool night air.

How long has he been watching me? And why? Oh, crap! I hope I wasn't drooling or snoring. She raised herself on bent elbows and asked, "Did you say something?"

He nodded.

She tilted her head to the side in question when he didn't elaborate. "Why are you watching me?"

He shrugged.

His silence was scaring her. And the raw hurt glittering in his eyes...what was that about?" "Hauk?"

"Will you be here when I get back?"

"What? Where did that come from?"

"This is the first time we will be apart since you first came to rescue me," he said, smiling. The smile she attributed to the fact that he still found it amusing that a woman would be sent to rescue a big, brave Viking man. But she noticed that his smile was rather sad, not reaching his expressive eyes, which regarded her gravely. "Will you stay?"

Ah, so that's what he meant by that single word I heard. "You think I'll use this opportunity to go back home?" She realized immediately what a poor choice of word she'd used, how he would interpret her calling another place home. "I mean, back to the future."

He tipped his mug up and emptied it, then set it on the floor. After that, he just looked at his hands that were folded on his lap, as if thinking of the right way to say or ask something.

She was pretty sure she knew what was bothering the man. "Hauk, I have no plans to leave while you're gone."

His eyes speared her with silent recrimination. They both recognized her response as what it was...an evasion. "No plans" didn't preclude her making a sudden decision to leave.

"First of all, I don't know if I could teletransport from here, or if I have to be at the point where I entered. I've told you that before."

"You also mentioned that your brother Torolf went forward, back, then forward again, all from different places."

Good Lord! Is he caching all the bits of information I mention

casually, giving them more importance than they probably merit?
He didn't comment at the time.

"You're right about Torolf. But we...my family...always believed that for safety's sake, a time traveler should stay close to the portal, or stay away from the portal, for that matter. Not that any of us have deliberately made such a trip, except for Torolf and even then what happened was an accident that..." She waved a hand dismissively. "I can explain later."

"I thought you came here to save me," he said, with the same sad/grim smile.

"I was *sent* here to save you," she corrected him.

"Ah, the godly mission."

She could laugh off Hauk's misconceptions, but she sensed he was serious, that something important was bothering him. "Are you going to have these fears every—"

"I fear nothing," he interrupted with indignation.

Another wrong choice of word! "Are you going to have these *expectations* every time you go somewhere without me?"

"Probably. Until or if..." He let his words trail off and looked at her, waiting.

He wanted assurances, she realized. But she couldn't commit to that kind of promise. Not yet. Maybe not ever.

Kirstin was not usually so bold or blasé about her nudity, but feeling Hauk's pain, she flipped the bed fur aside and slipped off the mattress to slide onto his lap. Modesty be damned!

He was surprised but opened his arms to her, wrapping the blanket around them both. She could feel his erection under her thighs, but sex was the last thing on her mind, at the moment. She insinuated her arms around his body so that her face rested on his shoulder and they were breast to chest. It was probably impossible, but she could swear she felt his heart beating in a fierce counterpoint to her own. They sat thus, in silence, for several long moments while her hands caressed his back and his hands did the same to hers. They soothed each other.

Finally, she leaned back and said, "I think I know what your problem is, Hauk."

"You do, do you?" He chuckled but did not argue over her saying he had a problem, as he usually would. "And what, pray tell, would that be?"

"You're falling in love with me."

"Oh?"

"Yes. And it frightens you. Not frightens like a warrior before a battle or facing death, but—"

"I do not fear death. Vikings do not fear the journey to Valhalla."

She tapped his lips with her fingertips to stop his talking. Vikings and their egos! "Love…the kind between a man and a woman…can cause the strongest person to feel anxious, or alarmed."

"Do not tell me! You are an expert on love, as well as ancient Norse culture, and illness, and jokes, and any other number of things."

She jabbed him playfully on the chin with a fist and laughed. "No, I'm not an expert on love, but teenage girls in America obsess over the subject. Teenagers are girls between thirteen and nineteen. Anyhow, I think I remember reading an article in a magazine one time about the different stages of love, everything from attraction to infatuation to falling in love to full-blown head-over-heels in love." She laughed softly and told him, "It was probably *Cosmo* magazine."

She could tell he hadn't understood half of what she'd said. And there was no way in the world she could explain *Cosmo* magazine without a background on feminism and modern culture.

"And where does lust fit into all those stages?" he asked, telling her that he'd understood more than what she'd thought. "Seems to me you have remarked on more than one occasion that love and lust are two different things."

"Lust plays in all those stages, with different effects."

"Truly, you are a font of knowledge, wife," Hauk said, squeezing her to soften his criticism, if that's what it was. "Tell me more." He was probably making fun of her.

She sat straighter, which caused his erection to show it was paying attention, too. Hauk put his hands on her waist and adjusted her position to ease any discomfort he might be feeling. "Go on," he said then.

"The first stage of love is one of attraction, what I call the butterfly period. In fact, some people get this fluttery feeling in the pit of their stomach, which travels upward, causing the heart to race, just seeing or thinking about the other person. They might even get goose bumps."

"My butterflies tend to fly downward," he teased.

"*Tsk-tsk!*" she chastised him. "But the butterfly effect isn't just physical. It's more like empathy. A couple can sense the other person's feelings, almost reflect what they feel. That empathy can be so powerful that it's almost painful in its intensity. In the latter part of this stage, the afflicted party would do anything for, would sacrifice anything for, his or her love connection."

"Hmmm." Hauk seemed to be contemplating how those descriptions applied to himself. He didn't agree, but he didn't disagree either.

"Everything in this first phase feels exciting and new. The air is crisper. The scents more intense and inviting. A person can't wait to see the other person again, even if they've just left. They consider that other person extra special by now, even if others don't agree. For example, I had a friend who fell in love with a guy who was a head shorter than her, with the world's worst comb-over on his half-bald head, and the personality of a stump, but she considered him a hottie."

"A hottie, huh? Am I a hottie?"

"Absolutely."

"But only in your eyes?"

"No. I'm pretty sure you would be deemed a hottie by most women of my time. If you kept your mouth shut. Your chauvinistic attitude would turn off some feminists."

"I do understand your meaning," he said. "Toste the Tall's first wife was a love match. Her shrewish nature turned away many a potential suitor, but Toste actually deemed her voice melodious. And she was skinny as a lance with no fat spots at all for a man to grab onto in the bedsport. Toste did not care."

She nodded. "Exactly."

"To be honest, I do recognize a few of those symptoms. Go on."

She wanted to think about what his ready acceptance meant, what emotions he was admitting to, but she would ponder all that later. For now, she asked, "You're not just patronizing me, are you?"

"I would if I knew what it meant."

She laughed. "Okay, stage two could be called Chaos. This is probably the point of falling in love, where you are now."

"This should be good," he murmured.

"A person falling in love begins to feel off balance, not totally in control. They'll feel nauseated one moment and in the next be in such a good mood they can barely contain themselves. Someone who avoids commitment, or has some obstacles to a long-term relationship, will panic now. They'll try to step back, but they can't stop thinking about the other person, even at awkward moments. Like in the middle of battle exercises, for example, thoughts of the other person pop into their heads. My brother Hamr, an ex-football player, once told me that thoughts of his at that time babe-du-jour came to him in the middle of a critical game and he ended up being tackled with a possible concussion."

249

Hauk put a hand to his forehead and groaned.

"What?"

"Do not take offense, Kirstin, but you do talk a great deal. Do all pro-fess-whores sound like you?" he asked.

Kirstin *was* a little miffed. "If you don't want to hear anymore, I'll shut up." She raised her chin defiantly.

"Nay. Nay, go on. It's just that I understand but half of what you say. Football, baby-do-sure, conk-us-on? Holy Thor!"

She smiled. "You're right. I forget sometimes that you don't know modern words. Suffice it to say, stage two can make a person both jubilant and anxious at the same time. That and all the other things I've mentioned are why I said that I think you're falling in love. You aren't at a stage of trust or commitment, which comes next. So, it was natural for you to be apprehensive about leaving, not knowing if I would leave, despite all these heavy emotions. Am I right?"

"Perchance," he conceded. "Have you fallen in love so many times yourself?"

"No. Several times I've thought I might be falling. Most recently, with the Navy SEAL that I told you about, I was very close to committing, but it was not meant to be, clearly. We wouldn't have been dating for three years, off and on, without taking the next step, if it was." She shrugged.

"That is unfortunate," Hauk said with a grin of insincerity. "You must admit, Kirstin, that love as you describe does not sound very appealing. What sane man would want to be in stomach pain with the urge to vomit, with insect wings and goose dumps afflicting his innards, and legs that go limp with weakness?"

"Huh?"

"In any case, I am still waiting to hear how sex fits into all these phases." He winked at her.

"That's the best part. Sex combined with love can make for

the most spectacular love play in the world, or so I've been told. And it gets better and better through all the stages."

"Well, why didn't you say so?" With a whoop of joy, he stood and, in one fluid motion, lifted her in his arms. The blanket fell away and he tossed her onto the bed, climbing up and over her. Once he arranged himself over her, he smiled and said, "I concede to your better judgment. I *am* falling in love." He arched his brows and waited for her response. When it didn't come, he asked, "Are you in love with me?"

"Hell, no!" she exclaimed, not about to profess the real deal until he did, and watched as his face fell with disappointment. He started to raise himself off her, but she put her hands on both sides of his face and told him. "Sweetheart, I'm already falling in love, like you. Hook, line, and Viking sinker. But it will take a little more work on your part to reel me in."

~

Like Kevin Costner in **Bull Durham**...

WHILE THEY RESTED for a while with Kirstin nestled in his arms, they both mulled over what they had admitted to each other. Falling in love was a new concept to Hauk. In truth, he wasn't sure he'd ever experienced love of any kind. Certainly not parental love, and while he'd indulged in a vast amount of lust, he couldn't honestly say he'd ever experienced a softer, compelling emotion toward any woman.

But wait...there was Bjorn. Hauk did love the boy.

A sense of relief filled him then, knowing he was capable of love.

At the same time, he was hit with the realization that Kirstin was "falling in love," not fully "in love" with him. Despite the fact that he'd admitted to the same thing, her halfway declaration rankled him. *Gods above! I cannot believe I am making these distinctions. My Viking comrades would laugh their arses off if they knew.* Hauk was not a man to shy away from challenges, and he determined that, by thunder, he would force Kirstin to love him. Nay, that was wrong. He would persuade her to love him. None of this "falling in love" nonsense! And then she would stay.

"Kirstin, are you awake?" he whispered against her ear.

"Barely," she replied.

That was good enough for him. "Do you recall something I said to you after we engaged in bedsport back in the tent?"

"Are you nuts? You expect me to recall something you said after knocking my socks off—"

"Nuts? And socks? What socks? You were wearing nothing at the time."

She rolled her eyes as if he was hopeless.

While, actually, he was hopeful, not hopeless, about the outcome of this night.

"Suffice it to say— "

"Holy Thor! Every time you say 'Suffice it to say,' I know I am in for one of your lectures. Keep in mind, sweetling, I only have a few hours till I must rise." He gave her a woeful look so she would not take offense at his criticism.

She pinched his arm as punishment, but then continued anyway, "Suffice it to say, I was probably in an erotic swoon, in no condition to recall bed banter."

He laughed. "You do have a way of saying things. Erotic swoon. I will have to remember that."

"You must have a better memory than I do, Einstein."

Einstein? Is she calling me by another man's name whilst in my bed? I knew a man named Einar. But, nay, it must be another of her pet names for me...an endearment.

"Prepare to swoon, sweetling," he said with a growl. Rolling her over, he arranged himself atop her body, fitting himself between her spread legs to accommodate him.

As his enthusiasm began to rise, she said, "You play dirty, Hauk."

He cocked his head to the side, then smiled. "I like the sound of that. Dirty sex."

"You're hopeless."

"Good hopeless or bad hopeless?"

"Definitely good," she said with a laugh.

"I told you that I want to make slow love to you. The kind that starts with deep, wet, tongue kisses, the kind you taught me to appreciate."

"Are you blaming me?"

"Nay. Thanking you. Do not be so testy." As I was saying, those kisses will go on and on and on until you are mewling your need."

"I do not mewl."

"A first then! Wonderful!" He smiled. "In all the times we've made love so far, I haven't really studied your body and all its secret places. For that I apologize. I promise to accomplish this with caresses that alternate between soft and skimming, with hard and squeezing. All this I will do until you are begging me to enter you, but I will make you wait while I pleasure-torture you some more."

"Oh, ho! So now you think you can make me beg. I don't think so. Maybe I will make you beg."

He grinned. "I can only hope."

"Oh, you!" she swatted his shoulder.

"Moving on," he was enjoying himself and did not try to hide the fact. "When I finally enter you, my enthusiasm will be raging for completion, but I will remain hard through many, many thrusts, long and short, gentle and strong, slow and fast till you are scream with your peakings, coming one on top of another."

"Holy moley, Hercules! You know, what you've just said here sounds a lot like what Kevin Costner said to Susan

Sarandon in the movie *Bull Durham*. You could say that Susan was in an erotic swoon, too."

"I am not even going to *try* to interpret what you just said. Now just lie still and let me do my thing."

"You have a thing."

"Ah, how quickly they forget!" He looked upward and sighed dramatically. "You told me I have a thing...the same night in the tent."

"Oh," she said.

As promised, he began to make slow love to his wife now. First the kisses, which started gentle and coaxing, seeking to make the perfect fit. And of course there were tongues involved. Both his and hers. Who knew that lips and teeth and tongue had such carnal spots! And that they were connected somehow to the genital area!

The ears, too! Holy Thor! He ministered to hers, wetting the whorls with the tip of the tongue, then blowing softly. She moaned and tilted her head to give him better access. When she did the same to him, he about shot off the bed, so intense was the pleasure. He might have moaned then, too.

Next, he ministered to her breasts, spending a goodly amount of time there once he discovered they were her favorite erotic place. Leastways, he assumed they were her favorite as she arched her back and thrashed from side to side when he suckled her, licking the nipple with his tongue, then nipping it lightly with his teeth. *Those blessed tongues again*, he thought with an inward grin. Then, she stiffened and reached her first peak.

Let it be noted, she was not lying there docilely as he played with her body. Her hands caressed his back. Her heels rubbed the back of his thighs. She anointed his belly with her woman dew when she deliberately moved her hips sideways against him, right and left.

Moving lower, he studied her female area, the blonde

nether curls, the pink channels. That rising bud which contained a woman's most sensitive spot, he'd been told, comparable to the male organ. He could hardly credit that, but he was no fool. He would treat it as such. And he was rewarded with her keening, "Oh. Oh. Oh."

At each part of her body that he kissed, or touched, or pinched, he told her what he saw and how beautiful or alluring it was. Mostly she just sighed or moaned or cried out with bliss.

Whilst teasing her female folds and that little bud, she reached another peaking, this time arching her body up so high she raised his much heavier body as well. If she thought that was the end of it, except for the intercourse to come, she was going to be surprised.

She was breathing heavily, splayed out on the mattress, while he was still kneeling betwixt her legs. Her eyes were closed, but she was not sleeping. Not by any means!

"Did you mention never having been shown your Viking S-spot?" he drawled out.

Her eyes shot open. "What? Not now! It's too much."

"Nay, sweetling. Now! And it is never too much."

She groaned again. He took that as her acceptance.

And so he showed her with fingers and tongue the famous Viking S-spot that only a few Norseman knew about. And she peaked yet again.

He gave her time to rest then. In truth, he needed a respite, too. His cock was bigger than it had ever been with a tiny drop of his male seed escaping the tip. He would need to complete the act soon or explode.

Once his heart stopped thundering, and Kirstin's did, as well, she opened her eyes, which were misty blue with her arousal. Her lips were kiss-swollen. There might be a sucking mark on her neck. And surely that was a sex flush coloring her face down to her chest.

"Do...it...now!" she demanded, locking her ankles over his buttocks and pulling his face down to, not kiss him as he expected, but nip his jaw with her teeth.

He laughed and entered her, then stopped laughing. The spasms of her inner channels were so strong he could not withdraw if he wanted to. But finally she settled down, and he was able to perform the age-old pattern of sex. The tightness! The friction! The slick heat! It did not last long before he reared his head back and roared his triumph.

He dropped down onto her, even though his weight was probably crushing her. Their two hearts seemed to beat together. He felt a completeness beyond anything he'd ever experienced in his life.

Raising his head, he looked down at her. Her eyes were open.

She cupped his face with her hands and said, "I love you, Hauk."

And he admitted what he'd known but refused to accept so far, "I love you, too, heartling. Gods help me, but I have fallen in love with you."

CHAPTER 19

Home Sweet Home...

Kirstin awakened late the next morning, alone, Hauk having left before dawn on his hunting trip. She stretched widely, noted the ache in her girl parts, and smiled. Good thing she'd have a chance to recuperate while Hauk was gone. She wondered idly if he was feeling a similar ache. She'd have to ask him when he returned.

The night before flashed through her mind, but she decided to wait until later to ponder everything that had been said and done. Deliciously, she added with another smile.

Quickly dressing, she went out and found work in the hall going on as usual and in the kitchen Frida was stirring something that smelled like stew over the open fire. Pointing to the food laid out on the table, the cook told her, "Eat, m'lady," then chuckled and added, "Looks like ye could use some sustenance."

Finding herself ravenous, Kirstin grabbed a slice of manchet break and a hunk of hard cheese. Munching on them, she asked, "Has everyone gone?"

"The master is long gone, and Bjorn is up the fjord fishing. Egil is about to leave, I believe. They were still loading the longship when I went out to the dairy a few moments ago."

Finishing the food, she told the cook, "I'll be back soon to help you. Maybe we can make soap today."

"Whatever you say, m'lady," Frida replied.

When she emerged from the back door of the keep, Kirstin saw Egil.

"You're about to leave?"

"Yea. I just came back to get some extra rope I need."

"How long will you be gone?"

He shrugged. "A few days, no longer than a sennight."

"I'll miss you." She gave him a hug, which she could tell embarrassed him, but in a nice way.

He was about to walk away when he turned and said, "I must say, it was generous of you to give Zoya yer amber necklet."

"What? I didn't give her anything."

Egil frowned and muttered, "Damn bothersome wench!"

But then Kirstin thought of something alarming. "Oh, my God!" She turned and began to run back to the keep, yelling over her shoulder to Egil, "Don't you dare leave until I speak to you."

Quickly, she made her way to the bedroom she had been sharing with Hauk where he'd placed his travel chest until he could regain his own bedchamber. She opened the lid and began to toss items here and there, searching for the pouch which had held the necklace, which she'd taken off after going to the bathing hut. She soon discovered that not only was the necklace missing, but her two arm rings, as well.

Had Hauk hidden them?

Or Zoya stolen them?

She could take no chances. She ran though the keep and out into the back courtyard again, then raced toward the fjord where the longship was still, thankfully, docked. When she reached the wharf, panting for breath, she told an astonished Egil, "Help me get on the boat and search Zoya's belongings. She's taken some important things from me, not just the necklace."

Nodding, with more swear words under his breath, Egil helped her over the wooden gangway to board the ship. A short time later, they'd searched all of Zoya's belongings, and her body, as well. Not only did Kirstin find her necklace, and the two arm rings, but a number of Hauk's belongings as well.

"Thank you," she said to Egil while two of the sailors held Zoya who would surely attack her. She spoke in a foreign language, possibly Russian, and was clearly hurling curses at Kirstin.

Kirstin put the necklace and two arm rings on, then picked up a sack of Hauk's belts and brooches, along with some gold coins and a silver chalice. She let Zoya keep the wrist watch she'd placed in Hauk's trunk when its battery ran out. With a look of disdain at Zoya for her thieving, Kirstin walked back to shore, listening to Zoya screeching the whole time behind her. Egil was not going to have a pleasant journey. Kirstin watched until the longship was out of sight.

Walking back to the keep, she felt like she was still floating in the afterglow of her night with Hauk. She'd told him that she loved him, and she did, which filled her with joy. And fear. Because she wasn't sure what the future held for them.

She shrugged. It was in God's hand.

Just then, she noticed some color off to the left, beyond the beached ships. She really hadn't explored much outside the longhouse. When she got there, she saw a carpet of moss near a bend in the fjord, surrounded by some hardy wildflowers, surprising for this time of year. She decided to gather a bunch to put in water, which would be a cheery sight. Besides, they would be dead once the first frost hit, which came early this far north. On the other hand, she thought, sniffing the flowers, which still retained some fragrance, maybe she could use them in the soapmaking she planned for that afternoon.

Sitting down on the velvety moss a short time later, her back propped against a rock, she thought this was a rather magical spot, the kind little girls would adopt to play pretend games, or a quiet place for older girls to read or write in journals. Looking more closely at the pile of flowers on her lap—Christmas roses, winter jasmine, and irises—she realized they were really rather pathetic, on their last legs, almost dry, not as vibrant as she'd thought. Still, she was reminded of her father's Blue Dragon vineyard which had a field of wildflowers which was never mowed and therefore provided lovely blooms during three seasons. Moss was abundant there, too, beside the pond.

She closed her eyes and imagined that field, picturing herself as a young girl just lying there on a green mossy coverlet in the midst of a floral bed, no doubt pretending she was some fairy princess, like Sleeping Beauty. Suddenly, a shiver rippled over her skin, and she folded her arms over her chest, her fingers inadvertently touching the arm rings.

With a gasp, she stood, realizing what could happen, but it was too late. Without any warning, she felt dizzy and fainted into the bed of flowers. A short time later, she was home.

But it wasn't Haukshire.

Sometimes, love sucks, even for a Viking...

THE HUNTING TRIP lasted longer than Hauk had anticipated, ten days. Not because they hadn't found a bounty of large game, but more because they had been so successful and wanted to bring these carcasses back to process for preservation. There would be plenty of time for another, even two additional hunting trips. It was always good to have more food on hand in case the winter was harsher than usual.

The twelve men in his party, divided into six groups, now carried on long poles and a sledge the gutted carcasses and skins of six deer, eight boar, and a moose. Some of them might return for a large bear they'd spotted, but first they would have to skin and cut up this meat and prepare it for drying, salting, smoking, or cold storage in underground pits. Later, they would stretch and dry the skins.

Still some distance from Haukshire, they were greeted by three whooping youthlings, Gorm and his former tormentors, now comrades-in-mischief, who had no business being so far from home, being not yet weaponed, but he couldn't dampen their eagerness. They were speaking all at once, elbowing each other, jumping up and down, and Hauk found it impossible to decipher what they were saying. In the end, Hauk realized they were simply excited about the outcome of the other hunting parties...fishing, birding, and small game. Apparently, the cold cellar was now filling with the meat of squirrels, geese, ducks, turkey, and sea birds. All kinds of fish had been dried and salted, including cod, haddock, mackerel, halibut, pike, perch, and flounder, according to the three scamps who tried to outdo each other in reciting the names of the catches. And they said that the younger children had been sent out to gather nuts and late mushrooms under Signe's guidance, which at the present filled two barrels. What these three urchins had contributed wasn't clear.

Hauk was only glad that Gorm had managed to fit in with the others. It could be a lonely existence being an outcast of sorts in one's own home. He noticed one of his men speaking to the tallest of the boys, a hand on his shoulder. Hauk, who'd assumed they were all orphans, decided this must be the father of at least one of them.

Haukshire would survive the winter, that soon became clear. Leastways, they would not starve.

The three boys preened with pride when Hauk told them they could help carry the weapons. Not that they contributed that much, but that was not the point, of course.

As they walked the last distance to the keep, Hauk wanted to ask about Kirstin, what she was doing, did she appear happy, had she mentioned him, but he feared what he would reveal of his feelings, or, gods forbid, what the bratlings might reveal. No doubt she had been putting them to work, and that was why they'd escaped to come meet the hunting party.

Despite how busy he'd been these ten days, Hauk hadn't been able to stop thinking about Kirstin. Their last night together had been nothing less than amazing, and in the end, her declaring her love, his doing likewise...well, what man wouldn't be anxious to continue the relationship, whatever it was? He couldn't wait to see her again.

But first, there was chaos when the hunting party arrived in the back courtyard and began to unload their animals. No time for thinking of anything else. Makeshift tables had already been set up when the small game had been cut up and prepared for preservation earlier that week. So, they laid out the deer first. The men did the cutting under Signe's supervision. He saw Frida point to a haunch of venison, and one of the housecarls carried it inside for her.

Hauk was pleased to have missed the processing of the birds. Didn't matter if they were turkeys or geese or smaller quail, plucking the feathers was a distasteful, tiresome business. There was no worse smell than scalded feathers. To him, leastways. Not that he'd ever done much with fowl, that being women's work.

Several dozen people, men and women, worked together efficiently at assigned tasks, including those from the hunting party who wanted nothing more than to bathe and relax in the hall with a mug or five of mead. He saw Bjorn and Thorkel carrying a large sow. "Hear you did well with the fishing," he said, squeezing his son's shoulder.

Bjorn grinned at him. "Yea, and it was fun. I'm thinking of going again tomorrow, up near the entrance to the sea. Someone mentioned seeing a shark."

"Mayhap I'll go with you," Hauk said.

The smile Bjorn gave him then made him feel both wonderful and awful, knowing how many years of these kinds of opportunities he'd missed by his own neglect. Oh, well! There was always the future.

A short time later, Hauk looked around, then looked again more closely, and realized Kirstin was not there. His hands and tunic were grimy from handling the wild game. So, he wiped his hands on his braies, then headed toward the back door of the keep. Kirstin must be inside, helping the cook ready a feast to celebrate the success of all the hunting, trapping, and fishing expeditions. He was a mite offended that she hadn't come out to greet him, but then he shrugged. Mayhap she wanted their reunion to be a private one. He could appreciate that, he thought with a grin.

On his way, he noticed several people staring at him oddly. Almost like trepidation. Or was it pity?

On entering the keep, he glanced around the kitchen and saw only Frida, who was cutting the deer meat into small pieces and tossing them into a cauldron, which he presumed would be some kind of stew. It was too late in the day to roast such a large haunch for the evening meal. "Frida! Where is my wife?"

"Ye doan hafta yell," she said.

"Sorry. Where is she?" He began to walk toward the hall.

"She's gone."

Hauk stopped in his tracks and turned slowly to stare at

the old lady who was wringing her hands nervously. "What do you mean, she's gone?"

Frida shrugged. "A sennight or so ago, when Egil was leavin' fer Hedeby, she disappeared."

"She's not here, at Haukshire?" he said dumbly.

"That's what I jist said, isn't it?"

He narrowed his eyes at her tone of voice.

"Sorry, but I been worried 'bout how to tell you. Everyone has."

"Disappeared!" he muttered. "How long ago?"

"Since the day Egil left, I already tol' ye that."

Hauk groaned. This must be a jest of some kind. He hoped it was. With a grunt of disgust, he turned and stomped into the hall which was mostly empty, then went to all the bedchambers, which were also empty. After that, he did a more thorough check of his bedchamber and the guest one he'd been sharing with Kirstin. The first was a mess of tossed linens and upended chests, thanks to Zoya, he assumed. The other was alarmingly neat and tidy, as if no one had slept here for days.

He frowned with confusion and went back outside to find Signe, who had been somewhat of a friend to Kirstin. He found her standing with Thorkel who was hunkered down a bit so they were eye level. Laughing, he appeared to be trying to convince her of something to which the wench was shaking her head. "Leave off, Thorkel, and go help Ketil with that moose. Your seduction can wait till later."

"You call that seduction?" Signe scoffed at Thorkel. She turned to Hauk then and explained, "He said he dreamed about me this past sennight. In particular, he dreamed of my feet."

Thorkel grinned. "In my defense, I dreamed of her feet up in the air whilst I made love to her."

"Hmpfh!" Signe said.

Thorkel winked at her.

"This is all amusing, Thorkel, but you are needed to split that moose. Heft half onto the table and hang the other half in the smoking shed."

Thorkel went off, giving Signe a little wave. "We will discuss this further this evening, my fair Signe."

Signe just shook her head at Thorkel's hopelessness, but Hauk could see that a smile was twitching at her lips.

Hauk took Signe by the elbow and led her away from the others. "So, Signe, tell me what happened to Kirstin."

"I do not know. She was here one moment and a short time later she was nowhere about. I think she may have gone with Egil."

"What makes you say that?" The last night he'd spent with Kirstin had been wonderful, for both of them. He was shocked that she would leave him, without warning, after that. But he had to ask, "Did she say anything to you that morning? Was she unhappy?"

"Nay. If anything, she appeared to have a secret smile on her face."

Of course she did. In truth, I had, too. "What makes you think she went with Egil then?"

"Well, she did go down to the boat before Egil left. Actually, she spoke to Egil out in the courtyard. She seemed to be alarmed about what he said, then ran into the keep and into the bedchambers to look for something. A short time later, she was screaming at Egil, who was already on the longship, as she ran toward the fjord, demanding that he let her board."

"All this you witnessed?"

She shook her head. "Some I saw with my own eyes. The rest I pieced together from what others said."

"And she left with Egil on the longship then?"

"I think so, but I wasn't watching at the time. I'd gone back into the keep to gather laundry."

"Did *anyone* actually see her on the boat as it left?"

"I do not think so." Signe furrowed her brow as she searched her memory. She frowned then. "Another thing. My Lady Kirstin was excited about the soap-making we were planning for that afternoon. Why would she leave if that was her intent?"

"Mayhap it was a last-minute decision," he offered.

"Egil should be back any day now. You will find out then." She shrugged and went back to the racks where she'd been hanging strips of venison for drying.

In truth, Hauk was hoping that Kirstin *had* gone to Hedeby with Egil, for whatever demented reason she might have, like a sudden need for beeswax, or fine fabric to make her strange undergarments, or more poultry to make chicken slop.

Otherwise, she was gone. Really gone.

His heart ached so much at that prospect he had to bend over to catch a breath. It had only been a few sennights since he'd first met her. How could he be so affected?

If this was love, he wanted nothing to do with it.

～

Who let the dogs out?...

KIRSTIN FELT HAUK KISSING HER FACE. Wet, sloppy kisses. Playful.

She smiled.

What a way to wake up! She kept her eyes closed and turned her face a bit, giving him better access. She'd been sleeping and was only half-awake now. Hauk must have returned from the hunting trip.

She stretched and yawned, feeling that continuing ache between her legs, a not unpleasant reminder of last night. She hoped Hauk ached, too, if that was possible for a man. She smiled some more.

Just then, she noticed an odd odor. Well, Hauk had been on a hunting trip and was no doubt a little ripe. Maybe they could go to the bathing hut together, like they had that other time.

But no, this wasn't BO.

It was…wet dog.

Her eyes shot open and she saw Loki and Baldr, her father's golden retrievers, whose damp fur was evidence of a recent dip in the pond. Which she could see over their backs. Their lolling tongues and wagging tails spoke of their happiness to see her. The dogs started to bark, loudly and continuously, ran away, continuing to bark as they ran, then came barreling back to her, yipping as if to give her some message. They ran away again and returned with her father, who was stunned at first sight of her.

Her father was almost sixty years old, and he wore his usual jeans and Blue Dragon T-shirt, but he could have passed for a Viking anywhere. With his long, gray-threaded, brown hair hanging in war braids on either side of a Nordic sculpted face, not to mention a tall, still buff body, he looked like an older version of the actor playing Rollo on that History Channel's *Vikings* series, which made her realize that if her father had been the one shot back in time, he would fit in the Nordic atmosphere perfectly, almost as if he'd never left twenty years ago.

"Sit!" her father ordered the two yapping pets, who did as he ordered, immediately, though they continued to bark. "And shut the bloody hell up!"

Whimpering to get the last "word" in, Loki and Baldr splatted out, putting their faces on their front paws, looking at him contritely.

"Dumb dogs," her father muttered, then turned to her

again. "Holy Thor! Is it really you, Kirstin? We have been so worried."

By now, she was standing, equally stunned. When her father opened his arms to her, she rushed into his embrace. He held her tightly and asked one question after another, not waiting for a reply.

"Where have you been, sweetling?

"Are you all right?

"Did you go back in time?

"Of course you did.

"The Viking in a cage…was he there? Did you rescue him?

"Torolf wanted to travel back to help you, if he could, but Helga said it would be over her dead body.

"Did you go back to our homestead, by any chance?

"But all these questions can wait. Come, let's go up to the house."

Her father pulled back to look at her then. That's when she burst out in sobs, crying, knowing that her heart was breaking. Yes, she'd managed to come back home, but that meant she would never see Hauk again.

They said that love transcends time. It appeared she would have a chance to test that theory.

CHAPTER 20

Heartbreak Hotel, or Heartbreak House...um, Longhouse...

*K*irstin was not with Egil when he returned the next day.

Egil told Hauk that he hadn't seen his wife since she'd disembarked from his boat here at Haukshire a sennight or so ago, carrying her stolen necklet and arm rings, along with a sack of Hauk's purloined treasures. Hauk told Egil not to discuss Kirstin's whereabouts with anyone or add to the speculation. Let them think she'd left Hauk by going to Hedeby and probably to her own land beyond that. Otherwise, Hauk would have to explain time travel, or try to.

Egil nodded and squeezed Hauk's arm in sympathy.

The tiny thread of hope that Hauk had been holding onto snapped, and he had to accept that his wife had time-traveled, away from him.

The only good news Egil had to impart was that Zoya was also gone, finally and forever, now in the hands of her brother. The Hedeby samovar merchant, who was not happy with his sister, would undoubtedly make her life miserable, or more likely, she would make his life miserable.

As the days and then sennights went by, Hauk became more and more woeful. Drinking to the point of drukkinness was not helping. To his shame, he realized he had been hoping she would return, magically, but time and her continuing absence convinced him otherwise. After that, fury filled Hauk, that his wife had deserted him, even though she'd promised she would not leave, leastways not without warning him first. *Pfff!* He felt like a fool. A cripple. Less than a man.

Women! Who can trust them?

The skalds would probably be telling tales of his humiliation, along with all those sagas about a caged Viking. He did not care.

He wished he could say he hated her now, but he didn't. In fact, in his more sane moments, he knew she was better off, safer, in those later times, under her father's protection. But in his less sane moments, which was most of the time, he was filled with a boiling rage. And, unfortunately, it spilled over to everyone who gave the least offense. He'd noticed how many people avoided him of late, even Egil, who approached him last night. "It's been almost three months now. How long are ye goin' to have this burr up your arse?"

"As long as it takes," Hauk had snarled.

Other than Kirstin's betrayal, and that's how he regarded her departure, he had many reasons to be happy, or at least gratified these days. Thanks to additional hunting, fishing, and birding expeditions, more than enough provender had been stowed in the cold cellars, the storage rooms, and the barns, even if the gods should give them the harshest weather ever. Egil had brought back a bull and another milk cow, six dozen chickens, and two of the most vicious goats, all of which provided even more sustenance for the winter which was already upon them. In fact, snow flurries were coming down now, and he expected the ground would be at least knee-high by the morning. He stomped his boots at the entrance to the kitchen, he stiffened when Frida called out, "Ye do know that the yule season is almost upon us?"

"Um...yea," he answered tentatively. "And so?"

"What plans have ye made?"

"Huh?"

"What kind of yule feast are ye plannin'? Will ye be wantin' the hall decorated? Gifts fer all the children and coins fer all the Haukshire folks? How 'bout guests? Will ye be havin' any yule guests?"

"Huh?" he said again.

Frida rolled her eyes and muttered under her breath.

"What did you say?"

She mumbled something again.

"Come now, Frida. You've never been afraid to speak your mind before."

Frida clapped her hands together over the table where she'd been doing something with oat flour, probably making the flat, circular breads with the hole in their centers, to be stored on a pole by the hearth, once baked. They were much favored by the Norse people because they required no leavening. Then she put her hands on her hips, and turned to glare at him. "If ye'd quit feelin' sorry fer yerself, and moved yer arse to see what yer people need, ye wouldn't be dawdlin' over the yule feast. Moonin' about like an orphaned calf, ye are."

If he wasn't in such a bad mood, he would laugh at the amusing picture she made. A woman of more than fifty years who was a head shorter than him, skinny as a broom handle, with flour dusting her face and hair. Even the brooches that held together the shoulder straps on the long, open-sided apron were covered with flour. She picked up a long ladle and shook it at him like a weapon. Was she threatening to knock him on the head with it if he didn't heed her words? 'Twould be like a puppy facing off with a bear.

"Move my arse, huh?" He arched his brows. "Have I not repaired all the cotters' homes? Have I not filled all the store-rooms with more provisions than anyone has seen at Hauk-shire in many a year? Have I not been a fair judge in matters of dispute? Are we not at peace with our neighbors, or least-ways not at war?"

She waved the ladle dismissively. "Yea, ye are to be commended fer doin' more than yer father did."

"Thank you so much for your wonderful compliment!"

"Doan be plyin' me with yer sarcasm. I jist meant that ye need to get yerself in order and stop with yer drinkin'. Another thing…"

He was the one rolling his eyes now.

"Mayhap ye need to find yerself another woman to plow. Mayhap ye shouldn't have sent Zoya away, gods forbid."

Nay, he did not regret Zoya's absence. And he was far from ready "to plow" another woman.

"Another thing—"

"Oh, please, not another thing," he tried to joke.

She didn't laugh. More waving of the ladle to get his atten-tion. "Ye need to find someone to perform a weddin' cere-mony. Mebbe during that feast ye haven't yet planned."

"Whose wedding?"

"Thorkel and Signe."

"What? He never said anything to me."

"And why would he when ye've been too fuzzy-brained and snarly these past sennights?"

He was about to argue that Thorkel had had plenty of opportunities to approach him, and that he wasn't fuzzy-brained or snarly all the time, but just then he was distracted by Gorm huffing and puffing as he dragged a huge, obvi-ously heavy bag across the threshold from outside. His unruly hair and grubby tunic were covered with snow flakes. Someone needed to show that boyling the bath hut again.

"What is *that?*" Hauk asked.

"I found this." He wiped his runny nose with the sleeve of his tunic. "Over by the place beyond the boats...you know, where all them purty flowers grow."

Hauk looked at Frida to see if she understood what Gorm meant.

"There's a pretty damp patch over by the upper fjord where flowers seem to thrive, without any care. One of yer grandmothers planted them flower seeds years ago."

This was all news to Hauk. He walked over to Gorm and dumped the contents of the bag on the floor. There was a gold chalice, one of his favorite belts, a handful of coins, and some sodden fabric.

"Thass the stuff that Zoya stole, isn't it?" Frida asked.

Hauk nodded slowly. This must be the bag that Kirstin had supposedly been holding when she got off of the longship. "Show me where you found it," he told Gorm. The hairs on the back of his neck rose in foreboding.

Shortly after that, they arrived at the spot that Gorm indicated. While snow was coming down more heavily now and starting to stick on the ground, this area was somewhat sheltered by nearby trees. So, at least for now, the mossy ground was bare, but the flowers long dead. There was nothing here. Certainly not the necklet and the two arm rings that Egil had said Kirstin was carrying, along with the bag, when he'd last seen her.

Hauk's heart dropped.

This was the place where Kirstin had left him, leaving behind the heavy bag that belonged to him. He didn't know why this particular spot would be Kirstin's point of return to the future, but he was convinced that it had been.

It was final then. Kirstin was gone. And she would not be returning.

So much for love!

~

This is what she'd wanted. Wasn't it?...

HER FATHER HELPED her walk across the lawn to the house. She felt kind of weak and leaned against his broad shoulder for support. While she no longer sobbed, tears did leak from her eyes.

She wasn't sure why she was crying. Well, yes, she did. It was Hauk.

I will never see him again.

What must he think about my disappearance?

He will think I left, deliberately.

After he told me that he loves me.

It must seem like a slap in the face to him.

And I told him that I love him, too.

He'll think I lied.

"Oh, Daddy," she moaned. "It is such a mess."

"Now, dearling, it can't be that bad. You are not to worry. We will fix everything. Just you relax and let your father take care of you," he said, kissing the top of her head.

If only he could! Like he did when I was a child. But I'm not a child anymore, and some problems are too big to fix.

As they approached the side of the old Victorian house, Kirstin noticed the warmer weather, compared to the cooler climate she'd just left. Being November, or at least it should be, the air was balmy, even for winter in northern California.

They walked up the steps to the wraparound porch and her father ordered the dogs, who'd followed them, "Stay!"

They plopped to the floor in a sunny spot, while she and her father crossed the porch and entered the kitchen..

Her stepmother, Angela, was standing before the commercial-sized gas range, stirring what smelled like her famous Shrimp Carbonara. Despite being more than fifty years old, Angela still looked as trim and professional in a designer track suit, her black hair perfectly coifed into a short bob, as she had when she was a Hollywood PR person.

"What was all that barking about, darling?" Angela asked, without turning around.

"Look what the dogs found down by the pond," her father said.

"Those dogs better not have caught another skunk. Last time they brought a dead skunk inside it took me a week to get rid of the stink."

Her father chuckled. "No, they found something better."

Angela turned around, a wooden spoon in her hand. Seeing Kirstin, she screamed, dropped the spoon, and ran toward her, giving her a huge hug and refusing to let go, despite her father laughing and saying, "Hold off, Angie, you're going to crush Kirstin."

Angela backed away, finally, but didn't release Kirstin totally. She held her shoulders with extended arms and said, "Oh, my dear, we have been so worried!" Kirstin had been fourteen years old when her father married this kind woman, whose family had owned Blue Dragon vineyard for generations. Her father had been a farmer back in his old country. He liked to say that love turned him from turnips to grapes. "Are you all right?"

Kirstin nodded, and her father pulled out a chair at the table for her to sit down. He sat on the chair closest to her and took one of her hands in both of his. Angela put a glass of water in front of Kirstin and sat on the chair on her other side. She poured iced tea for herself and her husband.

Kirstin drank greedily, not having realized how thirsty she was. God bless Angela for noticing. Angela also handed her a tissue.

"Tell us," her father urged.

Kirstin started from the beginning in the great hall of Uncle Jorund's Rosestead, leading to her entry in King Aethelred's Saxon castle. She told them that the arm rings that Storvald had made for her seemed to be the trigger for her time travel.

Her father gazed at the arm rings with some trepidation that she might somehow be shot back again. He was probably right to think she should be cautious; so, she picked up a dish towel sitting on the table and used it as a buffer to remove the rings and place them on the table.

She continued the story about how Hauk got out of the cage, and started to describe their escape from the castle and how they met up with Sweyn Forkbeard.

"Whoa, whoa, whoa, did you say you got married?" her father asked.

"Well, yes, but I'm not sure how valid it was...is. I mean there's no law regulating trans-century marriages. Ha, ha, ha," she tried to joke.

"Married?" Angela said, wide-eyed. "To a man in a cage?"

"He was no longer in a cage by then."

"How did you get married...I mean, who married you? Was there a law speaker?" Vikings, especially those of upper classes, usually employed a law speaker at one of their Things to perform the ceremony.

"No, it was a priest. Actually, an archbishop," she revealed.

Angela, who was a devout Catholic, looked impressed. Her father looked concerned.

"Does that mean that the marriage would be valid?" Kirstin asked.

"I would think so," Angela offered, tentatively.

Her father shook his head with dismay, then said, "Hold on with your story. I think we need something stronger than iced tea to hear this tale."

Soon, a decanted bottle of vintage Blue Dragon wine sat on the table and three wine glasses were filled to the brims.

As she continued telling them about her adventure, both Angela and her father intermittently asked questions. Her father wanted to know the details of the battle, what kind of weapons were used, and what size of longship Hauk had used when he kidnapped her. Angela was more interested in the ladies in the Saxon court, the food served, and wasn't it romantic that her husband had "kidnapped" her?

That latter remark of Angela's caused a grunt of disapproval from Kirstin's father. What man wants his daughter to be kidnapped?

Even though it was only a cursory summary she gave of the events, Kirstin noticed that they'd gone through one full bottle of wine and half of another. She was beginning to feel the effects.

Her father's brow furrowed with puzzlement, and Kirstin could tell he had a lot more questions. "Why did you say things were a mess when we were walking to the house? Why were you wailing like a cat with its tail caught in a trap?"

"Because I fell in love with Hauk."

"I knew it, I knew it!" Angela sighed.

Her father, who was not a sentimentalist, made a sound of disgust. "And did he fall in love with you, too?"

She nodded, unable to speak over the sudden lump in her throat.

"You said your return was accidental," Angela remarked. "Would you have tried to come back, deliberately, if given a chance?"

"I don't know."

"What a mess!" her father concluded.

SANDRA HILL

~

Vikings had busybodies, too...

"YOU SHOULD PLAN on going a-Viking first thing next spring," Egil advised. "Nothing like a little plunderin' to wipe the mind clear."

Didn't we bring enough plunder back from Aethelred's royal court?

"We could use snowshoes and travel north to where the polar bears roam. A white bed fur would make you forget soon enough." This from Horrick, one of his best hunters.

And freeze my toes, and another important body part?

Bjorn had another gripe. "I thought you were giving me a mother. Couldn't you have been nicer to her?"

I tried.

Frida didn't waste words, "Go find the girl."

As if I could!

"What you need is a good tupping," Thorkel said.

With whom?

The voice in his head had yet another opinion. *"Pray."*

In essence, everyone felt the need to give Hauk love advice. Was he so pitiful? He determined to stop acting like a lamebrained idiot. If nothing else, he should keep these emotions inside.

Hauk did not forget about Kirstin after that. Nor did he stop hurting at her betrayal, when he allowed himself to think about it. But he kept busy, from daybreak to bedtime, and could say that he was surviving. It helped that he gave Signe and Frida free rein to plan both the wedding and yule feast, which might have been a mistake since the entire keep, from the barns to the great hall, were decorated with evergreen boughs. And the sweet succulent scents that emanated from the kitchen tempted even the most hardened warrior who claimed a preference for a meaty bone of beef or pork.

To his surprise, his neighbor Ingolf, the one who lusted after Haukshire lands, invited Hauk to join his family at Stormstead for a yuletide celebration. The date did not interfere with Hauk's plans, but he had no desire to be away from his estate at this time of year. However, he felt the need to reciprocate the invitation, and, to his disgust, Ingolf accepted on behalf of himself and his family.

"You know why he's extendin' the hand of friendship, don't ye?" Frida said.

"Nay. Why?"

"He has two unwed daughters," Frida told him with a cackle at his obvious dismay. "If he can't get his hands on yer lands by force, he'll do it by marriage."

"You jest," he said.

Frida just laughed.

CHAPTER 21

Home is where the heart is...

Kirstin slept for twelve straight hours. Well, she got up twice during the night from her bed in her old bedroom, once to pee, and another time to get a glass of water to combat her wine-dried mouth. She had been both hopeful and afraid that she would dream of Hauk, but her slumber had been dream-free.

She finally awakened to the gleam of a morning sun and the sound of voices.

Lots of voices.

From a distance.

Downstairs.

Or outside.

Maybe both.

Lying still, with her eyes closed, she tried to discern the voices. There was Torolf. And Ragnor. And her sister Madrene. Her father must have called everyone last night, and now they were all here, or arriving, by the sound of car doors slamming. Each of them would be wanting to welcome her, but also to get the real story of her time travel.

Kirstin sighed. She wasn't sure that she wanted to be drowning in family so soon, but maybe it was for the best. The less she was able to think, the less miserable she would be. Or so she told herself.

By that evening, all...every single one...of her half-brothers and sisters were there. Even Jogeir. Actually all eleven of her siblings were halfies because her father had had so many wives and concubines, though thankfully not all at the same time; so, while they all had the same father, there were numerous mothers, most or all of whom had died or run off when they realized there were so many children to care for. Except for Angela. By the time they'd arrived in modern day California, her father had turned monogamist. No more extra wives or mistresses. Angela would never have stood for that, and hopefully her father no longer had the inclination to spread his virility.

Kirstin took a long shower, one of the things she'd missed most while in the past. She blow-dried her hair and pulled the long hair back into a ponytail. No make-up. Just some lip gloss and mascara to her blonde eyelashes. After that, she dressed in beige yoga pants and a multi-colored sweater which had been left here from a previous visit.

Finally, she was ready to brave the assault of her family. And it was an assault of sorts, a well-intended but almost overwhelming barrage of hugs, cries, laughs, questions, opinions, and enough food to feed a Viking army. It wasn't just Angela who'd been busy in the kitchen, but her half-sister Marie, the professional chef-in-training at some culinary school in Colorado, shared the stove. Marie must have hopped a plane as soon as her father called. Same was no doubt true of Dagny who'd come from FBI headquarters in Virginia. And now she sat talking to Torolf and Hamr, who'd come up from San Diego to welcome her home, along with Madrene, Ian, and Njal.

She'd already described her time-travel "adventure" twice now, but then she had to repeat it again for those who arrived via later flights: Kolbein, a priest from his parish in Florida, Lida, who was from New York City, and Jogeir, who'd come, not from his home in Iceland, but Chicago, where he'd been attending an international farm conference. Storvald was particularly interested to find out that it was the arm rings he'd made for Kirstin that proved to be a time-travel device.

Kolbein, of course, disagreed, and said it was God's doing, not some particular object, like a boat wreck, or lightning, or a piece of jewelry.

Kirstin wanted to ask Kolbein if that meant that God did not want her to be with Hauk, but she'd yet to discuss the emotional entanglements of her trip.

Her father walked up to where they were all sitting around the dining room table and passed around bottles of beer and glasses of wine before commenting, "So, did she tell you she got married?"

Everyone turned to look at Kirstin.

"No, she failed to mention that," Lida said.

"He must have been really hot. Bet he was Hollywood good-looking. Was he good looking?" Dagny asked.

"Like some kind of Viking god, I'll bet," Marie added, nodding her agreement at Dagny.

"Bet the sex was spectacular," Madrene remarked.

"Madrene!" her father rebuked. "Betimes you go too far."

Madrene just shrugged and grinned.

"And did she tell you she was married by an archbishop in the Saxon church?" Marie asked, coming in with a tray of cheeses and crackers.

Kolbein looked at Kirstin steadily and said, "Well, that settles it then."

Kirstin wasn't sure what Kolbein meant, and she wasn't about to ask. Not now, anyhow, in front of everyone.

Eventually, everyone who lived in the state left, each of them giving their opinion or advice. Despite her long sleep of the night before, Kirstin felt totally depleted...exhausted mentally and physically. All those who lived out of state stayed overnight. They were all in the living room, chatting, while her father streamed his favorite *Vikings* episodes, with the volume turned off.

But Kirstin didn't think she could talk anymore. She was about to sneak off when Dagny caught up with her and asked, "Do you still have that drawing I did for you when you described the man you saw in your dreams?"

Her question surprised Kirstin because she had totally forgotten that day when Dagny did a drawing for Kirstin based only on the dream image. "I think I do." She went up to her bedroom and pulled out a dresser drawer. Yes, there it was, at the bottom, under some underwear. When she went back to the dining room, where Dagny had laid out her sketch pads and charcoal, she put the rendering on the table.

"Well?" Dagny asked. "Does it look like him?"

Kirstin looked down, and her heart skipped a beat. "It does, and it doesn't," she said. "His cheeks are wider, but the bones are more sculpted in the Nordic fashion. The lips are wrong. Hauk's lips are fuller, and they should have a slight grin on them. The eyes...hmm, I'm not sure what's off. He has what I call talking eyes. When they look at you, you know exactly what he is feeling."

Dagny went to work, her fingers working deftly, following some more tweaks that Kirstin suggested. It took several tries, making corrections according to Kirstin's memories, before she was finished. When Dagny lifted up the final product, Kirstin just nodded, unable to speak at first over the lump in her throat. Finally, she said, "It's almost perfect."

"Good! Be careful in framing it. The charcoal could smudge if it's not done professionally."

Kirstin felt an odd sadness at Dagny's suggestion. It was as if her sister was assuming she would never see Hauk again and would want to have some memento. But wasn't that a given? Why would Kirstin even harbor a different opinion? She was home where she was supposed to be.

Wasn't she?

~

The road to recovery is a bumpy one...

LIFE GOES ON, and so did Hauk.

He'd finally resigned himself to the fact that Kirstin had left him and he would never see her again. There remained a dull ache in the region of his heart when he allowed himself to think of her, which wasn't often during his hard-working, demanding days, but the nights...ah, the nights were difficult, especially since he was no longer falling into bed only when he was blindfuller with drink. What he needed was a woman to while away those late hours, but that would have to wait until the springtime when he was no longer landlocked. For now, he survived. Even so, it hurt.

He swore to himself that he would never again in the future allow himself to be so emotionally entangled with a woman. Love? *Ha!* From now on, it would be lust, and only lust.

"Are you ready to perform our wedding?" Thorkel asked, coming up behind him in the great hall where Hauk sat at one of the far trestle tables.

"*Pff!* As ready as I will ever be," Hauk replied, knowing that his friend was taking great pleasure in Hauk's discomfort over such a duty. Usually the duty fell to the lawspeaker at the

Viking assemblies called Things, or Althings where many weddings took place, or at some royal estate where a lawspeaker was in residence, but since they had no such person here, Thorkel had asked Hauk if he'd perform the task for him and Signe.

Hauk had tried to pass the chore off to Egil. After all, Egil had been married enough times, and should know the words by now. But Egil had outright refused. "Me, I'd rather kiss a boar's arse as speak the ancient words afore a crowd of drinking Norsemen, not that I remember them," he'd scoffed.

Hauk's sentiments exactly.

Signe and Frida followed after Thorkel, one carrying a pitcher of ale and the other four wooden goblets. Hauk had asked them to come share a cup with him to discuss some plans to be made, both for the wedding and the yule feasts. The Vikings celebrated twelve days of yule, or Jol, from the solstice onward. The Winter Solstice, the longest night of the year, would arrive a mere two sennights from this Thursday, with much to be arranged.

If Hauk had a wife, she would be the one doing all this planning. Not him. Hauk didn't want to think about the irony of his actually having a wife, but having to do this anyway.

"You two still want to marry on Jul eve?" Hauk asked. "We could do it during the first night of the Jul feasts." Which made more sense to him, lumping all of these celebrations together.

Signe and Thorkel looked at each other and nodded at some understanding they must have decided on aforehand. He noticed that they held hands, even as they sipped at their drinks.

Signe spoke for the two of them. "We prefer our ceremony to be separate from the yule ones. It would have more meaning to us on a separate day."

Thorkel's face flushed and he took a quick swig of ale to

cover his embarrassment. It was obvious this was Signe's idea, and he was going along with her, to avoid an argument. Smart man!

"You do not have to worry about anything. The decorations, the food to be served, the music. We will do everything," Signe was quick to add.

Except perform the ceremony.

And was I supposed to be worrying about these things?

And what's this about music?

Aarrrgh!

"By the by, I hope no one is expecting us to hold a feast for twelve days. The first and last night will be it," he declared, and he didn't care if it went against tradition or expectations or anything else, or if folks started calling him "The Grumpy Viking," along with "The Caged Viking," or "The Forsaken Viking," all of which he'd overheard in passing. This jarl business was getting more involved than he'd ever imagined. He would resign, if he could.

"So, is Ingolf still planning a yule visit?" Thorkel asked, having the good sense to change the subject.

"Yea, he is. He and his family and guardsmen will arrive three days before Jul begins, in plenty of time for your wedding." He waggled his eyebrows at the two of them.

"How will they get here? The snow is thigh high, and even though we keep paths dug to the out buildings and cotters' homes, I can't see them tramping by foot through the snow." This from Thorkel, who'd had to supervise much of that digging.

"As long as there is a crust of ice on top of the snow, he will probably come in a sleigh," Hauk mused. "That means you must make sure there is room in the barn for the horses, both the ones pulling the sleigh and those ridden by any retainers he might bring."

Thorkel nodded.

"I will need to have the bedchambers and bed closets made up for all of them," Signe said. "What do you plan?"

Again, they expect me to be planning these things? By the gods, I wish I were off a-Viking, or wintering in the Rus lands. Anyplace without all these responsibilities. He sighed and decided, "We will let Ingolf and his wife have my bedchamber. His two daughters will share the guest bedchamber. And you and Thorkel will get Bjorn's bedchamber for the yule season."

"Nay, you cannot do that," Signe protested. "Where would you and Bjorn sleep."

"In bed closets. It won't be the first time for either of us," Hauk said.

"Really, Hauk, we appreciate the offer, but we had planned to use one of the cotters' huts," Thorkel said.

"Nay! This is our wedding gift to you, mine and Bjorn's."

They agreed, reluctantly, but thankfully, compromising that they would use that bedchamber for their wedding night only.

"Now, what about the food, Frida?"

"We will do several haunches of venison for the wedding. Signe is working with me on the menu. Then, for the yule feast, we will roast the traditional boar," his cook told him. Frida had been uncommonly quiet during all this discussion, up till now. No doubt she was still harboring ill feelings toward him since he'd snapped at her two days ago when she asked if he was ever going to look for his missing wife.

"You have everything you need?" Hauk asked her, kindly, wanting to make peace.

"I do, especially with all the extra vegetables and spices that Egil brought back from Hedeby." She did not mention all the game he and his hunting party had brought back as well. Ah, well, she would get over her sulk with a few honeyed words. All women did.

"Thank you kindly, Frida. I knew I could count on you," he said, smiling at her.

She lifted her chin and gazed at him haughtily.

Well, mayhap it will take a little more time.

Frida and Signe left then to various duties, while he and Thorkel finished the rest of the ale in the pitcher.

"So, do you think your wife will allow you to go a-Viking next spring?" he asked Thorkel.

"What? Of course." Thorkel appeared insulted before he realized that Hauk was teasing.

"Originally, I thought to go amber-harvesting in the Baltics, but with our success in replenishing the larders here this winter, I am more inclined to adventure. Maybe those lands beyond Iceland."

"Where Lady Kirstin came from?"

"Nay, not that," he replied. "'Twould be impossible." Which was more true than Thorkel could realize since Kirstin came not just from a distant land but a distant time.

"Do you think she will ever come back?" Thorkel asked.

Hauk stiffened. Thorkel pushed the bounds of their friendship with his question, just had Frida had. Everyone knew it was a forbidden subject. Even so, Hauk answered, "Nay. She will never return." Then he added, "Even if she did, she would no longer be welcome."

Signs can be interpreted **in different ways, but a sign from God? Oh, boy!...**

Everything Kirstin did for the following weeks was seen through a Hauk filter.

When she went to a supermarket, she wondered, "What would Hauk think of such abundance?"

When she drove to her apartment in LA to get her work

laptop and research materials, she smiled. Hauk would love driving a car. No doubt he would have a lead foot on the accelerator.

When she watched her father working in the vineyard, she wondered if Hauk's family had ever tried to raise grapes. Probably not, not that far north.

When Torolf and Hamr visited one weekend and talked about their latest SEALs' mission, she realized that Hauk would probably fit in well with his warrior skills.

The last straw was when she accepted and went out on a date with JAM...Jacob Alvarez Mendoza...the Navy SEAL she'd been dating off and on for years. She sat across from him in a Salina restaurant, and couldn't help but notice how attractive he was, and nice. But she felt nothing. He was not Hauk.

After that, she stuck pretty close to home...Blue Dragon, that was. For some reason, she needed the comfort of her family, especially since the dean of her college at UCLA, Dr. Carter, assured her that her substitute was doing a fine job, and Kirstin would be welcome back next semester. Dr. Carter was even more accommodating because Kirstin had mentioned that she'd found some new research material that would enhance her doctoral thesis, which was to be presented after the new year. And that was the truth, but in a way her supervisor was not aware. All that Kirstin had witnessed and experienced during her time travel would enhance her thesis tremendously. And she did work diligently on her laptop every day.

But then she started streaming some of the old *Outlander* series, particularly the episodes where Claire decides to go back in time, again, and she is planning all the objects she could carry with her, like penicillin. Which was fine for Claire since she was a physician. Not so much for a college professor of Nordic studies.

Even so, Kirstin found herself compiling a list in her head of what she would take if she were going back, not that she was actually considering such a ridiculous notion. It became a sort of game.

Yes, a few photographs. One of her entire extended family taken last summer, all fifty-some of them. One of the Blue Dragon vineyard, with the house in the background. And pictures of a few other modern marvels.

Some antibiotics and over-the-counter painkillers might come in handy, but they would run out eventually. Maybe she should research some primitive herbal remedies.

Kirstin wasn't much for make-up, but she'd always been embarrassed by her light eyelashes, which appeared nonexistent in some lights. So, a few mascara wands might come in handy. And flavored lip glosses, she thought with a smile; Hauk would get a kick out of those. She'd missed having a mirror, but she couldn't lug such a fragile item through time, and she wasn't out to change history, or anything, with modern inventions, but a compact one might be possible.

Maybe an old-fashioned self-winding wrist watch, rather than a battery one, would be helpful. Jewelry itself held no appeal for her, and she didn't have much of it, anyway.

Underwear! Absolutely, several sets of underwear, and maybe some fabrics and elastic and fasteners to make more. But, no, she shouldn't do anything to alter history.

Tampons would be so convenient, and she wondered if she brought some as samples whether primitive ones could be made. And even though she wasn't much of a gardener, she could take packets of seeds, all kind of vegetables. Her father would know which would grow there.

She even researched methods for making soap with rudimentary materials, like ash, the way people of that time period already did. She also learned how to add scents to soap.

She had to remind herself that this was all just a game, not something she was actually considering.

But then one day, her brother Kolbein, the priest, came to visit. While they had a few moments alone when her father had to meet with a distributor and Angela started dinner, they decided to walk around the property for exercise. It was chilly...it was, after all, December, even if it was northern California...and they both wore fleece jackets.

"Will you be here for Christmas?" Kolbein asked.

The question surprised her. "Where else would I be?"

He raised his eyebrows at her.

"Kolbein! You of all people have to believe that my return here was an act of God."

He shrugged. "Probably, but that doesn't mean you can't go back if you really want to, God willing."

"I can't believe you are even suggesting such a thing."

"It's obvious that you're miserable."

"I thought I was doing a good job of hiding it."

"*Pff!* Let me ask you a private question, sister. When you were in the past with your husband...and, yes, I refer to him as your husband...weren't you afraid of getting pregnant? Wouldn't that have precluded you from coming back? I doubt you would have taken the chance if you carried a child."

"None of this was my doing, the going or coming back," she reminded him. *Or my not being pregnant. I was playing Russian Roulette with sex, and I knew it.* "It was all God's doing, or so we've always believed when it came to our time-travel experiences, Kolbein. That's why I say God must have intended me to return to the future."

Kolbein considered her words as they continued to walk. Finally, he seemed to come to some conclusion, and he stopped to look at her. "Has it occurred to you that God deliberately kept pregnancy from you...even when you returned, and still could have carried Hauk's seed...so that you would be free to return. I doubt you would ever risk taking a child on such a trip. The choice is all yours. God is all about free will."

Kirstin felt a wave of dizziness pass over her.

Should I go back?

Can I go back?

"Maybe we should both pray," Kolbein advised.

They did. On their knees, even.

That night, for the first time since her return, Kirstin dreamed about Hauk again. He was not in the cage, of course, but he was not happy. The loving expression she'd last seen on his face was no longer there. Instead, he flashed her a forbidding scowl. Was that a sign that she should go back, that he needed her, or a sign that he no longer wanted her?

She did not know.

CHAPTER 22

Dashing through the snow...

*H*auk was having a good time at the moment, which surprised him. He wasn't happy, or even contented, not all of the time, leastways, but he was mostly all right with his world. For a certainty, he was no longer mooning about like an orphan calf, as Frida had once accused.

Speaking of his opinionated cook, he had to give her credit for the wonderful job she'd done preparing for the Jul season. Signe, too. His keep had never appeared better, and the vast array of foods he'd seen when passing through the kitchen would equal that in any royal household.

In essence, he was proud to be the jarl of Haukshire, something he'd never expected when growing up, or during the years he'd deliberately stayed away. Mayhap it was something related to what Egil had said to him yestereve, "All evidence of yer father living here are gone. 'Tis yours now, not his."

In any case, he walked into his great hall, where the three center hearths blazed with warmth, and the walls and tables were festooned with red-berried holly and evergreen boughs tied with ribbons of many colors he'd found for Signe in the treasure room. Mistletoe hung here and there in remembrance of the death of Baldr, killed by an arrow made of mistletoe. The tears of Baldr's mother supposedly turned the red mistletoe berries to white, forevermore. A ceiling-high pine tree stood in one corner decorated with small carved wooden statues of various gods, candles, ribbons, and bits of hardy food strung together, like dried apples and nuts. A huge wreath hung on the wall behind the high dais.

The air even smelled festive.

Several massive yule logs, with their carved runic symbols, lay at the ready. The logs would burn for the twelve yule days, representing light, despite the darkness outside, and hope for the end of long winter nights.

He went up and checked the low table, which remained still below the dais, even though the need for it was no longer there, with Zoya gone. He needed to see if everything was ready for the wedding to be performed this evening, not that he hadn't checked twice before. Yea, laid out on the white cloth were Thorkel's short sword, Heart Stabber, a bowl of grains, a small knife, a cup of wine, a polished stone, a hammer, and a leather thong. Oh, wait, there should be some coins. He dug into the leather pouch which hung from his belt and pulled out five silver pieces which he set on the table.

Hauk had to admit to being nervous about the words he would have to speak to seal the wedding vows. Mayhap he should go seek Thorkel to see if he was nervous, too, for different reasons. Hauk looked forward to teasing the long-time bachelor.

But wait. He heard a clatter outside the front double doors of the keep, which were rarely used, followed by the sound of voices. Oh, gods! He hoped Signe hadn't convinced Thorkel that he should put a row of yule decoration on the roof line all around the keep, as she'd threatened. She was the one who had gone a bit barmy with her decorating of his hall, even putting boughs in the garderobe. But outside? Nay, he had to put a stop to this madness. With the iced-over snow, the lovesick fool could fall and break his neck, and Signe would be without a groom for her wedding.

But then he heard the neighing of horses, and knew it was something else. His guests had arrived. Hauk had half hoped that Ingolf's party would not be coming, since they hadn't arrived when expected two days ago. Alas!

"Bjorn!" he hollered at the top of his lungs.

"Holy Thor! I'm right here," Bjorn complained, pretending to knock his ears which were presumably blocked at the loudness of Hauk's voice.

Hauk hadn't realized that his son was on this side of the hall, behind a pillar, playing the board game *hnefatafl* with Floki, a warrior-in-training of about the same age. He'd thought the boy was in the adjoining weapon room polishing a sword he'd given him as an early yule gift.

"Sorry," Hauk said. "Come, help me greet our guests."

Reluctantly, Bjorn ended his game and came up to stand beside Hauk. He could swear the boy had grown half a head taller, just since they'd been at Haukshire. He was growing into a handsome Viking and would soon be shaving that blond fuzz on his face, or leaving it to grow into a beard.

Together, they each opened a door and stepped outside. Thankfully, his men had dug out a wide space on this front courtyard, and kept the steps clear. Standing on the threshold, he put his hand on Bjorn's shoulder. "Behave," he warned under his breath. Bjorn was of an age when betimes he let out inappropriate remarks and thought them funny, especially if his friends were around. Same went for inappropriately timed body sounds.

"Who? Me?" he said, fluttering his blond eyelashes.

Hauk just smiled, and turned his attention to the scene

before him—an open sleigh with seating for four, pulled by two matched white horses. There were also four guardsmen riding handsome mounts.

Ingolf got down first, hopping with ease off the high riding board. The last time Hauk had seen Ingolf, he'd been a young man, and his father the jarl. He was in his fifties now, a graybeard. But he'd aged well. His white plaited hair and forked beard were well-tended, his body still tall and straight, all of which were enhanced by his fine clothing...a fox-lined, long cloak and polished black knee boots.

"Welcome, Jarl Ingolf," Hauk said, stepping forward.

"Hauksson," Ingolf said, meeting Hauk with extended arms which clasped his shoulders. "It is good to see you again."

"I understand my former steward Halfdan took refuge with you." Hauk wanted to get that issue out of the way right off.

"Hah! That wily weasel! I soon put him on his way. Last I heard, he was in Kauptang." Ingolf gave him a steady, assessing gaze and added, "I want no enmity between our clans. Yea, I have coveted some of your lands, but mostly it was because they had been so neglected. I mean no offense, but your father was not a good landowner."

Hauk nodded, even though he knew Ingolf was feeding him a load of dragon shit. Even so, he could play the game. "No offense taken. Hopefully, we will deal well with each other, now that I am in residence." He hoped Ingolf got the hidden message in his hospitable words, *Beware or suffer the consequences.*

Ingolf helped his wife and daughters down from the sleigh then and introductions were made all around. His wife, Revna, was much younger than her husband, probably in her late thirties, with flaming red hair, diminutive in form under a gray sable cloak. Hauk did not know if Revna was a second wife, considering the difference in ages, but then many older men preferred young spouses. More introductions were made, and many "Happy Yule" greetings exchanged. The two daughters, Gisela and Gertrud, were dark-haired and similar in appearance to their father, probably born of Ingolf's first wife. They could be no more than thirteen and fourteen. Thorkel had to be mistaken that Ingolf wanted a match between Hauk and one of his daughters. In fact, Bjorn was gawking at the younger one like she was a goddess vision come to life.

Thorkel and some men came up then to lead the sleigh and the other horses to the barns out back. Everyone else walked up into his keep while Ingolf's men carried trunks into the bedchambers being given over for their use. At the number of trunks, Hauk wondered how long they intended to stay, but he did his best to be hospitable.

He could tell that Ingolf was surprised at how well his hall looked. Hauk was thankful now that Signe had taken so much care with the decorations.

Had Ingolf expected Hauk to have been as careless as his father in tending his home?

Probably.

At least with all this company and busyness, Hauk would have no time to think about She Who He No Longer Mentioned or allowed to be mentioned.

What to do, what to do?...

IT WAS two weeks before Christmas, normally her favorite season of the year, but Kirsten couldn't get into the spirit. Just the opposite. Every Christmas carol heard on her car radio, every Christmas decoration she saw in stores, every greeting of "Happy Holidays" drove her deeper into a pit of depression.

Occasionally, she burst into a bout of weeping, without warning. She tried to hide it from her family, probably to no avail.

Her brothers and sisters tried to help. Lida wanted her to come to New York to see her Broadway show and meet a hot actor who was dying to meet her. *Yeah! Ha, ha, ha!* Storvald said that a special holiday program was being held at Rosestead, which she would love. Plus, there was a hot Maine lobsterman who was dying to meet her. *Yeah! Ha, ha, ha!* Marie wanted her to come skiing in Colorado. And meet this hot chef who was dying to meet her. *Yeah! Ha, ha, ha!* On and on they went. It was funny, really, but a bit sad that she was so pathetic.

"I'm going into the village today for a little Christmas shopping," Angela said now. "Would you like to go with me?"

"Sure," Kirstin said, but her heart wasn't in it. At least Angela wasn't mentioning any hot guy dying to meet her. Meanwhile, for the rest of the morning, she worked in the den on her thesis. All of her experiences those months in the past were proving invaluable in tweaking her thesis. It was a hundred times better. Pleased with the revisions, she hoped to present the proposal to her advisor soon. After that, it would go to her doctoral committee for review. Several weeks after that, she would defend her dissertation. Probably not until January or February, at the earliest.

She returned late that afternoon with a loaded shopping bag. She and her siblings didn't spend much on Christmas gifts, just small presents with some meaning. The latest Magnolia Table cookbook for Marie, a coffee table art book for Dagny, a Mead of the Month Club membership for her father, squirt guns for the kids, those kinds of things.

Angela was in the kitchen preparing dinner, a pot roast with mashed potatoes to satisfy her father's manly appetite, Angela said. Kirstin had offered to help, but Angela demurred, preferring to work on her own. So, Kirstin was in the den again, but now watching a season of *Outlander*, the same one, for about the tenth time.

Her father came in and sat on the hassock at her feet. Taking both of her hands in his, after glancing with raised eyebrows at the same old television show he'd noticed her glomming, he said, "I think it's time, don't you, sweetling?"

She cocked her head to the side. "For what?"

"To decide what you're going to do."

Kirstin's heart began to beat rapidly, especially at the somber expression on her father's face. "What do you mean?"

"Go back, my dearling daughter." He sighed deeply, and she could swear he had tears in his eyes. "It pains me deeply to lose you again, this time probably forever, but I think you need to go back to your husband."

∾

Dum, dum, dee, dum...

HAUK STOOD on the lower level, with his back to the high dais where Ingolf and his family, along with Bjorn and Egil, sat, waiting for the wedding ceremony and feast to begin. Thorkel and Signe in their wedding finery stood on either side of him close to the table.

"Hear ye, hear ye, all who gather here at Haukshire to witness the wedding of Thorkel Ivarsson and Signe Elsedottir." His people thankfully went silent. Actually, he'd warned Frida not to send in any ale until the end of the ceremony to forestall any talking or ribald remarks.

First, Hauk took the goblet of wine into his hands and said, "Take ye this wine which represents the nectar of Odin's Well of Knowledge. May ye have the wisdom to deal with each other with love tempered with patience."

Each of them took a sip, Thorkel's deeper than warranted,

causing some men in the crowd to complain, "Hey, where's ours?" Hauk placed the goblet back on the table, then picked up the hammer which he handed to Thorkel and directed him with a motion of his head to hit the rock which sat on the table, announcing aloud, "With this hammer of Thor, the mighty Mjollnir, will you, Thorkel, protect your wife and crush her enemies?"

Thorkel nodded and hit the stone. Much harder than needed, causing shards to fly everywhere.

Hauk just raised his eyebrows at his friend, whose eyes twinkled with mischief, and continued, "With these seeds may Frey, god of fertility and prosperity, bless your marriage with babes aplenty and much riches." Without thinking, Hauk tossed the entire bowl of seeds at the two of them, causing Thorkel to spit out a few that landed in his mouth. But then, Thorkel grinned at Signe and murmured, "Making babes? I cannot wait."

Signe blushed prettily and told Thorkel to hush.

Along the same theme, Hauk picked up Thorkel's short sword and handed it to him, saying, "From this day forward, Thorkel, will your shield cover your wife, will her foe become your foe?"

"They will," Thorkel said solemnly, sheathing his weapon to his side.

"Now, give me your hands," Hauk directed, and, taking the small knife off the table, he made a slight slit on each of their wrists. As the blood beaded a line on their skin, he used the leather thong to tie their hands together loosely, wrist to wrist, and pronounced, "With this mingling of your blood, do you, Thorkel, pledge your troth to Signe as your wife?"

"I do," Thorkel said, and winked at Signe.

"And do you, Signe, pledge your troth taking Thorkel as your wedded husband?"

"I do," Signe said, catching Thorkel's eyes with seriousness, which was more touching than any additional words they might have said.

"With my authority as jarl of Haukshire, and representative of the lawspeaker, I do pronounce you man and wife," Hauk said then.

The couple smiled at one another, then kissed, to the cheering of the crowd. Pitchers of ale had been carried in during this final part of the ritual, and cups were raised with cheers and toasts of *"Skol!"* and "Good Wishes" and several bits of marital advice that caused women in the hall to blush and slap their mates.

Signe and Thorkel had agreed ahead of time not to do a bride-running in this confined space, despite Hauk's attempt to do so with Kirstin that one time.

Of course, that prompted Hauk to think about his own wedding, which was much different than this one. No Norse rituals, or anything like that. Had Kirstin felt cheated by that lack of ceremony? Or had the lack of ritual given her an excuse to dismiss theirs as less than a real marriage? Is that why she found it so easy to leave?

Hauk shook his head to clear it and directed several housecarls to clear the table while Frida supervised the carrying in of a board the size of a door, holding the roasted half of a reindeer, including the head, two of the legs, and the tail. The crowd cheered. Efrim, Frida's husband, raised a cleaver and large knife in the air and began to carve the roast. This marked the beginning of the marriage feast.

Meanwhile, platters holding slices and hunks of the other half of the deer were being carried by maids, first to the high table, and then laid out throughout the hall. The parade of maids and housecarls from kitchen to hall was continuous, back and forth, for almost an hour, with Frida calling out orders like a Viking chieftain. There were horseradish and mustard sauces for the venison, manchet bread, mashed turnips, beets, carrots, bitter greens, pickles, boiled hen and quail eggs, and sweet honey cakes.

Thorkel and Signe walked around the hall, exchanging words with men and women here and there, before going to the high dais where a place had been set for them in the center of the table. Ingolf and his family sat on their one side, with Hauk, Egil, and Bjorn on the other.

Everything went smoothly after that. More than one person, especially the old ones, told Hauk it was the best fellowship Haukshire had offered in many a year, possibly not since his grandsire's day. They thanked him profusely for his leadership.

After the meal, some of them exchanged seats and Hauk found himself sitting between Ingolf and his wife, while Bjorn was entertaining the two daughters. Egil snuck off to drink with some companions and no doubt share exaggerated battle stories.

Hauk didn't trust Ingolf completely, but he appeared to be offering a neighborly hand of peace. For the time being, least-ways. They talked of shared interests...hunting, fishing, a-Viking exploits and future plans, gossip of King Olaf's court and Sweyn's reportedly having been named king of all the Saxon lands. Which of course made him think of Kirstin once again, for she had predicted just such a fate for Sweyn. He had to wonder if Sweyn's untimely death would follow also, as she'd foretold. Of course, he did not mention that to Ingolf, who, thankfully, didn't inquire about his absent wife at all, probably having been warned by others that it was a sore subject.

Soon, Ingolf's wife began to whine to her husband about being overtired, and the two of them made for their assigned bedchamber, along with their daughters. It must be close to midnight. Thorkel and Signe had departed hours ago. Which left just him and Bjorn. Hauk let loose with a jaw-cracking yawn. It had been an especially long day. But neither he nor Bjorn could leave until everyone else had departed, since the tables would have to be moved to open the bed closets.

"So, you have taken a liking for Ingolf's daughters?" he inquired.

"What? I was just talking to them," a red-faced Bjorn replied, as if Hauk had accused him of some more forward activity.

"I would hope so! That all you did was talk," Hauk teased. "I would not like it to be said that you were playing lewd fingers under the table with girls of noble birth."

"Lewd...lewd fingers!" Bjorn sputtered. "I do not even know what that means.

"It is a talent most Vikings develop," Hauk said, waggling his fingers, telling him it was best to practice, perchance on himself. Then he laughed, which left Bjorn to wonder if he was serious or not.

But Bjorn got the last "word" in later, after having realized that his father had made mock of him, when they crawled into a bed closet together. Apparently Bjorn had overindulged in boiled eggs resulting in his breaking wind, repeatedly, with the most foul fumes, even as he slept...and snored loudly! It got so bad—the smell and the noise—that Hauk had to find another place to sleep, and the only space available was atop some fabric and furs in his treasure room. Which turned out to be just fine, more comfortable than a bed closet, for a certainty, with or without Bjorn.

Of course, as often happened, once he lay his head down, exhausted as he was, he was no longer tired. Instead, his mind wandered in the quiet, and Hauk could not keep his thoughts from returning to Kirstin.

Tomorrow was the first of the Jul days, comparable to the Christmas Day that the papists celebrated to mark the birth of their Jesus Christ. Tonight was their Christmas Eve.

Would Kirstin be attending Midnight Mass with her family, as she'd once described the traditions in her time?

Would they all...the numerous members of her extended family, be converging on the vineyard family estate tomorrow...well, this morning, considering the late hour?

Would they be feasting in their own way? What foods would they serve in that new land? Wine, of course, but would there be mead, as well, and roast boar for the day itself? Had they abandoned all Norse Jul traditions?

There would undoubtedly be laughter and teasing and exchanging of gifts. Children screeching. Music. The raucous noises of a happy family.

Would she think of me, even once?

Or am I as forgotten as the ease with which she left?

Tsk, tsk, tsk! said that voice in his head, which had been absent of late. *Oh, you of little faith!*

What? What do you mean?

Some Vikings are thick as mud, the voice said, as if it was speaking to some other celestial being, then laughed.

Hauk decided he must be half asleep and this must be some kind of half dream, or else, more likely, it was the result of his imbibing too much ale and mead and wine this night.

As long as he was already acting demented, Hauk decided to go one step further and whispered, "Good night, Kirstin, wherever you are." Tomorrow he might wish her bad dreams or nightmares when his resentments against her returned, but for tonight, he sighed and repeated, "Good night, wife."

He thought he heard a sigh in his head, too. Was it a sign... a celestial sign?

CHAPTER 23

Even the longest trips start with one step...

"Good night, Kirstin, wherever you are."

Kirstin heard Hauk's voice clear as if he lay beside her, and she jackknifed into a sitting position in her bed at Blue Dragon. Although she'd been asleep, she hadn't been dreaming of him; so, where had the voice come from?

She lay back down and closed her eyes, wishing to call up his image, either in her memory, or in a dream, but there was nothing, except she thought she detected a repeat, in a hushed whisper, "Good night, wife."

Is it a sign?

Or is it just desperation that I'm looking for signs in everything?

She was planning on trying to go back to Haukshire in the morning, and she was unsure whether it was the right thing to do, or the right place, or the right time. A sign would be welcome to let her know she was on the path God wanted her to be on.

Speaking...rather, thinking, of God, Kirstin had gone to

Midnight Mass with her father and Angela earlier tonight. During the entire religious service, her distracted thoughts kept going to Hauk and her possible return to him, constantly praying, "Please, God, if it be thy will, help me with my journey."

Unable to get back to sleep, Kirstin gave up after a while and walked over to the guest bedroom, tiptoeing and opening and closing the doors carefully so as not to awaken her father and Angela. They'd all been up much too late, and it was now only four a.m.

The first thing that caught her attention on entering the guest room, after she turned on the lamp, was the long blue cloak and the medieval-style, silver gown trimmed with red and green holiday colors which hung outside the closet door. The first was a gift from Madrene, the latter being one of the gowns Kirstin used in her Nordic presentations, although it wasn't strictly of a Norse style, which favored open-sided aprons over long-sleeved gunnas, but more Saxon medieval.

During the past two weeks, Kirstin had been gathering all the items from her fantasy list, things she wanted to take with her. Somehow, she knew, or sensed that she couldn't take anything too heavy. Even so, the pile on the bed had grown and grown. She hadn't told her family, except for her father, what she planned, not wanting to make a fuss with tearful farewells, and she hoped to be gone this morning, long before any of them arrived for Christmas dinner.

Madrene had suspected what she was up to, though. The two of them had always been close that way, almost like twins, a connection of shared feelings. In any case, Madrene, who wouldn't be coming to Blue Dragon for Christmas since her husband, as well as Torolf and Hamr, were unable to get out of duty at the Coronado compound, had shown up suddenly yesterday.

"You know?" Kirstin had asked her.

Madrene had nodded. "When?"

"Tomorrow. Christmas morning. Hopefully."

Madrene, who'd been carrying a pink garment bag, said, "Show me what you're taking."

They'd gone up to the guest room where Madrene handed her the garment bag.

Kirstin had raised her eyebrows in question.

"An early Christmas gift."

It was a long, royal blue velvet, white fur-lined cloak with a hood. Gorgeous.

"Good Lord! Where did you get this?"

"One of those motion picture wardrobe shops. You know, the charity thrift shops that sell used costumes. I think this must have been worn by some Disney princess."

Kirstin had to laugh. "Madrene! I am so not the princess type." Even so, she wrapped herself in its lushness, covering her jeans and white T-shirt, and rubbed her face against the softness.

"Yeah, but you'll need something warm to cover you."

"It must have been expensive," Kirstin said, fingering the lush velvet.

"Nah! That's fake fur, in case you haven't noticed. And the hem is frayed."

"Actually, the cloak will come in handy for carrying all this crap I'm taking with me." Kirstin pointed to the items on the bed. "I had been thinking I would have to carry all this in some kind of messenger bag, strapped across my chest, but maybe I can put each of them in separate Ziplock bags and safety-pin them to the inside of the cloak."

"That might work. Is that what you're going to wear?" Madrene asked, looking at the full-length gown hanging on the closet door. When Kirstin nodded, Madrene said, "The cloak will match your eyes, and the gown will match your hair. Perfect!"

"Unfortunately, I'll have to wear boots or athletic shoes. No Cinderella high heels, or even ballet slippers, considering the fact that there's probably snow on the ground there."

Madrene shrugged. "Needs must."

"Do you think I'm doing the right thing?" Kirstin inquired as she hung up the cloak.

"I don't know." Madrene pondered the question, then added, "If it were me, and Ian were back there, I wouldn't hesitate for a moment."

Well, that was answer enough for Kirstin.

They both had tears in their eyes when they hugged before Madrene drove away a short time later.

There were also tears in her father's eyes, and tears streaming down Angela's face, when Kirstin left them in the kitchen at eight a.m. the next morning. She had refused to have them accompany her to the site by the pond where she'd returned nine weeks ago, and warned them not to come checking on her, at least not until later. She didn't know how long it would take, if it even worked.

As she trudged across the lawn, her cloak weighed her down even more than she'd expected, especially when her father had insisted on her taking a half dozen grapevines wrapped in wet paper towels inside a giant Ziplock bag. In the end, he'd even shoved a palm-sized, metal flashlight in her hand, in case it was dark where she landed.

It wasn't just her cloak that weighed her down. Her heart was heavy with both sadness, knowing all those she was leaving behind, but also with hope for what awaited her back at Haukshire.

When she got to the pond, she sat on a rock and arranged her cloak around her. Closing her eyes, she tucked the small flashlight under the rounded neckline of her gown, under her bra, then crossed her arms and clasped the arm rings, trying to picture the place at Haukshire where her time travel occurred. The flat mossy ground. The remnants of summer flowers, drying or dead. The fjord a short distance away.

Nothing happened.

She closed her eyes and tried again.

Again nothing.

She checked her watch. Only a half hour had passed. And she realized that she hadn't visited the bathroom before coming out here. So, trudging back up the lawn to the house, she saw her father and Angela peeking out the window, apparently heeding her warning not to come looking for her.

"Sorry. Have to pee," she said to the two of them, gaping at her silently as she passed by. It was a chore taking off the heavy cloak, and lifting the long gown, but finally she was done and trudging across the lawn again. Her father and stepmother hadn't said a word as she passed.

It was past ten o'clock when she resumed her position by the pond. She yawned, then yawned again, and no wonder. She hadn't slept much at all last night. She should have had a cup of coffee. A half hour more and many, many yawns, found Kirstin back at the house asking Angela for a cup of black coffee. She chugged it down quickly, even though she wasn't particularly fond of the beverage, and definitely not without sugar or milk.

"Maybe you should wait for another day," her father suggested when she set the empty cup on the counter.

"No, no! It took me long enough to decide to do this. I can't just stop."

"How long…" her father started to ask, but Angela nudged him with an elbow, whispering, "Shhh."

Thus it was almost noon when Kirstin found herself back by the pond. This time she knelt and closed her eyes, saying a prayer, except her hands were holding onto the arm rings, instead of pressing them together in a prayerful attitude.

"Dear God, please help me in this hour of my need," she repeated over and over. Again, nothing.

Just then as she bent forward, rocking in prayer, she felt the flashlight slip out of her gown, and it fell to the ground. Stretching out her arms to catch it as it rolled away toward the pond, she fell, flat on her face, the smell of moss and damp earth heavy in her nostrils. As she held onto the flashlight and pulled it toward her, it managed somehow to strike one of the arm rings. She felt a sparking kind of vibration, starting at the arm ring, then rippling like an electric shock up her arm, down through her body, and hitting all her extremities. Stunned, she slid halfway into the pond, wetting her head and shoulders down to her breasts.

Somehow, she managed to get out of the water and into a sitting position. But she felt dizzy, kind of.

"Oh, my God!" she muttered, blinking rapidly, as she saw stars, or was it snowflakes?

And then everything went black.

You've heard of the legendary Christmas Visitor...

IT HAD BEEN SNOWING STEADILY all day. Even so, Hauk and Ingolf had been walking about the estate, wanting to escape the stuffiness of the great hall and the fussiness of the women preparing for the evening yule feast. Besides, this being the longest night of the year, there would only be an hour or so of light today.

"Is that the bridegroom?" Ingolf asked with a chuckle.

"Appears so," Hauk said.

He and Ingolf had been amused earlier, at the noon meal, to note that the newly married couple hadn't emerged yet. Must have come up for air, or food, because he saw now that

Thorkel was out with some men making sure that all the paths remained cleared. Must be that he hadn't expended all his energy in the bedplay if he was doing such energetic work now. Leastways, Hauk would use that notion to tease him later when they sat down over mead.

"What is it about us men that we let women lead us by the nose...or rather the cock...into wedlock?" Ingolf commented idly. "The key part of the word being lock, if truth be told."

"You have a poor opinion of marriage," Hauk replied. "Has your experience been so bad?"

Ingolf shrugged. "My first wife, who died after breeding me two daughters and no sons, was a living nightmare. Never stopped complaining. A shrew she was."

"And your present wife? She does not seem so bad."

"She's not, but then Revna is too young to have developed such bad habits. Best to train them early, if we must wed at all. But we have been wed for two years now, and not a babe in sight. Mayhap she is barren."

"Would you put her aside for that reason?"

"Possibly. If I am not to gain any heirs, and Revna brings no lands, well, I would just as well be alone, without the burdens of a wife. Bed partners are available easily enough." He glanced at Hauk. "You disapprove? I would think your experience with marriage would have turned you against it, too."

"My marriage was not so bad...while it lasted." Hauk couldn't believe he'd said that, after all these sennights of rancor. Mayhap he just wanted to disagree with Ingolf, to be contrary.

"'While it lasted,' you say. See. That must be the key. Short marriages. Ha, ha, ha."

They'd just arrived at the wider, cleared space of the back courtyard. Going up to Thorkel, Hauk grinned.

"What?" Thorkel sniped. He'd no doubt been the target of

many jests from the men as they worked.

Despite the cold, Thorkel was wearing only a tunic over his braies, the exercise of shoveling no doubt heating him up. But that did not account for the pink dots coloring his face and neck and collarbones. "I am just admiring your sex flush," Hauk said.

The pink turned to rose. Thorkel knew what a sex flush was, Hauk having explained it with great glee once Kirstin had introduced him to the subject.

"I assume you will be wanting to take a nap after all this activity," Hauk continued, his lips twitching with suppressed mirth.

Thorkel told him to do something to his male organs that was physically impossible.

Ingolf was enjoying their exchange, adding, "If you get tired of your new bride, I have a daughter or two that would make an excellent second wife."

"Thank you, but nay thank you. My wife would have my balls for dinner if I even considered such," Thorkel said. "In truth, I am pleased with my current wife." He waggled his eyebrows at Hauk then and was about to walk away when he stopped dead in his tracks, staring off toward the fjord. "What in the gods' name is *that*?"

Hauk and Ingolf turned to see what had caught Thorkel's attention.

Even though the sun was overhead, there was still only a dim light, and it was hard to see clearly at a distance. Even so, it appeared to be a person, or creature, of some kind, covered with a blue cloak, lined with white. From its hood hung long wet strands of gray hair, or animal fur. Most unusual, though, was its gait. The creature trudged slowly along the path as if dragging a great weight, its head bent forward. In its one hand was a bunch of vines and in the other a strange light.

As it got closer, the men in the courtyard backed up.

"Mayhap it is a troll, sent by Loki as a yule visitor," Thorkel mused. "'Tis just the kind of thing the jester god would do."

Hauk and Ingolf looked at him as if he'd lost some brains during his long night of sex.

"Nay, I think it is a witch," said Ingolf. "I saw one at the Trondheim Althing five years past. She was an old crone who escaped afore King Olaf could burn her at the stake. Apparently, she had put a curse on the king's cock that made it make a right turn, halfway up."

Hauk and Thorkel looked at Ingolf with horror, then turned to watch the approaching apparition.

A strange tingling arose on the back of Hauk's neck, which slingshotted to all his extremities, raising all the fine hairs of his body on the way.

"Nay, 'Tis not a troll or a witch," Hauk said with a mix of shock and anger. "'Tis my wife."

∾

Not the reception she expected...

KIRSTIN TRUDGED UP TO HAUK, who was standing with Thorkel and some other man, the three of them just gaping at her.

"Hauk!" she called out. "Help me get this cloak off. It's killing me."

Hauk blinked with confusion at her demand, then stepped up and behind her to remove the cloak off her shoulder. He staggered and almost dropped the garment, surprised at its weight. No wonder! All the items she'd pinned inside the cloak, not to mention a partial soaking in the pond, must have made the blasted thing weigh at least twenty pounds.

She clicked off her flashlight and tucked it back inside her gown. Then she handed the grapevines, which had somehow fallen out of their Ziplock bag, to Thorkel, who regarded them as if they might be snakes.

Finally, she looked at Hauk and smiled. "Hi," she said shyly.

He raised his eyebrows, then glanced at her wet hair and the sopping cloak he still held. "Where have you been?"

She thought he meant where had she been that she'd gotten wet and told him, "I fell in the pond?"

"Pond? What pond?" He waved a hand dismissively then, as if it didn't matter. Which it didn't.

She sneezed. This was not the way she'd pictured their reunion. The kisses, and hugs, and declarations of love she'd expected were blatantly missing.

"Too bad you didn't come sooner," Hauk said. "You missed the wedding yestereve."

"Wedding?" she said dumbly and just then noticed a very attractive, nobly-dressed redhead standing at the entrance to the keep, along with two young, dark-haired girls. Then she looked at Hauk. Was it possible? Had Hauk gotten over her so quickly? Had he wed one of those females standing there? Yes, the girls were young, but men of this time period tended to go for adolescent girls in order to ensure they were getting virgins. On the other hand, it might be the mother, or older woman, he'd wed, not that she was *old* old, probably thirty-something.

Kirstin blinked away the tears that burned her eyes.

"Hauk was magnificent," Thorkel told her. "He said the words like he'd done weddings many times."

Kirstin gasped. It was true then. Hauk had married someone else.

"You pig!" she said and ran away, back the way she'd just come. "Oh, my God! Oh, my God! This was such a mistake. Can I go back? I have to go back. Oh, my God!"

Hauk didn't even follow after her.

"I'll show him," she muttered. "I'll go back and he'll never see me again." But halfway back to the mossy place, with the snow coming down more heavily, Kirstin sneezed, felt a cough tickle her throat, and shivered uncontrollably. Her cloak was back in the courtyard where Hauk had dropped it.

"Maybe I could warm up a bit first," she muttered to herself. But there was no way she was going back to face Hauk again, or to pass his bride. With that in mind, she headed around the side of the keep to what was the rarely used front courtyard. By now, she was covered with an inch of snow, even her eyelashes, and the cold was marrow-deep. She pushed on one of the two doors and stepped into the hall where the three middle hearths were blazing...and almost fell over at the heat.

But she didn't want to stay here where one after the other men sitting at the tables, eating cold foods, drinking, or playing that board game *hnefatafl*, turned to stare at her. Instead, she ducked into the guest bedchamber where, to her surprise, Signe was smoothing out the bed furs.

"Oh, my gods!" Signe exclaimed and rushed over to pull her into a hug. Immediately, Signe stepped back and observed her, "You're cold as an icicle."

Kirstin nodded and with chattering teeth told her, "Got wet. Lost my cloak. Freeeezing."

"Here. Let me get this damp gown off, and you can snuggle under the furs." Signe gave Kirstin's white lace bra and white silk bikini underpants a sharp look before pulling a linen bed gunna over her head and bundling her onto one fur and under another and she smiled as she helped take off the athletic shoes that Kirstin had chosen in lieu of high heels or ballet slippers. Fortunately, Signe didn't say anything, for now; Kirstin wasn't up to explaining, not with Hauk's betrayal occupying her mind. Signe also stared at the small flashlight that Kirstin had tucked in the center of her bra. She probably thought it was some kind of jewelry. "Thank you, Signe. Once I warm up, I'll be out of here." She sneezed once, twice, three times and wiped at her nose with the back of her hand. It was obvious that she had a cold coming on. No wonder, with her getting wet and with the chilly air.

Signe frowned. "Why would you leave again?"

"Are you kidding?" When Signe still looked confused, Kirstin explained, "The wedding? Does that ring any bells?"

Signe brightened. "You heard about that? Oh, I wish you had been here. It was wonderful." A dreamy expression covered her face, and Kirstin could swear there was a flush covering her face and neck...almost like...hmmm.

"Seriously, Signe? It's not like you to be so mean."

Signe put a hand to her chest, as if wounded. "Why is it mean to wish you had been here at my wedding?"

"*Your* wedding?"

"Who else's?"

"Hauk's."

Signe burst out laughing. "Thorkel and I wed yestereve. Where did you get such a fool idea that it was Hauk?"

Kirstin sat up. "Well, Hauk said it was too bad I'd missed the wedding, and he said it in a very snarky tone. Then Thorkel said that Hauk did a wonderful job saying the vows,"

Signe sat on the side of the bed and took her cold hand in both of hers, rubbing it to get the circulation going. "Hauk said the vows, which we repeated. He performed the ceremony, Kirstin."

"Oh."

"Who did you think he wed, pray tell, so soon after your leaving?"

Kirstin felt her face heat with embarrassment. "There were three women...well, a woman and two girls...standing outside, and..."

"That was Jarl Ingolf's wife and daughters. They are here

as yule guests."

"Oh," Kirstin said again.

"Have you any idea how distraught Master Hauk was when you left him? Like a bear with a thorn in its paw, he was. Growling at one and all. In truth, I saw tears in his eyes that first night when he went looking for you."

Kirstin got tears in her eyes then, too. "I called him a pig."

"Who?"

"Hauk."

"Ah. Do not fret. All men are pigs at one time or another. Promise him some good bedplay and all will be well."

If only it were that easy. Kirstin put a hand to her head and lay back down, pulling the top fur up to her chin. She pressed the fingertips of both hands to her forehead.

"Are you all right?" Signe asked.

"I have a headache. Feels like I have an axe in my head." *And I'm probably on my way to the flu.*

"I could look for some megrim powders for you."

"Actually, if you could get my cloak for me. It's out in the back courtyard. I have some Tylenol pills there."

"Pills?"

"Herbs."

Once Signe returned, dragging the heavy cloak, and raised her eyebrows at the vines which Thorkel had told Signe belonged to her "lady," Kirstin told her, "I'll explain later." Meanwhile, she asked Signe to open the cloak and lay it over the bed. Kirstin made quick work of getting out the baggie of pills and took two Tylenol, without water. Luckily, they were coated and went down easily.

Signe spread the cloak over the bottom of the bed and hung the gown from a wall peg, smoothing them both out so that they would dry as wrinkle-free as possible. "They're beautiful, m'lady," Signe said.

"Thank you. Oh, I almost forgot. I have a gift for you."

Kirstin sat up and pulled the cloak closer, then unpinned one of the Ziplock bags that held toiletries…a brush, comb, compact, and what she was looking for…a small bottle of Chanel No. 5 perfume. "Sorry I didn't wrap this."

Signe took the small glass bottle in her hand and stared, perplexed, not even sure how to open it. "Here. Come closer," Kirstin told her. Then she showed her how to open the bottle carefully so as not to spill any of the precious liquid. "You only need a little. Wherever you like. But I prefer the wrists or neck." She showed Signe how to do it with the glass stopper, and really only the tiniest dab was enough to fill the room with the floral scent.

"Ooh," Signe said with a sigh. "It smells like flowers." She looked at Kirstin then. "Thank you, thank you. I'll only use it on special occasions."

"Just be careful. Only a tiny bit goes a long way."

Signe nodded and asked, "Those silver loops…are they brooches?"

At first, Kirstin didn't understand. Then she laughed. "No, those are safety pins…fasteners. They're not worth much, where I come from. Unlike brooches, which can be valuable. Here, I'll show you how they work."

Signe was fascinated, and Kirstin gave her two, which could have been gold, by the expression on Signe's face. Perfume and safety pins…wow!

"Could you'd leave me for a little while, Signe?" Kirstin said then. "I need to rest until I get the chill off of me, and the pills take effect." Kirstin was already regretting her failure to pack cold medicine.

"Certainly. And thank you again, m'lady," Signe said, sniffing at her wrist as she stood at the open door. "What should I tell Master Hauk, if he asks?"

If he asks. Kirstin hesitated, then said, "Tell him I'm sorry."

Kirstin was lying corpse-straight under the furs, still

chilled and still suffering a splitting headache when there was a knock on the door and Bjorn entered. "Am I bothering you?" he asked.

"No, come in." She sat, pulling the fur up over her chest.

She could swear the boy had grown a few inches since she'd been gone, but then at his age, thirteen, boys tended to shoot up practically overnight. Her brothers sure had. And he was looking good, too, with his blond hair hanging in a long braid down his back. There was a peach fuzz on his cheeks that would soon turn into whiskers.

"You came back," he said bluntly.

"Yes."

"I was angry at you for a long time," he confided, shifting from foot to foot. "You shouldn't have just left."

"I know, but I had no control over it. It just happened. By accident, sort of."

"Oh. We thought you didn't care about us anymore and wanted to go home."

"Of course I care about you. You're like...you're like my son," she told him, and that was the truth, although she hadn't realized it until this moment.

He nodded, as if he shared the feeling. Without invitation, he plopped down on the side of the mattress and began talking about Gisela, one of Jarl Ingolf's daughters. He'd apparently developed a crush on her.

"Can you pull my cloak up here? I have a gift for you," she said with a loud sneeze. "This is the kind of shirt a guy your age and size would wear in my time." She took out a rolled up piece of fabric and shook it out to reveal a long-sleeved, black Grateful Dead T-shirt. At the same time, she pulled out a travel pack of tissues. Another thing she should have packed... more tissues.

His eyes went wide at first when he saw her gift, and then he laughed and pulled his tunic over his head and replaced it with the T-shirt. It was a perfect fit, maybe a little big, but that was okay.

"What do you think?" she asked.

"I don't know. How do I look?"

"Here. Use this," she said and handed him the open compact.

At first, he didn't understand that it was a mirror, to reflect his image. When he did, he was more interested in how his face looked. He declined to take the shirt off when he left, carrying his tunic with him. He couldn't wait to show Gisela. Kirstin had to insist he leave the mirror. She wished she had been able to bring him a pair of Nikes, which would have surely blown him away, but they would have been too heavy, on top of everything else she'd carted.

No sooner did Bjorn leave than Egil popped in. "Well, well, well," he said. "And how long are ye gonna stay this time?"

"That depends on Hauk. He didn't look pleased to see me."

"And why should he be? Ye nigh broke his heart."

"He told you that?"

"Hah! 'Tis not the kind of thing a man confides to another man. Nay, I know because I saw the pain he was in. Sick he was. Heart sick. I tol' Frida she should make him some chicken slop, but she didn't know how."

"I was in pain, too, Egil. Absolute misery. Why do you think I came back?"

He shrugged. "I do not know. I thought...we thought that ye decided to go back to yer jelly man."

"What? Who?"

"The master tol' me 'bout yer former mate, the jelly man."

"Oh, you mean JAM." She recalled telling Hauk about him, when he'd asked if she had a man in the future. "Jacob Alvarez Mendoza, JAM, was never my mate. Just someone I...no, I didn't go back to him. I mean I dated him once, but realized that we had no future."

"Dating? Is that like tupping? So, ye let the JAM man swive ye and then decided my Lord Hauk was a better swiver. Ye should have known that from the start if ye ask me."

"That's not it, at all, Egil." She inhaled and exhaled deeply for patience. Her head was starting to feel fuzzy, not just painful. She tried to look as sincere as possible before telling him, "Bottom line: I love Hauk."

"Good luck with that!" He looked at her and quickly added, "Now, don't be getting' all teary-eyed. Mayhap ye'll be able to melt that wall he's put around hisself."

'Well, in case I'm not going to be here that long, I better give you your gift now." Once again, she leaned forward and took one of the Ziplock bags out of the cloak.

"What is this?" Egil asked, taking the package she handed him.

"Oreo cookies. I know you have a sweet tooth, and these are a popular snack."

"Hmmm," he said doubtfully.

"Believe me, you'll like them. Best way to eat them is by dunking in a cup of milk."

"Milk!" he exclaimed as if she'd suggested some vile substance.

"Thank you for welcoming me back," she said then, but the sarcasm passed over his head as he waved good-bye.

Kirstin didn't bother to lie back down again, waiting to see if there were any more visitors. She wasn't disappointed. In came Gorm, the little boy who'd been abused before Hauk's return to Haukshire.

"My, my! Aren't you the handsome little man?" Kirstin said.

The boy looked fairly clean and his tunic and braies, though of a simple, brown homespun, were obviously new. He preened at her remark about his appearance, but then confided in a tone of disgust, "The master made me take a bath. Again! Called it the Yule Bath, but methinks he were just makin' mock of me."

"I see that you lost two of your front teeth."

Gorm nodded. "But I'm gonna grow other ones in that place."

"You know, Gorm, where I come from, children get a gift from the tooth fairy when they lose a tooth. I wonder if I might have something for you. Oh, I know. I brought some things that should please you as well as all the other children here. In fact, they are a special Christmas...um, yule treat."

Reaching once again into her cloak, she took out a bag holding several dozen items. Gorm leaned forward, studying what she held in her hand, sniffing the peppermint scent, clearly not understanding.

"These are called candy canes. I noticed that there is a yule tree out in the hall. These are meant to be hung from the limbs of the tree, and then on Christmas day the children get to take one and eat it." She pulled one out of the bag and put the end in her mouth, sucking on it and humming her enjoyment. "These sweet treats are best if you suck on them, making them last a long time. But some people just crunch them. Here, try one."

"They look like shepherds' crooks." Gorm took one and hesitantly put it into his mouth, right between the open space in his teeth. Immediately, he smiled and said, "Good!"

She could hear him boasting of his booty to his friends once he exited out into the hall, but then she worried that these "gifts" she'd been doling out might prompt even more visitors. So, she went to the door and locked it by pulling a bar against the latch. With that little bit of effort, she had to lean against the wall for a moment to steady her wooziness. If Hauk wanted to talk with her, he would have to knock.

He never did.

CHAPTER 24

If Dr. Phil were a Viking...

*J*ust as Hauk had been plagued by advice from one and all when Kirstin had disappeared all those months ago...nine sennights and two days, to be precise...he was plagued now by people...meddling busybodies, to be precise...giving him advice of a different sort. How to punish his wife. How to keep his wife. How to reject his wife. How to win his wife's affections. How to...how to...how to! 'Twas enough to drive a Viking man mad.

Signe was the first to approach him where he was shoveling snow from the path to the fjord. It wasn't as if the path hadn't already been cleared a number of times already, as evidenced by the waist-high banks on either side, but there'd been another snowfall. And it wasn't as if there weren't plenty of others to handle this chore. But Hauk needed hard work to deplete his body humours lest he explode with fury, or frustration, or mind-blowing something or other.

"Master?" Signe called out, as she approached. When he ignored her, she repeated, "Master?"

"What?" he snapped.

She flinched.

"I'm busy, Signe," he said, as if that was any kind of apology. "What is amiss now?"

"She's sorry."

"Who?" he asked, as if he didn't know.

"Your lady. She said to tell you that she is sorry."

"Pfff!" He would like to ask what she was sorry about. Leaving, coming back, lying, or something altogether different. "It matters not to me, Signe."

Instead of leaving right away, Signe shifted from foot to foot.

"What else?" he asked, trying his best not to betray his emotions by snapping again. He continued to shovel around Signe.

"She thought you got married."

Now, that surprised Hauk. "Is she barmy? Why would she think that?"

Signe gave some long-winded explanation that made no sense, ending with, "And that's why she called you a pig."

Hauk just shook his head, then sniffed the air. "Why do I smell flowers?"

"Oh, 'tis perfume that my lady gifted me. Isn't it wonderful?" She stuck out her hand for him to smell.

Truly, Hauk felt as if he'd fallen off a cliff into a land of the demented. He narrowed his eyes at her. This must be a magic trick Kirstin was employing, using scent on this wench to lure him back. With a snort of disgust, he continued shoveling, and Signe wandered back to the keep, muttering something about bull-headed men.

Next to offer him advice was his son who sought him out in the barn where Hauk was raking shit out of the straw in the stalls occupied by Ingolf's horses. His son was wearing a strange shert celebrating the dead, as if warriors would be grateful to be dead, although he supposed some would be, those who went to Valhalla. *Aaarrgh!* He had no doubt that this, too, was a scheming gift from his wife; so, he declined to ask the traitor about it.

"She says she feels like my mother," Bjorn told him right off.

Under normal circumstances, Hauk would have asked "Who?" but he knew and would not give her the satisfaction. Not that she was here to witness his disdain. Instead, he just ignored Bjorn and almost got kicked by the one of the horses who was not happy with his proximity.

"She did not mean to leave us," Bjorn continued.

That, he could not ignore. He turned, leaned on his rake, and glared at his son.

"Well, she didn't. She said it was an accident. Must be it was her One-God who decided to send her away."

"And was it her One-God who sent her back?" Hauk inquired, disbelieving. "And why?"

"I do not know."

Hauk handed Bjorn another rake and motioned for him to push the soiled straw toward an already large pile, which would later be spread on the kitchen garden. Bjorn complied, but then he turned back and said, "Don't send her away."

"What makes you think I have the power to do that?"

Bjorn shrugged. "Forgive her. That would be a start."

"*Pfff!* According to you, there is naught to forgive. She was not responsible for her desertion."

"Well, according to Egil, when dealing with women, the best course of action for a man is always to apologize to a woman, even when he is not in the wrong."

"Ah, and now Egil is the font of all wisdom. An Odin he has become."

"I am just saying."

It was not a surprise, therefore, when Egil showed up later

in the storeroom where Hauk had gone to get a barrel of mead for tonight's yule feast. "Do ye need help with that?"

Hauk nodded, and the two of them rolled the heavy barrel, which held a half-tun of mead, up the steps and into the outer kitchen and from there to the great hall.

Setting the barrel in one corner, for now, Hauk turned to Egil. "What? No advice from you, too."

"Hah! Ye know what I think of wimmin and their greedy ways. Nay, I would not be swayed by her declarations of love, if I were ye. Best to send her away, sooner rather than later."

"What declarations of love?"

"She claims to love ye, but then she was with that JAM fellow whilst she was gone, and you know what that means?" He raised his eyebrows as if they shared some understanding.

"I don't understand," Hauk said. "She said she loves me?"

"Yea."

Hauk's heart lifted, despite himself. "Why would she tell you something like that?"

"'Cause I accused her of bein' unfaithful with the JAM man, but she says they was jist datin', which I still think is suspicious. She claims datin' ain't tuppin', but I don't know about that."

Hauk put his face in his hands and counted to ten, under his breath. *"Ein, tveir, þrir, fjorir..."*

"Do ye have a head pain? The lady has a cure fer that."

Hauk raised his head. "Why am I not surprised?"

"You know, m'lord..." Egil began

Hauk groaned. He knew when Egil referred to him as lord or master, he was going to say something Hauk would not like.

"You know, m'lord," Egil repeated, and went on, "it occurs to me that ye are in a prison of yer own makin', no different from the cage ye were in back in that Saxon castle."

"Whaaat?" Hauk exclaimed.

"'Tis true. Yer in this cage, and each of the bars were put there by yerself."

"That is the most ridiculous thing I have ever heard."

Egil went on as if he hadn't even spoken. "One of the bars is yer excessive pride. Another is yer stubbornness." He began to count off on his fingers. "Third, there's a denial of pain, the heart kind. Fear is fourth…oh, yea, you have fear of rejection, again. Then, number five, is yer Viking manhood, or yer view of it, which makes ye stick to the old ways. Six is yer selfishness; things always have to be yer way, like returning to Haukshire, or kidnapping the lady." He waved a hand airily. "There are probably lots of other bars, but I'll have to think on that."

Hauk found that his jaw had dropped, and he was gaping at Egil. "I had no idea you had such a low opinion of me."

"Nay, nay, nay! You misread me, m'lord. A loyal comrade speaks the truth to help his friend. And none of the things I mentioned diminish yer goodness."

Hauk shook his head with incomprehension. "There is no cage, real or imagined. I am as free as I could ever be. What do you imagine I am barred from doing?"

"Going to yer wife, like ye know ye want to. Keepin' her with ye by any means, even up to beggin', if necessary."

"You just got done telling me that women are selfish creatures and that I would do best sending my wife away."

"Now that I think on it, I realize that ye were much easier to live with when she were around. When the lord is happy, his followers are happy."

"I'm happy."

"Pfff."

"Contented then."

"Pfff."

"Truly, you go too far betimes, Egil."

Something seemed to occur to Egil then, and he put up a

halting hand to Hauk. "Wait here, m'lord. I have somethin' to show ye." Egil went off to a nearby bed closet where he'd stored his sea chest. He came back with a black circle...nay, two black circles with white in the middle. "Eat that," Egil told him.

"What? Nay! It looks like dirt."

"'Tis is a sweet from Lady Kirstin's land. Called an Oar-yo. Taste it."

Hauk took a small bite, chewed, then popped the whole bit, which wasn't that large, into his mouth. It was delicious. "Give me another one," he said after chewing and swallowing.

"Nay. I only have so many and I'm am saving them to last for a long time."

"Why did my wife give you these sweets?"

"Probably so that I would soften you up toward her," Egil told him, but then added, "You should see the sweets she gave Gorm." Egil pointed toward the other end of the hall where the boy was on a wooden ladder propped against a wall next to the yule tree, leaning sideways precariously. A number of other boys stood at the bottom of the ladder cheering him on.

"Good gods, the bratling is going to fall and break his fool neck." He ran forward and hollered, "Gorm!"

Which was a mistake, of course, Hauk realized too late, his yell causing the boy to turn abruptly, lean in the opposite direction, and look down at him, the ladder teetering and starting to fall. Luckily, the ladder dropped toward the trestle tables in the hall, and not toward the ceiling-high tree which would have surely toppled over. As it was, the old ladder shattered into several pieces when it hit the table, but he was able to save the boy from injury just in time by lurching forward and grabbing his tunic by the neck.

Gorm's eyes and mouth were both wide when Hauk placed him on his feet. "Bloody hell!" the imp exclaimed. "That was a close one."

"I'll give you a close one, and watch your filthy mouth. That's no language for a child," Hauk said, taking the boy by the shoulders and shaking him. "You could have killed yourself."

Homing in on the least important thing Hauk had said, Gorm straightened and said, "I'm not a child."

Hauk rolled his eyes. "What were you doing?"

"Hanging the candy crooks on the yule tree...the way Lady Kirstin tol' me to. It's a tray-dish-on."

I should have known. Kirstin again. He glanced down at Gorm's hand which still clutched several of the objects in question, miniature shepherd's crooks, except they were white with red stripes. Dozens of them had already been hung from the branches of the yule tree. Even from here, he could smell the not unpleasant minty odor.

Once they'd cleared the ladder away, throwing the pieces onto the hearth fires, Hauk looked around, wondering what to do next. It was only mid-afternoon. Ingolf was sitting at the other end of the hall beside his wife and daughters who were working on some type of embroidery. He waved, motioning for Hauk to join him in a cup of ale, but Hauk needed to do something more mind-consuming. He'd love to go off to some private place and drink himself into a stupor, but there was no private place he could think of, except for the treasure room, and he wasn't about to hole himself in there at this time of day. Besides, getting drukkinn would only work for a short while; then he would have to face his problem once again. The most logical recourse would be to go to his bedchamber...the guest bedchamber...but that's where his "problem" was currently lodged. Mayhap it was best to take the bull...um, his problem...by the horns. Mayhap it was time to break out of his "cage." But he was a well-trained fighting man. He knew from experience that a warrior should not go to war unless he had a plan.

Hauk had no plan.

He also knew that warriors should be calm and collected before confronting the enemy, lest they be berserkers.

Hauk was no berserker.

And Kirstin was no enemy. Was she?

And forget calm and collected. He was as agitated as an unblooded boyling afore his first battle.

Without thinking, he stomped down the hall, through a corridor to the guest bedchamber, where he attempted to lift the latch. And found the door locked. From within. The latch would not move.

Should he knock?

Should he yell?

Should he kick the door down?

Just then, Signe rushed up, putting her forefinger to her closed lips. "Shh. Leave the mistress for now. She is not feeling well and needs to rest."

"She dared to lock me out."

"Nay. She did not lock the door against you. 'Twas all the others who kept coming to visit, giving her no chance to get better." She gave him one last warning look and walked away.

Somehow the servants had become the master in this keep. One and all felt no compunction about telling him what to do. Even so, he inhaled and exhaled, then decided to go chop wood. A lot of wood.

He was not done with his errant wife, though. Not at all.

ANIMAL FARM...

Kirstin awakened, feeling much better. The Tylenol she'd taken, on top of the stress exhaustion of her time-travel experience and Hauk's less-than-welcoming welcome, had all combined to knock her into a deep, healing sleep. Glancing at her watch, she saw that it was seven p.m. She must have been out of it for at least four hours.

It also became apparent to her, glancing at the closed, barred door, that Hauk hadn't come to her. Tears welled in her eyes.

With a stifled sob, she figured she had three choices: Continue to lie in bed, nursing her hurt feelings. Go back to the future and Hauk be damned. Or fight for what she really wanted, the fool Viking.

Well, screw the self-pity, and screw capitulation. I am woman...I am Viking...hell, I am Viking woman. Just watch me roar, baby!

Kirstin rose from the bed furs and shivered, not from the cold virus, but from the chill in the bedchamber. Usually, the bedchamber door was left open in the winter, even when occupied, so that the heat from the hall hearth fires would spread inside this adjacent room. As she relieved herself, using a pottery jar from under the bed, she noticed the noise outside her door...the sound of loud conversation and laughter, even music, possibly a lute. She realized this was still Christmas day, and the people of Haukshire would be enjoying their Jul feast.

And no one had bothered to invite her.

No, no, no! No self-pity.

Besides, she reminded herself, *I locked the door. Maybe Hauk knocked, and I didn't hear him.*

Yeah, right. Like a Norseman would let a locked door keep him from something he wanted.

Whatever!

Pouring some water from a pitcher into a bowl, she gave herself a quick sponge bath, using a piece of linen and the one and only bar of Dove lavender soap that she'd brought with her. After that, she put on her gown. It was made of silk in a shimmery silver color, with a green and red band along the edges of the rounded neckline and wrists and hem. Clearly a Christmas garment. A luxurious one, at that.

Luckily, it had a side zipper, which allowed her to fit the tight bodice over her breasts and abdomen, with a silver-plated belt cinching her waist. She would have to wear her athletic shoes, but they wouldn't be visible under the long skirt.

Next, she worked on her hair, combing out the tangles, then brushing the long platinum strands until they shone like...yes, silver, she decided, checking her reflection in the small compact mirror. She let her hair hang loose over her shoulders, held off her face by a pearlized, comb-style headband. Only the tiniest bit of mascara and cherry lip gloss completed the effect.

She picked up the arm rings and slid them to her upper arms, on top of the tight sleeves.

She was ready.

Or as ready as she would ever be.

She unlatched the door, inhaled and exhaled to steady her nerves, then stepped forward into the heat and raucous party noises. She almost turned back but decided it was do or die time, literally. She made sure to leave the door open to let some heat in.

As she walked along a far aisle bordering the fully occupied trestle tables, she greeted people she recognized here and there. But, mostly, like a domino effect, the hall became increasingly silent, everyone becoming alert to her presence and watching to see what her husband's reaction would be.

Hauk was sitting in the middle of the high table with Jarl Ingolf on one side beside his wife and one of his daughters. On his other side was Egil, Bjorn, and the other daughter, presumably the fair Gisela.

Hauk was laughing at something Ingolf said when his eyes wandered the hall and latched on her. He froze for a second, and in that second she saw the pain she'd caused him. But then, he covered that hurt with a sneer and turned to say something to Egil, who shook his head vehemently. He'd probably ordered Egil to get rid of the wench, meaning her.

Instead, Egil whispered something to Bjorn, who in turn whispered something to Gisela. They all slid down the bench, making room for Kirstin beside Hauk, who was clearly not happy about their actions, but seemed to decide against countermanding the order. Probably didn't want to make a scene, which was to her advantage.

Instead of going up the short set of stairs at Bjorn's side of the dais, she went to the other side, where she introduced herself to Jarl Ingolf, his wife Revna and her older daughter, Gertrud. "Greetings! Welcome to Haukshire!" she said.

"Happy Jul!" the guests replied.

The beautiful red-haired woman was clearly about twenty years younger than her husband, only a few strands of gray showing in her red hair, whereas her husband was totally white, from his prettily flowing hair to his intricately braided, forked beard. His clothing befitted a king, more suited to a royal court than a rustic northern estate. A vain man, to be sure.

"What marvelous embroidery you have on your gunna, Lady Revna!" Kirstin said. "Is that orphrey? I detect a gold thread in the pattern."

"It is," Revna said, her tone showing surprise and pleasure at the notice. "Do you do needlework, Lady Kirstin?"

"No. I wish I had the talent. But I am a great admirer."

"Come to the hall tomorrow afternoon, and I will show you some interesting pieces."

"Thank you. I will."

"Your gown is beautiful, as well," Revna observed.

Kirstin thought about saying something flip, like, "This old thing? I got it from a secondhand shop," but, instead, she nodded and said, "Sorry I couldn't be here on your arrival." Including Revna's husband and daughter in a sweeping glance, Kirstin added, "Is there anything you need?"

They all demurred.

Out of her side vision, she saw Hauk raise his eyebrows at her taking on the role of "lady of the manor."

Big deal! He should have come to her by now, not the other way around. He should be happier to have her back. He should stop acting like the wounded party, or the only wounded party.

She skirted around him, deliberately saying nothing, and spoke to Egil and Bjorn...and Gisela, after being introduced. "Have you eaten already?" she asked.

"Nay. They're just about to serve," Egil said, taking a long draw on his horn of ale. "We've been toastin' so far."

A lot of toasting, Kirstin decided, if Egil's boozy breath was any indication.

Well, the moment was at hand. She slipped awkwardly onto the seat beside Hauk, not an easy matter, being in the middle of a bench and him not helping. He didn't look at her, even as her leg was half-exposed when she lifted her foot up over her seat, but his jaw was rigid. He must be gritting his teeth.

Once she was settled, he motioned for two young girls to resume playing their lutes and told one of the maids to bring more ale for everyone. No doubt he wanted the crowd to resume their conversations and drinking and stop gawking at them on the dais.

And, oh, he was so handsome, she had to work hard not to gawk herself. His blond hair was clean and hung loose, except for the thin war braids on either side of his clean-shaven face that had been plaited with multi-colored crystals. His grayish blue eyes were clear and steady; if he'd been overindulging in alcohol, it didn't show. He wore a tunic of soft, dark blue wool with silver braiding along the edges, not a match for Ingolf's regal attire, but in some ways better. He must have raided his treasure room.

He turned to her then. And raised his brows in a haughty manner.

"Merry Christmas, husband."

"Oink, oink!" he said.

She could feel her face heat. "I said that when I thought you got married while I was gone."

"*Pfff!* In such a short time? What does that say about me? Nay, don't tell me. Oink, oink."

He was not going to let her forget that. Actually, he was starting to earn the name. "You should talk. How could you have thought I would leave, willingly? Without any warning? With no good-byes?"

He shrugged.

Typical man! Couldn't admit he was insecure. Just like women were.

Jarl Ingolf said, "You did not tell me, Hauk, that you have such a comely wife." He leaned forward then and winked at Kirstin.

Hauk stiffened at the wink.

Good. She leaned forward, too, and replied, "Thank you for the compliment, sir. Likewise, I did not realize you were so young. From the descriptions I had been given, I pictured a much older man."

Jarl Ingolf preened. "Mayhap they spoke of my father, who went on to Valhalla only two winters past."

"Are any of his wives still living with you at Stormstead?"

"Yea, my mother, along with his first wife, and an aged concubine."

Holy Sister Wives! "You should have brought them with you," Kirstin said.

Revna made a snorting sound which pretty much

amounted to, "Over my dead body!" Kirstin could guess what it was like at Stormstead with four females vying for household power.

"They would have been more than welcome," Hauk added, as if just now recalling his duties as a host.

"My mother is ofttimes bedridden," Ingolf told them, "but I will convey your kind words."

Nothing was said about the other two women.

That was one good thing about Haukshire. There was no strife among the women, although there would have been, for sure, if Zoya had stuck around.

"I bet you were sorry that you sent Zoya away," she blurted out to Hauk. "I mean, once I was gone, having another woman to..." Her words trailed off at the glower he cast her way.

"Is that how you justified bedplay with another man, so soon after leaving me?"

She gasped. "I did not...where did you get the idea..." She paused, then said, "Egil."

"Yea, Egil told me of your 'activities' with the JAM person."

"Activities! *Pfff.* We merely went out to dinner together."

"No swiving?"

"No swiving."

"And that was all? No touching, or rubbing, or kissing?"

"Well..." She could feel herself blushing. "There was kissing, but—."

He tossed his hands in the air in an "I knew it!" gesture.

"Oh, give me a break."

"Do not try to say he kissed you and you did not kiss him back. 'Tis ever the way with women to prevaricate thus."

"I did kiss him back, but only to see if he had any effect on me, like you had."

He rolled his eyes, and then there was a prolonged silence before he relented. "And...?"

"Nothing."

She couldn't tell if her answer pleased him or not, or if he even believed her.

There was another prolonged silence before she asked, "And you? Were you with any other woman? Did you kiss anyone?"

He gave her a disbelieving look. "As if there were any women here to kiss! Signe is the only passably attractive woman under the age of forty, and Thorkel would beat me bloody if I dared try her charms."

"There was Revna and her daughters."

He gave her another disbelieving look. "I would have had to act quickly for that to happen, if I had been interested, which I was not. In truth, I do not like adultery, nor am I inclined toward sex with children."

Who said anything about sex? "So, it's only for lack of opportunity that you've remained celibate?" *And not because you were faithful to me?*

"Do you deliberately bait me, Kirstin? Yea, I would have swived another woman. I would have swived fifty women if they'd been available and even moderately attractive, anything to wipe you from my mind. Are you happy now?"

Actually, yes. Well, not unhappy. Instead of answering, she stuck her tongue out at him. As immature as that was, she found herself immensely pleased that she'd rattled his chain.

Further talk was interrupted by the arrival of the house-carls carrying in the food, first to the high table and then to all the others. Some dishes were brought from the kitchen, under Frida's supervision, and others were taken directly from the hearth fires in between the aisles, where they had been kept warm since their preparation.

This being the Jul feast, there was a wider variety of offer-ings than the usual daily fare. Thick slices of roast boar sat on huge wooden platters, in some cases complete with the actual pig's head, feet, and tail. For those who did not like pork, alternatives were offered in the form of quail in a baked pastry, sliced venison tongues, a variety of smoked fishes, little herrings swimming in a tart brine, *hrútspungar* (ram's testicles pickled in whey and pressed into cakes), and *blodpolse* (a Viking version of blood sausage). Flat circular breads, similar to modern pitas or naan, were used to scoop up meat scraps or drippings, in lieu of forks or spoons. Tiny, pathetically thin wild carrots swam in a white dill sauce. Dots of butter adorned bowls of mashed turnips. Green beans dressed with hazelnuts, chips of crisp pig skin, and a rudimentary vinaigrette. Boiled and salted sea gull eggs. Condiments, such as horseradish and mustard, were provided, too. Honey oat cakes, and *skyrr*, a soft cheese with the consistency of yogurt, mixed with dried fruits, completed the feast.

Kirstin could smell spices like cumin, ginger, and clove on some of the offerings, and assumed Egil had obtained them, as well as some of the vegetables she saw, from his trip to the market town of Hedeby. "Maybe we won't need to import all this produce in the future. I brought a bunch of hearty vegetable seeds to be planted next spring," she said before recalling that Hauk wasn't interested in her plans, not in his present mood. So, she added, "If I'm here next spring."

"See, there you go again. No sooner do you arrive than you are threatening to leave again. How can I ever trust you?"

Kirstin was stunned at the vehemence of his reaction. "That wasn't a threat. I meant that I might not be here next spring because you don't want me here."

Instead of reacting to her words, he asked, "What is that red substance on your lips?"

"Cherry lip gloss."

"What? Do you bedevil me apurpose?"

"It's only lip gloss. Nothing devilish about that!"

"It is for a man with a passion for cherries."

"You like cherries? I had no idea." She batted her eyelashes with fake innocence, then licked her lips. Kirstin would have continued with her teasing, but Hauk turned away from her toward the food.

They put a little of each dish on their pewter salvers. Kirstin only picked at her food and sipped at her mead, while Hauk ate heartily and drank like a camel. Obviously, she was nervous. Obviously, he was not.

The pig!

No, no, no! She'd already used...rather misused that insult for him. The jerk, then. He was behaving like a jerk.

"Did you say something, dearling?" he asked with super sweetness, turning the table on her innocence act over the lip gloss.

"Nothing important...dearest." She oozed false sweetness, too.

"It sounded like berserk."

Yes, you're driving me berserk, you jerk. "I said it's not important," she snapped.

"Whoa! I did not mean to stir your feathers." He smirked, a clue that he was not displeased with the result, despite his lack of intent.

"I can't believe you're behaving so boarishly."

"Boarish, am I? I thought you apologized for calling me a pig. Make up your mind, wench. A boar is a pig, in case you did not know."

She barely suppressed a growl. "I take it back then. You *are* a pig. And you're stubborn as a mule. Mean as a bear. Fickle as a bull. Horny as a jackrabbit. Vain as a peacock. Sneaky as a snake. And...and..." She had to stop for a moment because tears were beginning to well in her eyes.

Hauk was no longer smirking. His head was tilted to the side, studying her with confusion, or concern, or something. He put out a hand, about to touch her arm.

She slapped his hand away and might have said or done

something more to show her opinion of his behavior, but she felt a tap on her shoulder. She turned to find Gorm standing there. The boy had washed his face and hands, probably on someone's orders, but he'd only gone so far, leaving his arms and the outer edges of his face and all his neck a different, darker dirt color. He'd plaited his hair into two braids that lay forward over his shoulders toward his little chest, which was commendable, that he'd made such as effort at grooming, except one of them was a good four inches shorter than the other. He was wearing a reasonably clean tunic over slim braies, with a length of rope for a belt. He was barefooted, despite the cold weather, and his toenails looked as if they hadn't been clipped in a very long time. A candy cane hung from the rope belt on the side, like a dagger. When he smiled tentatively, flashing those two empty spaces, his red tongue showed evidence of what he'd been eating, or overeating.

In other words, he was adorable.

"What is it, Gorm?" she asked.

He looked right and left, unsure of his welcome here on the dais, and Kirstin could see why. Hauk, Egil, and Bjorn had all moved around so they could see what he was about.

"Don't worry about them. You can talk to me."

"Frida said I should come thank ye fer all the candy crooks ye give me."

"It was my pleasure, honey." Kirstin glanced toward the tree and saw none in evidence. "And they're candy canes, not candy crooks. Did you share them?"

He nodded. "Frida tol' me to ask if ye have any more?"

That was clearly a fib, she saw as his expression perked up with hope.

"Nope," she said. "I see you have one left, though." She pointed to the one on his belt.

He nodded. "I'm savin' it fer my birfday."

"When is that?"

"I doan know...mayhap in the summer time."

"You're going to wait all those months?" she asked.

Hauk snorted his disbelief behind her, and Bjorn said something about how sticky his fingers would be by then.

"By the way, Gorm, how did your one braid get so much shorter than the other?" Kirstin asked

"*Pff!* Ye should ask! 'Twas Ubbi what did it. Three of his friends had to hold me down, though." The latter was said with pride.

"What did ye do to cause Ubbi to go after ye?" Egil asked.

Gorm hesitated, probably trying to figure what answer would serve him best, but then he admitted, "I mighta poured blue woad dye on his ballocks when he was sleepin'."

Kirstin put a hand over her mouth to smother a giggle. The others didn't even bother to hide their appreciation of the boy's mischief.

"Y'know, somethin' jist occurred to me," Egil remarked. "The bratling looks jist like ye, m'lord. I always disbelieved his mother's claims, but could he be another of yer father's get?"

"Who? Me?" Hauk scowled. "He doesn't look at all like me."

Kirstin wasn't sure there was a resemblance, except for the grayish blue eyes, but she could see that Hauk was not pleased by the comparison; so, she said, "Spitting image!"

Hauk directed his scowl at her.

What else is new? Scowls 'r Us.

"By thunder!" Bjorn said. "That would make the little guy my uncle."

They all laughed at that, except Hauk who was still scowling. And Gorm, who was frowning with uncertainty. But then Gorm brightened. "Does that mean the jarl is my brudder? Thor's Teeth! I'm gonna be rich. I'll have me own longship. When can I get a sword? Oooh, I can't wait to tell Ubbi."

Before Hauk could call him back and correct any misconception he might have about his family ties, the boy vaulted off the dais and ran toward the kitchen.

"Now you've done it!" Hauk said to her.

"Me? I'm not the one who first mentioned the resemblance."

"Everywhere you go, there's trouble," he grumbled.

She was offended at his easy dismissal of her. "Is that all you think of me?"

His Adam's apple moved several times as he thought about what to answer. "Nay, that is not all I think of you. I recall a day when I came upon you in the back courtyard where you were talking with Bjorn about an herb garden or some such. Your hand was on his shoulder as you spoke. You were wearing an old gunna of Signe's...a pale rose color...and your hair was bound high on your head and swished like a horse's tail when you turned abruptly to look at me. I was discouraged, having come from the barn where everything was in disrepair. But when you smiled at me, all my worries disappeared, and I felt such a warmth rush through me." He shook his head as if surprised that he'd revealed so much. "A good memory," he concluded with a shrug.

Before he had a chance to withdraw into himself, she said, "It's funny how it's the little things that stick in our brains. The memory that plagued me most when I was gone was of the day when we arrived at Haukshire. We'd just disembarked from your ship and you got your first look at your home after being gone so long. You were looking so forlorn and sad. I took your hand and laced our fingers together. You raised our double fist and kissed my knuckles, looking at me the whole time, thanks in your eyes. Then we walked toward the keep. Together."

Her words caught him off guard and he said nothing at first. Then he laughed. "That is some memory. I would have thought your favored remembrance would be of me tupping you like a…what did you call it…a jackrabbit."

"That was my second favorite memory." She didn't bother to look at him as she spoke. Instead, she was concentrating on the delicious but messy honey oak cake she was nibbling on, finishing off by licking her fingertips. When she noticed his continuing silence, she glanced his way and saw him staring at her with disbelief.

"What?"

"You say…and do…the most outrageous things."

She looked at her fingers, realizing what he referred to. "*Pfff!* It's not as if I was licking any of *your* body parts."

"I have a vivid imagination."

He seemed to be softening toward her. "Are you still mad at me?" she asked.

"Furious."

"But that would not stop you from a free fuck, would it?"

He winced at her crude word. "What has one to do with the other? A man has his brutish urges and must slake his lust in some way."

"Typical man! If you're going to say that all cats are the same in the dark, forget about it!"

"Huh?"

She shook her head at his hopelessness, or maybe at the hopelessness of repairing their relationship. "Sorry, Charlie, but I'm not making love with a man who doesn't love me, probably never loved me."

"I do not know about that. In truth, you missay me at every turn," he said with a lazy drawl that caught her attention and caused her to look at him suspiciously. "There are butter-flies fluttering in my belly. I am assailed by dizziness at odd times. And bilious? I could vomit here and now. In truth, I scarce know whether to oink or bray. Should I laugh or should I cry? That's how moodsome I've become. A sad, sad state for a Viking warrior!" He arched his brows at her as if asking if she understood. Then he got up and walked away.

She frowned, then recalled once telling him about a *Cosmo* magazine article detailing the symptoms of love. Was he saying he still loved her? And then just strolling off, as if it was of no matter.

No frickin' way!

"What are you saying?" she yelled after him.

Everyone at the high table and many of them below looked at her and then Hauk to see what was going on.

Kirstin stood and took her goblet in hand, raising it high. "I'd like to propose a toast," she shouted. "Here's to strong-minded Viking women." The women in the hall cheered, Signe loudest of all, and raised their arms in the air, taking long draws on their drinks. "And to the few, very few, rare men who have the talent to hold them."

The women cheered even louder, and the men not so much, as they peered at each other, wondering if they'd been insulted. Thorkel seemed to be shocked by his new wife's actions.

Hauk stopped in his tracks, turned to stare at her. "Is that a challenge, m'lady?" he called out.

"That is a dare, my friend. In fact, I double dog dare you."

"A dog now!" he said with disgust, not understanding, into the silence that had suddenly overcome the hall as everyone watched. He motioned with his forefinger, beckoning for her to come to him.

"Not a chance." She laughed.

He started to return to the dais.

She started to sidle toward the other end of the dais.

He changed direction, moving over in front of the dais.

She did an about-face, and went back the way she'd come, bypassing Egil, Bjorn, and Gisela. Jarl Ingolf appeared amused, while his wife was horrified by Kirstin's actions which she likely deemed unseemly. The two daughters were just confused.

Kirstin flew down the steps and ran up the center aisle.

Hauk leapt off the dais, which he'd just climbed, and came after her.

The crowd was in a raucous uproar, with cheers, laughter and bets being placed.

"A *brud-hlaup*! We finally get a bride-running! A real one this time!" someone hooted.

Another person contributed, "Best get the master's sword for 'im so he can smack our lady's arse when he catches her."

A female voice shouted, "*If* he can catch her!" And a number of other ladies cheered her on.

Kirstin stopped, picked up a greasy piglet head, and tossed it at Hauk, aiming for his face.

He caught it with surprise, then a grin. He was slowed down a bit as he had to find a place to drop it.

She almost escaped. Bolting through the open door of their bedchamber, she turned to slam the door shut, but Hauk got his booted foot in first. In a match of strength, she pushed, he pushed, and he, of course, prevailed. Slamming the door behind him, he grabbed her shoulders and pinned her against the wall.

Kirstin did the most unexpected thing then, unexpected to both her and Hauk. She began to cry...big, loud sobs that wracked her body and caused her eyes and nose to run.

"What? Are you hurt? Did I hurt you?"

She shook her head, not wanting to tell him that it was the pent-up fear and pain of the past few weeks and things not going as she had planned on her return. Relief, actually. Now that they were alone, together, there was hope. She could swear she saw tears in his eyes as well.

Carefully, without speaking, he wiped his hands, then hers on a piece of toweling sitting on a nearby shelf. He also dabbed at her eyes and nose with a clean edge, still pinning her to the wall with his body. Afterward, he bowed his head for several moments, as if in prayer. Then, ever so slowly, he raised his head and regarded her gravely.

She couldn't let him get all serious on her, venting about what she'd done, then her venting about what he'd done, and blah, blah, blah. Wasted time, wasted energy. Instead, she turned the tables on him by warning, "You better not plan on hitting my ass with a sword."

He blinked several times, puzzled.

"Like those dumbbells out in your hall suggested. You know, the bride-running crap."

He blinked several more times, then visibly relaxed with understanding. "Have no fears, my foolish, impulsive, stubborn, deluded lady." He paused and leaned down to nip her earlobe, blowing softly into the shell with erotic intent, before whispering, "I have other plans for your arse."

CHAPTER 25

Round one...

*H*auk wasn't sure what to do first.
Paddle the wench's arse.
If she'll let me.
Kiss her senseless.
If she'll let me.

But, of course, Kirstin took the action out of his hands. "Listen, sweetheart, since my abrupt departure and equally abrupt return are the big pink elephants in the room, let me assure you—"

"An elephant am I now?"

"Not you. It's a figure of speech. Never mind. I am never going to leave again. Even if you don't want me anymore."

"Kirstin," he said on a long sigh. "You came. You said you love me. You left. You came back again. You said you were sorry. Then you locked yourself in this room. You came out acting as if you'd never left. Then you get all shrewish on me and run away, crying. How can I trust what you say anymore?"

She bristled. But then she raised her chin. "What if I can prove it, that I won't be leaving ever again?"

"How?" He suspected he was falling into some trap.

"Release me, and I'll show you."

He hesitated, still wary of a trap. But then he muttered, "Damn me for a fool!" and stepped back from her.

Immediately she went toward the door and opened it. At the same time, she was pushing the two arm rings down from her upper arms to her wrists, then off. By the time he caught up with her, she was already poised over the closest of the hearth fires where one of the yule logs, which had been lit this morning, was still burning white-hot. Before he realized what she was about, she dropped both arm rings into the fire.

"Good gods!" he exclaimed as he came up beside her. "Have you lost your bloody mind?"

"No. I've found it," she said, smiling up at him.

It took him several moments to find a poker which had been moved to another hearth. The heat was so intense that he had to be careful not to singe the hairs on his forearm. Once he caught the two arm rings on the tip of the poker, the metal had already started to soften and reform into odd shapes. The rings would have had to stay in the coals for much longer before the silver would actually begin melting, but as it was, they would never fit over anyone's arms at this point, not even a child's.

Kirstin had already turned and was stomping back to the bedchamber.

Egil and Bjorn came up to him, both of them laughing like hyenas.

"Truly, m'lord, I have not had so much fun since...since..." Egil sputtered.

"...since Lady Kirstin was here before," Bjorn finished for him.

"I cannot wait to see what you two do next," Egil said.

"Nor can all the rest of us here in the hall," Bjorn added, waving to indicate the dozens of people in the hall who were blatantly eavesdropping. Ever since Hauk had gotten the appellation of Viking in a Cage, he'd been the subject of much mirth, and he was damn tired of being the source of everyone's amusement. He motioned for the musicians to resume their performance and told Egil and Bjorn in no uncertain terms to go back to their seats and lead the feast to its usual finish, which should be soon. Otherwise, he would be back, and it wouldn't be him providing the entertainment; it would be the two of them, singing, or dancing, or standing on their mead-sodden heads.

Hauk was left, still holding the poker with the dangling, misshapen arm rings in front of him. They were too hot to set down anywhere. After he followed her into the room, he kicked the door shut behind him and tipped the poker over the water pitcher where the rings sizzled as they sank to the bottom.

Only then did he turn to look at his wife who had the absolutely infuriating, galling, outrageous nerve to smile at him. She was half lying on the bed, propped against a pile of bed furs, her arms crossed behind her neck, and she was as naked as the day she was born.

And she was wearing a set of arm rings.

~

Round two...

ON THE OUTSIDE, Kirstin worked to appear calm and triumphant, but inside she was nervous and unsure how Hauk would take her grand gesture, which turned out not to be a grand gesture after all. Well, actually, it was, but she would need to make some explanations before he would realize that.

He did not look like he was in the mood for explanations. He put his hands on his hips and shook his head with disbelief. "Do you enjoy making mock of me?"

"I wasn't mocking you. I needed to make a grand gesture in order to get your attention."

"Hah! You had my attention when you came walking up the fjord path looking like a Valkyrie in that white fur. You had my attention when you came swanning into the Jul feast looking like Queen of the North. You sure as hell got my attention when you made that challenge toast."

"Well, how did I know that? That stupid shield of indifference you built around yourself was impenetrable. I had to make a grand gesture with the arm rings on the fire."

"*Pfff!* More like a grand jest. At my expense."

She sat up and held her arms out to him. "Take off your clothes and come make love to me. Afterward, I'll explain everything."

He shook his head. "You will not trap me by pulling on my cock." When she said nothing and didn't even flinch, although she wanted to, he said, "Aren't you going to threaten to leave again if I don't do as you wish?"

She did flinch then and lowered her arms, pulling the bed fur up to cover her breasts. She was embarrassed now. "Is that what you think? Is that how I acted all the time…as if you had to toe the line, *my* line, or I would threaten to leave? As if you always had to be on tenterhooks?"

"You make me sound pitysome."

"No, it makes *me* sound like a self-centered bitch."

He shifted from foot to foot. She wasn't sure if he was going to leave, and to hell with her. Or if he was going to give her…no, *them*…another chance.

"I love you, Hauk."

"Cherry lip gloss and love! You do not play fair." More shifting from foot to foot.

She shrugged. "All's fair in love and war," she quipped, and didn't even care that it was a cliché. "I brought you a Christmas gift."

"Is it cherry-flavored?" He didn't shift from foot to foot this time, but he did glance at the door, as if contemplating how quickly he could exit, gracefully.

"No, it's not cherry-flavored. Actually, the gift is from both me and my father."

A gleam of interest showed in his eyes. God bless the Viking man's curiosity! Why else would they have gone a-Viking and adventuring to new lands that frightened off most people of that...rather, this time period. "Hand me my cloak," she said.

He took it off the hook on the wall behind him and arched his brows at its continued weight. "What do you have in here? Stones?"

"No, but your gift is contributing to a lot of its heaviness."

"Is it a sword? A solid gold belt? A crown?"

The fact that he was joking...at least, she thought he was joking...gave her hope.

He laid the cloak over her lap and raised his brows at her clumsy attempt to keep the bed fur over her breasts. "You owe me at least the pleasure of your nakedness."

"And the pleasure of seeing my discomfort?" she added.

"True." He sat on a stool beside the bed. "Well?" he said, waving a hand toward the cloak.

She opened the garment and took out two large Ziplock bags, one from each side, which had been needed to balance the weight. There were six mini bottles or splits of Blue Dragon wines, reds and whites, each protected with bubble wrap. "These are samples of the types of wine made at Blue Dragon vineyard," she told him. "They're much smaller than regular bottles, of course. They're only intended for promotions or travel venues, like airplanes or hotel rooms." He had to be amazed at the very idea of bottles of glass holding a beverage, least of all her bringing them back to him or the sound of those other strange things she mentioned, like airplanes and hotels.

The wines had such names as Dragon Spit, Dragon Tail, Dragon Flame and Dragon Breath. She recited the names of each of them as she unwrapped them.

"That one seems appropriate," he said when she got to Dragon Lust.

She handed the bottle to him, but then had to show him how to open the screw-top lid. Over and over, he opened the lid and closed the lid, more fascinated by that modern invention than the glass bottle itself. Glass had of course been invented ages ago, but he wouldn't have ever seen anything so small or perfectly proportioned for holding a liquid. "Amazing!" he said and was ready to try the content.

"Just sip," she advised. "Maybe hold it in your mouth for a few seconds to get the full flavor before swallowing."

He did and then made an expression of pleasure at the taste before handing it back to her. She took a tiny sip as well, being careful to hold the bed fur up under her arm pits.

"Dragon Lust is a cabernet sauvignon. A dry red wine. Often served with red meats. Very popular."

She replaced the cap and opened Dragon Breath. "This is my favorite. A light white wine. Pino grigio. Goes great with fish or cheese, or just for drinking."

He sipped and said, "Good, but I prefer the first one."

"Do you want to try more?"

"Yea, but are you going to clutch that bed fur like a chastity belt the whole time?"

"I am if you're going to remain fully clothed," she responded as she opened another red, Dragon Flame, and handed it to him. "By the way, I have another present for you. A tattoo."

"You're giving me a tattoo?"

"No, I got a tattoo on my body, *for you*."

He considered that for only a second before asking, "Where?"

She fluttered her lashes at him. "That's for you to find out."

He muttered something that might have been "Wench!" or "Witch!" before chugging down the entire split in two long swallows, despite her warning to only sip.

She arched her brows at him.

"In every battle, a point is reached where one side needs to make the assault. Enough of these pricking little attacks."

"Do you consider this a war?"

"Don't you?"

"And the end result?" she asked. "Winner takes all?"

"Or loser loses everything," he said ominously.

~

Round three...

IT WAS TRUE. Hauk was tired of the games they seemed to be playing.

I love you. I hate you. I love-hate you.

Thrust and parry.

I want you. I don't want you. Whatever (her favorite, most irksome word)!

Stab and retreat.

Bestir me. Betray me.

Feint and spin.

I'll never leave you. Good-bye! Tra la la!

'Twas enough to drive a Viking into berserkness. If he wasn't careful, he would be howling like a wolf and biting his shield.

Another animal! Aaarrgh! I am doing it now, too.

With a muttered curse, he stood and undid his belt, holding her gaze the entire time. He tried to view her as a combatant he was about to duel, but it was difficult when she did not even try to hide her smile of satisfaction. A good warrior did not react to the enemy's taunts. So, he raised his chin and scowled her way.

Having taken that stand, he held her gaze as he lifted his tunic over his head and bared himself to the waist. He knew that she liked his body, and liked to look at it. She'd told him so many times. Bloody hell, he liked to look at her body, too.

She waved a hand, indicating that he should continue. As if she were the commander in this battle of wits...or witlessness, he was beginning to think.

Even so, he held her gaze as he shrugged out of his braies, and toed them off along with his half boots. *Take that, wench!* he thought as he brazenly exposed himself to her scrutiny.

With his hands on his hips, he continued to hold her gaze, or tried to hold her gaze, but it was difficult because her gaze kept flickering to his enthusiasm, which was standing out like a knight's lance about to wage an assault. Embarrassing, really. Well, not really. Try as he might, it was difficult for a man to remain angry and seemingly unemotional when he was betrayed by his favorite body part.

"Do you want me to explain about the arm rings?" she asked.

Unbelievable! I present her with all my magnificence, and she wants to chatter. "Do not dare!"

"What? You don't want to know why I had two sets of arm rings?"

"At this moment, I do not care if you have ten sets. Enough blather!" He picked up the top edge of the bed fur covering her and flipped it up and back to land at the foot of the bed.

"Hauk! I'm getting cold."

"You won't be cold for long. Where is it?"

"Where is what?"

"The tattoo."

"I was saving that for later."

"Well, there's no saving this." He cupped himself, then put one knee on the edge of the mattress and swung the other knee over her body, managing to land exactly where he wanted, skin to skin.

"I can see your point," she said, raising her hips a little, which caused his enthusiasm to become more enthusiastic, pressing against her belly.She was probably being sarcastic, but he was beyond caring.

"Are you still cold?" he asked.

"You're better than a bed fur any day, babe, but, yeah, I'm still a little chilled." She put her arms around his shoulders. "A few kisses might heat my blood."

"Kisses? I'm beyond that now."

"I thought you liked our kisses. I could reapply my lip gloss."

"Later," he said. "Must we talk?"

"Just one thing. I love you, Hauk. If we love each other, we can work all the little details out."

"The little details!" he exclaimed with consternation. "Like your deserting me? Like your pretending to melt your arm rings? Like you sobbing your eyes out when you're finally in my arms?"

"Minor speed bumps on the road to love," she proclaimed airily. "You do love me, don't you?" The slight quiver of her lips told him that she was actually unsure what his answer would be. Foolish woman!

"My hands are shaking. My brain is spinning. My stomach is churning. My knees are wobbling. My heart is racing. My cock is throbbing." He ran out of bodily descriptions and shrugged. "Must be love. Or else I'm suffering from *herfjöttr*, or war fetter, like some head-battered berserker." He paused to consider that last possibility. "Nay, it must be love."

"You're never going to let me forget that *Cosmo* article, are you?" She smiled.

His racing heart skipped a beat and seemed to grow and grow. If a smile could do that to him, he wondered what a more overt expression of her pleasure would do to him. He could scarce wait to find out.

He grew more serious then as he began to make love to his wife. He wanted to go hard and deep, to imprint himself inside her so that she would never leave again. A fanciful thought! Like those lamebrained poets who spoke of lovers becoming one. That's what she was turning him into...a fanciful dolthead. And so it was with special care that he made slow love to his wife.

And she returned that slow love right back at him. Kiss for kiss. Caress for caress. Moan for moan.

But then...

He couldn't believe it, but then...

As he wet her ear with the tip of his tongue, then blew it dry, over and over, an erotic technique he knew she enjoyed, as evidenced by her little sighs and shivers...but then she insisted on talking. "I had my brother make me a separate set of arm rings, not because I plan to go back, but just in case there is some emergency."

"Like?" he asked, meanwhile moving lower to lick her nipples into hard points. Another of her special erotic places that Hauk had discovered on earlier occasions.

She arched her back to give him better access and remarked, "Oh, I don't know. A plague or something."

"A plague! We have ne'er had a plague in the Norselands afore. Unless you know something that is to come in the future." He shot up to a sitting position, his buttocks resting on her thighs. "Oh, my gods! What will it be? Locusts? Boils? Frogs? Disease?"

"No, no, no! I don't know about any specific plagues. It was just an example of an emergency that *could* occur."

"I swear, you will be the death of me," he said, lying back down over her.

"I'm just saying we should have a spare set of arm rings put away in some safe place, in case they're ever needed."

"How can you make love and talk about other things at the same time?"

"I'm a multitasker," she said.

Is it a sign of intelligence or lackwittedness that I am beginning to understand her strange words? He smiled to himself and thought, *Whatever!*

"I missed this," she murmured as he licked her breasts.

"And I missed *that*," he choked out, well above a murmur, when she stroked him down below.

He kissed her endlessly and deeply and told her. "Your taste...I forgot your taste."

"I didn't forget yours," she drawled, later. And she wasn't talking about his mouth.

He wasn't able to say anything at all for a while after that. And they hadn't even mutually consummated their loveplay yet.

"Oh, I forgot," she said as he lay splatted over her. "You mentioned that you had something in mind for my ass, and I thought you'd guessed where I got my tattoo."

His brain was fuzzy from his lone peaking, and he probably had a sex flush covering his face and neck; so, only half attending, it was several moments before her words sank in. He raised his head and arched his brows in question. "You didn't!"

She nodded. "I did."

Without warning he rolled her over so that her body was face down on the mattress. And there it was!

His shield sign of chasing hawks tattooed on one of her nether cheeks. He spread her legs and knelt between them, lifted her hips so she was on her knees, too, her arse raised, to give himself a better look. He thought earlier of wanting to make such deep love to his wife that he would be imprinted inside of her. But she'd imprinted his sign on the outside of her body.

What a woman!

And she is mine!

His enthusiasm shot back with a vengeance. And he made love to her in what was to become his new favorite sexual position, one in which he could do the deed deeply and at the same time view the artwork on her arse. 'Twould seem he was good at multitasking, too.

"I love you, sweetheart," she told him as she drifted off to sleep a long time later.

"I love you, too, sweetling," he whispered, kissing the top of her head which rested on his shoulder, "for all time."

The next morning, they buried the arm rings beneath a tree in the mossy patch over by the fjord, which was not an easy task, considering the snow and icy earth. It was just a precaution that Hauk had agreed to, just in case someone (not either of them) needed them in the future.

Some of his people who watched from afar considered them addled by the love that clearly showed in their eyes. Thorkel thought it might be the sex flush which had moved to their brains. Egil wondered if they were digging for some treasure that the lady had learned of in her time travels. Bjorn had nothing to say; he was still asleep.

Thereafter, that mossy, flowery grove was said to have magical powers.

EPILOGUE

Time went by, in more ways than one...

Over the next five years, Kirstin gave birth to four daughters, two sets of twins, whom Hauk referred to as his "heartlings." Then she went on to have two sons. As decades passed, the timeswept couple were more in love than ever, their bond enhanced by their large family. Never once did Kirstin regret giving up her modern life, even as she missed her "other" family. Although she was said to complain more than once that she would give anything for a good shower, whatever that was.

Hauk's trading skills (dealing in amber and furs) brought prosperity to Haukshire which allowed him to expand his keep and outbuildings enough to rival a minor kingdom. His fleet of longships numbered twelve at last count, including two *knarrs* or merchant cargo ships. A village grew up in those surroundings to house all the new Haukshire folks, and not just seamen and their families. There were blacksmiths, ship builders, carpenters, woodcarvers, weavers, and other skilled craftsmen.

Kirstin made good use of their prosperity to better furnish her home with tapestry wall hangings and even carpets on some of the floors, which was unheard of for that time. Revna taught Kirstin's weavers how to make the intricate orphrey embroidery, and Haukshire fabrics became prized products in the trading markets of Hedeby, Birka, and Kaupang.

Of course, Kirstin, always looking for new "projects," pleaded with Hauk for "a few" sheep (they ended up with ten, and the frisky animals kept reproducing) to provide the wool to make the cloth, much to Hauk's disgust; for some reason, Hauk had a dislike for the wooly creatures, which he often said were "dumb as Saxon dirt." But there was nothing Hauk wouldn't do for his beloved wife.

Kirstin used those initial seed packets to grow vegetables and herbs, some of which thrived with her constant care. Even some of the grapevines managed to survive, and they made their first wine on the fifth year. "Tastes like dragon piss," was the general consensus, but it improved over the years to the point they no longer needed to import any of that beverage.

"Chicken Slop" with "spit balls" became a favorite dish at Haukshire. Kirstin gave up on correcting the mispronunciations after a while once she figured out that Hauk deliberately fostered those false ideas, one of his many ways of teasing her. Viking men were known for their playful mischief.

Hauk never escaped his experience in that Saxon cage. Over the years skalds not only told sagas of "The Viking in a Cage," but they embellished on it. To hear some of them, you'd think he had grown fur and animal parts by the time he finally escaped...an escape which was aided by a silver-blonde Valkyrie with wings, which allowed the two of them to fly out of Winchester Castle. Good thing he had a sense of humor, but then, Viking men had a great talent for laughing at themselves.

Bjorn became a skillful warrior, a member of the far-famed Varangians, travelling to many lands. Eventually, he left that band of fighting mercenaries and married Gisela. As jarl of Stormstead, after her father's death, Bjorn also flourished with three sons and two daughters.

Egil lived to a ripe old age of fifty-five and was said to be pleased in his final hour to die in battle (one of the many continuing wars with the Saxons), which entitled him to go on to Valhalla. No straw death for him!

The biggest surprise of all came with Gorm, who grew into an incredibly handsome Viking man, praised by his comrades-in-arms, loved by women in many countries. A rascal to the bone! In other words, a Viking. A lot like his brother Hauk, many people said. Gorm sought adventure every chance he got, and it was he who vowed to use the arm rings one day to travel to that new land of America.

Who knows! Stranger things have happened.

READER LETTER

Dear Readers:

Well, my goodness! Did you ever think I was going to write another new Viking book? Seems like forever, doesn't it? Well, it has been eight years since I've written any Viking novels, eleven years since I've written any books in this particular Viking series, the last ones being DARK VIKING and VIKING HEAT. I forgot how much fun these guys were.

Those of you who have been with me and my Vikings from the beginning, more than twenty years now, know that I pride myself on my Norse ancestry. I can actually trace my paternal family tree back to the tenth century Viking Rollo, first duke of Norsemandy. But besides that, research has shown me that these Vikings were brave, handsome, talented men with a remarkable sense of humor for their time. They were not the rapers and pillagers depicted by the biased monk historians of that time, or at least they were no worse than the Saxon, Franks, or other cultures back then. They were violent times.

In my opinion, my Vikings are different from many other

Vikings out there because of my unique voice for humor and sizzle. I hope you agree. Where else will you find a Viking commissioned by a king to find the witch who caused his cock to take a right turn, or a grief-stricken Viking berserker who is being counseled by a modern-day psychologist on anger management, or a whole series of Viking Navy SEALs, for that matter?

Y'know, there's nothing sexier than a man who can make a woman smile in bed. Boy, do my Vikings ever! I also often quote that old proverb, "When a rogue kisses you, count your teeth." Yep! You could insert "Viking rogue" in there, and it would be doubly true.

Historical accuracy is important to me, but I have taken some author license in terms of dates. For example, there was, in fact, a St. Brice's massacre, but it might not have been the exact year I've used.

I love to hear from you readers. Your opinions do matter to me. I answer every email. I can be reached at shill733aol.com, or on my website at *www.sandrahill.net*, or on Facebook at SandraHillAuthor. More than anything, I'd like to know what you'd like to see next. Gorm's story? Another Viking Navy SEAL or maybe some of the old secondary characters that never got their own stories, like Alrek the Clumsy Viking, or any of that rogue Tykir's sons. If you sign up for my mailing list on my website, you'll receive occasional newsletters with updates and gift offerings.

The books in my series can be read out of order, but, of course, it's best if you can go back from the beginning. One of the best things for me, as a reader, not a writer, is discovering a new-to-me author and being able to go back and glom onto his or her other books. That's what I'm hoping you'll do, go back and read all the books in this Viking Series II: THE LAST VIKING, TRULY, MADLY VIKING, THE VERY VIRILE VIKING, WET & WILD, HOT & HEAVY, ROUGH

AND READY, DOWN AND DIRTY, VIKING UNCHAINED, VIKING HEAT, DARK VIKING, and now THE CAGED VIKING.

As always, I wish you smiles in your reading.

—**Sandra Hill**

ALSO BY SANDRA HILL

Books in Sandra's Viking Navy SEALs series:

Wet and Wild

Hot and Heavy

Rough and Ready

Down and Dirty

Viking Unchained

Viking Heat

Dark Viking

The Caged Viking

ABOUT THE AUTHOR

Humor (and sizzle) are the trademarks of Sandra Hill novels, all fifty or so of them, whether they be about Cajuns, Vikings, Navy SEALs, Viking vampire angels (vangels), or treasure hunters, or a combination of these. Readers especially love her notorious Tante Lulu, the bayou matchmaker/folk healer, and often write to say they have a family member just like her, or wish they did. In addition, there are thousands of fans who devour her outrageous Viking novels, whether they be historicals or time-travels. Sometimes, the characters jump from one series to another.

Growing up in a small town in Pennsylvania, Sandra says she was quiet and shy, no funny bone at all, but she was forced to develop a sense of humor as a survival skill later in her all male household: a husband, four sons, and a male German Shepherd the size of a horse. Add to that mix now a male black lab, a male Labradoodle, two male grandsons (a rock musician and an extreme athlete), and a stunning granddaughter, who is both gifted and a gift, and you can see why Sandra wishes all her fans smiles in their reading.

GLOSSARY

Althing—an assembly of free people that made laws and settled disputes. It was like a Thing, but larger, involving delegates from various parts of a country, not just a single region. Forerunners of the English judicial system.

Baldr (also spelled Baldur, or Balder)— Norse god of light, purity and summer sun. Likened to the Christ god, Jesus. Son of Odin and the goddess Frigg.

Berserker—a Norse warrior who fought with a frenzied rage in battle, known to howl like a wolf and bite his shield

Birka—market town where Sweden is now located

Blindfuller—drunk as a lord

Braies—long, slim pants worn by men, usually tied at the waist, also called breeches

Brud-hlaup—bride-running, a Viking tradition in which the groom chased the bride, after the ceremony which was usually held outdoors. When he arrived ahead of her at the door to his keep, he laid his sword over the threshold. When she stepped over the sword, it was an indication that she accepted her new status as wife, not virgin maid. Often, being Vikings, the men smacked their brides over their rumps with the broad sides of their swords, just to show who would be master in their household. At least, my Vikings did, all with a sense of humor, of course. In some Viking rituals, the man would then swing his sword into the hardwood rooftree of the longhouse; the deeper the cut the more virile he was deemed to be, and it was a permanent scar of good luck

Cotters—laborers on farms or in village

Ells—measurement, usually of cloth, equal to about 45 inches

Fjords—long, narrow, deep inlets of the sea between high cliffs, usually formed by submerged glaciers

Foeman—enemy combatants

Frey/Freyr—Norse god of peace, fertility, rain, sunshine

Frigg—goddess, wife of Odin

Gammelost—Norwegian blue mold cheese made from soured skim milk; in the ancient sagas, it was said to be so foul it turned men into berserkers

Garderobe—indoor privy

Gunna—long-sleeved, ankle-length gown, often worn under a tunic or surcoat or long, open-sided apron by women.

Hedeby—market town where Germany is now located

Hersir—military commander

Hide—land measurement originally intended to represent the amount of land sufficient to support a household, equal to approximately 120 acres (49 hectares)

Hird/hirdsmen—troop, warband

Herfjöttr—a condition known as war fetter to the Vikings, similar to shell shock suffered by men in battle.

Hnefatafl—a Viking board game

Hordaland—Norway

Hospitium—a medical facility, usually tended by monks, like the hospitium associated with the minster in Jorvik (ancient name for York)

Housecarls—permanent troops assigned to a lord or nobleman's household

Jarl—high ranking Norseman, similar to an English earl, or a wealthy landowner, could also be a chieftain or minor king

Jorvik—Viking Age York in Britain

Karl—one rank below a jarl.

Keep—home, estate, or holding

Knarr—a larger Viking longship suitable for longer voyages and carrying cargo

Loki—Norse god known as the trickster

Longboat/longship—Long, narrow warship or trading vessel, powered by both oar and sail, made most popular by the Vikings

Lutefisk—a traditional Norse dish made of dried, salted, or aged whitefish with lye. In fact, its name literally means "lye fish"

Manchet—type of flat bread baked in a circle with a hole in center so they could be stored in a stack on a pole

Manchus/es (of gold)—a measurement of gold with seventy grains equaling to six shillings, or thirty pennies/pence (one shilling equals five pennies)

Mead—fermented beverage made of honey and water

More danico—an accepted practice of multiple wives

Motte and bailey—a high, flat-topped hill on which a castle or keep was built

Norns of Fate—three female beings who rule the fates of gods and men

Norselands—All of the Scandinavian countries as a whole... Norway, Denmark, and Sweden, which were known then by such names as Hordaland (Norway), Halogaland (northern Norway), Vestland (southern Norway), Jutland (Denmark).

Norsemandy—Vikings ruled what would later be called Normandy. To them, it was Norsemandy.

Odin—king of all the Norse gods, considered a god of wisdom

Orphrey—gold or silver-threaded embroidery

Runes—ancient alphabet made of sticklike figures used by Vikings and other primitive cultures

Rushes—Fresh sweet flag plants, incorrectly termed 'rushes," were periodically spread on floors as a floor covering. These reed-like plants were inexpensive and plentiful and, when mixed with fresh herbs, were a good way to cover dirt while sweetening the air. They were also filthy and bug-ridden at times, if not replenished periodically.

Sagas—oral history of the Norse people, passed on from ancient times onward, important when written materials or skills were unavailable

Samite—heavy silk fabric, often interwoven with gold thread

Sennight—one week

Shert—shirt

Shiphird—ship army

Skalds—poets or storytellers who composed and told the sagas, which were the only means of recording ancient Norse history since there was almost no written word then

Straw death—to die in one's sleep, not to be desired, a Viking wishing to die in battle instead and thus be led to a home in Valhalla

Surcoat—outer garment often worn by men over armor embroidered with heraldic arms, or sleeved or sleeveless garment worn indoors by men or women over a gown or other apparel

Thane—a member of the noble class, below an earl but above freemen, often a landowner

Thor—God of war

Thrall—slave

Tun—250 gallons, as in ale

Valhalla—the great hall where Odin welcomes Viking heroes who die in battle

Valkyries—a host of female figures who choose who may die in battle and who may live; they bring their chosen to the afterlife hall of the slain, Valhalla, ruled over by the god Odin

Vestfold—southern Norway in Viking times

Witan (or Witenagemot)—king's council of advisors, precursor to the English parliament

Made in the USA
Columbia, SC
22 September 2022

67674831R00231